Museum of Human Beings

MUSEUM
of Human Beings

a novel

Colin SARGENT

McBooks Press, Inc.

Ithaca, New York   www.mcbooks.com

Published by McBooks Press 2008

Dust jacket and text designed by Panda Musgrove.

Pictures used in cover collage:

Apache Medicine Hat: Plate V., *Ninth annual report of the Bureau of Ethnology to the Secretary of the Smithsonian Institution, 1887–88*. GPO, Washington DC.

Teacup: unknown origin.

Library of Congress Cataloging-in-Publication Data

Sargent, Colin, 1954–
  Museum of human beings / by Colin Sargent.
     p. cm.
  Summary: "Explores the fantastic life and times of Baptiste Charbonneau, the son of Sacagawea, the Indian woman who guided the Lewis and Clark Expedition. Raised in many cultures but belonging to none, Baptiste travels deep into the heart of the American wilderness on an epic quest for ultimate identity"—Provided by publisher.
  ISBN 978-1-59013-167-1 (hardcover : alk. paper)
  1. Charbonneau, Jean-Baptiste, 1805–1866—Fiction. 2. Quests (Expeditions)—Fiction. 3. Sacagawea—Fiction. 4. Clark, William, 1770–1838—Fiction. 5. Lewis and Clark Expedition (1804–1806)—Fiction. 6. West (U.S.)—History—To 1848—Fiction. I. Title.
  PS3619.A735M87 2008
  813.6—dc22

                           2008037492

All McBooks Press publications can be ordered by calling toll-free: 1-888-BOOKS11 (1-888-266-5711). Please call to request a free catalog.

Visit McBooks Press at www.mcbooks.com.

Printed in the United States of America
9 8 7 6 5 4 3 2 1

FOR NANCY

Acknowledgments

This story is a product of the imagination. Liberties have been taken in changing real-life names, events, and dates in creating this fiction. According to Duke Paul's journal, *Erste Reise nach dem nordlichen Amerika in den Jahren 1822–1824*, translated by W. Robert Nitske and edited by Savoie Lottinville as *Travels in North America, 1822–1824*, the duke did bring young Baptiste from St. Louis to Württemberg, crossing the Atlantic aboard the brig *Smyrna*. Duke Paul also took some luggage: "The alligators, too, had been activated by the warmth to leave their muddy river bed and stick their heads above the surface of the water [at the mouth of the Mississippi, off New Orleans]. Several of these creatures were shot [from the *Smyrna*], one of which, wounded in the head, was brought on deck alive. Despite the intense cold which we encountered on the journey while crossing the ocean, this alligator made the trip to France in a spare cask and was brought on the land alive."

Thanks to Warren Ferris's *Life in the Rocky Mountains*, first published serially in 1842–1844, Baptiste can be tracked event-for-event in the early 1830s, as he was in Ferris's company while the young *engagés* of American Fur experienced the great herd of buffalo, the Sioux party at the campfire, the Rendezvous at Pierre's Hole, and Baptiste's eleven lost days on the black lava desert. Baptiste's work for the U.S. Army is documented in *The Conquest of New Mexico and California, An Historical and Personal Narrative,* by Brigadier Brevet Major-General Philip St. George Cooke, 1878.

For the myth of the box canyon and others, I'm grateful to references including *Pachee Goyo: History and Legends from the Shoshone* by Rupert Weeks and *Shoshone Tales* by Anne M. Smith, which capture a thousand years of magic in their pages. Hunting texts such as Tom Brown's *The Science and Art of Tracking* and Paul Rezendes's *Tracking and the Art of Seeing: How To Read Animal Tracks and Sign* provided eyes to see the forest as it never could have been otherwise. A flux of countless other inquiries helped create an emotional mosaic of Baptiste so palpable for me that at least twice I found myself turning while driving to see if he were riding beside me in my car.

Finally, the Native-American signs at the beginning of each chapter—and those Baptiste teaches to Ekaterina—were compiled by William Tomkins, who as a boy lived among the Sioux and other tribes from 1884 to 1894. The fifth edition of his invaluable source book, *Universal Indian Sign Language of the Plains Indians of North America,* appeared in 1931. In his introductory notes, Tomkins wrote: "This language was not created by anybody living today. If it belongs to anybody it belongs to Americans, and it is for the purpose of having it carried on by the youth of the United States that this little volume is compiled." The signs described at the beginning of each chapter appear directly or barely adapted from Tomkins's guide. I can't think of a finer example of poetry in motion.

Museum of Human Beings

1

"ARRIVE"

—hold your left hand ahead of you, fingers together, right hand against your chest. Strike your left palm with the edge of your right.

Christmas Eve, 1805

Sleet pierced the air like volleys of arrows. Having already eaten their horses and with packs nearly slack, the party looked like Romani in their rags as they stumbled up the crooked mountain trail. The little one, strapped to his mother's back, nestled his head into the curve of her neck. Needles of ice stung his cheeks, and the salty tang of the yet-unseen ocean that his mother called *Paakate* tickled his nose.

But Baptiste was not to giggle or cry, his mother, Sacagawea, whispered. He was to keep silent, be invisible—a lucky, if forgettable, witness to the great expedition to the Pacific.

He squeezed his eyes shut to hold his tears. The ground began to shake with the drum of approaching hooves. Suddenly his mother stopped short, and Baptiste opened one eye to see Captain William Clark hold up his hand.

"Keep back," Clark ordered. "Leave this to me."

The explorers stood and watched a hunting party of thirty Chinooks arrive. Their leader slid gracefully from his horse. Baptiste could tell that the young *numah* standing at the head of his men was a threat. With a deliberate grin the brave displayed his teeth, carefully filed to resemble the bone points used to spear salmon and hares.

Baptiste watched Clark's Adam's apple rise and fall as he took a dry swallow and stepped toward his interlocutor.

Clutching his spyglass as if the lens could still keep his guests at a distance, Meriwether Lewis slunk into the shadows behind Clark and the interpreter Toussaint Charbonneau.

"I figure we can get away with half a dozen of those gewgaws," Clark said and bit his bottom lip, as was his habit. From a leather satchel his sergeant pulled six strands of the blown-glass Venetian beads they'd been issued by the Department of War to dazzle the savages.

"Yes, sir," Sergeant Gass said. "That's a pretty impressive knife he has."

It was a fishing knife, big enough to make short work of a halibut.

Clark's lower lip was bright red now, an oddity, in this thin air almost a sexual accoutrement.

"Watch his face, not his knife," Clark said.

But Sacagawea watched only Clark, with deep admiration. Her husband, the drunken Charbonneau, waited with stark raving disinterest. York, Clark's manservant, held his breath so his neck swelled like a tree toad's. Lewis took a second imperceptible step backward.

"Don't anyone move," Clark said. "Just let him walk around us for a while. He has to sniff us like a cur. See how his warriors are tense but he is relaxed?"

The Chinook glided within three inches of the six-foot, red-headed Clark. Though he stood half a foot shorter, the brave's conical grass hat made him seem nearly as tall. The blue clay smudged on his high cheekbones was much like the *a vee* Sacagawea had seen her father and uncles wear. A silver British dragoon's gorget swung from his neck on a strand of white shells. At the ready on his fur vest was a string of large, bone fishhooks. In spite of the cold, he wore nothing below his thigh.

"What could he want?" Captain Lewis, behind Baptiste now, whispered.

"Tell him we have brought things of great value for him," Clark said firmly, keeping an eye on the Chinook but nodding to Private Labiche, who translated in French to Charbonneau. Receiving the message in Hidatsa, Charbonneau's wife relayed it in Shoshone to the young brave, who made her repeat it three times before he shook his head and spat.

"Just give him something, quick," said Lewis in a bleating voice that did him and the party no credit.

"Compliments of the Great Chief of the United States of America." Clark slowly reached into a black bag held open by Gass and produced a piece of "solid water" for the Chinook leader, who, bored with mirrors, waved it away.

"No shit." The Chinook made a hawking sound deep in his throat. "*Wake.*" He spat in Clark's face.

Clark answered with a rusty *haw hoo* he'd cultivated in the Kentucky militia to impress young ladies in drawing rooms. Reaching back to grasp Lewis by the vest, Clark pulled his partner off balance, drew him close, and spat in his face.

"Was that really necessary?" said Lewis as he pitched back and wiped his cheekbone with his sleeve.

The brave grinned broadly. "Haw hoo!"

Clark wore the spittle like a badge of honor. "We're open for business. Let's see if he'd prefer the tobacco, or the vermilion."

Baptiste twisted around his mother's slender neck for a better view. Gass slowly pulled a pouch of the leaves that burned with a dark redolence. The brave refused it, along with the rich folds of blood-red cloth. He dismissed two silver trading amulets embossed with *The*

Lewis & Clark Voyage of Discovery. He pushed aside Clark's English surveying tools, as he had no desire to calculate their distance to Arcturus. He envied not at all the well-executed, steel-engraved illustration of President Thomas Jefferson, nor even Clark's final resort, their last crumbs of hard tack.

"*O'-koke.*" The Chinook leader made a sign and pointed to Sacagawea. Baptiste felt his mother quickly push his head down with the back of her skull as she retreated a step.

"What the hell?" Lewis blurted.

"Shh," Clark said.

The brave, barely older than Sacagawea, keenly focused on her with his half-drawn wolf eyes.

He stepped toward mother and child, and as they froze he took in Baptiste with a funny glance—*are you a raccoon trapped at the top of a burning tree?*—before descending to his knees in front of the young mother as if to pay her homage. But instead, his hands circled her waist, tracing the lines of her brilliant blue Lemhi beaded belt that denoted her and her son's rank as members of a royal family. Princess Sacagawea had worn it proudly since she was nine. Even her Hidatsa captors, who'd inflicted all other humiliations, hadn't had the heart to take it away from her.

"*O'-koke,*" he said. For me, *this.*

Clark, blind to the ornament's significance, forced a laugh, and the other men joined in. Loudest of all was Toussaint. Sacagawea untied the belt and handed her birthright to the young man. She kept her eyes on the horizon.

The Chinook wrapped the prize around his bicep and walked briskly back to his men. He yanked a string of greasy weasel tails out of his saddle bag and marched back to Sacagawea. Tossing the weasel tails at her, he mounted his horse.

"*Wake,*" she said sharply, remembering his word. When the Chinook turned back to her, the princess admonished him sharply in Shoshone.

He rolled his eyes but reached back into his pack and accorded her a scrap of dark blue cloth, which she folded over the weasel tails and tucked under her arm. "*O'-koke*," she said.

Baptiste thought he heard his mother laugh, but with a different tone. No one followed them when she ran into the woods through the branches, slipped across a mossy ledge, and hopped a rocky stream.

Watching the world bounce from his mother's back, Baptiste saw the men grow smaller and disappear as Sacagawea twisted up through some forested undergrowth to emerge atop a granite outcropping so high in the wind they could hear the Pacific roar even more clearly in the distance, though clouds prevented their seeing it. The Columbia River estuary lay like a trade-silver necklace below. Baptiste had never seen his mother cry, so he kept very still until he grew hungry. His mother's eyes were wet as she wrapped him in the scrap of blue flannel, nursed him, and tucked him into his papoose.

"They did not take my true treasure, little one," she said in Shoshone, then crooned to him in a low voice. "I carry you on my back. With soft deerskin I lay you on a slab of bark cradled gently behind my shoulders so your head will be close to mine, and ever you will see what I see. We will walk as one. We crossed the mountains as one. The wind will warm our passage. We will always be together."

Feeling the delicious warmth of the blanket surround him, Baptiste drifted off to sleep, barely able to reflect that often one's pleasures come from another's pain.

"Well done, Janey!" Clark said in the only language at his command when they returned at dusk, his endearment, the common one used by soldiers to address female camp followers, defiling mother and child in a single sweep. He ruffled Baptiste's hair.

"Because of your mother's salesmanship, the Chinooks left us fresh horses and an elk. The devils will even help us build a fort, for the right price, of course."

Sacagawea turned away.

Misinterpreting her sorrow and pretending she understood enough to bask in his praise, he said, "Aw, I'm sick of all this weather, too. The only relief we have from the snow is the rain."

"We must hurry," Sacagawea told him haltingly in the English she was determined to learn. She knew after a day or so the trading would wear off and the braves could kill them with a clear conscience. She made her two fingers "walk" in the air stealthily and then abruptly stabbbed the air with her fist.

"It would serve us right," Clark laughed. Then he leaned down and kissed both Sacagawea and Baptiste on the lips. No one else was nearby. Sacagawea stared at Clark with a lost look.

"*Compliments*," she said softly, and draped the weasel tails around Clark's neck. Baptiste tried to reach out and touch the black-tipped pieces of fur, they looked so alive.

"They stink to hell!" Clark smiled.

Every time the explorer put his face near Baptiste's mother's it became difficult for the boy to breathe. The tip of Father Clark's enormous hairy ear covered his nose.

At nightfall, the discomfited Captain Lewis was ejected from the shelter to take his damp grass mat and retire elsewhere. Sacagawea looked shyly into Clark's eyes as he took off his leggings and leather breeches.

Clark took her and her papoose to his blanket. Trusting Baptiste was asleep under the wool, Sacagawea untied her deerskin shift and let it fall open. Blue islands around her ribs from Toussaint's regular beatings had now turned to yellow and nearly healed.

"*EttsemiH*," she told Clark, "close your eyes." She softly repeated "compliments" as he drew her onto his lap.

They awoke at dawn to a commotion outside the shelter. A cold, clear air hit the trio as Clark threw off the blanket. It was the advance party who'd been charged with scavenging for food, returning pell-mell to camp, shouting, cheering. They had seen Pacifica, and their eyes were lit by the sea.

"Done," Clark said to himself. "After twenty-six months, we've made it." Then, more loudly, "This calls for a toast!"

"Not everyone here needs a toast," Gass said, scrunching up his nose as Toussaint Charbonneau shuffled in.

"A bonus would be *agréable*," Charbonneau said, via Labiche. "To reward he who brought you here."

"The terms of your remuneration were agreed on long ago," Lewis said, backing up.

Charbonneau studied Lewis resentfully for a moment, then lumbered away.

"And there's a giant fish on the beach, Cap'n," York said, "as big as any ship I ever saw on the Potomac."

"A whale," Clark marveled. "How far away?"

"Maybe five, six miles, Cap'n."

"Is it alive?"

"I think I saw it move."

"What did he see?" Sacagawea asked shyly, tugging at Clark's sleeve.

"A great fish," Sergeant Gass said, drawing in the dirt with his toe. "Large as this hole in the woods." He traced the edge of their grassy swale with his musket.

"Not a fish," Clark said. "A great beast that lives in the sea."

"Beaver?"

With a shake of his head, Clark waved her off. Then he motioned to Gass. "I need a few men to go back with me to see this whale," he said, dressing and seizing his notebook. "The rest of you wait here."

Still naked and barely covered by the corner of Clark's blanket, Sacagawea stood up. "No. We will come to see the whale." She dropped the blanket and clenched her fists.

Clark shrugged. "You can see it later. It is nearly a day away."

She crossed her arms. "We will see it now. My son will see the creature, and the great ocean, now."

"You will do what you are told." He started off with his men.

"We will see the great whale."

She dressed quickly and drew the papoose onto her back.

Baptiste could feel his mother's excitement as her quick footsteps slashed in single-file through the forest, but in spite of his best efforts to stay awake, the bouncing lulled him to sleep. He woke to the sound of her hard breathing as she ran to the top of a hill. He heard shouts and alarms from the men. Then the Pacific started spilling in, blue.

On the beach, Clark paced the mammal at 105 feet. Purple and distended like a huge rotting plum, the monster was an endless galleon with clouds of gulls for sails. The great swollen corpse produced an unfathomable stench, its melting flesh actually bubbling with the incessant attentions of sand crabs. Far from alive, much of the behemoth was nothing so much as a skeletal, open-air cathedral of gothic proportions that death was building, the remnants of its tail drifting back and forth in the waves. As Clark continued his necropsy, Sergeant Gass walked inside the mammoth rib cage.

Toussaint Charbonneau mumbled something in French and made the sign of the cross.

"Look, I'm Jonah!" Gass called through the big hoops of the carcass while the ocean splashed at his feet. The others headed inside to see.

Baptiste, free from his mother, toddled to the wall of flesh still hanging from the leviathan and plucked something sharp from its side. He already had it to his mouth before Sacagawea could stop him.

"What have you got there, sonny?" Gass asked as the child drew near, now holding it in his fist. "Let's have a look." It was blue and sharp, a tiny spearpoint made of delicate, flinty stone. With its ripping ridges, it was designed for killing birds, not whales.

"I'll be darned," Gass said, turning it over and handing it back to Baptiste. "I wonder how many years the beast wore that bauble in his flesh. Make a nice present for your da-da."

Baptiste wobbled straight through the troops, waving the stone, and before Sacagawea could stop him, he held it up to Father Clark.

No one dared to laugh as Clark awkwardly accepted the token and Sacagawea strode forward three steps before stopping. Then, blushing and confused, she turned to Baptiste and slapped him hard.

The sting traveled across Baptiste's face, which began to throb with pain. He was confused and inconsolable, even when his mother wrapped him in her arms and kissed his head.

That night, as the fire turned to embers near the shelter where Baptiste and his mother lay, Meriwether Lewis approached Clark, who was absently turning the blue spearpoint in his hand.

"This has gone too far," Lewis said and fidgeted. "I wouldn't cross Toussaint. Even drunk, he can relieve a buffalo of its hide in three strokes."

"You know what she's done for us," Clark said. "She is under my protection."

"I'm telling you as your commander, keep your hands off her."

"I don't give a shit for your command. My honor is defined by my surroundings. I will take care of her, and Little Pomp."

"You're playing with fire." Lewis grabbed the shard of blue flint from Clark's hand and tossed it into the ashes. "And you're putting the whole mission at risk."

"Exactly how? She's the guide, not the one you hired. Charbonneau's been nothing but dead weight and another mouth to feed, or shall I say, quench. The men call him 'Long-Way-Round.'" The grizzled Frenchman was certainly capable of leading parties he was guiding for days in order to pad his expenses and save himself the trouble of being responsible for the safety of amateurs in difficult terrain.

"Charbonneau is as much her owner as her husband. The only reason the girl knows her way here is, she was captured and raped, and she brought us back the way she was dragged. What would your cousin think? You're supposed to be married in six months!"

"That's worlds away. It has nothing to do with Janey. You're so wrapped up in your calculations you can't even take in the scenery."

"You can be a real scut-hole sometimes, Clark."

"And you can be a real priss. Just because you're too disillusioned and wormy to sample a ripe fig."

"Oh, all in the interest of science, I'm sure. You know, your log entries have been pretty sketchy lately. Senator Pickering and the rest of the world will insist on a full accounting of everything we did, and Charbonneau could make trouble for us."

"Aw, history in the making. I'll take care of it. Charbonneau doesn't scare me."

Belching, Toussaint Charbonneau lurched out of the dark and clutched Clark's wrist as he stooped to flick the spearpoint from the ashes with the end of his knife. He rubbed the flint in the dirt with the toe of his boot, then picked it up and put it in his pocket. Though he understood precious little English, he had no trouble detecting scorn.

"You'd better take care of your*self*," he growled, "'Da-Da' Clark." The trapper threw open the flap to the shelter and exposed his teeth to the shivering Baptiste. "*Et tu*, Bear Bait. You'd best remember where you came from."

2

"ABANDON/THROW AWAY"

—hold hands closed at left side near breast, then drop them down and to rear, at the same time opening them as though expelling some article.

Christmas Eve, 1809

Baptiste savored the scent of mulled cider as he edged nearer to the fireplace. He stamped his feet, cold and wet from the rain outside, until his mother grasped him to hold him still. Then the large white door opened.

"Isn't this a nice surprise, Julia!" Clark said to his wife as they entered the kitchen. By her expression it was obvious that the eighteen-year-old lady of the household wasn't so much surprised as horrified. Certainly she wasn't used to frequenting these quarters to receive guests. She clapped a hand over her mouth.

Breaking free and giggling, Baptiste ran to Father Clark and wrapped his arms around the lanky explorer's knees. Indoors, Clark resembled a stuffed condor. Candlelight magnified the shadows cast by his ears and nose.

"My little dancing river otter!" Clark exclaimed, wheeling him up and around so that for an instant the five-year-old was eye-to-eye with Julia.

"Look, *maman*, this lady's crying," Baptiste said in French.

"My compliments, Janey, welcome," Clark said softly.

"What did you say?" Julia sniffed and wiped her red eyes with a gauzy hanky.

Clark looked from Julia to Sacagawea. The nearer the Expedition had gotten to St. Louis during the closing days, the more distant he'd become. When his last chance to dispose of Sacagawea and Baptiste presented itself at the Mandan Villages, hundreds of miles upriver, he'd taken it and acted "like a gentleman," as Lewis recommended. *Gentleman, hell.*

With only hotel room ceilings to confess to after galas in Washington, his thoughts had often drifted to his Indian girl. Nostalgia had given him the bite after he returned to St. Louis, accepted an appointment to oversee Indian affairs in the new Louisiana Territory, and married, setting up offices and a museum commemorating the Expedition in a white frame house along the river.

So he'd written to Toussaint after three years, bribing him to bring the mother and child, offering education for the boy and "other considerations": $500.33 and 323 acres of land.

"I'm fulfilling a promise," Clark said.

"You made that promise in the woods, a world away," Julia said.

Julia's eyelids fluttered when she was agitated. *You are so exotic*, she thought as she studied the "squaw"—her maid had gleefully whispered the sobriquet—and looked down at her own pale, trembling hands. Beyond the girl's vitality Julia sensed a formidable, cunning intelligence, something that spoke of the genius of the woods. She closed her eyes for a moment, then lowered her voice. "What will my family think?" *All of St. Louis will know.*

Julia suddenly felt dizzy. She'd met her first cousin Clark when she was just twelve, and he thirty-three. "I'm going to marry you on your fifteenth birthday," he'd vowed. But he'd been a year late and a dollar short. *And oh, now this mistress.* Julia had been the loveliest maid since her mother to lead the Virginia reel back in Fincastle. She'd pictured her life spread before her as one perfect day after another, with no upset to the schedule, but this change of scenery made her head ache fit to bursting and made her strangely afraid. She allowed herself to look for a second at the girl's dusky majesty. *How different are you from me, dark where I am fair, round where I am hollow. You must be some sort of devil's familiar.* Then she took in the bare feet, was certain she detected a musk, and instinctively raised her handkerchief to her nose.

She shot a glance at her husband. *When we married you were vigorous, a world celebrity.* Now, as Julia retreated to become a pale figure behind an upstairs window . . .

Clark installed his second family in a shack barely eight feet in front of the chattel quarters, close enough that Baptiste could hear the slaves sneezing.

That first January, Father Clark often came at moonrise to visit. Baptiste was too sleepy to do much more than totter about when the explorer tapped his feet and snapped his fingers to the sound of Sacagawea's *muyatainka,* her little reed whistle carved with the profile of a raven.

But as the hours of sunshine grew longer and Sacagawea began to open her door to the spring air, Baptiste practiced some steps in the shaft of light that fell on the crude floor. On May Day, merrymakers spilled into the garden. Clark spied Baptiste watching from behind an azalea.

"Aha!" Clark clapped his hands. "Come on out!"

With a studied grace, Baptiste bowed and strode toward him as if he were gliding across a proscenium.

When the delighted crowd clapped, he started to skip, then turned toward them and recited a short poem.

"Wonderful, Pomp!" Clark called to the boy, then waved toward his friends. "And this distinguished company is, of course, the circumstance!" The crowd laughed politely at his witticism.

"By your leave, sir!" Baptiste bowed again. The attention warmed the boy all over, and as he departed he promised himself he'd always please Father Clark and oblige his acquaintances.

But Sacagawea wasn't so pleased and quickly pulled her son into the thorny bushes behind the woodpile. She squeezed his upper arm.

"*Yokopekka*," she hissed. "Wise ass." Then she hugged him gently and clasped her hands over his heart.

"Little One," she warned, "you must be careful how you answer the *Taipo*, even when he's friendly. They want you to be smart enough to help them, but not too smart. It doesn't make a good impression."

They were happy, the two—and when Clark visited, three—of them until the next winter Sacagawea began to get sick in the mornings. A storm blanketed St. Louis in snow. Baptiste, now six, heard stamping and yelling below the loft under the eaves where he slept. The horrid Toussaint had been summoned by Clark from the woods, where he'd been trapping along the Missouri near Fort Mandan. Baptiste couldn't make out what they argued about. His mother pleaded, "No, no, no." Then his time came.

"*Mon fils*, so this is where you hide," Toussaint bellowed.

Baptiste felt a sour reek envelop him as Toussaint scraped his way up the ladder. The fog of the man. Was it possible for a human being to sweat rum? Toussaint's head popped through the transom and caught sight of Baptiste; he trapped his eyes. The firelight emphasized the yellow scar that ran straight down Toussaint's cheek and snagged at the right side of his lip in a permanent snarl. Something dangled from his neck. A blue stone, but sharp, like something dangerous. And familiar.

"Leave me alone," Baptiste said.

"*Mon fils,*" Toussaint said. In the darkness the boy scrambled away from his hairy arm, but Toussaint was accustomed to working with desperate animals. His grip on Baptiste's calf was forged iron, like one of his traps. Baptiste shook it loose and scurried back into the corner, out of his reach. "Rascal," Toussaint said, making the sign of the cross for luck before disappearing below.

Baptiste spent the night huddled into his corner with his eyes shut tight. The next morning his mother and Toussaint were gone. So were her cloak and pots, and the gourd she used each morning to dip water from their bucket. The room was completely empty except for a large brain-tanned bag—her "possibles"—left on the crude wooden table. He'd never seen his mother go anywhere without it.

When he picked it up for a look inside, her precious whistle fell out. Baptiste blew into its emptiness with his finger covering the last of its holes and heard its simple, pure scree. When he held it down against his chest and blew more softly, it produced a lower tone as he saw two orioles fly past their window. He stuffed it into the bag, which he slung across his chest and over his shoulder. Carefully pulling the door closed behind him as his mother had taught him to do, he stepped into the yard.

He could see tracks heading north, where clouds darkened and massed beyond the icy cliffs that lined the lower Missouri. He could almost hear his mother whispering, always instructing, *See these pretty sweeps in the snow? They show I was struggling. It's where he dragged me. Here's where we got on the horse.*

· · ·

When the sun began to fade and his mother hadn't returned, Baptiste wailed so mournfully that an exasperated Clark, hearing the boy from his library window, stepped out onto the terrace.

"Stop the racket, Pomp," Clark said. "You'll scare the horses."

That caught him up short. When he wasn't studying at the Roman Catholic School or tracking game as his mother had taught him, Baptiste would often fall asleep in the stables, near the great beasts he'd come to adore.

"Sir, I can't find Mother."

"I think she's gone for a while to see her people. Don't worry, she'll be back in the spring." Father Clark smiled, but Baptiste recognized it for what it was, a baring of teeth.

"But Mother told me only I was her family."

Clark's eyes widened. He stared at the boy for a moment.

"It's snowing. Come into the house out of the snow."

So this was the reward for silence.

Surely Mother will be all right, Baptiste thought. *She told me the forest is her home, the trees are her counsel. She'll come back for me. Father Clark disappeared for three years, yet here he is before me.* Adults were curious. They disappeared all the time.

"Come on, Pomp, right this way. Come in where it's warm. Hepsibah, I'd like you to give Pomp a bath, then give him some warm milk and apple betty."

"Yes, Genr'l," the cook said. "Over here, child. Will you look at those eyes. Why you carrying on like this?" She fixed him a bed behind the stove.

Baptiste knew she meant well, but the only thing that consoled him was looking out back at the shack where his mother and he had spent their tranquil days.

· · ·

The big white house was full of rules, with many rooms denied him. Baptiste learned in the kitchen, after watching a succession of silver trays borne up and porcelain chamber pots borne down, that Mrs. Clark was becoming too delicate and sensitive to leave her second-floor apartment. She'd long since stopped playing the pianoforte Clark had imported from Germany with great expense and fanfare.

The luminous instrument in the forbidden parlor seemed like the grandest thing in the world to him and represented all that was fine and beyond his grasp, much more inspiring than the rude mission altar where they took communion. Sometimes when the house was quiet, he'd steal up to the piano and study his face reflected in its ebony surface.

"Get out of there!" Hepsibah said, catching him one afternoon. "This is not the place for a *shetani* like you!"

"No one's here. I wonder what kind of sound it makes."

"*I'm* here! Now you just get away from there."

With his little finger the boy traced gold leaf letters in a scroll above the piano's grinning mouth. The florid characters transfixed him. Painted in the lacquer was a funny name with lots of s's and z's that he couldn't pronounce, and it was born in a city called Hamburg. He wondered how far it was from Missouri.

"Don't you hear me?"

Baptiste did not move.

Then suddenly, light on his feet, he stabbed a single key in the low register. He held the key down as the thrumming waves of sound filled the room. He imagined the vibrations traveling from the soul of the wood across the cities and rivers to the place where his mother had been carried away. It was a black sound, resonant and lasting, like a great river roaring under the stars. He would relish the sound for weeks to come.

"Yer a bad demon," Hepsibah said.

She grabbed him by the ear and dragged him back to the kitchen. When he looked up he was surprised to see that instead of a stern face he caught the trace of a smile, and the boy wondered if maybe bad wasn't always so bad.

"Devil!" Hepsibah scolded him severely the next week. "Why do you think you can go to bed with those raggedy fingernails?" He knew her harsh words were at odds with her amiable nature.

She endeavored to teach him table manners, and eventually he was allowed to participate in the *petit déjeuner* that Clark and his two boys, Meriwether and Preston, enjoyed in their lemon-lit breakfast room. Neither the absent Miss Julia nor the vanished Sacagawea was mentioned during these merry celebrations, where a good deal of time was spent joking and scheming over tea.

Winter turned to spring. Baptiste began to pester Heracles.

"Where is my mother? Doesn't she miss me? When will she return?"

But the foreman just shook his head. Nor would the other servants tell him anything, though sometimes he saw them smirking. He dared not ask Clark, who had begun treating him brusquely but at least without averted eyes.

One day, in a moment of tenderness, Clark called Baptiste into his study and motioned for him to sit on his knee.

"Your mother, Little Pomp, has passed," he said.

Baptiste burst into tears. Clark reached to touch his shoulder, but the boy pulled away.

"Mother can't be dead. She promised she'd be back for me." Baptiste took in a gasp of air. "*Why* did she die?"

Wiping his eyes and looking up, the boy's attention fell on Clark's chin, oddly unshaven, flecked with stubbles of rust and gray, and close enough to receive a kiss. He saw a port wine stain on his normally snowy cravat. Baptiste sniffed—he'd never before detected *that* strong smell from the explorer. Clark smelled like Toussaint.

"I'm sorry, Pomp," he said. "She died of . . . an adult disease."

Sacagawea was just twenty-five.

"But you have a sister, Lizette!"

Baptiste turned when he heard a commotion outside the door. Now the embarrassed clerk of Fort Manuel, in the Dakotas, entered and stood behind Clark with an infant in his arms, so young she could barely open her eyes. Lizette was wrapped in a blue cloth that Baptiste recognized as the same one that had once kept him warm. He caught his breath and involuntarily reached out to touch it, thinking of those weasel tails so long ago. His throat swelled and got salty, but he refused to cry.

"I will adopt Lizette, Pomp, as I have you," Clark said.

Sacagawea had been hastily buried under a pile of rocks outside the stockade. As usual, Toussaint had fled the scene.

Hepsibah took immediate charge of Lizette and delighted in her gurgling smiles and strawberry curls. Sometimes Baptiste felt he could hear his mother singing when his sister laughed, and he didn't feel so peculiar. But before he and Lizette even got to celebrate her second birthday with sponge cake and candles in the kitchen—when the house servants began to whisper that her red hair was taking on an even more vivid hue instead of darkening—the drunken Toussaint was summoned again. He disappeared with Lizette before dawn.

"Where is she?" Baptiste asked Hepsibah, who with her daughter Lottie was soaking clothes in a tub of hot water reeking with lye. "Does anyone know what happened to my sister?"

"Best you mind your own business," Hepsibah said. "Unless you want that old Toussaint come some night and get you."

"Maybe eat you," Lottie said.

"Where's Father Clark?"

"He's gone to Washington." Lottie stuck out her tongue and licked her lips. "Don't you know anything?"

Fearing Toussaint might take *him* away, too, Baptiste worked all the harder at school and resolved to follow every household edict he could divine. When Clark returned a few weeks later and no search for Lizette was launched on his orders, Baptiste was alarmed by how little protection the general's doting affection offered. At the morning meal he'd always looked so forward to, sharing the passages he'd mastered at the mission during the great man's absences, the boy was only able to stare down at his plate.

"Pomp!"

What would it feel like to be deaf and dumb? Baptiste wondered.

Clark shouted at him, "I've asked you twice to send round those strawberry preserves."

When Baptiste still couldn't look up, Clark reached over and gently lifted his chin.

"What is it, Pomp?"

"Where is Lizzy?" Baptiste asked almost inaudibly.

"Damnation," the explorer said, pushing his chair back and throwing his napkin down on his plate. "She's fine and just where she's supposed to be."

"I want to see my sister. Is she going to be gone forever like Mother?"

Clark stood up to leave. "I'm very tired, Pomp. She's well provided for. We'll have no more on the subject."

The nine-year-old learned, as all who grieve must one day learn, eventually to stop asking. Five years flowed by like the murky waters of the lower Missouri.

As school progressed, Baptiste continued to advance, with honors. His only hope was to distinguish himself in Clark's world. He launched more deeply into the study of the classics beyond the French, English, Mandan, and Shoshone he'd grown up speaking. To his surprise it became easier; languages were a delicious place to hide. His school-master was impressed.

"Son, why on earth would you want this?" He pointed to Caesar's *Bellum Gallicum*, which Baptiste had just borrowed. A younger priest leaned over and whispered to him.

"Oh!" he said. "So this is the half-breed prodigy. I understand you've read much of our library."

"Only in Latin," Baptiste said. "But if I might try the Greek . . ."

"But they're heathens," he said, then chuckled at the boy's discom-fiture. "You'd better come with me." He took Baptiste to the attic library reserved for the initiates. For a moment Baptiste was fearful, but the old man smiled, pointed to a chair, and left him alone to con-sider the dust covering the long oak table. Cracked brown texts of the *Mathematica*, Plutarch, and Ptolemy had faded blue ribbons bound within, to mark favored passages. Tracts in Old and Middle English slept undisturbed in great stacks. Shining at the end of a shelf were St. Thomas Aquinas, Thomas Hobbes, Einhard's *Life of Charlemagne*.

The more I read these, the more you will admire me and be my real fa-ther, Father Clark. Baptiste devoured everything he touched, peered intently at the clothing and deportment of sophisticated gentlemen through the ages, cartoons in black ink. The only pages he flipped over were illustrations of primitive peoples.

He worked long into the evenings in his little alcove behind the stove. If he kept reading, the world would offer limitless possibili-ties. Outside the window, vines crept over the shack where he and his mother had lived.

The priests generally praised Baptiste for his scholarship until some-thing "turned up missing," as Father Neill called it—slates, a fragment of chalk—whereupon all eyes turned to him. If a pane of glass were broken, he was shown the rock. In spite of this, the fourteen-year-old was surprised when his instructor approached him while he was reading, reached toward him as if to ruffle his hair, and took hold of his ear.

"What is it, Father?" Baptiste asked as Father Neill splashed him through the mud past the dooryard of the Roman Catholic School, four doors down Constitution Boulevard, and up the stairs into the East India tea store, where Mademoiselle Vachonne had let Baptiste sweep her floor on Saturdays for a penny.

"You know damn well what it is," Father Neill said. "There's been a pilfering."

"But I didn't take anything!"

"You come inside right now, young man. Your benefactor will meet us here."

"What's wrong?" It was raining, Father Neill was angry, the world was crazy.

"Not another word!"

The door slammed, followed by a silly jingle. There in her oddly quiet world was the *mademoiselle,* dressed in black and purple like a wild turkey at a funeral, her knuckles white against the glass counter. Her eyes glittered.

"*Voleur,*" she hissed.

Clark entered and remained in the doorway while he waited for Baptiste to translate the French of his accuser.

Baptiste did so, his face hot. *Why would I steal your stupid teas?* The Missouri backwaters smelled better.

"With my compliments," Clark said to Mademoiselle Vachonne, dispensing a full silver dollar into her spidery hands.

Sputtering gratitude, the storekeeper rubbed Clark's wrist as if she might catch some of his good luck that way.

"Tell her you're sorry, Pomp."

I will not, sir. He waited for Clark to say, "How dare you treat my son this way!" but when the explorer looked away, Baptiste realized it hadn't even occurred to Clark to defend him. How could Father Clark be so mistaken? Baptiste circled to look Clark in the eyes. Then he wheeled around to take in Father Neill's disapproving face.

"But, sir," he whispered, "I didn't take anything!"

"Now that's enough of that," Clark said, nodding to Mademoiselle Vachonne. "This gentlewoman believes you stole it, and we have to take her at her word."

So believing was seeing now.

"But, sir."

"Let's not be impertinent," Clark said. "Now you come with me outside."

"She's simply wrong, sir!"

Clark laughed and lowered his voice. "Don't worry about it, Pomp. That's just how some people treat Injuns."

So I'm an Indian.

As Baptiste fled out the door, he looked back to see Mademoiselle Vachonne smiling.

How is it I can feel shame even though I'm not a thief? Baptiste wondered as he raced across the puddles back to the compound, slipped behind the stables, and leaned over to sob where no one could hear him, a duty to which he applied himself with violence before gasping in the cold, nearly unbreathable air. He spent half the night alone in the rain. How he hated Mademoiselle Vachonne for introducing that word to his home.

From this moment on, I will double my efforts to make you proud of me, Father Clark, or at least notice me, he vowed. *I will become a gentleman as you have never seen.* Each high mark he got at school, Baptiste came right home to proudly show his parent, but Clark withdrew further into himself. Each time he brought back a bag of fowl, or a saddle of venison, to grace their table—for Baptiste had become most adroit in the woods—Clark neglected to praise him, or barely nodded his appreciation.

Since the War of 1812, the general had enjoyed life as governor of the Missouri Territory, but a string of intrigues was keeping him up at night. Superfluous around the compound, Baptiste spent more time in the stables, fantasizing that Clark was taking some pride at least in his growing mastery as a horseman. But after Clark fought for Missouri to win statehood, only to lose both his wife and the election to become its first governor, the general stopped coming to the stables altogether.

Julia Clark simply failed to take a breath one morning.

Little in the household changed after Mrs. Clark's death, partly because she herself had had no impact on the household affairs for so many years, and partly because Clark, in attending her funeral in Fincastle, had chosen and later brought back his second wife, Mrs. Clark's near-identical cousin, Harriet Kennerly Clark, who resembled Julia in temperament and constitution as well as visage. If anything, Clark became even more detached at the arrival of his new bride.

Maybe he just needs cheering up, Baptiste hoped. But when he played a merry tune outside the explorer's study, Clark became impatient and slammed the window.

One evening, Baptiste became so discouraged at being shut out that he threw his whistle into the bushes. Lottie slipped out of the shadows, came into the yard, and placed the little reed into the palm of his hand. He felt a strange lump in the back of his throat as she stood close to him beneath a large oak tree.

"You're all alone in this world, ain't you?" she said.

She held a piece of sorghum candy out to him, but when he reached for it, she clasped her hands behind her back and teased, "I *heard* you was a thief."

Baptiste slapped her hard with the back of his hand and a red welt appeared on her cheek as her eyes filled with tears.

"I didn't mean nothin," she said.

"I shouldn't have done that, Lottie," he said and reached his arm around her thin shoulders and drew her close. As he kissed the top of her head he could taste the tang of the smokehouse mingled with the sweetness of the jasmine flower she'd tucked behind her ear. He felt his pulse quicken as her warmth surrounded his, and he grew unmistakably aroused. She tilted her head up in the moonlight, and as he kissed her yielding lips she untied the top of her jumper and eased it off her shoulders. He was in a hurry to see her beauty. He'd peeked at her lovely thighs before when she'd gone down to the river and hoisted up her skirts, but his fortunes had ended there. Now, delicate and coffee-colored, her small breasts melted into vermilion nipples. He tasted salt on them as she tugged at the hem of her dress. Then he was inside her, and though he felt thrills of excitement and surface ecstasy like starlight skipping across the river, he knew it was passion but not exactly love and guessed it was the same for Lottie. For a long while, Lottie was as quiet as the river beside them. Lying beside her, Baptiste felt himself relieved of some of his anger, but as he looked over at his old friend, he thought maybe he really was a thief. He didn't know what to say, so when he got up he said, "I'm sorry."

"I'm sorry, too," Lottie said, struggling into her dress the way his mother used to. He and Lottie were sorry the next night, too. Whenever he kissed her, it felt like falling. Sometimes they'd stop for months at a time for fear of getting caught. But like his mother and Clark, they knew how to be lonely together.

In contrast with little Meriwether, who hadn't yet acquired his enthusiasm for school, Baptiste's thirst for knowledge was unquenchable. By the time he finished his final classes he had no linguistic peer. The thrill he felt at the ceremony was tempered somewhat by the absence of Clark, who'd been called out of town on important business. Clark had long stopped coming to breakfast, and the youth rarely saw him because of his frequent trips to Washington for meetings with members of the Cabinet.

Because I can write in more than a fair hand, Baptiste reflected, *one day I might accompany Father Clark as his diarist on these junkets.*

The night Clark returned, Baptiste's presence was respectfully requested at the great man's study.

Baptiste arrived fully prepared to talk at length on any subject Clark chose in order to show him his years of education had been money well spent. Instead of shaking his hand when he held it out, Clark pushed a piece of gold into his palm.

"It's time for you to learn your father's business," Clark said.

Almost beside himself with excitement, Baptiste glanced up at the maps and the gilt-edged books behind Clark on the walls, but when he returned to the explorer's face he realized that was not at all what he meant. The general was talking about Toussaint Charbonneau. Baptiste's heart sank.

"You'll have to get ready posthaste, Pomp. You're starting at dawn tomorrow at John Jacob Astor's American Fur."

3

"TRAP"

—for iron traps, touch or point to something made of metal. Hold closed hands side by side, knuckles touching, index fingers curved and touching; then bring sides of indexes together to close jaws of trap.

Baptiste made it to camp just after nightfall. Fire flickered against the shapes of men as they flensed flesh from fur. To Baptiste, they looked like lost souls in an engraving from the *Inferno*, the Cantica from *The Divine Comedy* by Dante.

"Took your time getting here, did you?" said William Sublette, a powerful, leonine Kentuckian in his mid-twenties, after peering at Baptiste's letter of introduction. "Says here the general thinks you can hunt. Well, we'll know directly."

Baptiste said nothing.

"Not very brawny, are you?" Sublette said with no attempt to mask his dismay. *Another half-breed, the Missouri basin's teeming with them. Look at those switchy eyes. Maybe he can cut.* "You afraid of work?"

Baptiste shook his head very quickly and smiled.

"Afraid to get your hands greasy?"

Baptiste said nothing.

Sublette's gaze locked on Baptiste's leg. "Let me see that thing. What's that, an elephant knife? Hand it over."

Most people didn't see the blade his mother had taught him to strap almost invisibly to his calf.

"Antoine!" Sublette yelled across the fire. Two heads popped up. "Over here, now," he motioned, and hawked a flume of spittle that the two approaching young men nimbly sidestepped.

"These are the two goddamn Antoines," he said as he tossed back the knife, which Baptiste caught so indifferently the three men exchanged a quick look.

"Most rockheaded rascals ever to shit in the woods. Best of all, they don't understand a thing I say. Right, shitheads?"

The Two Antoines grinned and nodded as one.

"No possible use to me, and even less so to your girlfriends, am I right?"

More grinning and nodding.

"Pile wet skins on dry? That's right. Keep nodding. Yes, you do that, too!" Sublette lifted the flap of Baptiste's jacket pocket, which partially covered a well-thumbed book covered in leather, then spat again.

"See if you can help 'em coax the backbone out of that elk."

"Yes, sir," Baptiste said and returned with the two young men to where they'd been kneeling beside the magnificent bulk of an elk and the dark stain its soul made on the forest floor.

"Hey, is that the Book of God you got there? 'Cause I'll tell you right now, I'm a church-going man myself, but I don't have any time to waste, listening to some Bible thumper," Sublette called after Baptiste's retreating figure.

Baptiste stopped for a moment. *Candide* had become a bible to him.

The trio of young men worked with a will while Sublette watched from the other side of the fire. When he disappeared from view all three smiled.

"*Quel direction de compas* are we headed tomorrow?" Baptiste asked the Two Antoines, whom he'd run into at the blacksmith's shop countless times, their faces streaked with smoke and sweat. He hadn't seen them lately—so he was glad to find where they'd turned up. *Maybe they couldn't stand the heat.* If they were going to pretend they didn't understand Sublette's English, he certainly wasn't going to let on that they were old friends. The elk was well excavated now, and they tossed pink lungs and what seemed like miles of bowels into the pile of offal.

"Twenty miles yon," they replied. "Close to the caves of the Manitou."

"Manitou are enormous ghosts, neither men nor animals, with elk antlers sprouting from their skulls and arms," Baptiste's mother had often told him. "Thousands of years ago, they were painted with great reverence by your forebears inside the clefts of white cliffs along the lower Missouri River."

To reach the top of the Manitou Bluffs, three days above the meeting of the Kansas and Missouri rivers, worshippers and blasphemers alike had to pass through a series of limestone caves before a final turn through a narrow passage opened to the sunlit peaks where the Manitou drawings were visible. At least, that was the short cut. Like manhood, the tightest space was barely wide enough for a boy to fit through. Thus, only a handful of white men had seen them. A row of lofty cedar trees provided shade atop the sheer white cliffs.

Baptiste knew that Clark and his ilk, misunderstanding the nature of the Manitou, believed these chimeras to be the product of devil worship, a notion so romantic he chose not to disabuse them of it. In point of fact, they were more like the sketch work of kindly spirits. There were stars, lost caribou antler-feet, unfathomable crosses and circles from the depths of the heavens.

One of the pictures showed a bison with images of his entire future projected inside him. Another showed a school of flying fish with men in their mouths. Still another was a smile without a face, a black demon with a white bladder, a man with a foot enchanted into the hook he'd caught himself with, all "vurry vurry coeureous," Clark had written in his journals, having, in his ignorance, stumbled precisely upon their spirit—a certain curiosity of the heart.

Trapping for weeks on end in the area, Baptiste learned to climb up through the cliffs and sit high in the great wind when he wanted to be alone. It was here he'd disappear to most often. Three hundred feet above the river, he was free to conjure mournful tunes from his whistle, chew sap and slippery-elm gum, and smoke the Virginia tobacco he found himself trading a good deal of his take for.

Baptiste's first hunt was most successful. The game was lush, there wasn't time to despair over his fading hopes of becoming Clark's secretary, and he'd made a kind of peace with Bill Sublette that would help him through the rigors of the next two years. By the time late-summer 1823 rolled around, their boats were filled to the gunwales with fox and beaver pelts as they began their return down the Missouri for St. Louis. Then, just a week out of town, a passing trader stopped to tell them the rumor that a spy from Germany, sensing instability and the opportunity for a possible land grab, was among them just to monitor America's control of the woods. Lively japes danced across the campfire as first one hunter, then another, claimed to have figured out the dead true spit and skinny about what the interlopers were really up to.

"Goddamn Teutons. Have they hunted their own land bare? What right do they have to ours?"

"Maybe they want to establish dominion here."

"They're welcome to this hell hole! Let's trade it for Munich. Isn't that where they make the beer?"

"Whoever he is," the visiting trader said, "he has letters of passage from General Clark and the Secretary of War."

"But why would General Clark ever invite him here?" Baptiste asked.

"*Reales* make anyone smile sweet and pretty," Sublette said with singular authority.

A few days later, as night fell, Baptiste heard a gasp from Sublette, then a huge roar of laughter. Sublette pointed toward the horizon while the Two Antoines raced to the top of a boulder for a better view.

There, cresting the top of an outcropping and magnified by the setting sun, was a green and gold cart pulled by horses and adorned with a small bell that tinkled with each squeak of the carriage springs on the rocky slope as it made its way toward them. With strings of beasts tied head to tail, and attendants stationed along the way, the deputation looked more like a caravan from the spice trades through lost Araby than an encounter on the lower Missouri. Hooves lifted and stalled in the shimmer. Baptiste half imagined the snort and spit of camels with black tongues and leather bags laden with aromatic incense.

He couldn't help it. He and the younger Antoine shinnied up a tree in jig time, a skill they'd learned when charged with watch duty. After a hand signal, Baptiste pulled out his whistle and made a crude approximation of the call to hunt that made his lofty partner laugh so hard he fell into a nest of yellow jackets.

While Antoine danced to avoid the wasps, waving his hands wildly, a grinning Baptiste accompanied his every move with a lively air.

As the brougham drew nearer, four flamboyantly dressed men ensconced upon red-tasseled cushions came into view, followed by nearly a dozen mules, wagons, and two dozen woodsmen on foot. One man, with a tall plumed hat, obviously had the role of driver. Another was dressed like an English huntsman straight out of Baptiste's schoolbooks in a very precious and shiny pair of black boots and a long tarred moustache. *The German—he must be a nobleman.* The third was clearly playing the role of artiste, with smock, oil paints, and studied eccentricity—and the fourth, Baptiste realized with horror, was none other than Charbonneau.

"The great Toussaint Charbonneau," Baptiste heard the men below joke as the two parties mingled for shared amusements along the side of the river. *I'll say nothing but instead will watch you, so great is my shame for you*, Baptiste thought as he slid twenty feet back to earth with his toes barely touching the branches, landing directly in front of the man he loathed in his heart.

Toussaint's eyes opened a bit as he recognized Baptiste. Sliding from his saddle, the reprobate came forward and drunkenly embraced him.

"*Mon fils*," he said for the others' benefit, clanking his mouth and rotten teeth on the rim of Baptiste's canteen, which he'd grasped without invitation. He spat the liquid out in disgust when he realized it was water and grabbed a more likely vessel from his companion's shoulder. "Time for a toast!"

I know you can read my eyes, so I will let you. Why have you not yet died, old man?

Each one in Baptiste's party was introduced to the two Europeans in turn. Though Baptiste was too embarrassed to be caught staring at them, the continental nobleman and his artist friend didn't look like spies to him, because if he'd been in that line of work he would certainly have been quieter in his dress and added some camouflage to his carriage.

"*Enchanté*," Baptiste greeted them. "Pleased to meet you."

The artist, Vogelweide, took a step back in amusement. After combing the Mandan Villages unsuccessfully, they'd now chanced upon exactly the specimen they were looking for.

"Here's a live one," he said in Latin to his superior and pointed to the whistle hanging around Baptiste's neck. "So he was the source of that racket."

"One man's racket is another man's music," Baptiste replied in Latin, marveling at language's power to be either a wall or a way to move between worlds. In Clark's case, wasn't his limit of English actually a moat, surrounding him with a deliberate murkiness?

"*Sauvage savant,*" the grandee said to the artist, flashing a smile and returning Baptiste's bow. But he said nothing else. With a shrug, the artist disappeared into the coach and produced half a dozen botellos of wine.

"Care to join us?" he offered Baptiste in English.

"No."

Nearly stumbling across tree roots in their courtly jackboots, the Europeans disappeared behind the flap of their elongated Moroccan tent, which had required two hours and seven men to pitch.

Baptiste laughed with his fellows at the Europeans' clumsiness in the natural world, but judging from the glances the two had thrown his way he felt an eerie premonition that their predatory prowess in a civilized setting might be considerably more evolved.

4

"WOLF"

—hold your right hand with palm outward near your right shoulder, first and second fingers extended, separated and pointing up; move your hand forward, upward.

"SPY"

—make the sign for WOLF.

September, 1823

Upon his return to St. Louis, Baptiste busied himself repairing fences on Clark's property. To bunk down, he dragged a cot into his mother's old shack, with no one stopping him. He was just drifting off to sleep one night when an enormous hand reached around his shoulders and stood him up. Heracles had never handled him so roughly before. Even after fifty Missouri winters, Lottie's father was strong enough to tear off one of his arms like a squab's wing. Baptiste worried that the gentle giant had discovered his trysts with his daughter, but the big man's expression gave nothing away.

"Git yourself cleaned up," Heracles said and pushed him toward the water bucket.

"Where are we going?" Baptiste asked while he dressed and again as Heracles dragged him across the yard to the lights of the white house.

"I ain't going nowhere. The genr'l has sent for *you*," was all Heracles replied.

The horses had been put away, but Baptiste could see a group of people in the mysterious salon. Figures moved in the semi-darkness, with several looking through the windows as he approached the front porch.

This was the first time he'd been invited into Father Clark's world through the street entrance. Baptiste passed the fanlights and side-lights and Georgian trimmings into the foyer, where a tall cherry clock ticked. Everything here had been designed to welcome people who regularly wore shoes.

"I believe we have a guest," Clark joked benevolently.

Blinking, Baptiste nearly tripped on the thick cushion of Persian carpet. Candles in crystal prisms flickered in chandeliers that seemed to lean toward him. He felt himself sweat.

"My God, he's lovely," said a woman with a soft brow and rosy cheeks. "Don't you think so?"

Her eyes glowed below a turban of green satin. She flapped open a fan with a single practiced motion. Baptiste didn't dare look directly at her. He smelled her instead. There was a murmur of general agreement about his presentability. Who was he to disagree? Shouldn't an exhibit be presentable?

"Where are your manners?" Clark said. "Give your regards to Duke Paul . . . now let me see if I can do it . . . what's the rest of the horseshit? *Ah!* . . . Friedrich Wilhelm, Prince of Württemberg."

The tall, leering man to whom Baptiste's adopted father motioned was distinctly familiar. Baptiste looked down. Of course he could say hello, but he didn't. Father Clark, in a deeper voice, commanded him to repeat the Prince's name and greet him. Baptiste looked at the gangly man with blue skin and tried, fluently this time. His name was a mouthful of bees.

Duke Paul was evidently pleased with his effort, because he straightened himself and approached the youth. He looked directly into Baptiste's eyes, or tried to. Baptiste focused instead on the wallpaper floating behind him above his shoulder and to the left—a barque in full sail disappearing behind a screen of evergreens. In the doorway he saw Lottie sneaking a peek at him, too. The aristocrat leaned a good deal closer to him than he'd have liked, smelling sour and slightly musky beneath waves of what Baptiste took to be perfume, verbena and lavender.

"Could you look at me directly, please?" Duke Paul said. He glanced at the artist, whom Baptiste also recognized, and nodded in Baptiste's direction, "*Enfant charmante et fourbe.*"

"*Pas si charmante,*" Baptiste said. *To hell with you.* Baptiste stared right at Duke Paul's watery irises until he jumped. There was a burst of laughter, and Father Clark patted Baptiste on the back. Outside, rain began to fall.

"Gentlemen, may I show you the culmination of my life's work?" Clark said. "It's not much, but it passes for entertainment here."

Duke Paul edged closer to Baptiste as the entire party followed their host down the creaking, talking boards toward the museum's ell, where Clark's exhibits awaited them: silver foxes drinking from dusty mirrors, framed charts, pastel drawings of the Snake River, fossilized pemmican, and other ephemera from his historic expeditions, including the birchbark canoe Baptiste had been instructed to tell visitors was his birthplace, though it was not. *Poor Clark.* Baptiste felt something vaguely approaching pity for the man when he was in here.

At the mouth of the ell, on a lectern, was Alexander Mackenzie's *Voyages from Montreal, on the River St. Lawrence, Through the Continent of North America, to the Frozen and Pacific Ocean*, published in London in 1801. Baptiste knew the words of the big green book by heart because they were among the first he'd been taught to read. How could it be that Clark—so enchanted early on with his little Pomp, and so kind—was trotting him around like this now?

Duke Paul, with long strides, pulled up beside him again. As they considered the exhibits in turn, he laughed and clasped the boy's elbow.

In the shadows, Baptiste glimpsed Lottie, whom he knew was charged with keeping the display cases dusted, though not necessarily in the evenings, darting from darkened doorway to doorway as his group passed. How long had he not been listening to the elders ooh and aah as Clark droned on? He noticed it had stopped raining and fog now steamed up the window panes.

"Here," Clark intoned, "all we had was bear oil. We were out of food. And then we found a stray colt, way up in the snow."

Baptiste turned away. He didn't like the part about the horse.

"I butchered it without delay, and with good fortune and good spirits we in our advance party had horse for breakfast the next morning."

"Do you remember that, my *fauve?*" Duke Paul said, turning to Baptiste.

My fauve? When did I become a wild beast? If Baptiste didn't remember the colt's death he dreamed of it. A rabble of unshaven men chased the animal higher and higher up the frozen mountain until he finally turned around, his chest heaving, the snow knifing through his fetlocks. The men trudged slowly toward him, alone in the snow. *Who knows what a great leader he might have been. But they ate him,* Baptiste remembered. *So did I.*

Duke Paul drew Baptiste by the sleeve to a corner of the exhibition hall and bade him sit on a rawhide bench below a row of war bonnets hammered to the wall. As the foreigner slid in beside him, Baptiste thought of a copperhead slipping through cattails.

"At last," Duke Paul said. "The young Charbonneau. Is it true you're the son of my guide, yet you live here as Clark's son?" He looked the boy deep in the eyes. "Will you take me to the Manitou, the pictures of the Deavil?" he said, making light of Clark's infamous misspelling of the word devil in his journals.

"I have never seen them, *monsieur*," Baptiste lied.

Baptiste looked across the exhibition hall to where Clark and the other guests talked in two small groups. He caught sight of the canoe in its cradle of hemp, and as he watched, it seemed to move as the crowd passed beneath.

All of these great hunters and explorers were unaware of Lottie, who like a shadow had slipped to within inches of them below a slab of basalt to hear what they were saying. She sat down, catlike in her blue kitchen dress, the only one she had, her long arms around her knees.

"The cliffs of the Manitou," Baptiste told Duke Paul, "because of their occult nature," he said in French, "are impossible to find."

"*Enfant charmante!*" Duke Paul exclaimed. "You must one day take me there! I've spent the last two months looking for them!"

You were barely twenty miles from them.

"You can look for the cliffs of the Manitou. But you cannot find them before they find you," Baptiste said. *I will never take you there.*

"Perhaps all I need is the right guide," Duke Paul said.

"Why are you here, sir?"

Duke Paul brightened at the boy's directness. "Because I am nephew to the King, I will never be king myself, so I am allowed wanderlust to find my own place. I am unable to stop traveling and filling up my notebooks with all things rare."

He said he'd been to Brazil the year before, and Lima, and Port au Prince. Baptiste could smell the bear-loneliness of a man who had come all this distance to chat with strangers. The European's pale blue eyes surveyed him below a high forehead and a sweep of black hair that curled on each side. His moustaches curled upward a la mode, and he wore his white collars below his cravat, eccentric, like pictures of Lucifer Baptiste had seen in Scott's *Lessons*. The Duke explained that he and Vogelweide, his illustrator, had been to the Rio Plata, too, and the Amazon Basin in Brazil, studying Indian religions and, with Latinate precision, cataloguing the magic and phosphorescent plant life that took him to other worlds. "We are going back to Germany for a while." Duke Paul stared into Baptiste's eyes, which the boy boldly gave him this time. "You would be under my protection, and educated at court. Would you like to come?"

Duke Paul took a figural silver box from the folds of his vest and, with a dainty motion, dabbed a pinch of ground herbs into his nostril. He sneezed violently and then laughed when Baptiste looked alarmed. With exaggerated care, the duke tenderly used his long-nailed little finger to open Baptiste's lips, then tucked a small wad of the snuff inside his cheek.

"Our secret."

Within seconds Baptiste began to feel queer. His heart pounded in his chest as the blood behind his eyes seemed to heat up and evaporate. The effort it took not to move. But Baptiste felt his power growing. Something he didn't particularly like about himself had been piqued by the prince's interest in him. Maybe he was Duke Paul's Manitou. He was certainly neither man nor beast, but the first all-American half-breed, primogenitor of a new species. He looked at a grouse hen sitting on a nest of dried straw under a bell jar and wondered if his mother's hair, had she been so preserved, would by now have lost its sheen and turned gray.

Duke Paul stood up abruptly, almost martially, and strode to Clark, who nodded with him in animated discussion. Then Clark motioned for everyone to gather in the salon.

"Come here, with us," Clark said to Baptiste. "These gentlemen propose to take you to Europe and see how well they can educate you. Do you realize what an opportunity this is?"

It was the same dream you dangled before my mother, Baptiste realized suddenly, *and look how it turned out for her*—not so much a mistress as a fetish to be displayed and occasionally taken off a shelf to be handled—dead at a score and five. He felt squeamish that Duke Paul was attracted to him, but was anything ever free? Yearling that he was, he came to the cocky conclusion, *I can handle this dandy. If Father Clark is willing to cast me off, there's certainly nothing left for me here in St. Louis. Maybe it's all some kind of test.* "Exactly what will be expected of me?" he asked.

"You'll have to study, of course," Duke Paul said.

"May I learn to play music?" Baptiste said, his eyes lighting on the closed piano.

"Oh, you'll learn many things," Vogelweide said.

Clark looked around briefly as if he'd just joined the conversation. But he'd been here all along. Everyone had. A deal was being struck. *No matter,* Baptiste thought. *I will become a true gentleman, the equal of my white brothers. Nothing will stop me from becoming a gentleman.*

He stood up and bowed. "Thank you, sir," Baptiste said. "I will be honored."

An Indien at court. Baptiste looked again at the barques on the wallpaper, forever sailing with no land in sight. He could outswim any Creole, Frenchman, or brave he knew, but he didn't know water that immense and duplicitous. Crossing it would be like dying.

"Well," Clark said. "I think a toast is in order. Duke Paul?"

The duke winked at Baptiste. Glasses were being charged. Duke Paul put a drop of wine in a goblet and handed it to his new protégé, but Clark—whose views were well known on the subject of intoxicating "aborigines," as Duke Paul called them—shook his head no. Duke Paul slowly pulled the glass away. "Oh, of course not. How rude of me."

The next morning, Baptiste packed his possibles bag and in the pre-dawn darkness went to tell Lottie about the great opportunity that had been presented to him. In his self-absorption he imagined she might implore him to stay. But then he chided himself: *Other young men have already shown interest in her. I know she won't be lonely.*

She was carrying a pail of water when he found her. He reached over to take it from her, but she pulled away. In the distance, her father, Heracles, stood watching them.

"When are you coming back?" she asked. Her arms strained from the water as she walked.

"I don't know."

"Will you receive wages?"

"Duke Paul says I'll be educated at court."

"Yes, but is he paying you money?"

Of course, he hadn't asked. They walked a few more steps. Lottie dumped the water into a sluice for the animals and turned around.

"You'll be the slave," she said.

5

"OCEAN"

—make the signs for WATER and BIG.

In bright sunshine, Baptiste walked back to the house, where Duke Paul and Vogelweide watched from the porch as Heracles loaded skins, maps, an elk head, and other curiosities into a huge trunk lashed to their coach. Clark leaned out of the door.

"Goodbye, sir," Baptiste said.

He studied Father Clark carefully during these last moments. Clark didn't seem to know what to do. Certainly he was relieved Baptiste was going.

"My little dancing boy," Clark said, a shadow passing over his face. "You will do us honor."

"It will be my honor to paint him," Vogelweide nudged. Clark laughed.

"Don't worry," Clark said to Baptiste. "He means he'll paint a picture of you!"

Do you really think I'm that stupid? You really don't know me at all.

Baptiste watched Duke Paul sweep inside the coach, his servants climbing on top. How Lottie's eyes narrowed when Vogelweide got on board and then motioned for Baptiste to follow.

Clark frowned. Baptiste knew a rule had been broken. It was only the first. The coach began to roll, and Baptiste settled into the redolence of incense and leather and the "Europe" of the two men, both a head taller than he.

Behind him, Lottie skipped a few steps as if to follow the carriage, then stopped, her blue dress wilting on her frame. Heracles returned to work. Clark had already closed the door.

January, 1824

Baptiste woke on the brig *Smyrna*, pickled as a pike.

He stirred to the haunting sound of abakuas drumming their leg irons and singing in the Guanabacoa slave port. *This can't be Havana.* He tried to open his eyes, but his eyelids hurt, full of grit. He realized with horror that he'd lost weeks on end in a haze of rum and snuff. His tongue a big, dead, scaly fish stitched to the floor of his mouth, he listened to the mournful chants of thousands of coffled souls who'd survived the Middle Passage out of the millions captured. Their voices faded in the distance, then surged with hope, then faded again: the wretches were unable to name the body of water that separated them from home.

For a moment Baptiste felt blessed. He was, at least, headed in another direction. Oh, precocity of his innocence: He was crossing the blue Atlantic to discover . . . the Old World. Again he was being carried, with someone else the guide. *What do you think you're doing, my nestling?* Baptiste could almost hear his mother whisper. He wondered if he, too, would ever return across the Sargasso Sea. Lost between midnight and misapprehension, he drifted back into a troubled sleep.

At daybreak, water slapped below decks, and above, sailors shouted and moved tackle about on the quarterdeck with determinate thumping. The *Smyrna* lifted with a wave, and once again Baptiste felt the sensation that he was moving. Forcing one eye open, he caught sight of Vogelweide's long, tubercular back as the artist completed his toilet, a single drop of perspiration running down the channel of his spine toward his arse. His bony shoulders slumped forward, and his narrow fingers, unlike Duke Paul's, tapered into long nails yellowed by tobacco and uncertain health.

The three of them had squeezed into the supercargo's cabin. Baptiste nurtured his semiconsciousness while the blush of sunrise on the horizon became more distinct through a porthole. A long walnut table, surrounded by weighted ship's chairs, seemed to lean against the motion while, on its surface, a spyglass in a leather box rolled back and forth. He tried . . .

But he couldn't go back to sleep. Sounds grew too loud: the rasp of Duke Paul's razor as he preserved the flourish around his moustaches, Vogelweide's oily chuckle as he washed beneath his hairy arms—*what was funny about soap?*—and through the wooden rafters of his prison of motion and time, he could still hear gulls, far away.

Baptiste was fully awake now, but he lay very still. The two Germans talked softly in their native language as they padded about. Like giants in a fairy tale, they seemed very, very tall.

"*Der Indianer, das dornröschen—dann, Prinz Kinderschänder?*" Vogelweide said in a lewd voice, pointing to Baptiste while he feigned sleep.

"*Nur keine solche eile,*" Duke Paul answered him curtly.

Then Duke Paul, wiping his purple neck with a towel, leaned down and pulled Baptiste's toe. A snake of a smile moved across the nobleman's face. A brass lantern swung across the ceiling but he ducked it neatly and let it pass in front of his face again—a smooth traveler.

"*Mon fauve*," he said to Baptiste in the courtly French with which they habitually addressed him. "You'll find it better in the fresh air. Come on."

Duke Paul offered Baptiste his arm, and as Baptiste got up he realized he wore only the Duke's ivory silk *inexpressibles*.

"*Estraunliche*," said Vogelweide. "He finally wakes."

Baptiste accepted a pewter stein from Duke Paul, slopping with tepid grog. He drank it thirstily while they watched. It dawned on him why the two men seemed so tall. He'd slept on the floor. A single bed was built into the cabinetry below what must have been Duke Paul's red satin coverlet. Books and charts shifted behind glass doors on shelves built between the beams. Duke Paul guided him to a hatch in the transom, which he pushed open, and a gust of frigid air rushed in. Baptiste poked his head through to look outside. They were no more than a mile from a long sandy beach roughened by evergreens bobbing slowly in the opposite direction.

"Florida," Duke Paul said. "We'll head north along the coast until we're above Bermuda; then we'll tack east northeast until we catch the Gulf Stream and the trades."

Two figures fishing on a catboat threw a skein of nets behind it just this side of the collapsing waves of the shore. Baptiste heard the fishermen talking over the water, their voices amplified over distance, though he could not decipher their syllables. He felt a soft sorrow for the shore. He could swim there from here.

"With my compliments," Duke Paul ventured in English, handing Baptiste a small pile of linens from his trunk, exquisitely folded.

"Thank you."

At first Baptiste was honored that the duke would give him things of his own, but then, gauging their size, realized they fit too well. Had Duke Paul taken the care to have new garments tailored for him? In any case, it was possible he kept a set of clothing at the ready for any prospective Métis who might deserve his attentions.

Baptiste recalled now with shame that he'd been sick in the street four nights earlier on the docks at New Orleans as he'd descended from Duke Paul's carriage. They'd so softened him with mulled wine that Vogelweide had laughed, "*We* will be your Lewis and Clark."

Such a "voyage of discovery" he'd never considered on the cliffs of the Manitou. His mother had often told him he was the grandson of Chief Red Hook, a sachem. His uncle was the great witch Cameahwait, in command of more Shoshone than there were people in Württemberg. If accidents of birth were important, Baptiste was closer in his line of succession than Duke Paul was in his. He pushed away thoughts of his mother's eyes.

"Perhaps we can convince him to wear proper boots," Duke Paul called over to Vogelweide as he looked at Baptiste's calloused feet. The two men watched him dress.

Discomfited, he followed them past the sail locker, crossed a passageway covered with rope faked back and forth, and climbed a narrow ladder toward the sunlight. Sailors turned away and snorted as he passed by, but Duke Paul pulled him ahead, nodding to them, and finally they were on the deck.

Baptiste took in a deep breath and looked about. *A ship is a* tso'a-ppeh, *a spirit captured and chained by the wind.* Though the touch of shore might mean its death, *shore* was the sound it made as it moved through the waves. The creak of oak and canvas was everywhere, under pressure, as it glided forward, the only direction the future permitted.

A short man with a complexion so dark and movements so explosive he reminded Baptiste of the Two Antoines' smithy boss strode immediately to them.

"Our host," Duke Paul leaned over as he spoke. "Captain Stanhope."

"How do you do?" Baptiste said and then regretted it when Vogelweide snickered at his attempt at civility.

"Mmph." Captain Stanhope dismissed him with a glance.

Baptiste's filmy new clothes fluttered, and his face got hot. He felt humiliated in the mariner's presence: Stanhope had merely approached them in order to greet Duke Paul, who'd paid him handsomely for their passage. No one had paid the good captain enough to speak to the jeweled monkey.

"Baptiste." Vogelweide motioned him to the rail. "Come here."

Baptiste felt the silk of his finery sliding over his legs. During their ablutions, Duke Paul had sprayed something green at him from a bottle. So malleable was he, he hadn't even asked what it was. But when the bergamot fragrance hit him he did not jump because something was changing in him, as if the perfume were a magic mist with an unexpected outcome. Now what he loathed the most, that which demeaned him most profoundly, was to be considered, because he was a savage, accidentally charming. He reached Vogelweide and looked at the shore.

"Do you want to go back?" Vogelweide asked him.

"No."

"Look!" Vogelweide leaned over the rail. Porpoises were following the *Smyrna*, twirling and reveling in her wake. "See? Over there! That one looks like you."

The artist pointed to a shorter one trailing the school.

"See? He cannot laugh."

Baptiste tried not to smile, but he had him. Vogelweide sloughed his cheek, and he jumped back.

"Must you do that?" Baptiste said.

"Why does it bother you?"

"It's wrong."

"Who told you it was wrong? The priests at your school? Aren't you Christian?" Vogelweide leered.

"Oh, I'm *often* a Christian," Baptiste said. Even Toussaint, the rapist, had insisted he be baptized when he'd first brought him to St. Louis. "In St. Louis, no one dares not to be a Christian."

Vogelweide's mouth barely opened. Then he approached the boy's ear. "So you'd rather I didn't touch you . . . here?"

Baptiste sidestepped him so neatly Vogelweide's hand still floated in the air.

"You see? Nothing happened," Vogelweide teased. "I have a reward for you."

And now the other half of the transaction, Baptiste thought. *I wonder where I'll wake up next.*

He watched Vogelweide walk briskly amidships and return with Duke Paul. What was this "reward"?

Stand your ground. Baptiste suppressed the urge to run away as Duke Paul reached into his waistcoat while the transparent sea swelled and lapsed behind him. The catboat and the fishermen were far behind them now. He watched the beach bobbing behind Vogelweide and could make out piles of seaweed and three white trees. A gull swirled in front of the *Smyrna* and dropped down in the water, splashing for fish. He knew he could still swim away. They were only a mile from shore.

"Now I want you to try this."

Duke Paul, at his shoulder, nodded approval as Vogelweide took out a small vial the color of gentian violet. He poured some blackish fluid into the cap and held it out. Both men stood silent now.

If this were a dare he would show no fear. Baptiste took it and swallowed.

"How does it taste?" Duke Paul asked.

"Like honey," Baptiste said, "and sugar."

"Anything else?"

Baptiste's eyelids fluttered like Julia Clark's.

"Don't worry, belladonna won't hurt you."

Baptiste tasted something from far away. "Behind it there is something very bitter."

Duke Paul lowered his voice. "Venetian women put drops of the distillate in their lower lids to dilate the pupils and make their eyes seductive and luminous."

"Why have you given it to me?" Baptiste's heart thumped. He took two steps toward the rail, but Vogelweide stopped him.

"In Maraca Ibo, the deadly nightshade, which gives us belladonna, has a structure that's like a hand," Duke Paul said, holding his forearm up in the air. "In the palm of that hand is a violet flower with five leaves." He opened his fingers dramatically. "The roots yield a 'tea,' Brunfelsia tea. We've only given you a tea, *fauve*. In a little while you will feel how wonderful it is to be alive." Duke Paul moved closer and patted his shoulder. How could he have reached him before he could pull away? The duke's eyes brightened. He sketched a bow and left.

"What will this really do to me?" Baptiste asked Vogelweide.

Vogelweide studied him. "Nothing will happen today," he said. "Tomorrow will be different. The third day it will be over." He reached over and lifted the boy's eyelid. "I'd like to paint you when you are afraid. You know, you're really quite lovely when you're not so guarded."

Baptiste determined at that moment never to be caught off guard.

That night, Vogelweide and Duke Paul dined with the captain in his stateroom, while a cabin boy a few years younger than Baptiste brought him a pail of food from the crew's mess. Baptiste felt nothing from the drug but imagined he could hear laughs and stories from the royal party more acutely as they throbbed through the wood. He couldn't make them out but was surprised at their volume. He found himself in an odd humor.

"Come in," he said to the boy with waxen features and curly hair.

"I shouldn't!"

"It's all right. I'm allowed to be in here."

"I'm *not* allowed, suh." The youth's eyes begged Baptiste to dismiss him.

"What's your name?"

"Reehl. I have to go. Here's your Injun pudding."

"*ReelIhavetogo?*"

"No. Name's Reehl. I'm not 'lowed to pass through the door that leads to the fancy cabin, nor enter any of the offisuh's quartas, or they'll whip me to next Sunday, suh. Then, when we get back home and they tell my muthah, she'll make their whippin' seem like Sunday dinnah. You get the ideer."

Baptiste had a little trouble following what the boy was saying. He'd never heard this flat, nasal manner of speaking where the letter "r" was inexplicably dropped from some words and attached to the end of others.

"Where's home?"

"Salem, and in Salem we don't let the Injuns inside our house."

"Here, *you're* not allowed in," Baptiste laughed. "Look." He demonstrated how easy it was to pass in and out of his stateroom while Reehl's eyes rocked. Baptiste took the pail from him. It was a golden mélange of cornmeal, eggs, and molasses.

"Did you think this was all I could eat?"

Reehl turned red as a pomegranate. "Cook's joke, suh. It weren't my ideer."

Baptiste stopped smiling when he realized he was taking the same high tone with this boy that the Germans were taking with him. "Do you know any Indians in Salem?"

"Oh, no, suh! We've killed you all!"

"With this pudding?"

"That's more than I get in three days, and it's bold good, too."

Baptiste felt himself losing his balance. He shifted his stance.

"Suh, are you ill?"

"Why do you ask?"

"The other men, suh. They say all the savages who are taken to Europe nevuh survive the city sickness. They say you're going to sartan death."

"Certain death?"

"That's what I said. They was saying you'll die just like the prince and princess of Hawaii died last wintuh aftah sailing the *Cleopatra's Barge* all the way to London to see King George. Operas and waltzing at the royal castles and all. Both dead."

"Surely their crew didn't die, too?"

"All of 'em died. Measles."

In the darkness of the rocking ship, with the whale lamp casting a dull glow, Reehl's warnings of deadly pestilence in Europe seemed compelling.

"Have some of this." Baptiste held out the pudding. He didn't have to ask twice—Reehl rammed his dirty hand into the pail.

"If you don't mind my asking, why are you heah?" Reehl licked his lips and reached for another scoopful.

Baptiste straightened. "I'm getting an education at the court of Württemberg."

"The tars say that you make a right propuh *gweedoon*. You could make your fortune."

When Baptiste realized what he'd said, he grasped the boy's collar. But he could tell he didn't know what it meant.

"You may tell them I am no sex slave."

"They are wrong, suh?"

"I am nobody's *guidoune!*"

"Yes, suh. I'll tell them, suh. As long as you're not afraid of making them wrathy."

Reehl made the sign of the cross and spat for friendship. Baptiste spat, too.

"I'm not afraid."

6

"MEDICINE/MYSTERIOUS AND UNKNOWN"

—hold right hand close to forehead, palm outward, index and second fingers separated and pointing upward, others and thumb closed; spiral hand upward right-to-left.

In the deep of night Baptiste awoke to find Duke Paul and Vogelweide snoring in their bunks. He stood up but found he had to reach over and touch the long walnut desk to steady himself. Pulling the lantern toward a looking glass, he noticed that his pupils nearly obliterated his irises. He drank some water from Duke Paul's washstand, then felt the need to relieve himself immediately. In the moonlight, he slipped outside and climbed the ladder to the deck. Making his way to the rail, he sensed the boat rocking violently, as if in a storm, but his eyes told him the sky was calm and the sea glassy. He glanced down and his hands shimmered as if underwater. So did the narrow planks of the deck washing over his feet. He considered returning below but decided he'd suffocate if he spent another second in that stateroom. Instead, he climbed into a canvas sail bag and dozed off.

At dawn, he felt fresh, alert, as if he were seeing his first sunrise, though the sailors on deck seemed blurry. With Duke Paul and Vogelweide recording his reactions, he began to notice smells that seemed familiar though he'd never smelled them before. Of a sudden he felt he'd known poor Captain Stanhope for years and attempted to engage him in vigorous conversation, alternately crying and laughing. He all but kissed the man. The sailors, aloof in his presence, were now his brothers. The adventures they'd shared together! His skin tingled as though covered with ants.

A special breakfast of salt ham and bread with root vegetables had been prepared, no doubt, in his honor. This delighted him, though it was difficult to eat because the ham waltzed about on the plate.

Before long, Baptiste began to believe that sly Vogelweide must have arranged the pieces of ham so that they looked like faces. When Baptiste marveled aloud that his tubers were taking on obscene shapes, Vogelweide and Duke Paul laughed all the harder.

"Well, there are certain aphrodisiac effects," Duke Paul said, looking down at Baptiste's nankeen trousers.

"The belladonna has juicy black berries, the Devil's cherries," Vogelweide said. "It is said they are fatal to children." He whispered something to Duke Paul.

"Not now. Maybe tomorrow," Duke Paul said.

Baptiste felt himself slipping into a dream, although he still heard them speaking. For once, he didn't care what his standing was. He'd been carrying a bag of distrust all the way from St. Louis. Now he put it down.

Today, it seemed, Vogelweide was going to paint him. They went below, out of the sunlight. The artist sat him on the green horsehair of the supercargo's window seat. Baptiste was familiar with the ship now, and prolix.

"Have you any talent, Herr Vogelweide?"

"Stop fidgeting."

Baptiste tried to oblige him, but he itched all over.

"And take off your shirt."

The boy's eyes adjusted to the dark. As if Vogelweide were slowly painting him into the scene, Duke Paul appeared dimly in the background. The duke watched as Baptiste pulled off his roundabout and tossed it to one side. Then Baptiste took off his tunic. One of the two men made a low sound of appreciation. It didn't matter: Reehl had explained it, in his way. Baptiste was already infected. In the darkness of the cabin he felt Duke Paul move a step closer, hunting him with his eyes.

"You're so exotic, you think you're so beautiful," Vogelweide clucked. "If you think that dusky skin and hair 'blue as a cormorant's wing' is going to get you somewhere, just know I'm keeping my eyes on you. What kind of *sauvage* do you think you are, anyway, with that nose? You've got some Gaul! More indeterminate than Indian, if you ask me. Hold up your arms."

Without grace, he complied.

"Hairless as a child," Vogelweide said.

"There are little wisps," Duke Paul said, now inches away.

It was Baptiste's shame that he did not reach for his knife, but his mind was racing ahead. He would never make it to Stuttgart, where the Duke's mother lived. These gentlemen might very well kill him. They already thought of him as dead. In his intoxicated state, he thought this odd, too.

"Breeches," the painter said.

"No," said Duke Paul. "Paint him like this."

It was like standing on top of a cliff and feeling the dizzy pull that makes the uninitiated back away from the edge. The trees far below whisper, "We are soft; we will catch you with our boughs of fir." But the trees were lying. Ignoring Duke Paul, in his self-loathing, Baptiste took a running leap over the edge: his pantaloons were soon a pool of silk on the floor. *What do I care? Am I not a savage?* These men considered him so incapable of modesty he would answer their insult. He quickly unbuttoned his linens, and a moment later he saw Duke Paul lower his chin to his chest and close his eyes.

"All elbows and shoulder blades and jaw line," Vogelweide said. "Gamine and sensual, the new specimen. What a marvelous belly. Look at the angle of his bones, the planes of his buttocks."

Baptiste didn't answer, because it was easier to pretend he wasn't there if he didn't speak. This was not at all like flirting with Lottie. With Lottie it was all juice and roses, but these overtures held hints of violence and degradation. He was falling, pulled down by the vertigo. And to his mortification exhilarated at the bottom of his thoughts for having made Duke Paul blush. *Is this what you want, Baptiste?*

He had never stolen from the East India store. But here, with no one watching him but two lunatics enamored with his darker below, afraid of the measles and other European vapors, afraid of his own shame and excitement, he forgot Lottie and the Creoles. He forgot his mother, and he knew Clark had forgotten him. He began to steal from himself.

"*Quel picrelle,*" Duke Paul said. "What a compelling complexion, rubicund but neither Latin nor Oriental, skin finely textured as that of *l'enfante.*"

My skin again, Baptiste thought. "He'd saved his hide" suddenly had an entirely different meaning for him. It horrified him: Even if he died, he knew the two Germans might preserve his corpse. He saw himself spiked and stuffed, on display with a taxidermic grimace in a grimy school for boys in Düsseldorf.

From that moment on Baptiste spoke boldly to the duo. Without the shackles of inhibition, he relaxed and began to adopt Vogelweide's air of Weltanschauung.

He'd learned this German word, and others, by listening intently to every syllable Duke Paul and Vogelweide uttered during their private exchanges. For days nothing had made sense. Now, though he didn't understand a third of what they said, he was encouraged. He would keep whatever knowledge of German he had a secret for as long as he needed it. *Perhaps one day, in my hearing, you will say out loud your plans for the Indian boy.* He even made the pretense of asking Duke Paul when he might learn German. The duke seemed only mildly pleased.

"In good time," Duke Paul said as he looked at his nails. "When we reach the castle."

"Perhaps German is a little like Latin?"

"Nothing could be further from Latin," Duke Paul said.

Over the next week Vogelweide painted Baptiste three times in the most idealized chromes of cinnamon and gold. In one portrait he painted him beside the lovingly lifelike head of Duke Paul, already completed at a separate sitting. He could not help but elongate Baptiste's nose and give a romantic aspect to his mouth and eyes. In his neglectful manner, barely in the room with Baptiste as his brush whistled across the canvas, Vogelweide answered his questions. With the deftness of his paintbrush he slowly put the Duke's arm around him.

"One of the young seamen was telling me—I am not expected to survive the passage?" Baptiste asked.

"You would be unusual if you did. Who knows? Maybe you'll linger for weeks, even months, in Europe when we get there. Maybe longer." Vogelweide grinned. "A long life for a souvenir."

Baptiste pushed down his anger. "Just how durable a souvenir are you?"

The painter took a draught of a smoky substance from a dark green bottle covered with scratches. A coiled hose transmitted smoke to his lungs. Baptiste noted that Vogelweide exhaled in threes—Father, Son, and Holy Ghost.

"I am the invaluable traveling companion," said the painter. "I became indispensable in Leipzig, when Paul's military obligations were nearly complete. In spite of his size and courage, His Grace had determined himself that he was unfit for such duty, and as I was principal aide-de-camp, his military advisors were only too happy to facilitate his release via an accelerated promotion schedule," he laughed scornfully. "Besides, with Napoleon gone, was there anyone interesting enough left to bother fighting? Instead, His Grace decided he'd be far more useful pursuing and developing his intellectual talents, so he embarked upon the study of botany and zoology under Gay-Lussac. Head up."

Baptiste moved as commanded. Vogelweide approached him, handed him a bumper of rum, and set his head in an attitude, arranging his shoulders in yet another unnatural position. The painter put a hot bearskin over his shoulders, and it itched.

"Duke Paul found that *living things* were the fruits of his passion." Vogelweide very gently sloughed his hand over Baptiste's sleepy left nipple, which now stood at attention. The youth jerked back. "Now there's a little warrior," Vogelweide said and went back to his easel.

"Will I be assigned a tutor at court?" Baptiste asked, looking down.

"I've made you no promises, Baptiste. But Duke Paul will keep his, unless he flattens you and puts you into one of his books. You will be examined by the foremost scientists of the day. We will see how rapidly you can learn, if at all. If you fall sick, we will study your reactions and do everything in our power to effect a cure. An *Indien* with fragrance of contour and the chasteness of Romance. Your General Clark was most enthusiastic about this."

"Varus, Varus, where are my legions?"

"Aren't you the dark thinker! Now suck on your lips a bit so they'll shine."

"But it was understood?"

Vogelweide kept painting.

That night, after a dinner of pickled herring, Vogelweide produced a new gift for Baptiste from Duke Paul, a cobalt-hued tonic.

"Tomorrow, '*fauve*,' we will be in le Havre de Grace," Vogelweide said. "You must not address Duke Paul once we reach the shore unless he requires an answer from you, and even that will usually come through me. But he should like you to know that his feelings for you are most warm. Immediately upon arrival you will begin your studies, though we are disappointed that you have asked for no books to read thus far. Now down the hatch."

After Baptiste swallowed with a loud gulp, Vogelweide quickly handed him another bumper of rum. Baptiste watched the stars through the portholes as they skidded across the night sky, then slowed down.

Duke Paul entered through the cabin door with more of the blue elixir glinting in a glass. Raising this to his lips as well, Baptiste could have sworn he saw the constellation *Lupus*, the wolf, in its depths.

"What is it . . . your highness?" he asked.

"It's called *Ayahuasca*, 'Vine of the Dead,' from the Amazon forests of Peru and Ecuador."

"A plant," Vogelweide said, adding to Duke Paul in German, "for the boy in a vegetative state."

"Vine of the Dead is most certainly not a plant but the bark of *Banisteriopsis caapi* entwined with leaves of *Psychotria viridis*," said Duke Paul. "We powder it to make a slurry, strain it, then sweeten it with Damascus rue to drink it."

"Naturally," Baptiste said.

"Fourteen grams this time?" Vogelweide ignored him.

Duke Paul nodded. "Five grams rue."

"What else is on the menu?" Baptiste asked.

In front of him Vogelweide took the rue from a jar among his paint supplies and stirred it into still another glass.

"You'll find nothing else is necessary," Vogelweide said and held out the new mixture. Baptiste downed it.

"Now this is very tasty!" he said.

Duke Paul's smile exposed his rodentlike lower teeth. "There is a beautiful flower in the Amazon Basin that smells like a rotting corpse. The Vine of the Dead is not so beautiful, and the stench is infamous, but the taste is sweet."

Moments later Baptiste's eyes widened as the walls of the cabin dropped away. He felt more than naked, as if he'd peeled off his skin like wet clothing, exposing all of himself to the breeze. The stateroom chairs seemed to be plotting with each other; upset that he'd discovered them, some of them lunged toward him like small animals. He sensed his body accelerate toward the horizon as though he were flying. Jungles, mountains, isthmuses flew below his feet in ecstatic colors, as though spilled out of a jar. When one tries Vine of the Dead, a lovely inflection, soothing and deadly, suggests, "Wouldn't you like to come with me?" While he considered this offer, recollections from years dead and gone heaved into view as though part of the present: Clark's desk; Toussaint's black teeth; his mother's eyes looking kindly down at him from within a statue of the Virgin Mary, who now had brown skin like his mother's. His mother *was* the Virgin Mary. Sweat trickled down his temples. *What is happening?* Duke Paul approached him and kissed his mouth, his neck, the small of his back, and his heels. "I admire you," the duke said, "and will never abandon you."

Then he turned Baptiste over and pushed himself into the boy.

Baptiste was surprised that he felt nothing but a mild revulsion at first, and then it actually did hurt. At the last moment he broke the tips of his fingernails trying to pull himself away across the ship's deck. He thought the cabin door hit him, though it could have been something else, and he fell unconscious. By the next morning his nails were blue and black. There was a long scratch against his cheek, too, and it was difficult to walk three steps without retching.

But in his mind Duke Paul never really touched him. His mother made sure of that.

After breakfast, when Duke Paul, Vogelweide, and Baptiste walked on deck to get some air, Baptiste saw young Reehl trailing behind him but avoiding his glances. Or was he the one following Reehl, begging him to look him in the eyes? Later, in mid-afternoon, Baptiste, Duke Paul, and Vogelweide found themselves far forward at the rail, where Reehl was repairing a sail with two other sailors. The other tars affected an air of curiosity, but Reehl never looked up from his long needle.

"When we get to shore, you're not to reveal that trick of yours without one of us speaking to you first," Vogelweide said.

"What trick?"

"That French tongue."

"But I *am* half French," Baptiste said.

"We've got all too many Frenchmen over here. What draws the audience is Indians."

"But why me, in particular?"

"Why, it's your mother, of course!" Vogelweide rolled his eyes. "Who is more romantic, and a sylph of Nature, than the great Sacagawea? The finest *schlosses* will adore your stories about her! You do have some prepared, I hope, though they're going to want you to do it in pictograph, I suppose."

"*Crisse moi patience!*"

Vogelweide put his arm around his head as if to comfort him, but behind him Baptiste felt the sailors stiffen in revulsion. He was a country that was being discovered, *terra incognita*. Ships approached his bays, inlets, straits, throats, lagoons, swamps, and mossy creeks. He was all that remained of their New World, but they had no interest in saving him. He doubled over with the dry cough he'd suffered since

Duke Paul had raped him. *Do that again and I will kill you, Duke Paul,* he thought, but stopped himself. *We have made a deal. I must weigh the consequences and form a plan. Duke Paul will most certainly do it again, but in return I will learn about the wonders of Europe.* He rubbed his hair. It didn't make any more sense to him than it did to his mother: To enter society, you had first to surrender your self-respect.

"Why do you never speak of your mother?" Vogelweide asked. Baptiste had been so deep in thought he was surprised the painter was still beside him, somewhere between his two worlds. Vogelweide's voice sounded distant, fathoms deep, as if calling from below a wave. *What do you care about my mother, Vogelweide? Don't mention her. And stay out of my head.* His temples throbbed and his eyes felt hot.

"She was a witch," Baptiste said.

"Even out here, your eyes flash like a lynx's."

He became the wooden Indian he'd seen in front of the shop in St. Louis.

"Your mother was . . . a clairvoyant? Did she show you this?" Vogelweide reached for his palm. "Do you see this? You have no lifeline."

The oldest of the sailors bolted up rudely. "Everybody has a lifeline, sir. Even this Injun, sir."

With luck I won't have a lifeline. With luck I'll die right now. Baptiste stood still as the tar walked over and carefully inspected his palm. The others, with Reehl excepted, followed his voyage of discovery. The sailor scratched his chin.

"Let me see the other hand," he demanded.

With that Baptiste fell into a fever and dreamed of his mother.

7

"HORSE"

—hold left palm edgewise, back of the hand to left, in front of left breast. Place the right index and second fingers astride the left hand.

February, 1824

Baptiste woke with a start and realized he couldn't move. His hair was matted and he smelled as if he'd been exhumed from the grave, steeped in the true "fragrance of romance." Lucacz, the second mate and ship's surgeon, tossed him a wet rag. Baptiste pressed the thankfully cool cloth to his forehead.

"You've been unconscious for eleven days," Lucacz said. "Dead, we thought."

"Was there a battle?" Baptiste half-remembered the feeling of compressed air and a roar as though it would never stop. Cannon.

The surgeon grunted. "A kind of battle. The consul fired nine guns to welcome Duke Paul, but as he requires eleven, he could not be prevailed upon to disembark. We were stuck out here on ceremony—four hours in the harbor, with rigging rattling, on anchor detail. Our sailors could not get their grog." He rolled his eyes to indicate the ugliness that might attend to such a delay. "Finally the consul got wind of it and fired another eleven."

"Where is the royal party?" Baptiste asked.

"They've been in town, suh!"

Baptiste sat up to see Reehl standing in the passageway.

"Open the hatch," Reehl said. "The *winnder!*"

Turning, Baptiste reached behind and pushed open a porthole that filled the stateroom with icy salt air. Through it, he saw ships' masts and stone chateaux rising to the top of a snow-covered hill. He saw women wrapped in blue and plum *douillettes,* and then he saw a coach glide to the head of the quays. Vogelweide stepped out of it in a long bangup. Baptiste rolled back onto the hammock that had encased him like a chrysalis. For one moment more he allowed himself to close his eyes.

"Get up, lie-a-bed," Vogelweide said as he strode in, grabbed Baptiste by his hair, pulled him to the doorway, and threw a bucket of water over him.

Beside him, Reehl stood at the ready with a sea sponge and a sliver of lye soap. They helped Baptiste to stand up.

"Avoir l'air de la chienne à Jacques," Vogelweide said.

Baptiste laughed and started to wash up. "I must look a fright, like 'Jack's bitch.'"

"As it seems you'll be with us a while longer," Vogelweide said with good nature, "you might as well get into these."

He opened a trunk and folded back some tissue to expose a full dress Ojibwa funeral suit with headdress. Baptiste had seen one such outfit at Clark's museum. It had nothing to do with his culture, so he put it on. This was his curtain call.

Reehl's eyes bugged open. He was about to say something, but Baptiste stopped him short by asking him, "How have you found Le Havre?"

"Oh, I don't leave the ship, suh! I'm perfectly happy right here."

Baptiste was dizzy but felt gusts of health returning. Vogelweide left, returned, tossed him his bag. "Deavil take the hindmost!" he laughed as he ran down the gangplank and into the dark blue carriage. Baptiste wished Reehl and Lucacz well as he flew down to the slippery stones of the quay and followed the painter inside. To his relief, the stevedores loading the *Smyrna* for her return passage ignored him entirely as they continued with their work.

The interior of Vogelweide's hired phaeton was finer than any he'd ridden in before. The canopy was upholstered in silk brocade. The velvet seats were tufted with heavy buttons, embellished with tassels, and braided in silver. The burled wormwood was flecked with gold.

"*Wo ist* Duke Paul?" Baptiste asked in the rudimentary German he'd picked up during the crossing. There was no longer a reason to keep his growing knowledge of it a secret. Vogelweide turned to him, quick as an adder.

"So. You're using the Duke as he uses you," he said in French, with Baptiste following.

"I'm sure I don't know what you mean."

"Ha!" he said. "What a sly student. Funny that the first 'German' you've learned is how to lie. Is this the gentleman you hope to become?"

How could you know me so well, or at least the worst part of me? Baptiste swallowed. "I came here to be educated. Did you think I covered my ears when you talked, or did you believe you could select the 'education' for 'the boy in a vegetative state' as well?"

Vogelweide whistled, softened his tone. "Duke Paul is with the consul, up there." He pointed to the slopes of a soft hill that hung over the harbor. Plane trees lined the shore below it, and to the left, the ghost of an orchard covered the hillside. With a tut from the coachman, their two black horses plunged into their harness, and they started off over the cobbles.

"Tomorrow, we'll be in Paris," Vogelweide said. "But tonight we dine at the consul's. Are you hungry?"

"Most famously."

"I have a remedy for that," Vogelweide said, and at his signal they turned left onto a narrow *rue* which ran out from the mouth of the harbor like a spoke of a wheel. An old yellow lighthouse appeared at times through gaps between the buildings. Soon the parti-colored signs of inns and shopfronts flashed in front of them until Vogelweide stopped the carriage below a sign marked *Louis le Desire*.

"This place was called the Blue Boar when Napoleon was in favor," he said, pointing to the sign. "Now, with the Prince of Wales and the Bourbons in control, they've painted it over. Do you see?" With his finger, he traced the outline of the boar's tusks in the air. "Le Havre blows like the wind. Across the street, the Virgin Mary has reemerged as Duchesse d'Angouleme. The eagles that were omnipresent in the shops here have been painted into *fleurs-de-lis* . . . look! The instinct for adapting, for survival here, is strong."

They stepped from the coach and entered Louis le Desire. Baptiste clung stolidly to his slow German as they took their seats. Vogelweide spoke like a banging gate. Baptiste tried to mimic him.

"Duke Paul is not expecting us?"

"Not for hours. And he's not expecting you at all. You've made quite a recovery! But we'd better air you out."

The dark, cool room was dominated by a central beam hung with dried herbs. A small tavern table had been drawn up beside a huge stone hearth adorned with gleaming copper pots but thankfully empty. Baptiste's newly tanned rawhide costume creaked as he lowered himself into his seat. The innkeeper, missing so many teeth his mouth was a black maw, approached and spoke exclusively to Vogelweide, though he stole anxious glances at his more spectacular guest.

"He is from the jungles of les Etats-Unis d'Amerique," Vogelweide said confidentially, "and you will be the first to serve this very gross monster some of your fine ale."

"*Honors, monsieur*. But . . . he looks sick," the man said.

"A difficult passage, eh, *monsteur?*" Vogelweide winked. He kicked Baptiste until he scowled.

"Can he speak?" the man asked.

"He hasn't said a word yet," Vogelweide said.

Baptiste reached up to take off his headdress. With the movement of his hand the innkeeper jumped, and from the tail of his eye he saw two young maids giggle. They'd been taking turns looking at him from a doorway near the kitchen. Baptiste smiled, and the smaller one blushed. She wore a light blue frock, and her hair was in braids.

The afternoon passed without the shadow of excitement but for a stop at a cobbler's. There Vogelweide bought him a pair of bright red Arabian slippers he insisted the boy wear at the bottom of his funeral togs. Baptiste glowed with the residual perspiration of his sickness. The pointed tips of his slippers curled skyward.

They arrived at the consul that night. By then there was a soft sleet. Everything at the top of the hill had an orange tinge, as if they were engraving the evening into copper. Below, in a sweep of masts, were the quays of the district Saint-François full of ships along the curve toward the soot-blackened lighthouse that marks the mouth of the Seine.

Even up here on Pavilion Poulet, high on the hill of Ingouville at the consulate, they could hear the voices of men loading things onto the shore far below. Or so it seemed. Stepping out of the coach, Baptiste saw the lights of a departing ship high on the horizon as it entered the atmosphere. The *Smyrna* was about to become one of the stars. To the east the view darkened over the forests of Montgeon as the Seine snaked its way toward Paris.

"Tomorrow we'll follow it, then after Paris we'll pass through Luxembourg the next day and cross the Rhine into the Black Forest," Vogelweide said.

"And live *tranquillement* ever after."

"Dear God," Vogelweide said. "Look at you. Maybe you ought to go to bed."

"Maybe you've forgotten. I've been in bed for eleven days."

"Put your hat back on." Vogelweide began to smudge war paint on the boy's cheek.

"Shoshones don't wear such a thing!"

"We're not going for *réalité* here," the painter said. "We're going for theater."

British bailiffs conducted them through the door. Three or four chambers deep into the Ingouville chateau, Duke Paul greeted Baptiste enthusiastically while the young guest received only the guarded approval of the Consul, a combed wild boar of a man with a tiny hatred in his eyes. Baptiste regarded his host carefully. The man wore a plaid cummerbund with a matching cloak over his shoulders and what must have been women's shoes. He seemed worried Baptiste had outdressed him. After a slight nod from Duke Paul, Vogelweide took off Baptiste's headdress and put it in a chair.

At dinner, Baptiste listened with no small interest to Duke Paul regale the small assemblage with his travels and the story of his discovering Baptiste in the American wilderness. Questions landed on his shoulders like sparrows.

"What tribe are you from?"

"I am what they call Washi, Your Excellency."

"Oh! What is a Washi, young man?" his wife, primed with paint and powder like the British men o' war below them in the harbor, asked.

Baptiste felt Vogelweide, to his right, imperceptibly shake his head. Duke Paul smiled serenely at his host. And like a flash he understood the gist of Vogelweide's slight squeeze at his elbow. He wasn't half as valuable a prize to Duke Paul in front of his host if he were a half-breed.

But he felt naughty.

"We're neither this and neither that, we Washi. As we carry the faults of both our forebears, the French and Indians, we are often shunned. We are generally introspective and intelligent. We are rarely killers and indicate our Washi-ness at a great distance to a hunting party by dismounting from our horses, taking our blankets, and flapping them in the air to signify our silliness, our surrender, our unthreatening predisposition.

"We are the root for your English phrase for indecision, 'wishy-washy,' *madame*, so isn't it interesting that you know a little of my language," he said and then disappointed them further by using a knife and fork to eat. He felt Vogelweide behind him grasp both of his arms.

"This *Indien*, when he is not piss-drunk, is really quite a sentient be-ing," he said.

Vogelweide pushed him out into the hallway and down the steps. "Duke Paul is most disappointed in your performance tonight," he said in a harsh whisper. "You've given ammunition to his critics who would savage him."

Baptiste stumbled down a set of stairs into long stone stables. The pungent tang of horse dung rattled him out of his stupor. "Here are the true sentient beings," Baptiste said. As his eyes became accustomed to the dim light he gazed along a dozen doorways filled with the most graceful horses he'd ever seen.

"These used to belong to the *huissiers*," Vogelweide said, "the finest hunters this side of Paris."

Then an old man in a faded uniform rose from a straw bed, ap-proached, and bowed.

"Monsieur Selicor," Vogelweide introduced him, "stablemaster del Couteau d'Ingouville."

With great ceremony the man bowed again. His hair was uncombed and white. A dull film covered his eyes.

"I sketched him yesterday," Vogelweide said. "See? He still wears the colors of Bonaparte's Old Guard."

"*La Garde muert, mais il ne se rend pas!*" Selicor said.

Vogelweide left Baptiste with Selicor, who showed him many of the horses, dark heads and eyes in each of the cool stalls.

"You fought at Waterloo, sir?" Baptiste asked the old man in his most formal manner, trying hard to impress.

"Still fighting," he said. "Why do you speak such sissy French if you are a savage?"

"I am neither sissy nor savage, though I look like both. Can I help?" Baptiste was soft with a brush; the horses walked right up to him. "This is just a costume I had to wear for my performance."

"I'm not surprised. Nothing is as it appears in Le Havre. Look at me. But do you have any other costumes? Like 'Horse,' or 'Man'?"

"'Gentleman' is not as easy a costume to don as you might think. That is what got me banished from the dinner party tonight."

"What got me here," Selicor said, "was I found I liked the smell of horseshit better than dead soldiers." He motioned Baptiste over to three bales of hay, reached behind the uppermost, and produced a bottle of Bordeaux. "You know your horses," he began.

"All my life."

"Let's see if you know your wine."

An hour later, Baptiste knew his wine a little better. Selicor said, "You remind me of my youngest son."

"Does he love horses?" Baptiste asked.

"That one, he was half horse," Selicor said as a chestnut mare stretched her head beyond her stall to nuzzle the back of Baptiste's neck, "like you. His commander told me personally how bravely he fought. But he never came home from Russia. Is there anyone waiting for you to come home, *Monsieur Indien?*"

"My parents are dead," Baptiste said quickly.

Selicor gave a quick nod back. They walked a little farther and reached the final stall. Baptiste looked inside but couldn't see anything. He waited for his head to clear. "My word," he muttered, looking more deeply into the darkness. "Who is he?"

By midnight, Selicor had retired and Baptiste was still currying the long midnight back of Sorcerie, the champion stallion who was the mount of the captain of the British bailiffs. He brushed his neck, his chest, and his fetlocks. Then, with the collective health of the horses around him, he fell asleep in the hay stall, drowsy, aware of their solemn eyes.

He dreamed of his mother and her Shoshone digger forebears, who ate dull roots, had no written language, and had no weapons persuasive enough to stop a buffalo. Instead, they ran whole herds of buffalo off the sides of cliffs. Some of his mother's people wondered why she hadn't led the whole Voyage of Discovery off a cliff at the Pacific's edge.

Early the next morning, he helped Selicor conduct stables. The cook brought bowls of coffee and milk for the stable lads, who jumped when Baptiste addressed them in their own language. They generously shared their breakfast with him. Baptiste did what he could to make himself useful, riding two mares for exercise and helping Saladin, a shifty Arabian stallion, to realize he could run away *with* a rider as well as *from* one.

The black and white dog of the consulate was very affectionate, too. When Baptiste was summoned to carry luggage, she followed him as he fetched box and valise and transported them down from Duke Paul's apartments to the livery and their coach, taking care not to be stepped upon. She was not a great beast but was rather lithe, and he thought she could have survived out on the lower Missouri without too much trouble.

Among the boxes and traveling cases, he found his possibles and now wore his clothes from St. Louis, the Ojibwa costume rammed deep into his kit. For all he knew, the Consul ended up with the headdress.

With a dusting of snow so fragile that it melted as it drifted onto Duke Paul's hat brim, they were off with abbreviated goodbyes. Most considerate in making no remark about Baptiste's conduct the night before, the duke reflected once inside the carriage that he'd stayed at the consulate a number of times. "They're always so respectful and have the best parties," he said.

This gave Baptiste pause because if a prince, requiring eleven guns, however tardy, must hunt around to find respectful people and feel a pang of loss upon leaving them, what a dry hunt life must be for lesser beings, where a respectful cousin must be spotted like an antelope across the plains standing upon a great rock, daring you to rush to him only to find him entertaining other guests.

Just as the carriage began to roll toward the woods of Normandy, Baptiste saw Selicor walk up with Sorcerie clopping behind him on a long lead. Duke Paul suppressed a grin. Vogelweide left them, strolled to the old man, and shook his hand. Selicor fixed the long stallion to the back of their coach. Duke Paul nodded to Baptiste.

"He's yours," Duke Paul said.

Like Le Havre, Baptiste shifted his colors to gratitude.

"You bought him?" Baptiste asked.

Vogelweide laughed.

"You must be joking. To my knowledge, Duke Paul has never bought anything. When the Consul discovers that Sorcerie is no longer in his stable, he will only be too happy to have had the privilege of accommodating His Grace."

8

"ASTONISH"

—hold palm of left hand over mouth. Raise right hand. Denotes great surprise, great pleasure, or great disappointment.

The trio did not stay long in Paris because all agreed that Sorcerie would fare better the more kilometers they put between him and his old home.

"Next time," Vogelweide said loftily, "maybe the consul will remember to properly welcome a royal party."

Hopefully with the cannons aimed skyward in salute and not at us, Baptiste thought.

Entering Germany through Luxembourg, they descended into a valley below the Rhine made stark by black branches and melting ice. Until now, Sorcerie had danced behind their carriage. Approaching Stuttgart, Baptiste couldn't wait any longer. "I could ride him in so he won't stumble in the carriage ruts," he said.

"This isn't a backwater like St. Louis," Vogelweide said. "We have canals, cobbles, and proper drainage in our city—"

But Baptiste wasn't listening anymore. He'd already flown out of the carriage and was on Sorcerie's back. Galloping free, he felt the horse responding to the gentle pressure of his knees. Sometimes Sorcerie twisted his great head to look him straight in the eyes.

"You can ride," Vogelweide said as Baptiste pulled up close to the carriage. "You must teach me."

Baptiste laughed. "As if you would ever trade a soft cushion for a hard saddle."

Vogelweide made a great show of a sketch he'd just made of Sorcerie rearing, his forelegs clawing the sky. He folded it and gave it to Baptiste.

"How could you ruin it like that?" Baptiste said after salting it away in his bag.

"I didn't want you to feel bad when you folded it later," Vogelweide said. "Well, off to the 'stud garden.'"

Stuttgart was so named because it was once a farm used by an eleventh-century prince to raise his horses. In the distance, the valleys folded themselves into hills and there was the stone city, sparkling with red tile roofs, Franconian timbers, and narrow alleys. Their way was festooned with banners showing the city escutcheon, the very image Vogelweide had dashed off for Baptiste.

"Forger," Baptiste said. "Imposter."

Riding through the portcullis into the Old Castle sprawling over the west side of Stuttgart, Baptiste felt something harden in him. No one expected anything of him, for they considered him a savage and imagined he had no conscience. Only Vogelweide suspected he had a heart. He'd behaved appallingly at the consul's. Inside these cold granite walls, who might punish *"fauve"* for doing whatever his unchecked nature directed him to do? He found the prospect of giving in to this impulse most despicable: He could be the scourge of court, his skin his passport, the *innocente arriviste*. He began to loathe this part of himself most of all.

◆ ◆ ◆

He plunged immediately into his studies, which included Spanish and Italian beyond Latin and German, as well as pianoforte and violin *ex nihilo*, from scratch, a far cry from his reed flute. Because of his devotion to the horses, he was given a small room directly above the stables, but he often stayed with Sorcerie in his stall. When he buried his face in the great beast's neck, he almost felt at home.

On Baptiste's first journey out into Stuttgart, the first blushes of spring made themselves known. Vogelweide, acting the role of guide, pointed out several nesting storks to him, perched on high-pitched roofs, mounds of feathers and long bills.

"They're good luck, an ancient fertility symbol," he said and laughed.

They walked along the Neckar River into the inner city, a cluster of tiny buildings like old cuckoo clocks, framed with crudely adzed logs from the Black Forest. Some had steeples, while others rose sharply to an arch. The facades leaned over them as they approached Strasse Lorinten and the commercial district.

The identities of the businesses stood out as cartoons carved in relief, as many of the villagers couldn't read. They passed a bakery, and carved in its crossbeam was the story of the wheat being scythed, crushed at a mill, baked, and proffered with a solicitous bow to an appreciative customer.

They walked over a tiny bridge above a narrow black stream, crossed a courtyard Vogelweide called Green Dog Fountain, though neither a green dog nor a fountain lurked close by, and stopped in front of a haberdasher's.

"*Vortreten*, if you please," the tailor snapped and directed Baptiste to a short stool. Baptiste was so surprised at his tone he very nearly hopped atop its height.

"What do you think?" the impatient retailer said, hardly soliciting Vogelweide's approval as he slapped a linen sample on Baptiste's back. "Yes? Or would you prefer the silk with the damask? Come, come!"

With a red face, the little man followed suit with wools and weaves.

"I suppose . . . I'll try that one," Baptiste said tentatively, having crossed a bridge of his own of sorts—from this moment forward he would address all Germans in their native language.

"*Which* one? Mary's blood," the man continued, measuring Baptiste with practiced sighs of discomfort, jotting down the particulars in a small book. Then he snapped his head up and put his hands on his hips. "Will there be anything else?" He looked pointedly at Vogelweide. As the pair stepped over the threshold, he rolled his eyes. "*Anything at all? The account of Duke Paul, I presume?*" he called after them.

Instead of offering a riposte, Vogelweide simply nodded and continued out with Baptiste. As they left the shop, the tailor all but slammed the door behind them. Vogelweide stroked his chin. Baptiste had never seen him go so long without a sarcastic joke.

"The tailor seemed a bit rough with the scissors," Baptiste said finally.

"There was an unpleasant famine when we left for America . . . and many are still hungry," Vogelweide said. "We were hoping it would all have blown over by the time we got back, but that may not be the case." A stork took wing above them and with slow flaps wheeled out of sight. "So much for luck," he shrugged.

"Just how bad was it?" Baptiste asked.

"Well, we didn't actually lose any from our household."

Baptiste stopped walking. He was surprised that he could still be put off by Vogelweide's carelessness.

"It's Duke Paul's prerogative," Vogelweide said, "to travel. Famines come and go. I mention it only because you may detect traces of a general feeling of resentment."

So not all the staredowns from the villagers were at me.

"Duke Paul will make it up to them," the painter said. "With a little bread," he tossed a coin into a mob of children, all wearing wooden shoes, "and circus," he said, patting Baptiste on the back. The rest of their walk, Baptiste felt oddly taller than Vogelweide, though the painter towered over him.

The next day they set off to explore the southern part of the city. The carriage pulled into a courtyard facing an imposing stone surgery. It was much more impressive than the clinic the nuns ran next to Baptiste's school at the convent in St. Louis. Vogelweide led him in, and Duke Paul, who was sitting at tea with a tense little man in a green suit, looked up. Vogelweide took out some American tobacco and, smoking, struck a picturesque pose. The doctor put on a white gown and conducted Baptiste into the *experimentill* quadrant.

An assistant in a filthy jacket approached the specimen and led him to a *versuchstadium*. Then a curtain before him parted to reveal a murmuring assemblage of between fifty and seventy-five men of science looking up at him from an amphitheater. He tried to turn around, but the Duke held up his hand in restraint, then slowly joined him on the platform to applause before descending down a set of circular stairs to greet his peers. He warmly announced three among them, the Drs. Gall (their host), Carus, and Spurzheim.

"*Homo sapiens Indianus . . .*" Duke Paul theatrically called up from a sort of orchestra pit. "*Nova varietas. Somatotype mesomorphia,*" he said and returned to the stage. "Black hair and skin the color of cinnamon." Baptiste picked out the word *gracilis*, the gracefulness of muscle.

The assistant helped Baptiste remove his shirt. The crowd rumbled. *Vogelweide and Duke Paul have it all wrong,* Baptiste thought. *The Germans don't just want a spectacle, they want nudity.* He felt a needle bite his forearm, but the torches burned so brightly above his head that it was hard to see what was happening. Duke Paul drew his blood into a glass tube in front of the rapt audience. He continued to rhapsodize: "*Natura quae creat et non creatur,*" a nature that creates but is not created. Vogelweide, standing by the curtain, did not smile so much as expose his long teeth.

Duke Paul held the vial aloft and observed, "A general thinness of the hemoglobin leads to *akrasia,* mental fragility, coupled with reduced intelligence." Baptiste grimaced upon hearing the word "idiot," the same in German as it was in English, as Vogelweide had been only too happy to point out during the crossing.

"Most significant," Duke Paul said, "this subject is the offspring of the American Indian squaw Sacagawea, whose innate sense of direction enabled her to lead Lewis and Clark to the Pacific."

Baptiste strained to pay attention. What did they think about his mother? That she was a homing pigeon, a bat? Duke Paul caressed the faint hollow where Baptiste's nose descended from his brow.

"This is the point where magnetite granules accumulate," Duke Paul said. "It is this magnetic center which affords the savage the directional power to determine which way is north."

Baptiste looked out at the deputation of Germany's foremost researchers. His face felt hot, his head pounded. *You starve your people but call us savages. You ghouls in white gowns accord us with directional instead of deductive powers because you're terrified we can think like you but, unlike you, have souls. Are we birds, then, flying north? My mother certainly had gifts, but her ability to lead Clark to the Pacific was hardly a matter of science.*

She was retracing a horror path when she "guided" the Expedition to the sea. With the acuteness of a blinded victim she remembered the terror of her last "sights": the cave where the Hidatsas had sold her to Black Cat, with his Mandan braves staring and laughing. She remembered the great mossy rock where she hid when she tried to escape her captors. She remembered the bend in the Snake River where they beat her. She remembered every spot along the Snake where the conquerors raped her. She remembered the cave where she begged them not to slit her throat. She remembered the way the long purple robes of the Cascade Mountains descended into the Basin from the elevated spot they'd taken her to, her last look into her village. She remembered the last time she heard Sparrow Hawk's sobs after they beat her with clubs. She remembered jumping off a cliff after breaking away from them and trying to run away with Sparrow Hawk. She remembered her tears of joy at seeing her brother Cameahwait escape into the woods. She remembered the cries and the hot waves of crackling smoke and the eye-sting of her village burning. She remembered the spirit tree where she and the girl called Sparrow Hawk were playing when she first set eyes on them. She remembered hearing a funny swishing in the grass.

Baptiste broke into a sweat thinking of his mother and Clark. He didn't know why, but whenever he felt this angry he heard the roar of a waterfall. As the probing fingers of the German phrenologists crawled over his head like spiders, he wondered at what these madmen were pretending to detect. There was a buzz in Baptiste's head. He calculated the value of his music lessons.

As the three left the hall, a broadsheet advertising the demonstration of the spectacular agility skills of the *Menschenfliege*, the human fly, caught Baptiste's eye. Something about the face on the poster struck him as vaguely familiar. As he drew closer for a better look at the sketch, it occurred to him that the hapless exhibitionist resembled none other than the younger of the Two Antoines he'd known from American Fur.

On the morrow, without fail, a pupil of the Duke of Saxe Weimar will demonstrate the spectacular agility of *aborigine americanus* by climbing the *Gerdanigspielturm* at the top of Strasse Dorendorn. You will witness the monumental courage and tenacity of the *Menschenfliege*, the human fly, to celebrate the first day of our wonderful new Stuttgart Volksfare.

Boy, aren't we getting around, Baptiste thought. *I hope he's learned to lay off the 'strap.*

They drove past the *Gerdanigspiel* pinnacle on the way back to the old castle. *What a relief,* Baptiste thought as he looked toward the summit. Tiny windows with enormous sills and lintels bulged at regular intervals all the way to the top, just four feet apart. It might as well have been a ladder.

Slippery tiles near the apex looked a bit tricky to negotiate, but a wrought-iron retaining wire was reassuringly embedded in courses of bricks that ran all the way up to the finial, a bloated copper burgher with a full belly and a salacious grin.

The cast sculpture's coarse mouth and drooping eyes glinted sparks in the sunlight. His hideous form stood in relief, a stark contrast to the lovely, wild Black Forest, which stretched to the horizon in a sweep of evergreen. With all the red fox, weasels, deer, hares, wild boars, and wildcats so close at hand, it seemed odd that the civilized villagers had been inspired merely to deify an awkward grocer. The only thing apparently missing was a human fly.

Baptiste grinned. How could the *Deutschvolks* imagine it was so hard to climb such a thing? *Maybe because they grew up believing it.* He might have worried further about Antoine's new role as human fly had it not been such a cakewalk.

9

"GIVE"

—extend flat right hand, back of hand facing right, in front of body at shoulder height. Move hand out and down.

The following morning, Baptiste advanced through the *strassen* of Stuttgart aboard Sorcerie as he pranced behind Duke Paul's royal carriage toward the foot of the tower. Here, atop a dais in front of the crowd at the *volksfare*, the mayor of the city announced Antoine and the challenge he would undertake. If Duke Paul recognized him, he didn't let on.

The mayor roused the crowd by recounting how two university students fell to their deaths attempting the same climb the year before. That lit Antoine's candle. He sprang along the platform and got an extra leg on the podium before leaping across ten feet of nothingness to the building. He was already on the way down when he got a mouthful of ivy and barely got his arm around a granite lintel. From there he moved skyward, inchworm style, for three storeys.

Resting, Antoine looked out at the crowd, which now spilled over into the wine bowers of the Schillerplatz along Konigstrasse. A stork flapped so close to his back that he nearly fell off. As Antoine wheeled around to catch himself, Baptiste felt the impulse to call out to him but then decided it was better to leave him to his new life.

Maybe we'd both only feel shame at what we've become, Baptiste thought.

"Behold the *menschenfliege*," the mayor said. "We understand that at the half-year he will climb the unscalable wall of Ludwigsburg."

Antoine smiled broadly and bowed to the crowd.

What is the lifespan of a fly? Baptiste wondered.

Antoine seemed to realize he'd better not make his ascent look too easy, because when he hit the slippery tiles at the top of the tower, he dropped down a few storeys and made the appearance of scrambling for footing. The crowd gasped. Antoine scrambled some more.

"Where is the miracle?" Baptiste said. *For one thing, hasn't it occurred to the crowd that various carpenters had to have been up there to construct the tower?*

"Jealous you didn't think of it first?" Vogelweide snorted, looking down from his opera glasses.

Triumphant at the top, Antoine ritualistically spread his arms as if to jump, a daemon in the *Inferno*, pinions fluttering (though he was more demonstrative than demonic).

The crowd whooshed and clapped—except for a girl in a hooded cloak of green brocade who stood just outside their circle and looked up at the dizzy heights, transfixed. Watching her, Baptiste had the distinct impression that far from being terrified, she was studying Antoine's every move as though she might dare assay such a climb herself. The more mysterious, she seemed immune to the clapping around her. As she smiled, shook her head, and turned away, she tucked a small slate under her arm. Even in a crowd, she seemed detached—and wild as a fawn.

◆ ◆ ◆

Baptiste heard the strange girl from the square before he laid eyes on her again. She was but a trail of music floating from another chamber at the far end of the castle. While Maestro Klenze sat stoically on the bench discussing posture, pedals, and dynamics, and patiently explaining once again why his pupil wasn't yet ready to touch a low C, Baptiste had to concentrate in order not to surrender to the strange sense of yearning the distant notes brought out in him. The music abruptly stopped. Light footsteps approached.

Ekaterina entered the room flushed, eyes glowing with the *Moonlight* Sonata.

"Frau Klenze," the maestro said slowly, careful to face her directly, "my new student." He nodded in Baptiste's direction.

Ekaterina's shoulders shook slightly as Baptiste attempted the deepest of bows.

"We won't be hearing from him for a while," the maestro smiled.

Ekaterina nodded gravely. Then she clasped the maestro's wrist, wheeled about, and went back to her salon.

Baptiste didn't mind the maestro's silent lessons. From the first the maestro taught him to be very stingy about sound. "Silence can be very lush, very delicate," he said. "Everything disappears if you rush to your quarry."

The old man might have been a concert grandmaster himself had he not been so badly disfigured. Maestro's body seemed to travel in three directions. His left eye swept up to the rafters, while his right guarded his passage downstairs. He deferentially aimed his face straight ahead when speaking, but that made things worse: Then you knew he wasn't looking at you.

Ekaterina, to whom he'd taught musical composition since age seven, had been too delicate to interest the palace guards. She had a pointed chin and pale blue hands that barely showed at the ends of her sleeves.

The prodigy had never spoken nor heard a word, but by her bright look and uncanny ability to read lips by age four, her wealthy parents soon divined she possessed a superior intelligence and curiosity, resulting in her learning to read and write both German and French before age six—even though born deaf—and spicing her silent "conversations" with flashes of the new sign language that was developing throughout Europe. She was never without her slate and chalky fingertips, and though she tried politely to remember to wipe the keys, sometimes in her haste to go to her next frenetic activity she'd leave a trace on the piano.

Her widowed father had been the maestro's patron. Upon becoming gravely ill, he'd prevailed upon his beneficiary to become his daughter's protector. Against his better judgment but to please his friend, the maestro married the girl fifty years his junior. Ekaterina was but fourteen.

Now she was eighteen. As the scent of lilacs sweetened the air, Baptiste was aware of the warm place where Ekaterina stood, what clothes she was wearing, what she'd chosen to eat. He began to see her in places other than the music room: in the courtyard, at chapel, looking at him through arrow loops while he pitched hay for the horses. She rode, too, though her horse could scarcely have felt her weight on its back.

"You and the deaf girl Klense are getting along well together," Duke Paul said very quietly late one night. Baptiste hated even to hear him say her name.

Duke Paul was under great inducement to marry Princess Sophie von Thurn und Taxis. As his older brother Eugen had already wed, Paul was his line's last chance to bring a new marriage alliance to the kingdom, and Vogelweide told Baptiste the duke felt as though he were "a wild beast in a cage."

Imagine that, Baptiste thought.

"Sophie is cold as a snowstorm," Vogelweide said. "Their parents have been planning this for years. This situation is very troubling to Duke Paul."

But Sophie would be Duke Paul's guest at Baptiste's first recital, and there were many arrangements to be made.

With Duke Paul thus occupied, Ekaterina began to help Baptiste with his practice. They shared lunches together: *schupfnudeln*, noodles with red sausages; *maultaschen*, square dumplings served with fried onions and cheese; and *kasspatzle*, Swabian cheese noodles she enjoyed wrapping around cubes of sugar. This reminded him of the wad of sweet spruce sap his mother had so loved to chew.

Baptiste took advantage of these interludes to teach her *his* sign language. Long before the Europeans developed sign language for the deaf, the people of the Great Plains had communicated with their hands while hunting or hiding. Perhaps it was the first American dance.

Ekaterina's eyes misted when she watched him perform her first four choices: FOREST, DREAM, SKIN, BEYOND. For YES, Baptiste showed her, simply cup your hand and hold it up, as if the phrase just implied holds water. NO occurs when you abruptly splash the water out of your hand: "That doesn't hold water." Ekaterina devoured it.

At night, walking with him on the battlements, she requested STAR. He stood behind her and inhaled the sweet fragrance of the skin at the nape of her neck. Taking her hands, he signed NIGHT by shaking her wrists gently while crossing her forearms, then with her right index finger and thumb extended her hand skyward in a quick arc.

To make a bright star, he showed her, *snap your thumb against your finger to make it twinkle.*

Baptiste's eyes welled up when he realized she could only see, and would never hear, the snap. He felt a confusing storm of emotions, and in that instant he knew why his mother would turn away to cry.

What happens when you love someone? Baptiste wanted to share Ekaterina's every breath. He studied her every peculiarity. When she was angry, two vertical furrows darkened her sweet brow. Ekaterina had opinions about everything, preferred green to any other color. She wore tall men's boots when riding. As proof against the cold spring air, she asked for Baptiste's caftan, her slender shoulders disappearing under its great floppy collar.

Ekaterina liked wind too much. She searched for the draftiest places around the castle until even Baptiste was cold. She "listened," which meant she watched Baptiste's lips, with ferocious intensity when he carefully told the tale he claimed his mother sang to him as a lullaby, about the time "when Glooskap lashed the wings of the ancient wind bird Wuchowsen together and made our lakes and seas dormant and putrid."

"But why would anyone stop the wind?" Ekaterina wrote on her slate, in French.

"He was angry because Wuchowsen flapped too hard and nearly overturned his canoe when he was trying to fish. He politely asked Wuchowsen to flap his wings more softly, but he refused. He many times politely asked him to stop. But the immense bird drew himself up and said, 'No one was here before me; since the dawn of time, before any voice was heard, I thought to flap my wings; my cry was first to pierce the air—and forever will I flap my wings for my pleasure.' Wuchowsen was unreasonable."

The tiniest suggestion of a smile crept into the corners of Ekaterina's lips, and Baptiste felt as moved as one feels when a wild creature agrees to accept food from your hand. If his pleasure was tempered a bit by a slight pang of guilt because this story he'd attributed to his mother was not Shoshone at all, but rather a yarn from the Northeast tribes he'd read one rainy afternoon in the Museum of Human Beings, he consoled himself with the fact that he wouldn't be the first lover to woo a maid under, if not false, slightly embellished, circumstances.

Ekaterina loved to read with him below some catalpa trees beyond the castle but would often disengage from her book and try to confound him with a difficult concept, as though they'd been in mid-conversation. Looking up provocatively from *Othello*, she challenged him, scribbling furiously on her slate, "What do you call people whose skin is dark?"

He performed the signs: BLACK WHITE MAN.

"Rain," she demanded.

He closed his fists over his head. Then he slowly lowered his arms and released his fingers. Twice.

She moved her lips to request "mother." With a cupped right hand he gently pulled three times at his left breast. Then she tried it. Watching Ekaterina's hands, Baptiste remembered something he'd said to his mother in their little shack while she was teaching the signs to him.

"How stupid!" he exclaimed. "Do you prefer talking with your hands, Mother? Is this why you never speak around Father Clark and his wife?" Her slap stung his cheeks. Then his mother turned away and he saw her back shake the way it did each time Father Clark left their hut.

"Love," Ekaterina wrote on her slate.

He took her slender hands and made an X just north of his heart, then pulled them into his chest and, looking deep into her eyes, held them there so securely that she blushed.

10

"SNAKE"

—hold right hand at right side, waist high. Move hand one foot forward with a wavy motion.

June, 1824

The ladies of court didn't think much of Ekaterina, if their own vocabulary of gesture revealed anything. She dressed like a child, she did not comport herself like a lady, she ate so robustly it disgusted them. Like a ghost, she walked all over the castle at night without fear of falling. Only when Baptiste overheard one of the women call her a little mouse did he realize that Ekaterina had been the Indian of the castle long before he arrived.

Some mornings Ekaterina crept down to the stable and helped Baptiste curry Duke Paul's horses, and in return, he taught her riding tricks on Adelaide, the very large bay that was her favorite.

One night Baptiste saw a graceful figure in his doorway, her waist kept tiny by the tapeworm she, as was the fashion in court, swallowed. He knew in an instant it was not Ekaterina. This courtesan had undone her hair, a tumble of blonde curls. Her full lips turned up at each side in a wanton smile. He was both attracted and repelled by the possibility that those lips carried death from traces of arsenic she tasted on a regular basis to give her flesh a luminous pallor. Vogelweide had told him of an unfortunate sea captain who'd taken gravely ill upon returning after three years in Java to embrace his wife. She'd taken up the arsenic habit while he was trading for pepper, so he hadn't developed the immunity that the daily traces of arsenic had afforded her lover.

The arsenic had the additional side effect of making ladies' lips appear blue. To counter this, they applied a concoction of fish scales, emollients of bear grease, and dye which slithered on those lips and made them gleam.

The apparition glided to his bedside. "Ravish me, savage," she said.

It was Kirsten, the young wife of Karl Voorheis, captain of the palace guards. Karl was at least six feet four, with black moustaches and thick forearms, a favorite for his ribald stories and capacity for drink. *What on earth made Kirsten notice me?* Baptiste wondered. She put her finger to her lips and came over to his bed.

Undesired love had forced itself upon his mother. Baptiste's own compromises with Duke Paul were enough of a weight on his conscience. Love with a stranger repulsed him. Kirsten leaned over him. Her hair fell over his skin.

"I am yours," she said and put her pale hand on his chest. She slipped her shoulders out of her gown. She told him the compelling reasons they should *ficken.*

"What about your husband," Baptiste said.

"He's not interested in a *ménage à trois,*" she laughed lewdly. "Oh, so you're not so wild you can't be shocked. Don't worry, Karl's of no concern to us."

"He's of great concern to me."

"Oh, so *Herr Indianer's* position is not so innocent as he suggests.

Perhaps you do know your way around castle politics, now that you haunt the royal apartments, studying under Duke Paul. But does that mean . . . you only like the men?"

For a flash Baptiste saw the face of the cabin boy, Reehl. Duke Paul had visited him twice since they'd come to the castle. He'd endured it to keep up his part of the bargain, but he wasn't finding it any easier to enjoy. Neither was Duke Paul. The royal's now constant state of inebriation was rendering him all but impotent.

"Don't worry," she whispered. "You won't get into trouble. Wouldn't you like to touch Kirsten?" She sat on his bed and slipped off the rest of her robe, so gauzy it seemed like mist at the bottom of a waterfall.

He shook his head. Kirsten flushed quickly, then stood up and began to stroke her own thighs. Why did he feel the need to apologize? He took her hand and gently kissed it. He was a terribly disappointing *Indianer*.

She was still for a moment. "This is our secret—that you did not defile me?" she said. Then she shrugged and pulled her robe over her shoulders.

A few days later another *frau* found her way to his bedroom, like a stalking leopard. He refused to touch her, too. Within a fortnight, seven young *frauen* had come to see the dangerous *Indianer* in the middle of the night. He'd become the leader of a secret society he abhorred. Whenever he passed, they flushed and giggled.

Word got around the castle. In time, while refusing to touch any of these young women (though they boasted otherwise), he'd become the castle Lothario. Another transformation was taking place, too: In a matter of days many of the younger women at court had begun to carry purses decorated with the tips of little hawk feathers. Kirsten and a few of her friends suddenly were embellishing their tiaras with diminutive feather headdresses. He laughed—*thousands of years of proud Indian history and tradition, and I've become an opportunity to accessorize!*

Ekaterina wrote on her slate, "See what you're doing to us! Perhaps no woman can call herself sophisticated unless she has a savage by her side for comparison. If you hadn't come to our land we'd have had to invent you." *These ladies think you're the grit around which the pearl of their culture forms,* she reflected, looking at Baptiste, *but it's you who are the pearl.*

"You have yet to try a feather on yourself," Baptiste pointed out, admiring the braids in Ekaterina's hair.

One morning before dawn he and Vogelweide were dispatched on horseback by the Duke to deliver last-minute invitations to a banquet. To his delight, Ekaterina accompanied them. They rode below the fog into the bottomland along the Neckar.

A flock of birds splashed out of the river as they approached, and Baptiste saw Ekaterina follow their flight with her sweetest of eyes. He remembered this was what his mother's name, Sacagawea, meant, both Bird Woman and a sense of "birds taking flight when disturbed by a sudden motion."

A quarter mile later, Vogelweide pointed out an old red roof on the edge of the Schillerplatz. "The home of Herr Schiller," he said.

They cantered below some cattails. They crossed a dirt bridge with arches and stanchions bearded in moss. Sorcerie's head and shoulders were so tall they floated above the narrow doorways along the Schillerplatz. Villagers opened their windows. A large head came to a second floor window. Vogelweide waved.

"Is that the great philosopher?" Baptiste asked.

"No, idiot. He is long dead. I think that's his son."

Baptiste watched the man condemned to be the son of Herr Schiller, his life defined by another person who no longer walked the earth. *How soft the word was, son, and so utterly useless.*

"Sons don't count," Baptiste said.

11

"**BIRD**"

—with flat hands at shoulders, imitate motion of wings. Small birds rapidly, large birds slowly.

July, 1824

The young *Indianer* was as much enchanted with Ekaterina as he was unsure of himself. He was foolishly saving himself for the one he loved. Should he not show Ekaterina his feelings? The lonely women of the court had at least risked ridicule, or even worse, the genteel rejection, for him; did he not owe it to Ekaterina to take the same risks for her favor? He determined to climb in through her window on an upper floor of the old castle.

At nightfall, Baptiste crossed the courtyard to the other side of King Wilhelm's apartments. Narrow windows reflected the moonlight, and after crossing a buttress he worked his way around to Ekaterina's casement.

The window was already half open. He was transfixed by the loveliness of the scene before him. Everything in her room was asleep and bathed in a silvery light: her pitcher of water; her comb; her violin, its wooden case snapped shut. Tiny flowers slept in a vase and on her bedspread. Rising with a start, she seemed fearful, but she pulled her satin comforter aside. Her warmth enveloped him the moment he entered her bed. When they kissed, his lips traced the shape of her small mouth and chin.

That night, they merely clung to each other. Ekaterina's toes barely reached below his knees. He held her and thanked God for her.

The next night when he slipped through the window, Ekaterina laughed silently, took her chalk, and wrote, "A little bird who just flew off told me you might come. You must be cold." She held out a cup of wine. Looking deeply into her eyes, he drank it thirstily and wiped his mouth with the back of his hand. She settled into a cushion, leaned back, and signed to him, TELL ME A STORY THE BIRD WOULD HAVE TOLD.

Kneeling directly in front of her and taking her hands, Baptiste spoke deliberately so she could taste the words as they escaped his lips. He was stunned by her gaze. As he spoke, he realized no one had ever before devoted such focus to him and him alone as Ekaterina was doing now, drinking in his eyes, fascinated by the supple movement of his lips, bathing him in the warmest of attentions. He felt hypnotic as a cobra, and he wondered if perhaps the sinuous creature were as seduced by his power over the enthralled as they were by his icy stare. Stroking her palm with his thumb, he pulled her into the dream:

"A long, long time ago lived a beautiful maid, a beautiful maid. She rose from the crypt where her ancestors slept, slept deep in the long ago. She longed to spend her days in a tree, a great old tree, with leaves to adorn her; she would dress in leaves and be kissed by the breeze."

He paused for a moment to watch Ekaterina close her eyes in pleasure. Then she smiled and returned to him, and he continued.

"Floating inside her arbor, swaying this way and that, her feet were invisible, this way and that. She sang sweetly among the branches, but her loneliness cut through the night, a song through the night."

Baptiste now narrowed his eyes.

"Her song was heard by a handsome brave: From a forest afar beyond night's great lake, he followed her song, so brave was he."

Ekaterina shivered and her shoulder shook.

"His words flew so softly, they were lost to her ears; she could not hear, so strange was he."

Baptiste waited, then struck. It was almost too easy, but he was powerless against his own lust.

"From their union a child was born, a child was born. The babe could not see, so blind was he, but awed was she by his sight. He could see what would happen, not near but far, what was near the young babe could not see. He knew the wolf, the bear, the stars; but her leaves he could not see. In autumn she waits by the tree, the tree that cries its leaves, but never again could he find her, as her leaves he could not see."

When he looked into Ekaterina's eyes he saw tears. When she saw his confusion, she giggled. On her slate she wrote, "I know you must think I'm silly. Where did you learn that?"

"My mother taught it to me."

"Your mother must have been so wise. She must have loved you so very much. I know what it is to feel so happy and sad at the same time. How did she express this to you?"

"When my mother was reunited with her brother, the great chief Cameahwait, whom she thought had been murdered, she put her fingers in her mouth, like this," Baptiste said.

He demonstrated his mother's familiar gesture, which had made him burn with shame whenever she performed it in public—because it seemed so ignorant and melodramatic—by putting his second, third, and fourth fingers into his mouth and sucking on them.

Ekaterina, without taking her eyes from Baptiste's, slowly reached up to his hand, gently pulled his wet fingers from his mouth, and put them between her own sweet lips. Then she led him to her bed, her cheeks wet. He explored her lips, her pale neck, the great urgent depths of her kisses. He kissed the wisps of flaxen hair behind her ears and traced the hollows along her ribs to her lovely small breasts. He tried to breathe in every inch of her body. When they became one, and breathed as one, he felt a sense of freedom greater than he'd ever known on the cliffs of the Manitou. Afterward, they fell asleep in a tangle of limbs.

He woke when the moon had traveled halfway across the sky. He found a small door swung open that conducted him up a back staircase to the top of the battlements. His little bird was up there to feel the wind. He approached her very quietly and she barely started when he wrapped his arms around her. She pointed into the black air above the drop to the river and cemetery below.

IF I FELL, WOULD YOU FALL WITH ME? she signed.

YES, he answered, then "twinkled" it.

She smiled, looked down, and crushed herself into his body. WHAT BLISS, she signed to him. Her sweet melancholy was manifest at this height, and when he kissed her very hard she caught her breath, as if the stars and the trees in the distance might hear. A moment later, when he motioned for them to move away from the edge of the wall, she squeezed him so hard he imagined himself losing consciousness and balance. As he reached up to steady himself he hit some tiles and twigs from an empty stork's nest—unlucky bird, he thought briefly— before finally finding a handhold. He gently led her back to bed, and after making love again, they fell asleep in each other's arms.

Upon waking just before sunrise, Baptiste was startled to find Ekaterina curled up in a blanket, looking at him. All the windows were flung open. Her right hand was stained with ink, and there was a quill and an empty ink bottle on her table. Folded into his coat she'd slipped seven pages of a ballade she'd written for him.

After lessons the following day they walked through the courtyard together. Ekaterina, slate in hand, wanted to know if he missed the forest.

I TAKE IT WITH ME, he signed. JUST AS YOU CAN STILL FEEL MUSIC AFTER IT'S BEEN PLAYED.

She pressed her lips tightly together and furrowed her brow.

"How long do you suppose music stays in a room after it's been played?" she wanted to know.

The answer was forever, but he didn't have the heart to tell her. He shrugged.

"How long?" she wrote again, angry at him for taking his hearing for granted.

"I don't know," he said. Instead he told her about the difference between elk tracks that were two minutes old and those that were two days old. He told her about knowing where deer had been and where they might appear again the next day. He told her what few secrets he knew.

In return, Ekaterina wrote him about her father dying. "I laid my head on his chest. I heard the last great beat of my father's heart. It was the only sound I am certain I have ever really heard." She slid her hand up his belly to his chest and tapped his breastbone three times, slowly. "Until you came I felt alone," she wrote. "I will one day be free of the stinkpot world of this castle forever. I will live in a tiny cottage in the wood, surrounded by creatures who communicate in ways other than cruel jokes and nasty whispers. They think just because I can't hear that I don't know what they're saying," she scribbled on her slate. She looked at him, pursed her lower lip, and wrote, "They boast that you have loved each of them in turn and decorate themselves with feathers to signify this. Is this true?"

Baptiste burst out laughing and turned his hand over seven times. "Eight ladies make this claim!" Ekaterina scribbled.

As his hand flipped over a final time, she threw her arms around his neck and kissed him. Then she made the European deaf sign for BELIEVE.

By the end of their walk he'd told Ekaterina about Clark and Toussaint. He told her about legends like Haih the Raven and Wotsia the Fox, who really only tricks himself. He told her about Akilinek, "the fabulous land beyond the sea," which was really the Fourth World where his mother stayed. He told her about the times he felt as though he could turn very quickly and nearly catch his mother watching him. He fell in love with Ekaterina's steady blue eyes as she "listened." A wonderful future began to unfold for them. He could train the castle horses and be with Ekaterina forever. It would be his greatest pride to be able to sit beside her during mass.

The next morning, Ekaterina found him and in a state of agitated excitement wrote on her slate, "You've given me so much." She tugged at his wrist. "I want to show you something."

12

"DARK"

—make sign for NIGHT and SAME; or hold extended hands in front of and close to eyes.

He followed her down, down, down, past the servants' quarters, below the scullery, below even the place where the maids threw the night soil in long septic furrows, to the mouth of a cave below the old castle.

Where can she be taking me?

Baptiste was far too proud to tell Ekaterina that while he loved the night, he felt a distinct aversion to being confronted with the forced darkness below the earth.

Could fear be inherited? If so, his fear of caves came from his mother.

"Dear son, be wary of the dark places where Haih the Raven flew. My first nights with Hidatsa captors were in such a black cunt, and I could hear the Knife River snickering in the moonlight outside the cave's mouth."

Every time Baptiste closed a door he felt as though he were cutting off more air. It became harder and harder to breathe. The feeling of rocks closing in only made it worse.

But the cave was important to Ekaterina. The *Schacht* she seemed so desperate to reveal was hidden still farther below three floors of slimy granite stairs that had turned white near the river due to efflorescence of calcium seeping in during the last five hundred years.

"*Kleine halle*," she scribbled in her notebook, "a fifty-kilometer network of tunnels. Artifacts of torches and remains of prehistoric dwellers have been found here." Then she raced ahead down another flight of stairs, familiar as childhood.

Ekaterina motioned for Baptiste to push open an oak door that led to a natural cavern behind the dungeons. In utter blackness the door's bolt shot so loud he was surprised he couldn't hear an echo.

Nothing was in front of him—everywhere. It was a black rose, blooming. Here Ekaterina was the guide, conducting him into her silence. He reached for her and felt her breath against his neck as she stopped as if to look at him. Then she pulled his arm. Their feet splashed through a sludge of black water. She turned right, descending stairs.

He whistled for bravery but the blackness swallowed the sound. He counted steps, then lost count. Ekaterina took him deeper into the *schacht*, its *stalaktiten* dripping into invisible waters, reflecting nothing.

After an interval she began to walk extremely precisely. Curious, he risked a step to the right, sank knee-deep into a pool, and ripped his trousers. Or had he not ripped them? Was he bleeding, or was it some subterranean stream that was so damp? In this starless *Höhle* one might only learn later, up above, what had really happened. Information down here being indefinitely postponed.

He yanked his leg free and shook it in the pool of Ekaterina's deafness, her speechlessness. Nothing pounded in his head.

Now you know something of my loss, my love, even though it's a different sense, Ekaterina thought, in deep communion with Baptiste's acute deprivation. *Feel how the* untergrund *cradles you.*

She gently reached up and closed his eyelids. Then she moved softly away, just a step, because he could still detect her perfume. Foolishly he held his hand out and called to her.

"My love, I can still feel you smiling," Baptiste enunciated to the blackness. *Haih, I know you are here, too.*

Ekaterina fully clasped his hands and led him out.

Baptiste's practices accelerated. Inspired by Ekaterina, they weren't simply music "lessons"; he was playing piano and violin, on average, eight hours a day. He dreamed that somehow just by feverishly piling up a mass of notes, he might break through the barrier of silence that had tortured Ekaterina since birth. Maestro Klenze took care of the Italian and Spanish, too, while he was on the bench.

To judge by the maestro's long silences as he gazed through a window over the Neckar River, Baptiste was not a complete joy to teach. But the "dexterity of a cunning savage" in the young man's fingertips allowed him, after scores of failures, to fly over *pianissimos.*

It was not considered a fault if you hit a key so softly no one could hear it. Sometimes as Baptiste practiced, he tried to make it as if he weren't there. But few things could be hidden from a mind as reflective and penetrating as Maestro Klenze's.

"I want to thank you for taking care of Ekaterina," he said quietly one morning after Baptiste finally finished a drill that was not an insult to his instrument.

"I'm sorry, Maestro, please let me explain," Baptiste said and looked down at his hands.

"You don't have to explain," the maestro said. "When I made the promise to her father I had not thought of the implications of it. It was only to make her my ward. But this place has become a cesspool. My dying friend seemed to have a prescience of how bad it was going to get, with no morals, no care. I had no thought to fear for her until she began to mature. Then the world seemed to become so much more . . . dangerous."

The old man carried no illusions and never supposed he could have delighted Ekaterina as a young husband might have. Moreover, who would look after her after he died? This *Indianer* was adroit and oddly sincere, and certainly he loved her. *One day, I might think of Ekaterina's future as a sort of duet,* the maestro thought.

"I will take care of her," Baptiste said, beginning a five-finger exercise.

"I will hold you to that promise."

The old man nodded, then walked to the window. His wiry, twisted frame expanded and contracted with three long, slow breaths before he wheeled to face Baptiste, almost in waltz time.

"What's that—what on earth are you doing with your hands?" he demanded of his *Indianer.*

"I was just resting," Baptiste said.

"Better you cut them off," the maestro smiled, "than rest like that."

Ekaterina, by contrast, had both talent and skill; endless hours of watching the maestro's hands had given her an intimacy with ivory in place of sound. The keys seemed to reach out to be touched by her fingers, and she in turn learned to stroke them with infinite variations of pressure, so that even a single key could release a thousand different vibrations.

Baptiste practiced all the harder to earn not just the maestro's, but her, approval. She did what she could to help his lost cause, placing her head against the side of the piano to feel the sounds. After *des leçons horribles,* where the maestro criticized him for ponderously clubbing the keys, she comforted him, writing quickly on a sheet of paper:

"If playing 'with feeling' is a fault, no doubt it is a fault of mine, too." Then they looked at each other and smiled, because he'd seen her fingers glide over the keys like hummingbirds. "To me, your playing is like my winds on the parapets." She closed her eyes and hugged herself as if facing into the force of nature she so adored.

This note Baptiste folded to match Vogelweide's drawing of Stuttgart's rearing war horse. He slipped it into his possibles bag.

But even Ekaterina advised him to veer away from complicated compositions for his first piano recital. He was, more properly, to gambol in the phantasies. At last he chose Fantasia in G Minor, infamous for its brilliance and lack of industry. There were just two dangerous parts in this work. Properly rendered, eyebrows would be raised, especially if the renderer were an *innocente arriviste*.

He'd soon find out. The recital was just a week away. Every day brought it, and Ekaterina, closer.

In the meantime, he still had responsibilities. Stresemann, his stablemaster, told him he'd be in charge of morning stables "from tomorrow forward."

"Thank you."

Baptiste had seen his wife's creamy bosom the week before. Another of his night visitors, she was half undressed before he could even begin to object. He'd rehearsed his speech to Stresemann, about how sorry he was for (not) touching her. These Europeans were so unusual he considered taking one of them back with him to show the savages.

A dream about his night visitors disturbed his sleep, perhaps a premonition that these delicate *frauen*, with their delicate modesty, might mean trouble for him.

In the dream he was a blacksmith and was therefore required to "shoe" each of them. As he finished hammering the exquisite small curves of silver onto their feet, he released them and watched them, otherwise nude, taking their first tentative steps on the cobblestones of the inner bailey.

+ + +

Baptiste hurried through his music lessons one morning because he'd arranged to meet Ekaterina on the ramparts. Flying up the stairs, he turned in the gloom to find himself eye-to-eye with Kirsten's husband.

"Savage," Karl Voorheis said, stepping forward from a group of three guards he'd obviously brought as witnesses.

Baptiste took in the two-foot crimson plume atop Karl's silver in-laid casque, made of horsehair and more garish than any headdress in Clark's museum. Epaulets strutted on the shoulders of his tunic like a pair of ring-necked pheasants.

"I've been looking for you."

Baptiste swallowed hard, realizing Karl had donned his full battle uniform. "For me?"

Even if Catamount is so full after a kill he has to lie in the river to cradle his belly, still will he rise and snarl if Coyote tries to pick what's left of the fly-encrusted carcass, Baptiste recalled. *And if Coyote turns up his nose to the meal and walks away, then contrary Catamount's rage only grows.*

"You have been too free," Karl said, "with what is mine."

"Sir, I just want you to know I have the highest respect for you and Kirsten."

"*Kannibalisch,* how dare you invoke the name of my purest treasure?"

A few snickers wafting from the guards turned Karl's face bright red. This encounter wasn't going as well as he'd expected. He'd planned only to frighten the *Indianer.*

"I'm sorry for any offense I've given you," Baptiste said.

Karl opened his mouth to accept the apology, but one of his party cut in.

"Ah," the guard said. "So you're admitting you *did* give offense. Sounds like this must come to blades."

Karl's sword rasped as he reluctantly unsheathed it. They were halfway up the castle wall against a walkway that made the deepening purple sky behind them seem almost theatrical.

"But, sir, I have no weapon."

A saber was extended toward Baptiste hilt-first. He raised his hands in refusal.

"You're too good to honor my sword?" the guard said. "You are decidedly not a gentleman."

"If honor matters," Baptiste said sincerely, picking up the sword, "this is not a matter of honor, and it's certainly not a matter of skill because I've never held such a weapon."

"I'll gut you regardless," Karl said, a bit uncertainly.

"I've done nothing wrong, sir," Baptiste said and remembered with chagrin it was just what he'd said to Clark at the East India store in St. Louis. In a single leap, Baptiste was up on the rail, standing. Unwisely, he exaggerated his relaxed position.

Kirsten arrived at the run, flushed with embarrassment, holding her skirts in her hands. Karl's face now deepened to purple.

What, have you dressed for the occasion? Baptiste thought of Kirsten. *This is getting messy.*

Karl slashed twice at Baptiste's knees, which he evaded with a jump and a nimble sidestep. Then the wind was sucked out of the crowd when Baptiste, finally irked, thumbed his nose at *die Regeln des Krieges* and kneed Karl in *die Nüsse*. When the bigger man bent over howling, Baptiste ignominiously leaned in and bit the fleshy lobe of Karl's right ear. With bright blood dripping from teeth to chin, he beat his chest, spat the slimy flesh into the crowd, and leered from side to side, every inch the "savage."

"Bis zum Tode, Indianer!"

The silver swing of Karl's lumbering, meat-cleaving hack cooled Baptiste's cheekbones as he stepped aside to watch Karl's enraged momentum carry him over the rail.

The guards and feather-bespangled ladies in waiting ran to the edge and looked down. Karl clutched his mangled knee with his left hand. "I knew you didn't have it in you to fight like a man of honor," he cried, shaking his right fist.

Of course you did. You addressed me as a savage.

"*Untier,*" Kirsten said to Baptiste, then turned to the guards. "You've let this filthy monster embarrass us all."

At that moment, Ekaterina slipped up the stairs and ran silently to Baptiste.

"What are you doing here?" Kirsten said, turning on her.

HURT? Ekaterina asked Baptiste with her hands. Baptiste flipped his hand over in the negative.

"Oh, so that's how it is, you little *schlampe,*" Kirsten said.

Baptiste knew he'd made some serious enemies.

Baptiste and Vogelweide conducted final preparations for his recital in Duke Paul's laboratory. The minutes rushed forward as they heard the crowd assembling in the grand hall. With slotted spoons they held the cubes of sugar over their drinks. Then they applied one of the new friction matches to the sugar and watched it blacken, then drip slowly into the absinthe. It was much more efficient than using a candle, and the sulfur sparked with a pleasant *pffft*. Baptiste sipped the mixture. It helped him hear the individual steps of the guests and the swish of their Trafalgar dresses.

"Is Sophie here yet?" Vogelweide asked Duke Paul.

Ignoring him, Duke Paul fumbled with the settings of the de-oxidation lamp they'd acquired in Frankfurt a month earlier because they'd been told it would stimulate the growth of herbs. Vogelweide walked over and assisted him. Baptiste imagined he felt a warm flash on his right side.

"Ha!" the artist said.

The supernatural ray spread its vapors over the floor. Baptiste plunged his arm into the light, which became violet-colored, and then withdrew it quickly, widening his eyes, which he knew made him more deliciously savage-like and more likely to be taken to meet Beethoven in Malta if he played well tonight. Beethoven was spending the season at Malta. Though Lord Byron had been lost to fever while playing the revolutionary, at least Lord Elgin might still be found in the Greek islands.

There had been hints of an archaeological tour during which Baptiste might perform a series of recitals at the various consulates in the Levant and North Africa. He considered this a probable divagation because it would allow Duke Paul to escape Sophie for up to nine months.

Their wedding was now a fait accompli, but at least it might be postponed. Sophie's family had already spent a fortune refurbishing Ludwigsburg, the four-hundred-room baroque castle north of Stuttgart, to create the "gilded cage" Duke Paul wept about during his unguarded moments, which were many now that he had increased his laudanum dosage from twenty to forty drops.

To anyone but Duke Paul, there were many advantages to Ludwigsburg. It was cradled within an enormous nature reserve, where squirrels and deer were used for target practice. The handful of guards who presided over the park lived in rustic ecstasy in the renowned hunting lodge, Schloss Favorit. Schloss Favorit was visible from a white rock high in the countryside where Baptiste and Ekaterina liked to ride, though they were discouraged from going there through the woods as they were full of Gypsies.

Softened by the green distance, Schloss Favorit seemed a wonderful place. If Baptiste were allowed to bring Ekaterina and Sorcerie there and continue his studies, he might be happy forever.

"If we go there," Duke Paul had confided to him, "you will be my warden of the forests."

Now Baptiste stood up, looking empty.

"Are you ready?" Vogelweide asked him.

"No!"

"Then there will be some adventure this evening!"

"You *can* play, can't you?" Duke Paul asked, looking slightly alarmed.

They went downstairs into a glittering audience that caught its breath when Duke Paul stumbled. Baptiste and Vogelweide all but carried him to the front of the receiving line.

Here, for the first time, Baptiste was close enough to Sophie to see her crooked teeth. She was already one score and seven. It was an emergency that she was not married.

"My darling," Duke Paul said, "I'd like you to meet my great friend, young Baptiste Charbonneau, who breathes the spirit of the New World into these rainy days."

Her eyes glowed in their sockets, feral and defensive. She peered at Baptiste far more acutely than any of Duke Paul's scientific colleagues had.

"Perhaps the spirit of the poppy as well," she said.

Vogelweide coughed.

Baptiste stood still under her gaze. Vogelweide, flanked by Prince Maximillian of Wied and a red-faced American, broke in.

"His Royal Highness Prince Maximillian and young Henry Longfellow," Vogelweide said and grasped Baptiste by the arm. He pulled him toward some stairs behind the stage.

"You'd better play your best tonight," Vogelweide said and pointed out a bearded man with large hands surrounded by young women in the corner of the room. "Herr Goethe."

They disappeared behind the curtain and Baptiste felt better, alone for a few moments with the piano, which was so much like being alone with Sorcerie in his stall. He sat down and stretched.

"Good luck," Vogelweide said with momentary warmth. He disappeared into the hush of the curtain being raised and the lights going out.

People above him leaned down from gilded galleries. It was like the first night he'd spent alone on the banks of the Kaw River. He pretended he was alone with the stars. He slipped into the phantasie's *allegro ma non troppo* passage that bestows nobility on anyone's craven technique. No matter how badly Baptiste played, this was Beethoven.

He paused romantically, but without swagger, where the music sweetens almost with a chime after some dark clouds at the *ritenuto* comment, and in the afterhush he knew the piece was his to lose.

The big rocks were ahead, though, covered with seaweed. He dangerously felt nothing in his wrists as he accelerated through the *poco piu animato* prelude to the three crescendos where there was no opportunity for deliberate thinking, where every novice pianist met his Waterloo.

He charged through everything with anger and brilliance and knew now that he was going to make a horrible mistake. He was giddy with the knowledge of it. He would rightly be discovered as the "thief" of the East India store, an absurd pretender.

He continued *con bravura* and broke into a clearing, where all the trees fell away. He staggered in disbelief into the *leggatissimo* of that clearing as the applause began. It swept over the grand hall and covered his mistake, in the lower depths of his left hand, a single missed key resulting in a dead thud like the sound of a Bible falling from the top shelf of a rich man's private library.

Five, maybe six people heard it. Maestro, surely. And the satisfied Vogelweide, who'd doubtless warmed the edge of his chair listening for it. The applause continued to crash into the grand hall like the sea.

Duke Paul was wet with it. "*Fauve*, you are a sensation," he said.

"Not all sensations are pleasant," Vogelweide said. "I, for one, have never particularly enjoyed the writhings of a dancing bear."

"How do you like your beast now?" Duke Paul said almost directly to Sophie as he strode to the stage. Playing the fool he kissed Baptiste's hand. Then he asked the audience if he should play something more.

The maestro, sitting out of view from the others in a darkened chair, nodded uneasily. Ekaterina smiled. Only she had considered this eventuality.

He played the piece she'd chosen, a Scarlatti passage that was all touch, like butterflies landing everywhere. Years later, he would still remember its name: Sonata in E Major. He would always hear it moments before something revelatory was about to happen.

13

"SECRET"

—hold extended left hand, back of the hand up, in front of left breast.
With right thumb and index finger make sign for LITTLE TALK under
and close to left palm.

March, 1825

Baptiste's enthusiasm for their tour in the Levant was dampened when
he learned that Ekaterina could not attend with them as part of the
musical presentation. She had fainting spells, and the palace physi-
cian had insisted she stay in bed until her strength returned, but her
sweetheart was not to worry, everything was fine. Refusing to cry, she
handed him this note, tied with a ribbon to her own violin, which she
presented to him for his travels:

> Go, go, my dear Baptiste. You are the New World and the
> one they want to see. Engage in some plundering of Europe
> yourself. Then return to me.

Baptiste was touched. *This instrument, a precious token of your love, will be my constant companion.*

They reached Malta after minor concerts in Gibraltar, Rome, Crete, Tripolezza, Argos, Idria, and as far up the Adriatic as Valona, aggravated suppers, really, presided over by the local consul and his family after a day's hunting for Roman artifacts with Duke Paul and Vogelweide.

No treasures had revealed themselves yet. Lord Elgin had proved elusive. But tonight they would have Beethoven. They had received the letter in his hand that he would leave his seclusion to attend. No one had seen him in months. He was rumored to be working on a new symphony, his tenth. In all their peregrinations through the Levant over the last six months, Baptiste had never seen Duke Paul so sanguine.

"This is wonderful," Duke Paul said. "Now the great master will see the power of our lessons."

"You are truly the favorite of the deaf," Vogelweide said to Baptiste.

Through the windows of the German consul's villa they watched as an overdressed servant in a *dghaisa* dispatched by Duke Paul weaved across the Grand Harbor with invitations to the admirals on the British men of war anchored in clusters below the *kafés* near fleet landing, who would, thanks to Beethoven's kindness, now most certainly attend with their staff officers and families.

"The entire English community will be there tonight," Duke Paul said, flushed with pride as much as drink. "The Italians will come, the Dutch, the Saracens, they never miss a spectacle . . ."

"Perhaps even a few Maltese." Vogelweide swung a blue cape over his shoulder, casting a brief shadow over half the room. "But first we'll have some horse races." He looked at Baptiste. "Coming?"

"Just a moment."

"Well, we've waited long enough for you to finish scratching your love letters. Just follow the crowds."

Vogelweide pulled the door shut after the Duke.

Baptiste turned back to writing his fifth letter to Clark. The Roman Catholic School, and over a year at court, had made him most expert in corresponding in a florid hand that concealed rather than revealed. But he had no illusions. During his long nights on the azure Mediterranean, he'd realized what he needed, as much as Ekaterina's love, was Clark's approval. If Clark could only see what a gentleman he'd become, a post could still perhaps be found for him at his side. Malta, some lost part of him calculated, was the shortest route back to St. Louis.

His first three letters, addressed "Dear Father," had gone unanswered. So had a fourth, with the salutation "Dear Governor Clark." This new missive hoped to find "General Clark" in good health. *If I could just divine who Clark believes he is to me, if I strike precisely the right chord, I might learn who I am myself,* Baptiste dared to hope.

Now Beethoven was thrown into the bargain. If Baptiste made a good account of himself tonight, he'd be more than just a stage amusement, "The Savage." He'd be a modest ambassador for Clark's Missouri.

He wrote to Clark that Beethoven would inspire him to discoveries of his own. As always, he sent his best wishes to his brothers Clark, and to Lottie and her parents. Then he got dressed to see the horse races.

Above the *kafés* of Valletta, Malta's fortifications surged skyward to the Grand Bastion, the top of which, the Barracca, cast a shadow over the flat plains and the grandstands of the athletic fields. Baptiste, Duke Paul, and Vogelweide joined a swelling aggregation of colonials and visitors in the stiff heat for the final event, the Consul's Cup. Eleven horses would thunder across the flats point to point.

"Sir Alfred's horse," Duke Paul said of a witchy Arabian whom Baptiste had already noted. The horse arched his back, hating the weight of his rider, a Moroccan in a blue fez. The rider's eyes were nearly solid white.

"Has he owned him long?" Baptiste asked.

"Never mind that," Vogelweide said. He turned to a steward. "Who is riding that long chestnut with the blue blanket?"

"That's Lef'tenant Walley-Pierce, from His Majesty's ship *Aspire.*"

"I daresay," Vogelweide said.

In his white Royal Navy choker with gold epaulets and regalia, Walley-Pierce stood out from the sea of mufti.

"I know him as Lord Walley-Pierce," Duke Paul said.

Ladies whispered behind their fans as Walley-Pierce wheeled his horse toward them. His very short hair seemed out of place for a line officer. His horse danced closer in the wavering heat. Slight, lithe Walley-Pierce moved with such lifelong assurance he soothed the whole crowd, not just the horses around him. Just as he passed, he turned his head to Duke Paul's party and his eyes met Baptiste's.

This young officer is no older than I, Baptiste reflected. When Duke Paul turned his head toward Baptiste, Walley-Pierce broke into a canter and entered the mélange of horses about to let fly.

With a soft report they were off.

Muscles compacted and elongated, while inexperienced Maltese horsemen damaged their mounts with whipping. The Arabian jolted immediately to the lead. Behind the din of hooves lay the blue fez, rolling in a half circle before stopping.

Vogelweide handed Baptiste his empty glass to refill, along with Duke Paul's. In this heat everything was sticky. Baptiste filled the glasses with the Madeira so pale they called it rainwater and watched as four mosquitoes landed on his arm. He discreetly slapped them away. The Arabian drew farther ahead. No wonder. He was not racing but fleeing. The hatless Moroccan held on in terror.

"What are you playing tonight?" Vogelweide leaned over. "Not *Moonlight* again."

Baptiste most certainly would not butcher the *Moonlight* Sonata in front of its creator.

"Something new. But I'm terrified of it."

"Oh, we have a remedy for fear," Vogelweide said. He patted him on the knee and reached inside his vest pocket.

"No." Baptiste felt giddy with the freedom to refuse.

Ooooh. They'd heard the same expostulation in Rapallo, during the religious fireworks. They stood up to see the Moroccan fall, wriggling under the hooves. No one seemed shocked to see the man trampled, and Walley-Pierce, aboard his inferior mount, surge to the front and finish first as though he owned it.

A great cheer erupted. Dozens of spectators foamed about Walley-Pierce, shaking his hands and slapping congratulations on his horse's withers and saddle. "God Save the King" wafted through the air while in the distance, an attendant knelt over the broken figure of the horseman.

"I'll be right back," Baptiste said and left the shade of their platform, bumping down the stairs. He could have caught the Arabian stallion on the track, but he let His Majesty's Royal Navy, in the form of two scrawny sailors, try to catch him. In seconds he reached the rider.

The fallen man was unconscious. The flush of cholera darkened both his cheeks, and he was covered with sweat. Instinctively Baptiste stepped back. *Why put a sick man on a bad horse?* By now two other men, holding handkerchiefs over their mouths, were calling down into the black pit of him as if he were at the end of a dark hallway, a flickering candle.

Then Haih the Raven blew the candle out.

The poor rider's yellowed eyes rolled back in his head. But it was worse than this. Feeling the Moroccan's spirit rise out of his chest, Baptiste was now confirmed in the knowledge that Haih, who assumed many shapes in darkness, had begun to follow him.

The horror of seeing the jockey die may have infected his performance, which was held in the cathedral the British called Ingalls Hall. But then it was doomed from the beginning.

Seven o'clock came and went without Beethoven arriving. Sensing the night was a disaster, Duke Paul and Vogelweide continued drinking in the foyer. Cleared throats, craned necks, and murmurs of disappointment forced the concert into being, with the curtain revealing Baptiste at his piano on the stage, pushing the loud pedal up and down as if to make the piano breathe.

Above him in the nave, a carved wooden Jesus, his painted eyes rolling back in his head, twisted bravely on the cross, but he could offer no succor.

Perhaps the piano will get up like a moose in a forest and walk away, Baptiste thought. The torches in the hall, except for the one directly over his head, were extinguished. No Beethoven.

He lost track of time. Immediate darkness closed around him the way it had in Ekaterina's cave, and he felt an unquenchable loneliness. So now, in Malta, in this cave echoing without Beethoven but with the sound of dozens of guests shuffling out of their seats to leave, he began to play as he caught sight of still another group in mid-departure, led by a woman in a sapphire dress set nearly on fire with a blaze of jewelry, her dark hair pinned high in a modish Apollo knot.

The first dress his mother ever owned was blue, too. In St. Louis she'd begged Clark for white women's clothes, so he gave her the one dress his wife hated most especially and had discarded, faded periwinkle with an exhausted bonnet. *When Mother wore it,* Baptiste remembered, *even I thought her a monkey because of her filthy feet.*

At just twenty-two her teeth had blackened. Was she really chewing the same lump of spruce sap she seemed to have chewed since childhood? She was certainly never without it. Her smile the sweetest black cave.

We don't say "goodbye," do we? Instead, we just walk away, without comment, to reduce the seriousness of our departure. We'll be right back, we're only stepping over here, into this cave. Goodbye. The absence of it slammed back to Baptiste like the theme of a fugue. Goodbye. His mother couldn't have brought herself to say "goodbye" to him to save her life.

She was just this side of here. Death being the temporary condition that it was.

He played on. Just as he had promised Vogelweide, it was something new. He didn't give a damn what it was. Maybe it was his goodbye symphony. He finished to polite applause, rose, and bowed. What was left of the audience got up as the torches were re-lit by the Maltese Friars and the doors were flung open. All of a sudden the cathedral's great interior seemed to dissolve into deeply polished bronze.

He disappeared behind a curtain, grabbed his violin, descended a flight of stairs, and entered a series of hallways, catacombs with religious denizens painted in frescoes along the walls. Around a corner he could hear Vogelweide braying to the exiting crowd. Hello, Mrs. Spencer-Smith. Thank you, Governor Ball. Baptiste couldn't breathe. *Far too many critics.*

Baptiste headed toward the back of the cathedral through a small room and stumbled into a heavy old man bent over double and followed by an assistant who was fiddling with a woolen pelisse. As Baptiste offered the elder his arm he looked into a pair of sharp eyes. *It couldn't be Herr Beethoven.* Certainly no witch doctor could have believed in such a thing.

As the composer straightened, Baptiste realized he was taller, and more urbane, than he'd imagined. Beethoven wore a dark blue tunic with a white cravat. He leaned his walking stick against a dusty lectern as his assistant retrieved a chair from a corner. Beethoven dropped into it splay-footed and sighed.

Baptiste had never seen a man so tired.

"I am sorry to have missed you at piano," Beethoven said, looking at Baptiste's violin case. "What have you got there?"

Baptiste realized he would never play piano for Beethoven. But here, in this anteroom, with Duke Paul and Vogelweide out of earshot, he hastily snapped open the violin case and raised Ekaterina's gift to his chin. Upon Beethoven's nod, the door clicked shut as the servant considerately left the young man alone with the master.

In a flash Baptiste saw the composer's hell. Wherever this man went, he was forced to sit politely and smile while others butchered his compositions. *Maybe it's a blessing you are losing your hearing.* Beethoven barely raised his hand, and Baptiste began.

He played a fragment of one of his mother's tunes as Beethoven watched his every move. The composer seemed troubled by his fingering and the way he held his left arm.

"Thank you," Beethoven said when he finished. His low rumble sounded like large pieces of furniture being pushed across the floor below.

"Could you hear *any* of it?" Baptiste asked.

Baptiste's heart hammered. He stood close to the composer to hear his answer, even though he was not deaf.

"I heard you," Beethoven said, "or someone like you." He paused and said in a more kindly tone, "I don't have to hear it, young man, to hear it."

Beethoven clasped his pelisse and stood up. Upon opening the door, they found a throng of fawning gentlemen rushing up to greet him, among them Vogelweide and Duke Paul. Beethoven patted Baptiste on the shoulder and began his escape. But he turned abruptly back and looked sharply at the two toadies whom he realized were with the young man. He leaned into Baptiste's ear. "Why are you wasting your time with these moldering fops when you could be in the New World? You don't belong here. Go home to *Amerika*. Remember where you came from."

14

"NAME"

—make the signs QUESTION, YOU, CALLED—as in "What are you called? What are you named?"

Baptiste walked alone into the night and joined the crowds of sailors flooding Valletta. So close to the water, the *kafés* were positioned to jump the poor tars, then pick their pockets.

There was no more honorable a way to lose money than to toast the King's health with these tars. Perhaps he could join them and travel the world. With whiskey his rough frigate. Dragging his violin behind, he slouched into Sinbad's Locker.

"Hi, stranger," a sailor drinking at a tavern table said. "Where are you from, stranger?"

"That's a right proper fiddle," another of the tars said before he could answer. "But I prefer to keep mine in my pants."

"I prefer to keep mine . . . in your wife's pants," said a third as two powder monkeys approached Baptiste.

"Jesus wept," said one boy.

"Look! 'E's the very spit," said the other, who crossed himself.

"Of what?" Baptiste said.

A very old sailor got off his bench and joined them, surveying his face. He made the sign of the cross. "Our bowsprit." Embroidered on his black cap was the legend HMS *Powhatan*. Two other sailors crossed the bar to see. "Where did you say you were from, stranger?"

"St. Louis," Baptiste said. "In the New World."

"Ha," the old one said softly. "I'm stranger than you. I'm from Poland." He pointed to another tar who was finishing a plate of eel with half a hand. This personage smiled very broadly and waved his flipper. "He's from Java."

"Visit any waterfront, we're from everywhere but here. All of us is the same for bein' different," said a sailor with cobwebs tattooed on his elbows, who handed him a glass. "We share many fathers but one mother, the sea." His breath was so strong Baptiste had to grab a rail behind him for balance.

As absurd as these limeys were, they made Baptiste feel nostalgic for his old comrades at American Fur. He drank the rum the sailor had offered him. When he thought of what Beethoven had whispered, he ordered another drink. Maybe Beethoven was right and his European experience was a disastrous experiment, the only bright spot being Ekaterina.

Slowly, the room tilted as Baptiste descended into his rum. Two sailors broke into a lonely tune about a beautiful girl left back at home, and the image of Ekaterina on the castle battlements, waiting for him, came to him with so much force that he found himself wiping tears from his face. Now this was music. What a laugh. No one listening to his concert had been moved like this.

Noting with care that he had imbibed too much at this establishment, Baptiste drifted across the alley into a rum hole bearing the appellation Welcome Sailor. Finally he settled into Davey Jones's Stand Easy. An old salt at the bar eyed him up and down.

At this, the barkeep leaned over. "Watch him," he said in Italian. "He's one of the Jettatore. He'll give you the evil eye."

"Ha!" the old man snorted and hissed in that peculiar mix of Italian and Greek common to Sicilians. "And with this bile he calls beer, this one will give you the evil *head*."

"There he goes," the barkeep said. "It's his curse to curse even when he doesn't mean to curse."

"Show me a sailor who isn't cursed and I'll show you no sailor," the Jettatore snapped.

Baptiste moved closer to hear the two men better.

"Don't look at him directly," the barkeep said. "And don't listen to his compliments. They're the deadliest of all."

"To your health," the Jettatore said very softly, raising his glass.

The barkeep wheeled on the old man. "Aren't you supposed to hold a curtain between yourself and anyone you're talking to?"

At this he threw a wet towel at him and turned back to Baptiste. "They project the *mal occhio*, the bad eye, even when they don't intend to, though this old man, I think, knows perfectly well what he's doing. Every time he sets foot on my threshold I can depend on my night's take being cut in half."

"That's because you cut your brandy in half, and half again," the old man said.

The barkeep edged closer, spoke under his breath. "Children or animals make the best victims. The most sincere praise of a Jettatore can bare a tree of its leaves, render a man impotent, smother a newborn babe, sour the milk in a goat's udder." He paused. "You hear me, sir?"

Baptiste nodded and kept on drinking that he might keep his one chance to impress Beethoven forever ahead of him. He kept on drinking knowing that any of these tars was better than he, because the great one had not listened thoughtfully to them and yawned. By now his head had begun to throb. He snagged his violin and a half-empty bottle by the neck and stumbled into an alley to piss.

"Offering a drink to a stranger," a musical voice said from behind him, "makes for a fast friend."

Even in this state he recognized Lord Walley-Pierce. The alley glowed around the young man, washing him with moonlight.

"I heard you play," he said. "You are astonishing."

"Merely astonishing," Baptiste agreed and steadied himself against a lamp post.

"I hope your duke wasn't too disappointed that his celebrity guest didn't deign to attend," Walley-Pierce said after leaning in and helping himself to a drink from Baptiste's bottle. "Frankly, I don't understand all the gush about that German anyway. Give me a good English drinking song—a tot in a tavern." Walley-Pierce turned to the forest of masts in the harbor and saluted in the direction of a frigate draping signal pennants and a Union Jack.

"Is that yours?" Baptiste asked.

"My ship has yet to come in, but that's the slop bucket my father is certain will make a man out of me."

Baptiste said nothing.

"So what is your relationship to the prince? Protégé, specimen, ward, slave—?"

Baptiste stopped him before he could say "toy" or "pet."

"We're just—fast friends."

Walley-Pierce eyed him carefully and took another swig from his bottle, leaning in. "Your eyes are the color of my favorite tea in a little shop in Bury St. Edmunds; if our travels might once again coincide, it would be my pleasure one day to take you there. Listen to us! It's almost as if we're plotting a rendezvous! Do you know what? We should climb up here to the top of the Grand Barracca, because the view is incomparable there."

The Englishman trotted up three stairs, then turned, catching his balance.

"My lord, you are drunk . . . as a lord," Baptiste said.

"And you're tight as a fiddler. It's better that way. Come with me."

Like St. Peter, Baptiste dropped his nets and followed.

Have I sunk so low? he wondered as the pair stumbled their way across the cobbles and up the famous steps of Valletta. *Am I really this base?* There was no mistaking Walley-Pierce's intentions, even through the fog of flip and loneliness. *A disappointment to Clark, I turned to Duke Paul. A disappointment to Duke Paul—why not the execrable Walley-Pierce? Ekaterina would surely despise me if she knew what I was doing.* It was not the first time that Baptiste had wondered during low moments if he truly hadn't become a "right proper *guidoune*" by his own choice since he'd so often bent to the desires of Duke Paul. *Why haven't I put an end to it? Must a slave fall in love with his master? Does the done become the doer?* He shuddered at the thought of his abominable disaster at piano a few hours earlier, with the whole world turning away. *Why not experiment,* he argued with himself, *if I'm so bloody worthless?* Then, too, he knew he was not immune to America's secret love affair with royalty. At the lemon-lit *déjeuner* in the wilds of St. Louis, hadn't even the homespun Clark family bragged that their imported piano might once have belonged to "a German countess"? Baptiste brushed the sweat from his brow. He realized he'd fallen a step behind the lucky lord and all but called out from his own animadversion, "Lead on, good sir! Let's find out if I am a *finocchio* once and for all!" *What would Ekaterina do if she knew about this? I wonder what her sign for whore is? Well, she's the one who chose not to come, isn't she?* Even with that fleeting thought he saw the image of his mother, condemning him with a knitted brow. *Well to hell with her, too.*

A dozen steps up to the great height, Walley-Pierce stopped, catching his breath.

"Why don't we go instead to Calypso's Cave? The night is still young, and I'm not really prepared for such a climb."

Must it be a cave?

Baptiste, though drunk, was chilled at the prospect of visiting the landmark he'd twice refused to tour with Duke Paul and Vogelweide, but was intrigued at the prospect of seeing the spot where the witch held Odysseus spellbound for seven years with the promise of eternal youth.

"It sounds like the name of another tavern," Baptiste laughed.

"Right."

"But isn't it a long way?"

Walley-Pierce stopped and leered. "The great Sacagawea's son is not prepared to travel?"

"I might have slept instead."

Baptiste could barely stand up. He had a fleeting pang of regret at the thought of Duke Paul and Vogelweide already warm and snoring at their place in Palazzo Parizo. *Of all things, why a cave? Because it has to be a cave,* his mind countered with tipsy logic. *Mother never completely made it out of her cave. It's time you really faced what you haven't dared to fear . . .*

"Normally," said Walley-Pierce, "I'd dismiss it as a tourist attraction, but at this hour we should have it to ourselves." He grinned. "And there are some very fine excavations there superior to those at Skorba."

Descending the wide marble steps of Valletta, Baptiste and Walley-Pierce approached the town docks crowded with *luzzis,* fishing boats. Then the harbor opened up, and the Moorish dome of Fort St. Angelo slid in front of them like a golden moon.

Walley-Pierce kicked a boatman out of a drunken stupor and arranged for their passage to Gozo, the rock that huddled treelessly on the dark side of the main island. Within minutes they were on the boat heading out into the channel. High above them they could hear lovers talking from the top of the Valletta lookout.

"Your Duke Paul admires the ruins, I understand," Walley-Pierce said as they slipped beneath a dark wall below Malta's lighthouse.

My Duke Paul.

Baptiste gripped the gunwale and looked ahead. The Maltese had painted the dark Egyptian eyes of Osiris on their prows for a thousand years. Even the smallest watercraft looked out with them. Their boatman, just to be safe, had lashed an alabaster Virgin Mary to an iron spike above his bow to guide the way.

Baptiste hadn't realized that Gozo, hiding like a highwayman behind the main island, was so large. No one could see them. All the lights, domes, and ships disappeared. They glided through Ramla Bay and came ashore on a red beach.

"*Sahha,*" the boatman waved as they disembarked. Walley-Pierce stumbled off the boat without even turning around.

The boatman spat into the oily water and shifted his helm in the blood heat. As he headed back for the harbor, they walked straight into the darkness.

Up on the hump of Gozo they encountered tiny scraps of white marble dotting the night fields. They reminded Baptiste of cotton. They were all that was left of the Trilithon altars, part of Xaghra.

He looked out where the edge of the island dropped off to endless indigo, then ink. In the stars of the night sky, just like in St. Louis, the same three hunters stalked the same timeless bear.

"Here, below this lookout, is your Calypso's Cave," said Walley-Pierce.

Baptiste climbed over a sheep-eaten berm and sensed the ocean double its sound. "Where?" he called out.

"Down here," Walley-Pierce said. He led Baptiste down a narrow path edged with rocks.

Like grief, the waves had carved deep passages into the coral. Baptiste slid down behind the retreating shadow of Walley-Pierce and jumped down to the red-sand basin.

"Are you coming?" Walley-Pierce called back.

Walley-Pierce strode ahead. His heels sucked in and out of the sand. He turned right, right, right, like a magic incantation. Baptiste saw his white shoes disappear into the darkness.

When Baptiste caught up with the Englishman he turned and saw a turquoise grotto surrounded by wet sprays of coral. Tiny stones smoothed by the sea shifted as the ocean boomed outside the cave. With the passing of each wave, the stones slowly rose and fell, as though the cave were breathing.

Walley-Pierce slid his hand around Baptiste's neck. "The nymph goddess Calypso watched Odysseus's ship sink in a storm out there. She brought him in here, as I've brought you."

"Don't."

Walley-Pierce reached to unbutton Baptiste's tunic. Up close, and this late at night, the Englishman wasn't so clean or shaven, so the stubble of his beard felt rough when he put his lips on Baptiste's. *I can almost feel you watching me, Ekaterina.* How could a deaf and dumb girl seem to be eavesdropping on them from this great distance?

"I'm sorry. I'm afraid I've misunderstood your intentions," Baptiste said.

"You mean you're afraid you haven't."

Baptiste took a step back. Walley-Pierce followed him. "I've told you. No."

"No, *my lord*." Walley-Pierce stood very close. They were the same height.

"It will be our secret."

Now Baptiste laughed. He was already an expert at secrets. He got up and walked toward the brightest part of turquoise and watched the stars get lost in the eddies. The waves rose and fell. So did his breath.

Walley-Pierce was now behind him, parting the long black hair behind his neck. Baptiste felt his tongue and was revulsed.

"I see," Walley-Pierce said. "Only his master's *guidoune*."

Baptiste considered his relationship with Duke Paul a business arrangement. Walley-Pierce had nothing to offer him but shame.

"I suppose now I'm supposed to demand satisfaction," Baptiste said.

"You may have your satisfaction," Walley-Pierce said, "after you satisfy me."

Baptiste felt bile rise to his throat. Among the Shoshone, homosexuals were respected for their sorcery. Most were witch doctors prized for the sanguinity of their spells and their intelligence in general. These witch doctors often adorned themselves as women and kept to their tents, earning higher privilege for communing with the spirit world than the greatest warriors might for vanquishing their enemies. But privilege did not figure into Baptiste's present situation. Nor did desire.

He thought of, but did not move for, his knife. Again he felt a murderous rage inside him, and the sound of a waterfall roared in his ears. He could certainly kill Walley-Pierce. His arm leapt with the thrill of it.

But then he'd be hanged, or worse, imprisoned, or put into an institution where they'd study the savage even more minutely. How would William Clark react to the sensational broadsheets recounting the trial? Surely the horrific and thrilling details of a duel would find their way back to St. Louis. To top it off, it wasn't even Walley-Pierce's fault. *Why should I be surprised to find another European trying to seduce me?* Baptiste reflected. Didn't they have anything else to do, or was this just the manifestation of the impulse to colonize that came to these civilized creatures naturally? As inviting as it might be to kill Walley-Pierce, it was a more piercing triumph . . . *not to!*

"You don't deserve to have me cut you down," Baptiste said, relief surging through him because in this unholiest of holes he'd stumbled upon his way by exercising control.

"Just my luck to find a civil savage," Walley-Pierce said. "Too much brain and not enough brawn for my taste, anyway."

Baptiste walked out of the cave. He'd been to deepest darkest civilization and found it already fouling him. The noise of the waterfall had roared him close to madness. But his head began to clear during the hot swim to Valletta.

15

—hold right hand palm up in front of neck. Move outward in sinuous motion.

October, 1825

By the time they reached the swart meadow that rolled up to the old schloss in Stuttgart, Baptiste knew something was wrong.

Ravens sat on every fencepost. A messenger rode up to them in the loud dark. He handed Vogelweide a note. Vogelweide glanced at it, and whispered into Duke Paul's ear. Duke Paul turned his head toward Baptiste. The men stood up quickly in the carriage. Duke Paul got out and walked over to the rider. Then he motioned for him to dismount and give his horse to Baptiste.

Baptiste tore kingdom come in tatters flying to Ekaterina.

He opened the great oak door to her apartment, automatically putting Ekaterina's violin back in its place. What he saw was ghastly. Everywhere but the bed on which Ekaterina lay had been scrubbed clean. The smell of this room was not of life, but of carbolic acid and lye. Heaped in a chair was the green cloak he'd first seen Ekaterina wear to watch Antoine climb the tower. Her few possessions loomed in the candlelight and became important: her washbasin, her music stand, her riding boots in one corner. In the other corner, sitting with his head in his hands, was the maestro.

Baptiste forced himself to look at the small shape under the blanket. When he raised the blanket, he saw Ekaterina's dear face was drawn and empty. Clasped in her arms lay his son. Like a door clicking closed, he felt his brain shut down. He couldn't breathe. He shook Ekaterina and put his ear against her nose.

His newborn's arms were spread out wide, as if caught in surprise, as if he might be falling.

"Nobody would help her," the maestro said. "Once they saw the baby's ruddy complexion, they knew he wasn't mine and they wouldn't touch him. The midwives said he was unclean; the ladies at court had whispered he carried a disease from across the sea."

Baptiste's son was still. Then his knee kicked. Deer Baptiste had killed often did that, running from the black forest with their hearts pounding long after they were lost in that forest. *But the beautiful ones never get away.* Had he been hours too late? Minutes? As wildly as his head spun, he knew it was ignorance, and not simply Kirsten and Karl bruiting rumors about, that had killed his son—not to mention his own absence in the Levant and, most crushing of all, Ekaterina's choosing to keep the baby a secret from him. Her letters had been so light and cheery.

Baptiste picked up the infant and was astonished he was not yet cool. It was horrible luck that he had no name. *Mother would have said his spirit is gone.* He saw the veins on his fragile, fine eyelids: blue lids shut forever. Tiny, icy moons graced his fingertips. Petechiae covered his body like continents on a world he would never travel.

Baptiste looked wildly about, as if he were falling through ice into rushing black water. Ekaterina had told him to leave, but should he have listened to her? Was it worth it, playing in the Levant as Duke Paul's consort? Was he absolutely happy in his selfishness? Like Duke Paul, he had traveled the world and let his people suffer. *I could have saved both of you. This is your fault, Baptiste. Yes, look at what you have done.* But another voice, one he abhorred, cautioned *do not look at him or you will go barking mad.*

Here, finally, was the Germans' Red Skin. His son's mouth was open, but he'd barely had the breath for his first scream.

"Ekaterina will be buried next to her father. The priest from town has ordered the babe to be buried in the grounds below the river," the maestro said. "He was not baptized."

The graveyard below the river lay behind the old stone pest house, where the citizens of Stuttgart had burned stacks of victims killed by the Black Death. The place howled with loneliness. "No, they will not bury my son there." Baptiste reeled at the horror of it.

"*Pompey.*"

He could have sworn he heard his mother's voice, coming from somewhere in the shadows behind him, near the door. Just as suddenly, he remembered the ghost of his own voice, asking so many times in the little shack behind the big white house, "Mother, tell me how it was again, when I was a baby."

And every time his mother would say, patiently and without variation, because she knew he would listen and accept no inconsistencies, "*I carried you on my back. With soft deerskin I lay you on a slab of bark swung gently behind my shoulders so your head was close to mine and ever you could see what I saw. We walked as one. We crossed the mountains as one. The wind warmed our passage. We will always be together.*"

With this ringing in his head he took a step toward his son's body. "He is only sleeping, like his mother," he said to the maestro. *Didn't he understand?* He calmly wrapped his son's stiff figure, using Ekaterina's hooded cloak for a shroud.

The glory of a son: Baptiste marveled at the distance he had traveled. Just as he had swum a long way to cross the harbor at Malta, his son had swum a long way to get into this room.

"Where are you going?" the maestro said. Baptiste patted his arm as he passed him and broke into a long, woodsman's stride, carrying his child.

Once he reached the castle grounds, he tightened the shroud and swung the papoose onto his back. Then he set off for the woods. Just as his mother and he had done to begin the Expedition so many years ago.

He walked across the black field and turned along the Neckar. As the white rock loomed out of the darkness like the bow of a ship, he ducked into the woods and kept walking.

For the first few days he heard voices calling out. Long after the voices stopped, he continued deeper into the forest. Hearing only the crash of his footsteps, he moved swiftly, feeling alone but resolute in his decision never to let them bury his son near the pest house. Instead, his son needed to be elevated long enough for his spirit to make its escape.

Baptiste also feared the symmetrical lines of Stuttgart's burial stones, which in their regularity might seal his son's spirit forever below them, like ice covering a river. His mother's people insisted on a random pattern of graves, and they did not rush to bury; at times taking up to a year for the ceremony to be complete. He remembered his mother telling him that if a child died among her mountains, his parents, if the season permitted, built a tiny ghost teepee out of twigs in front of their own and lovingly placed a bowl inside it for ghost food beside the elevated infant. If good fortune prevailed, grieving friends killed a rare white buffalo calf and draped it over the corpse to preserve its innocence. Then they waited. Once they were sure his soul was free, they covered his remains with a pile of stones, often with his means of transportation to the Fourth World, such as a canoe, sticking halfway out of the ground. The Mandan hills half sprouted with mossy boats planted desperately askew amid the graves of loved ones in the high wind. Ekaterina would have approved.

He had so failed his son in life, he would not in death. How many times had he cursed Toussaint for being a bad father, but at least under his neglect he'd survived. How had he ignored the signs of Ekaterina's pregnancy? What other secrets had she hidden from him in her letters? What selfishness and self-absorption in him had missed the hints? The enormity of it became clear. *I am a true Charbonneau, worse than Toussaint. My son died.*

Though Baptiste could not bury him in the most desired way here, at least in these woods he would have a chance. Surely the boy's spirit would have time to escape and he'd be free, and in any case he would no longer suffer the presence of the barbarians who had stood by and watched him die, his lovely ruddiness being his only "illness."

Baptiste kept walking deeper into the woods, far from the castle now but still taking the trouble to hide, possibly from his own grief. By night he and his son slept under a bed of leaves, though it was getting colder as winter approached. The ground was already hard below them. They walked and slept, walked and slept. Then one night a great wind stirred, and Baptiste bolted up from under his blanket of leaves, looking around.

Nothing, once again, was creeping up on him.

It had been over a fortnight, and he had walked far. Must he continue? His chest ached from a kind of dry crying. A great tiredness slipped into his limbs. The leaves moved about and with a will of their own began to cover him again. *Soon*, he prayed, *the ghosts from the*

Fourth World will come and join us together. Or Jesus Christ, whom he had always considered one and the same. As he lost consciousness he felt the ghosts settling and coming toward him and his son through the branches of the trees. He was glad. He wanted to die himself and enter the spirit world, because "if the dead be truly dead, why should they be walking in my heart?" Like a wolf, he let out a low, broken howl and waited for his son's spirit and his own to rise and walk with the dead. He heard riffling sounds that night, the sound of wings. He kept his eyelids closed.

He believed the spirits took his son that night but left him behind as Washi trash. Whatever the case, he woke the next morning to find himself under scrutiny by the great and solemn eye of a squirrel. How long had the squirrel been considering him?

He was a red squirrel, and close enough for Baptiste to see the three shades of rusty silver that made up his tail, the two white lines denoting his kill zone. The watchlike ticking of his tiny heart, which tensed muscles just above his ribs with every beat, seized Baptiste's attention. The squirrel chattered quite specifically to Baptiste, but he couldn't make it out.

Who are you, Tame Sir? Baptiste thought to his new friend. *And what do you want with me?* Baptiste drifted back to sleep.

Then he heard footsteps in his dream. He woke up looking directly into the squirrel's eyes again. To the squirrel's surprise, Baptiste made no effort to move. *Haven't you heard my warnings?* In a flash the squirrel ran up a tree. There he was, dangling in the canopy of branches covering Baptiste's lost forest.

The author of the footsteps approached Baptiste, now at a run. Others followed and looked down at him below the supernal gaze of the squirrel. Insects crawled over Baptiste, and he did not scratch. He fascinated these wanderers in rags. Then a woman among them made a low moan and untied his child from the sling still lashed to his back. Baptiste did not try to stop her.

The tallest of the group looked down at Baptiste and rubbed his pointed beard. "We will have a *kris*," he said in German inflected with Eurasian rhythms that reminded Baptiste of the Turkish he'd heard in Malta.

"Or we could kill him," a man beside him said.

They were Romani, Gypsies, with their raven hair and moustaches, their faces greasy with sweat. They looked hungrily at him. The only thing Baptiste had heard Gypsies ate was little children.

A woman in an emerald dress, indigo coat, and olive bandanna circled him, her hair a wild tangle. She threw a glance at him and held her nose. "It is not a good idea to kill him," she said. "His ghost will follow us through the woods."

She squatted beside him and peered so deeply into his eyes he grinned back; he was too weak even to move his head.

"I knew it," she said. "He has the *glamour*."

Having the *glamour* in your eyes was apparently bad. More wanderers crowded around Baptiste. He had to be watched because of the evil spirit that possessed him. It could only be scourged out by The Evil Eye, which the woman in the green dress now generously applied to him. She threw up her hands.

A few feet away, the woman who had taken his baby cried out. "King Caumlo," she said, "he has broken the infant's arms."

"What is the child's name?" King Caumlo asked.

"I do not know," Baptiste said.

He fell unconscious and woke only when the claws of the squirrel gripped his chest. Something bright flashed by his side. The vagabonds had started a fire. King Caumlo still stood over him.

"Meriwether," Baptiste said.

The giant slowly smiled. He helped Baptiste to his feet and then turned to the others. "See?" Caumlo said. "There's plenty left in him."

The woman Caumlo called Svigula came over and grinned at Baptiste. She spat three times on her granddaughter's hair to protect her from him. Then she led him to his son's grave. She and the others had buried the infant near a chestnut tree that would shelter him with its great arms. Baptiste felt ashamed he had concealed the real name he might have given his son: Cameahwait, after his mother's brother.

With warm soup, these Washi of the Old World brought him back to life. They were Transylvanian Gypsies from the mountains near Cluj, on the other side of the Danube.

"They are looking for you," King Caumlo said. He was easily six inches taller than the others. "They have already questioned us. Any problems and they always come after us."

Baptiste fell asleep again. That night as he slept by the fire he was visited by Red Squirrel a third time. Why did the animal look at him so long and intently? Emboldened, the squirrel began to follow him wherever he went.

Baptiste worked to repay his rescuers for their kindness, and once when he brought fresh water in a pail from a stream he heard Svigula tell Caumlo, "There is truth and there is the *gadje*. He is like us." They could see he was at home in the woods and welcomed visits from the Fourth World.

Whenever Svigula gazed into her glass ball, she said she could see the future. She kept it wrapped in a piece of indigo velvet as if it could see, like a giant eye.

Objects shimmered inside it like a camera obscura, but it bent time, not light. She only revealed it on the heels of the evening and would not declare a thing about its contents until she had told Baptiste how it had been handed down for five hundred years by the Hindi, her forebears.

"Liar," King Caumlo said to her with love, as if it were a caress. "You are a lying bitch." He turned to Baptiste. "They say we Gypsies forged the nails that held Christ to his cross. That's why the *gadje* condemned us to wander the earth without a homeland forever."

Baptiste wondered what the Washi had done, or, for that matter, the Shoshone. As far as he could tell, his mother's biggest crime had been to aid the Corps of Discovery in their search for the Pacific.

The grateful *Indianer* carved a bow and prayed for the spirits of his game to be released as his arrows struck. Then he hunted for the King's deer. Four days in a row he returned to camp carrying a young deer on his shoulders.

"You are a warlock," Svigula said.

"You are dust under my wheels," Baptiste answered according to custom.

"Let us eat your offal, and deepen its pungency with soured wine," she said, "Brother Baptiste."

They moved from place to place in the forest for the pure joy of it. In time they began to travel north. Memories of the castle, softened by forest leaves, seemed a world away.

Darkness assumed many shapes. Haih the Raven knew this and hid in these shapes. Baptiste began to believe that it was Haih who put his son in the black canoe.

When winter snowstorms laid them low, they hid deep in the forest when they didn't simply follow the Danube. More bands joined them and left their company as they moved along, each speaking a different shade of German leavened by their ancient Punjabi. Warmed by mead and campfires, their stories agreed in this: Their tribe had come here as part of the *Aresajipe*, the vast movement of central Asians in the wake of the Ottomans during the fourteenth century. "We fought Suleman the Magnificent for the *gadje*," Svigula said. "So that now they can spit on us here."

Baptiste was happy to learn from them. Among other skills, he was taught to pick pockets by a gypsy from Izmir with hands so soft he could take all the clothes off a sleeping man without awakening him.

In Luxembourg he demonstrated this for Baptiste in the spring, "skinning" a drunken commissar who'd fallen asleep on a park bench in Vianden. Outside of Clervaux another band joined them. Chained to the back of their caravan was Rinko, the dancing bear, who had horrible breath and exposed his genitals whenever he drew himself up to scratch his back against the bark of trees. As a cub, he had been led by a leash across hot coals while accordion music was being played.

"He is old and ugly, but the *gadje* pay to see him," King Caumlo said.

When Rinko's trainer was too drunk to squeeze music from the box, Baptiste picked up the keyboard with the bellows attached and tried his hand at it. He found he enjoyed the mournful gaiety of its wheeze. In time, the job of playing the accordion fell to him.

Now, all he had to do was hit a few notes and the great old smelly bear would remember his pain and try to walk without letting his feet touch the ground. Little children mistook his grimace.

"Look!" they laughed. "He smiles as he dances!"

The bear's eyes blinked. Baptiste squeezed the box and the old fear came back to him; Baptiste remembered all the doctors running their hands over his head.

Baptiste stayed with his friends through a summer and a second winter and huddled with them during the biting cold. But near a river below a village in Alsace he told them he could no longer make the bear dance.

"It's time to go," he said.

Svigula nodded.

"Baptiste," she said. "Come with me." She guided him into her cabbage-smelly wagon, foul, dark, and smoking with incense. She bade him sit down. Svigula poured him a mug of wine. Then, out of her rag sleeves, she pulled out her Seeing Eye.

After obsequies to Osiris, she took it out of its velvet pouch. It reflected Svigula and the far corners of the wagon. Then it misted over, as if a rainstorm were going on inside it.

"Not much of a crystal," Baptiste said.

"Be quiet," she said.

Then something like green flame flickered inside the glass. Had someone opened a flap in the caravan wagon? Baptiste did not know where this new light came from. Svigula spat. "Stuttgart," she said.

"Where?"

But he had already seen it. The beauty of the city below shimmered in minute detail, the red roofs, the green sward, the old castle, the Schillerplatz. Was the ball projecting the future or simply the things he'd seen?

"Look," Svigula said. "It's you."

The ball misted over and he could have sworn he saw Vogelweide's portrait of Duke Paul with his arm around him. The painting seemed to be in a museum. The museum was on fire.

Explosions disturbed the ball, and troops marched beneath its smoky surface. Svigula twisted her wraith of hair. Now men in leather jackets in the mouths of giant steel birds flew over Stuttgart while the city exploded below. He did not tell Svigula he had seen pictures like this on the stones high above the banks of the Kaw River. He had dreamed of it, too, while sleeping under the bed of leaves.

"Does it always do this?" he asked.

"When you are around, it does," she said. "Do you know what it means?"

"No."

"Be careful," she said. "You are like us, your people like ours." She reached behind herself and produced a small wooden box from under her blanket. "This might help you."

She took his hand and slid a topaz ring over his finger.

"What will it do?"

"It will look pretty on your finger! Did you expect a magic ring?" She snorted a laugh, blew wet breath on his hand, and held his ringed finger up, glancing coolly inside the stone the way a thief looks into a drawing room he's considering breaking into. Then she smiled. "One day you will need to sell it," she said and stood up. "But don't. It must never be sold. It must only be given away freely. Think of us then."

He felt so moved by her gift that he opened his possibles bag, hoping he could find something to give her in return.

"You're looking for something for me, aren't you?" Svigula said, eyes sparkling. "But I've already made my selection." From deep in the folds of her skirt she produced the old twig whistle his mother had left him. She stroked its rude edges and blew on it.

As he left the wagon it pleased him to think of his mother's spirit as a tourist exploring the German wilderness. Through her curtain Svigula called out, "Baptiste. You will get lost only when you leave the forest."

The next morning, he embraced his friends and tossed a crust of bread, his breakfast, to Rinko. Baptiste waved goodbye and started down a wooded path.

It would be a pleasure to hunt for a while on his own on the way back to the castle. As the caravan disappeared behind him, Red Squirrel raced up and jumped into his pocket.

Since he'd been gone for nearly a year and a half, no one recognized him as he approached the *Altes Schloss*. He washed himself in the stables, careful not to look in Sorcerie's stall. Then he went up to the laboratory and found Vogelweide.

"Well, well, well," Vogelweide said. "Late for dinner again." He stood up. "We looked for you until the snow came. Then surely you were dead. We mourned you and had a drink in your honor."

"Several, I'll venture," Baptiste said.

Vogelweide shrugged.

"Where is she buried?"

Vogelweide pointed to the distant white rock that had been their favorite. "In the *wiese*. Beside her husband. He didn't last a month after she died. He felt he'd let his old friend—as well as the three of you—down." He paused. "He said to give you this," he said, handing him Ekaterina's violin. Then he brightened. "You're just in time for a wedding." He waved his hand in front of his nose and sniffed knowingly: "You'd better clean up."

On the way out the door, Baptiste passed a looking glass and barely recognized himself. He'd gotten older, and more sturdy. His time outdoors had roughened his skin. Inside Baptiste's old room above the stables, Red Squirrel rushed under the bed and looked up at him with his shiny black eyes.

Vogelweide led Baptiste to Duke Paul's library after dinner. Significantly, they offered him nothing to drink. So he asked. Vogelweide prodded Baptiste with questions about his winters, but Duke Paul seemed barely in the room.

"Did you know," the duke said finally, "that I'm to be married?"

"Yes, sir."

"You'll attend dressed in the uniform of our royal guard."

"By your command, sir."

The next morning Baptiste conducted stables as usual. Sorcerie had been traded to a Russian prince early in his absence. He smiled at the thought of how much he was learning about the term "Indian giver" from Duke Paul. He felt Ekaterina's absence keenly everywhere he went in the castle. Still, it was impossible to ride horses joylessly. He rode Ekaterina's enormous bay and felt a good deal closer to her when he climbed the hill and cantered in the rosy morning hours around the great white rock.

April, 1827

Duke Paul was scheduled to marry Princess Sophie in the presence of 2,804 guests, royalty who were traveling to the ceremony from as far away as Russia and India. Vogelweide archly showed Baptiste a letter to Duke Paul from General William Clark, who sent his regrets. He watched Baptiste unfold it and study the wax that had sealed it and hidden its contents as it crossed the ocean.

Baptiste walked to a window and sat down on one of Duke Paul's embroidered cushions. The letter was very formal. Nowhere did it make mention of him. Then it struck him. How often over the years had Duke Paul corresponded with General Clark? Had he been enquired after?

He asked Vogelweide about it, but the expression on the painter's face did not encourage him to peel this persimmon. He had learned something from his friends in the woods: not to beg for bad luck.

A week passed. Duke Paul refrained from visiting Baptiste's chamber until the night before he was to be married to Princess Sophie. Then, late at night, the duke appeared at his door.

"My responsibilities are forcing me to do what I would not do," the duke said.

Baptiste marveled at how this sentiment was within a few words of the way he'd consoled himself after Duke Paul had violated him on the *Smyrna*.

"My heart yearns for the wilderness, and the places we might travel together, *fauve*."

Did Duke Paul actually expect him to feel sorry for him? At least in this funk and state of inebriation the predator could no longer stalk him. Awake, they sat across from each other like two chess pieces on a board left overnight. And drank. Two bottles, then four. At six a.m. Vogelweide discreetly entered the room and began to lead the pale duke away. But Baptiste stopped the pair.

"A moment, your highness. I'd like some money, please," he said simply, without rancor. All night he'd prepared for this, reflecting, *it's just commerce. Mother was probably too naïve to ask for money.* Maybe Clark would have valued her more if she'd dared ask for it. Only the weak wait for a gift to be tossed like a crust of bread. Why, he wondered, had it taken him so long to learn that in civilization, unlike in matters of the heart, it seemed that cash had to be part of the equation for any real understanding? To the rich and powerful, it was in the demanding that you set your own price—and therefore your value. "Ninety guilders."

"But nothing could possibly have happened," Vogelweide scoffed.

Duke Paul's eyes opened wide. "You're no fun," he said to the *Indianer*, then turned to Vogelweide. "Pay him."

"Viper. You really have become a Gypsy," Vogelweide said.

"You heard the duke," Baptiste said. "I'll thank you for my wages."

Baptiste watched the wedding from the upper reaches of the balcony of a cathedral so immense that little clouds formed near the sprawling vaulted ceiling. Duke Paul walked with his royal retinue to the altar and stood beside Sophie.

Vogelweide appeared midway through the ceremony, lounged disrespectfully beside Baptiste, and sketched caricatures of the guests around them, as if the events below were nothing more than a play they were attending. As the celebrants began their vows, he peered over the rail and hissed, "An attractive couple, a paean to Lutheran piety. Don't they look just like brother and sister?"

With every phrase, every motion, and every antiphonal question and response of the ceremony, Baptiste ached for the life he might have had with Ekaterina.

Baptiste drifted for a time at Ludwigsburg, and he did indeed become Duke Paul's warden of the forest. Duke Paul spent day after day in his library, scribbling missives and accepting no visitors while the duchy awaited news of an heir, which seemed the whole point. Baptiste came in once a week and transcribed voluminous notes for the duke's journal.

The countryside breathed a collective sigh of relief when rumors of a pregnancy began to circulate. A great cheer went up when Sophie gave birth to little Duke Maximillian Friedrich Wilhelm IV. Happiest of all was Duke Paul, his mission fulfilled. He, Vogelweide, and Baptiste moved out of Ludwigsburg the next day.

"Well, *fauve*," Duke Paul said, "anything else you'd like to see here?"

They were approaching Stuttgart by coach. As they crested a hill the blue reflection of the Neckar rose into view. Vogelweide, who had been snoring in the seat across from them, woke up as if they'd hit a stone in the road. Baptiste dared say nothing but felt the hair rise on the back of his neck.

"No?" Duke Paul said. "Then let's return to your Manitou."

"What do they call the heir?" Baptiste asked Vogelweide just two weeks later as he handed him books, trunks, and instruments to carry to their coach to begin the expedition. Baptiste tried to push the image of Clark turning away as he left St. Louis out of his head.

"'They' don't call him anything. I believe Sophie calls him Maxi, but I've never heard Duke Paul refer to him at all, except in the abstract," Vogelweide said.

"Another beautiful family," Baptiste said, picking up a bag. Then he stopped. "My God, man, how can the duke just leave Maxi here?"

"The Duke feels his son will have to learn his own way out of prison," Vogelweide said, "just as he has."

"Has he?" Baptiste asked.

They set off for Paris the next morning during a thunderstorm, the first leg of their trip to New Orleans. The rain hit their roof so hard they nearly had to shout to hear each other.

"We miss the woods, don't we, *fauve?*" said Duke Paul, looking back toward the castle. "My son will have a kingdom to dote upon him. We will have the trees."

"You'll have to brush up on your English," Vogelweide said to Baptiste.

"And you your painting."

"You've survived Europe," Vogelweide laughed and slapped him on the back.

The rain drummed on the roof of the carriage. The boy who had crossed the Atlantic with Vogelweide was long dead. A man was returning in his place, with business to attend to. In fewer than thirty days, they would be in New Orleans. Slowly Baptiste reached across the carriage. Then he surprised Vogelweide by warmly shaking his hand.

16

"ICE"

—make signs for WATER, for COLD, and bring hands together, as in FREEZE OVER.

May, 1829

They set sail in late spring and hailed Hispaniola, the island where Columbus first landed, three weeks later. But instead of continuing directly to New Orleans, Duke Paul insisted they stop here for specimens of *Sauromatum venosum*—voudou lilies.

"A lethal dose of their extract is given to workers nearing the end of their usefulness," Duke Paul said. "Zombies, they rise exhilarated and work in the night fields until they die."

"Intriguing," Vogelweide said and pulled on his newly trimmed beard. "I'm willing to bet that a little drop will be quite stimulating. Talk about a last hurrah."

"Great. Then, when your time comes, the taste won't seem bitter on your lips," Baptiste said blandly. "Besides, your breath already stinks like a corpse."

Just then Vogelweide spied Red Squirrel peeking up at him from beneath the flap of Baptiste's possibles bag. "You haven't brought that rat across the ocean with you!" he said. "Just what the 'New World' needs, more vermin."

"Funny," Baptiste smiled, staring him down. "I was thinking just the same thing!"

As they entered the port of Santo Domingo, still Spanish in demesne though occupied by Haitian troops, two gannets large as hunting hounds flew across their bow. It had rained for the last three days of their crossing. Now their brig steamed as they approached the shore, a proper apparition for those watching them arrive.

What struck Baptiste most here, beyond the frightful vegetative rot of the place, was the heat. Sunlight dazzled the surface of the water and glittered on yellow stone buildings. How strange it was that ice, which had so numbed his toes in the Black Forest with the Gypsies, had so much value here. The ice in the rum Duke Paul, Vogelweide, and he enjoyed with their host, Don Santiago Verazon, had to be brought by ship all the way from New England and kept under armed guard.

Baptiste watched the ice arrive each morning through his bedroom window at the Alcázar de Colon, the Moorish palace that had once been home to Columbus's son, Don Diego.

"Another son with an axe to grind," Vogelweide jibed.

"Well, at least we had fathers," Baptiste said. "Exactly what graveyard did your mother choose your name from?"

"Your German has greatly improved," the painter said, "though your manners have not."

Sailors in striped shirts and red stocking caps raced against time to rumble the blue squares of ice down narrow gangplanks and into the ice house, a building fashioned out of blocks of coral and lined with sawdust. Among clouds of pink oleanders Baptiste could see clouds of vapor as the ice evanesced into the atmosphere.

This frozen gold meant the difference between tainted butter and spoiled meat in the tropics. The keeper of the ice was a tall West Indian who wore a bright red uniform with gold tassels and violet epaulets. He was proud of his position and strutted back and forth in front of his warehouse in possession of his bright key.

I've been on ice long enough, Baptiste thought, watching him. Which made it all the more frustrating that Duke Paul elected to stay and collect yet more botanical specimens in Santo Domingo for another six months.

The delay began to bother Vogelweide, too. Or perhaps it was the sleeplessness of Santo Domingo. Even snug in their beds in the palace, they were close enough to the jungle plantations to hear the laborers sing their *cantos de hacha*—axe songs. They sang them all night long, with only Duke Paul able to sleep, exhausted from long entries in his notebooks, and of course his rum.

"Why must they keep us awake like this?" Vogelweide asked of short, white-haired Don Santiago, who said the former slaves, still shackled to their fields whatever the regime, were singing to find a happy rhythm to work with. But Vogelweide wondered instead, were these axe songs really fantasies about killing their former captors?

What most disturbed Baptiste was the odd, buzzing sound of the *guira*. The field workers created this instrument out of hollowed gourds. It was then rubbed and scraped with a stick. Properly scraped, it made a nightmare sound.

"They are not insects," Vogelweide moaned. "Why do they want to sound like insects?"

"Because insects will suffer no lord and master," Baptiste said.

He watched Vogelweide's eyes flicker open.

"What's that about insects?" Duke Paul said.

They reached New Orleans on November 5. Baptiste could tell by the way Vogelweide draped himself over the cassapanca in the front hall of the Hotel St. Charles that they would be here a while, too.

New Orleans was a pleasant distraction for those with the nocturnal energy of zombies. While Duke Paul delayed further with voluminous expedition plans and visits with descendants of French counts and countesses, Baptiste haunted the lonely streets of the Vieux Carré at night, his heart still flinching with the otherworldly scratch of the *guira*.

There seemed to be an elastic sense of independence here. The streets teemed with Frenchmen, Spaniards, Germans, English, and Creoles, but most interestingly, *personnes de couleur libres*, Africans who spoke refined French and conducted themselves with sudden style.

On Gellatin Street behind the French Market, Baptiste fell in with groups of sailors as they haunted the night cafes along Smokey Row toward Bienville, Conti, and Dauphine streets that led to St. Louis Street and the florid pink whale oil lamps of the St. Louis Hotel.

One night he wandered so close to the hotel that he couldn't help but walk inside. Conscious that he'd been drinking, he spoke directly to no one but instead breezed past the clusters of gentlemen checking their ladies into rooms, crossed a black and cocoa Aubusson carpet in the lobby, and took refuge in a dark leather chair next to a fireplace.

On one side of the chair was a potted palm the size of a sycamore. On the other side a brass tree stood with swinging rods on which copies of newspapers from London and New York were hung. Beside the brass apparatus was a stack of the New Orleans *Picayune*, fragrant with fresh ink.

And there he saw it, three pages into the *Picayune*—below an article on a demi-octoroon suicide and opposite an item about Jim Beckwourth, the son of an English viscount and a black slave who had somehow managed to become a Crow sachem—a short announcement that President Andrew Jackson would be traveling from Washington to St. Louis to celebrate his sixty-third birthday with William Clark. The gala event would be held on March 15, 1830, at the home and museum of the great explorer.

Baptiste could hardly contain his excitement. If only they could leave New Orleans early enough, he might be reunited with his adopted father before the President's birthday; indeed, he might be at Clark's side for this historic reception.

"Surely you would enjoy seeing him as well," Baptiste said to Duke Paul.

Instead of answering when they might start the expedition, which Baptiste had promised to guide up the river as far as St. Louis as payment for his passage to America, Duke Paul ensconced himself even more deeply into their apartments at the hotel, lost in his journals.

Vogelweide passed by Baptiste's room one night and saw him packing. The painter slipped very close to him.

"Don't go yet, please. Duke Paul *ist erkranken*," he said in the parlor German all three used as intimates, though they casually switched to French in town. "He can't sleep. His refreshments have not agreed with him. He is incontinent. He is in no shape to travel. Please, you owe him this much."

Owe him? Are you rotty? Baptiste thought. *But if I hadn't been abducted by this feeble monster I'd never have learned the piano or violin. I'd never have seen Europe. I would never have met Ekaterina or Svigula. I never would have fathered and murdered my child . . .*

"Just give us a while," Vogelweide pressed. "You did promise to help us start out."

"Assuming we do start out."

"We will," Vogelweide said. "We just have to offer him a little assistance now, from administration to toilette."

Baptiste helped Duke Paul all he could by day, but at night, frustrated with the nobleman's delays, he began drifting and drinking out of boredom. With alcohol whispering into his ear, he spent a lot of time following the wisps and trails of music that insinuated its way through the shadowy streets behind the French Quarter.

The music led him to Congo Square, near Orleans and Rampart

streets. It was where the Creoles, who were given Sundays off, were allowed to congregate by day or night, speak as they liked, and even sing the songs they only half remembered from their ancestors' childhoods in Africa. Passersby barely frowned when their music descended into undulating voudou rhythms. Vogelweide, had he ventured near enough to hear, would doubtless have been annoyed to learn he'd been followed by the scratching sound of the *guira*.

In Congo Square, Baptiste found the people very friendly, and he returned their kindness after a few nights by playing Ekaterina's violin for a few of them, most memorably Swinbot, a round young man about his age with great dark cracks on his skin from working in the sugar fields of Port au Prince.

A Haitian émigré, Swinbot had ears for all Baptiste's stories and regaled him with his own, always in French and sparkling with black magic. They took to each other immediately and became fast friends.

Besides, as drunkards, they shared a common passion. But one couldn't be halfway through his third bottle of Shambro with Swinbot before the *loa*, or spirit, of some object would make the poor man's brain start to dance.

One afternoon, they had to duck into a doorway because in the queer New Orleans sky a thunderstorm appeared and began to conduct its affairs in the brightest sunshine. Swinbot laughed and pointed.

"Oh, it is the devil beating his wife," Swinbot said.

The next night, they were drinking on a set of elegant stairs so well into the evening, and so discreetly, that no one should even have heard them, much less been bothered, when the door cracked like the flash of a knife and a maid in a nightdress stood aiming a broom directly at Swinbot.

"Get along," she said.

Swinbot, who smiled with equanimity when passersby spat near him to show their disdain, now jumped like a puma and angrily knocked the broom out of her hands before running away.

"What were you afraid of?" Baptiste asked him a few blocks down the street.

"Pointy end or bristly, a broom sweeps your life away," Swinbot said.

With the tone of a professor, he was at pains to describe to Baptiste the minute diminutions of color accorded to "Negro claret." People of mixed race were called mulattoes, quadroons, octoroons, and even demi-octoroons, carrying one-sixteenth black blood.

"You never lose your blackness, no matter how many times they try to cut it," Swinbot said. "Cut red blood just once," he teased Baptiste the next night in Congo Square, "and it very quickly thins to nothing."

Hearing singing and laughing, Baptiste turned to the right. A final green ray of the sun illuminated the deliciously curved shoulders of a lovely young girl passing through the square, then faded.

"What are you called if you are seven parts Nereid?" Baptiste asked about the girl, whom he took to be a prostitute. Her skin was translucent, and her hair the color of a sunrise that made sailors take warning. Compared with the other whores who bubbled around her, she had ethereal grace. These girls had just entered the square from Rampart Street, under the low-slung branch of what looked to be, impossibly, a eucalyptus tree bearded so thickly with moss it had to be parted like a curtain upon entry, as though they were in the world's largest drawing room. Swinbot didn't need to ask Baptiste which girl he'd meant.

"Well, let's find out!" he cried. "Rowena?"

The girl grinned, abandoned her grace, and tripped over to Swinbot, who addressed her with obvious appreciation and familiarity as her friends shrugged and continued on their way, one of them sticking out a pointed tongue.

When Rowena drew directly in front of them, Baptiste realized what had made her look so otherworldly was partly the slight sapphire tinge she'd added to the paint on her face. From habit he stood up in her presence, and this tickled Swinbot, who pointedly did not. Instead, he kept his seat on his rock and looked up at her as she steadily met his gaze.

"Do you have any shades in you, girl, to make you proud?" Swinbot said. "You're so wondrous pale, but you do have those lips."

Rowena looked at him and did not answer.

"And in this light, those eyes aren't blue," Swinbot said.

She smiled and brushed his hand off her dress without anger. The maestro would have applauded her gift for silence.

"Oh," Swinbot laughed. "Let me introduce you to my quiet friend. But he's not quiet when he plays that violin." He pointed to the case which hung from the bottom of Baptiste's left hand. "He sounds like a bird," Swinbot said. "He makes the music fly."

"Such a lying bastard!" Baptiste laughed. "He's never sat still long enough to hear me play."

"Would you let me hear you?" she asked.

Now Swinbot stood up. He threw Baptiste a giant wink. "He will, after you show him some of the city. He's only just arrived."

"That's not necessary," Baptiste said.

"Oh," she said. "So you won't accept pay? Take it from me, that's a bad policy."

"Ever the coquette," Swinbot said. "But my friend, he doesn't just play the violin, he makes it sigh and moan."

"Who's playing the coquette now, with all the smutty talk?"

"At least I'll show you how to make it scream in pain," Baptiste laughed, "for I am out of practice."

He put the bow to his cheek and played a song that Rinko the bear used to dance to, but more slowly and sadly, with odd little stops and a lilting, Gypsy air. Svigula always called it the tree song and would ask for it by saying, "Trees!" It was a pleasure to go running into the trees with this girl, who clapped sweetly with her delicate hands when he finished.

"Where are you staying?" she asked, spoiling the moment.

Baptiste told her. He thought he saw her eyelids flicker.

"Well," she said, seeming to calculate something. "Just a few hours from now, you might walk me home . . . after I finish work." She turned and unselfconsciously disappeared through the lace curtain of moss, the night still young.

Baptiste dozed fitfully on a stone bench on the square before giving up at nearly three a.m. and drinking the rest of his bottle of rum. Then he saw Rowena's face, an apparition in a crimson dress that matched the stain on her lips that made her skin more pale.

"Come with me," she said. She seemed in a hurry. She and Baptiste walked until it started to rain. By now it was so late he wanted to sleep, but there was still farther to go. The rain fell like bullets, so he put his coat over her shoulders and felt a chill upon remembering it was the same motion he'd used in lending his coat so often to Ekaterina.

He followed the little slaps of her feet in the puddles until she ran up a flight of stairs. He heard the sounds of a piano throbbing through the walls of the narrow building. *Now what is this?* Baptiste walked up the stairs beneath an entablature proclaiming his arrival at Mahogany Hall.

To his delight, Rowena crossed the room and swapped seats with the pianist, a dusky man who walked blinkingly toward the bar. Hanging over the rails of a gallery overhead, several whores in white pinafores looked down. From the other side of the room a whole new sound came from the piano, and to Baptiste's amusement the mysterious Rowena had set it in motion.

Immediately he was at her side. The sound was so horribly regular it astonished him until he saw her feet pumping and a big wooden planchette with pegs on it turning and activating the keys. Her back shook from laughter, and he laughed, too, because it was all so monstrous.

"Una Cosa Rara," he laughed. "I know it!"

In Baptiste's coat pocket, Red Squirrel must have known it, too, because all of a sudden he began to chatter and tried to put his head up to see. Baptiste quietly buttoned the pocket, drastically reducing his pet's views of Mahogany Hall.

"Does it play just one song?" he asked.

"It knows twelve songs," Rowena said as the barrel churned its way through the *valse* like a steamboat chugging down the Mississippi in a muffling snowstorm, inexorably smashing through rocks and twigs on the way to its destination.

"Anything in its way had better get out of the way!" Baptiste laughed, and Rowena, glowing and laughing, pumped all the harder as a small crowd grew around them. Baptiste had heard of towering organs like this in France, but never anything so compact as this Harmonitronic, as it was styled in bright gold leaf, the filigree beneath it suggesting that it had originally been commissioned for, and had somehow been misplaced by, His Royal Highness The Prince of Wales. *What is it about gold and pianos?* A shadowy vision of that first piano in St. Louis crouching in the corner of Clark's salon edged into Baptiste's thoughts as he took in the upper half of Mahogany Hall's more garish update, in solid rosewood, as it reached halfway up to the gallery on the second floor.

"Excuse me, sir?"

A stern Spanish madame confronted Baptiste with an empty tray, so he ordered a phlegm cutter, rum and whiskey, just the thing to warm him up from the rain so he could linger in Rowena's presence and hear the end of the *valse*. Sliding beside Rowena on the bench, he watched the wooden mechanism whirl like a Spinning Jenny. His heart almost stopped when the armature disengaged, banged out of gear, and twickered to a halt.

"That was beautiful. What are the other eleven songs?" Baptiste asked as the madame approached him again. He realized that like the music, he had run out of time.

"Come back tomorrow night," Rowena said, "and I'll play you another."

17

"PERHAPS/OF TWO HEARTS"

—hold right hand over heart, pointing to left, fingers separated; then by forearm movement roll the hand back and forth. When expressing many conflicting emotions or doubts, vibrate or roll the extended hand to represent deep consideration.

December, 1829

Baptiste came back the next night after midnight, and the night after that. On the fourth night Rowena rose from the bench and bewitched him by enlivening the song with a lovely dance, her silk slippers barely touching the floor.

Mechanical as the piano itself, the madame appeared. "His glass is empty," she said, stopping Rowena in mid-twirl. "He must buy you both another drink."

He and Rowena began to meet in the afternoons, too, and walked the docks to see the ships disgorging bolts of silk and piculs of peppercorns from the China Sea. Swinbot, in charge of one of the crews, waved and said, "Look at you, a *swanga buckra* now with your beautiful woman."

Rowena skipped ahead of them to join a group of urchins playing with sticks and a hoop in the street.

The two men watched with fascination as the littlest ones pushed each other aside to be closest to her, yearning for her touch on the tops of their heads. "All God's creatures are seduced by that little witch," Swinbot said.

It seemed that every living thing was drawn to Rowena. It wasn't her beauty, however otherworldly; it was her joie de vivre that colored her every movement. She could appear ever excited and never jaded, one second the coquette and another the guileless child.

"Now let me see your squirrel," Swinbot said.

"He's sleeping," Baptiste said. "Don't you ever sleep?" But he obligingly reached to unflap his pocket.

"Don't let him out all the way," Swinbot said. "I just want to give him this. Come on, *jumbla, jumbla.*"

Swinbot reached into his red lacquer snuff box and with a quick motion slipped a sliver of acorn to Red Squirrel.

"What poison are you giving him?" Baptiste asked.

Swinbot took the lid off: frog bones, spoonfuls of ashes, crackly chicken skin, a hank of horse hair from an animal he had befriended in Cuba.

"What are those?" Baptiste pointed.

"Jaguar teeth."

"Are you going to cast a spell?"

Rowena returned and shook her hair, the sun sparkling on its ruby glints.

Swinbot smiled.

Two weeks into his friendship with Rowena, Baptiste showed up at Mahogany Hall already deep in his cups. He'd heard all twelve of the songs and demanded to hear a thirteenth.

"It takes three men to change the wooden rollers. They're kept in the barn," Rowena said.

"Then I'll help," Baptiste said and slipped unnoticeably as he reached over to rest his hand against the piano. It was just a gesture; he thought nothing of it. But now the madame approached Rowena very quickly and whispered something into her ear.

"It's time for you to go," Rowena said.

Only now did the other girls look up from their pillows at the edge of the long Oriental carpet, because Baptiste was about to be thrown out of Mahogany Hall.

"I'm sorry," he said and bowed, but perhaps a bit too grandly. His head pounded softly; when had that started? Then he lost his footing and the floor rushed up. He raised his eyes to find Rowena standing over him, well into a flap with the madame. He knew he was drunk now and tried not to make things worse by attempting to speak. But he was full of gratitude. It astonished him that anyone seemed to care what happened to him.

"Get him out," he heard the madame snap while more girls crowded around. "*Afueras de aqui.*"

"I will, he will," Rowena answered her. "Just as soon as he can stand up."

"You are supposed to entertain young men with *money*," she said. "This isn't a cheap hotel. You other girls, help him out the door."

"Wait a minute." Baptiste reached for his wallet, and upon seeing it, the madame warmed him with a smile. He looked at Rowena and fished for one of the bank notes Duke Paul had given him to help underwrite the expedition. "I can pay."

Rowena took him into her room and reached over to draw the curtains. She crossed in front of the bed and with a businesslike little skip stepped out of her dress. She seemed even more vulnerable in her chemise, which was trimmed with lace at her knees. Above it, in faded cotton, she wore a bustier with a red sash and mother of pearl buttons down the front.

She took one of Duke Paul's bank notes without comment, stopped, and said, "Sleep first. You look tired. Just for a while."

She helped him take off his boots, and then his socks. She pulled a blanket over both of them, as if they were children. Then she kissed him. He felt as though they were in a boat, paddling slowly out of the room and into a dark place on the ceiling. Outside, he could hear the soft jounce of coaches passing by, a clatter of horses. He put his arm around Rowena and fell asleep.

It was nearly morning when he stirred again. Rowena was not in bed, nor in the room. But then he saw her look at him through the doorway, and moments later she slipped in beside him, her warmth familiar and sweet as the Kaw River in July. She kissed him gently on the neck and over both his eyes. Her smell dominated the alcoholic waft he'd brought in the night before and made everything lavender and verbena.

When he woke up again, sunlight was everywhere and his beautiful creature was standing unashamedly naked in the window, the blinds thrust open, waving at a man outside, reminding him unpleasantly of the girls he'd seen among the quarters of the red lanterns in Germany.

"Can't he see you?" Baptiste asked. "Must you be so bold?"

"I've known him since I was a child."

With a wet cloth she briskly washed under her arms and between her legs before pulling on her bloomers, a white lace pinafore, and a smock trimmed in jet beads and fragile lace. She wrapped an embroidered Spanish shawl over her shoulders.

"I'm hungry," she said. Her feet were still bare. He marveled at her painted toes. "Wait here," she said and disappeared down the hallway.

Baptiste wracked his brain to conjure up details of the night before.

Had they made love? If they did, he did not know it. Yet there was a warm feeling in his chest a little unlike anything he'd felt before. He was going down the long black slide from drink, and here was this girl to save him.

She returned with a hunk of bread and cheese wrapped in a napkin, as well as hardened crumbs from cakes and desserts abandoned by gentlemen and their "ladies" the night before: rum cakes, the brown ice and sticky residue of a half-uneaten crème brûlée, stiff cookies touched and rejected, bonbons that the cats had softly walked through on the way to more animate treasures. Another napkin revealed still more "lagniappes," as Rowena called them, whore treats, hardened bits of food with sorry stories to tell: a desultory chunk of sweetbread, a praline shard. She laughed and clapped her hands as Red Squirrel danced beneath a broken crust of wild blackberry pie Baptiste held just beyond his reach.

"Beg!" she cried.

Baptiste brought out his pocket tickler and offered her some rum to go with it. She took a healthy draught, showing her lovely neck.

Then the sun rose higher through the curtains and warmed the bed on which they sat, eating sour desserts from the night before like children at play. Baptiste had rarely felt so completely at peace. Rowena bent her head over and kissed him, and he took his first full breath since he'd come back to America. Then he kissed her back.

Each lover has a different essence, he reflected. In this case he tasted filo, tar, and warm honey.

"Why are you so nice to me?" he asked her.

"I liked you the moment I saw you." She shrugged and handed him his trousers. "I like . . . the cut of your jib."

She was no stranger to the waterfront.

"But I was drunk, three sheets to the wind. My jib, last night, had no 'cut' at all."

"All right, then," Rowena laughed. "I liked the cut of your bank note."

He rose, kissed her, and dressed. Then, looking into the liquid brown eyes of his friend who seemed somehow so familiar, he kissed her again.

For just one moment, he was not Baptiste, but simply a man holding the very slim waist of an exceptionally striking and gentle young woman in his arms. He had spent a morning so free of care, the result of which released such a rush of freedom, that his heart sailed. Maybe he did after all possess a jib that had been luffing and was now catching freshets of wind that would pull him forward. He didn't care about Duke Paul or Clark or St. Louis or Ekaterina when he was in this girl's arms.

"I have to go," she said finally, buttoning her blouse and straightening her skirt. "Oh, that's pretty!" she said, softly touching his ring.

Impulsively, Baptiste had the topaz ring off his finger and put it on hers before remembering Svigula's warning to never pawn it away. He half reached over to take it back, then smiled that superstition had such a grip on him. *How many taboos from how many civilizations must I embrace?* he thought. The gypsies seemed so far away . . . It was so loose on her ring finger that she quickly put it on her thumb.

"Could I see you tonight?" he said, realizing that even though he hadn't sold her the topaz, a transaction was being conducted.

She stepped close to him and kissed him. With an expert caress she sloughed his cheek.

"You may visit me . . . very late."

"I'll be here," he said. She walked him to the door. In the upper hallway the other girls were waking up in their eyelit-laced nightclothes, stretching, belching, cleaning dirty china with weary passivity, and doing other things invisible to their benefactors by night. Lovely putains bent over to hidden tasks, skirts hiked up and tied behind them as they washed the dark fir floors.

They walked downstairs, and he said goodbye. His friend, his savior, flashed her red hair and climbed the staircase, glancing back devilishly at him as she hit the top of the landing and stood beside a large golden mirror.

My god, she is beautiful. Baptiste now remembered the night before. She had made love to him, and skillfully. What combination of talent and artifice did she possess that enabled her to keep her air of freshness? Or was it just his wishful thinking? He was ashamed he felt so good, and he wondered if Ekaterina would think him disloyal if he embarked on an entirely new life. This girl might save him from his darker nature, his bitterness; all of a sudden his prospects spilled with new sunshine.

The madame now pushed him out the door. "Rowena?" he called behind her, blocking the door's swing with his arm. The madame, with the strength of a galley slave, clutched his arm and closed the door back on him. Then she cracked the door open. "Rowena—is that the name she's using this week?"

Instinctively he reached for his pocket tickler and felt the hot rush of rum renew the beating of his heart. To his right, he heard a splash of gray water poured from a bucket held out a window by another girl who brushed aside a curtain festooned with heavy gold tassels more appropriately draped over a casket.

A voice giggled from a window above, and he saw Rowena again, the object of his passion. She tossed him a scented handkerchief, and he caught it as it fell through the lazy New Orleans breeze. He inhaled the smell and closed his eyes. Then his eyes opened wide. He knew the truth before she said it. It was as though an icy hand clutched at his heart.

"I ought to have told you my real name," she called down. "Lizette."

That night he returned, stone sober. He waited impatiently at the front door, gave the madame a piece of eight, and strode past the other girls and up the stairs to the room of the one he'd known as Rowena. But another girl was in there. So he stood at the end of the hall and waited, unable not to hear the muffled grunts and sounds behind the doors.

Finally Lizette emerged from a room two doors more distant than he expected, her red hair lighting up the hallway. Still draped over her was a besotted customer grinning gratefully and tucking in his shirt. The man lumbered like Rinko the bear while Lizette dragged him toward the stairway and dextrously negotiated for further payment. Money passed into her hands, and she tucked it into her blouse. She caught sight of Baptiste and ran over to him. She stopped when he didn't smile.

"I must talk with you," Baptiste said.

"Not all night, I hope, dark sir!"

She turned to pull him into the room that was still full of her musk, and that of her clients, but he didn't move. He desperately did not want to alarm her, so he smiled. Now the sense of his melancholy, and the blackness of his mission, overtook her automatic joy.

"What's wrong?" she said, straightening her stockings. She seemed changed, capable of defending herself, and not surprised. He was not the first man in her life to utterly cool toward her in one day.

"Could we sit down over here?" he said gently and motioned to a black window cushion. They walked over, and he pushed the window all the way up so that he would not take in her scent. All the while he remained astounded at his stupidity. Upon first seeing her red hair, and her redder maidenhead, so silky—he'd thought of Raphael's paintings. All he could think of now was something much closer to home.

He couldn't bring himself to address his little sister, his mother's lost daughter, the child Toussaint had stolen in the night, by name. Instead he asked, "How long have you lived here?"

"I was born here," she said.

"No one was born here."

A faint sense of suspicion entered her eyes. "Why do you want to know? What's it to you?"

Baptiste turned to see Lizette's employer standing at the top of the stairs. The madame wore an inky dress with white lace that looked like spume on the shore of a great rustling silk ocean, but she had made no sound. She shrugged, turned, and walked down the stairs. Every girl had a story.

"Can't you remember anything?" he asked.

"I am a lost princess from a forgotten island kingdom," Lizette laughed. "My parents were the children of French plantationers, and too young to take care of me. Perhaps they tried to look for me when I was little but were lost at sea . . ."

"What do you really remember?"

She looked at him, and then she looked away.

"I remember a river, a long trip on a barge, and then an orphanage." She paused for a moment. "It wasn't really an orphanage, it was more of a farm. All of us had to get up early and work." She looked down at her topaz and stroked her manicured nails. "I ran away at twelve," she said, remembering men's hands. "A gentleman picked me up and introduced me to the finer things of life. He dropped me here in New Orleans. I guess I got too old for him. Then I met Francesca."

"How do you know your name is Lizette?"

"Lizette was what they called me on the barge."

Though she couldn't name it, Baptiste was sure the city before the river glimmering behind the curtain of her memory was St. Louis. He didn't mention Toussaint during his questions, which he gently put forth, because he believed she was safer never to know him, and no doubt he had disposed of her at the earliest opportunity. *She must never know me as well.* She tried to touch Baptiste as he talked with her, but he stopped her hand so suddenly she drew away from him and regarded him with care, like a wounded animal. As he stared into her eyes, he heard the sound of a waterfall.

"This is all I have," he said as he tucked a wad of notes into his mother's possibles bag. It was the rest of the funds Duke Paul had entrusted him with. *Now I am finally a thief in every sense of the word.*

Lizette picked out the money and tucked it into her bodice.

"This is dirty," she said, dropping Sacagawea's purse in the slop bucket.

Baptiste quickly retrieved it. In the end, he thought, Lizette considered him with complete accuracy as just another selfish man who had molested her the night before.

"I will never forget you," Baptiste said.

She shrugged.

"I will send you more when I can. Goodbye," he said and headed down the stairs.

Lizette bit her lower lip from habit, puffing it up. Two lovely blue veins stood out on her slender hands like forks of a river.

18

"ANGRY/MIND TWISTED"

—place closed right hand close to forehead, with back of thumb touching same; move hand slightly outward and by wrist action give small twisting motion.

Baptiste walked back out into the streets hung heavily with Spanish moss and returned to his hotel. In the lobby was Vogelweide, dressed in a blue and green ball gown, with two men at his side and Duke Paul sleeping restlessly in an adjoining chair. Vogelweide fluttered his fan at Baptiste as he stalked by. He climbed the stairs to the third floor, where his single room was, hearing the waterfall. Now there was nowhere he could go without hearing it.

He unlocked his door, entered, locked it, and sat on his bed. All of a sudden his breathing became shallow and he struggled to draw in air. It was the same feeling he'd had upon seeing Ekaterina's lifeless body holding onto his murdered son. He opened his door to stop the room from closing in on him.

In the middle of the night, he woke up, lit his candle, reached into his bag, and pulled out the newspaper page he'd folded over beside Vogelweide's drawing:

On the 15th of March, 1830, a reception. In St. Louis: from Gov. William Clark, Missouri, renowned explorer, cartographer, and Superintendent of Indian Affairs, for President Andrew Jackson on his 63rd birthday.

The next morning, while assisting Duke Paul, Baptiste learned with dark exultation that their expedition would indeed begin on Saturday, and that he was in charge of the working party as chief guide. They would take a steamboat only to Baton Rouge and then travel by river raft the rest of the way to St. Louis. He'd long anticipated this and had made arrangements to meet his men later that day at the blacksmith's on the Rue Chartres that doubled in the evening as a saloon.

"We'll have an early start tomorrow," Baptiste told Duke Paul.

Vogelweide, a man again, looked up from his sketch book as if someone new had just entered the room.

Thursday found Baptiste occupying himself with the packing of provisions and hiring of the last of their crew. Vogelweide merely raised his eyebrows and disappeared after Baptiste told him the supplies would cost more than he'd anticipated.

Returning just before dusk, he approached Baptiste and handed him a silver card case. Upon opening it, Baptiste saw the extra funds he'd requested folded around a small stack of gentlemen's cards bearing the name *Graf Raymonde de Lucasse, Herzog auf Madagaskar*, the Duke of Madagascar. In the Levant, Vogelweide had first conferred this "title" upon Baptiste when sneaking him into the royal apartments above the English consul's at Gibraltar.

"A little money, a little identity," the painter said. "These should prove useful to you. Colonials think they're the same, anyway."

"A gift and a slap," Baptiste smiled. "Thank you and leave me alone."

"You're welcome," Vogelweide said in English, baring his teeth.

After dinner, Baptiste climbed the carpeted stairs to his room. With no more tasks to preoccupy him, he dreamed only of sleeping now.

With the door swung full open into the empty hallway to assure the clearest breathing air, he snuffed his candle, climbed into bed, and fell asleep with the newspaper page draped over his chest. He dreamed with a different anticipation about the interview he would have with William Clark. It was no surprise to him that Toussaint was such a blackguard. He'd been born that way. But the great William Clark was not his father but just another *Taipo* whose capacity for careless evil was so boundless it seemed as though it were the one mountain Baptiste could never climb.

Yet climb it he would.

In Clark's pallid kindness, in his stodgy ignorance, was more negligent cruelty than Baptiste had ever imagined in a gentleman. But seeing Lizette, and consummating his savagery with her, darkened his thoughts of Clark to pitch. He was afraid of what he would do to Clark when he saw him. But now life's lazy stream had forced Baptiste's purpose into rapids. He rushed to him. He was rushing to his tormentor over a deadly gush of water.

They were over half way to St. Louis when they saw the phantom, standing like a young deer behind a screen of trees. Upon Baptiste's catching sight of him he made a great show of disappearing, but Baptiste continued to feel his presence as he trailed them for several days, watching them as they progressed along the river.

Duke Paul and Vogelweide had not the slightest knowledge that a young brave had become a shadowy member of their party. When they stopped, he froze behind a rock. When they slept, he shook his way under a pile of leaves not a dozen yards away. It was his choice to

approach their fire one night and consider them at close range, with re-
flections of the campfire dancing on his deerskin smock. Red Squirrel
raised his head and twitched his tail. Baptiste watched Duke Paul lock
eyes with the youth.

"Baptiste," Vogelweide said. "Look. He might as well be you—fifteen
winters ago."

"Come here," Baptiste called to "himself" in Mandan, but the boy did
not respond. Baptiste had wondered for days whether the boy following them was Chuckalissa or Choctaw, thinking back to the detailed
drawings in Clark's Museum of Human Beings. For a moment the
youth looked as if he were going to say something. Instead, he backed
away.

"Ignore him," Baptiste said to his companions, "and watch what
happens."

Not a leaf crashed, nor did a branch crack, as the brave circled the
fire and stood directly before them. Baptiste studied his face. They'd
traveled quickly through Vicksburg and Helena without incident,
but who knew? This curious boy might have started tracking them as
far back as Natchez, or at least near Memphis, when they'd stopped a
week at Reelfoot Lake. Baptiste had certainly felt the growing presence trailing them, hiding. Now that they were above St. Genevieve,
Missouri, the young brave had become more daring.

By the time their caravan got into their pirogues to continue upriver, with their diminutive coach behind them on a somewhat larger
barge, the brave was walking beside their boats in plain view and after
so many miles of silence brashly calling out to them from the grassy
riverbank.

They welcomed him aboard, and through sign language and a few
awkward syllables Baptiste determined only that his spirit animal was
Muskrat, his name was Nalowepa-wa, and he would catch many fish
for them to make their travels easy.

To demonstrate, the boy dove off the pirogue, passed below their bow, and disappeared. Three minutes later his brown head burst out of the river in a dull green wave. Gasping and smiling, he flipped a wet river salmon right on Duke Paul's lap.

"So he's courting us," Vogelweide said. "Like a house cat presenting a mouse."

"Rather more like the mouse hunting the cat," Baptiste said.

As they continued upstream, Vogelweide sketched Baptiste and Nalowepa-wa attempting to converse. When Baptiste looked in the artist's book he was only slightly surprised that Vogelweide had re-drawn the back of his shoulder into a boulder, and his head into an overhanging branch on the river that came perilously close to marring Nalowepa-wa's unwrinkled face, completed with loving detail.

A few days later, after a hunt, Baptiste decided to check in on Vogelweide's larger execution of the same portrait, done in oil. Circling the easel, Baptiste saw dark, lush leaves in the foreground of the paint-ing below crepuscular clouds shot through with divine sunlight. Apart from Nalowepa-wa's image, the background of the scene made him feel as if they were in the *Aeneid*. Vogelweide was unable to see anything himself for the first time but instead had brought a limited number of remembered landscapes with him which he could superimpose over any scene.

"This is a most beautiful rendering," Baptiste said, "of Carthage. Or is it Sicily, after Aeneas has discovered Dido?"

"Ha!" said the painter, looking intently into the work. "Where ex-actly is it Sicily?"

"Where it is not Amalfi," Baptiste smiled. "Don't misunderstand me. I think it is wonderful. A painting should contain what we can't see."

"Athens in the wilderness," Vogelweide laughed. "My own genius continues to astonish me."

Nalowepa-wa was full of questions, and so deferential to Baptiste for his craggy ways of the world that Baptiste increased his drinking so he would not exactly retain a clear image of him. But like Jesus, this boy was his savior, his stand-in. As the nights passed, Baptiste argued with himself about whether he should warn Nalowepa-wa about the pitfalls. But Baptiste's concern for the prospect of Nalowepa-wa's further adventures evaporated when the young brave surprised him with Red Squirrel's pelt after the boy had caught and eaten the pet. Nalowepa-wa now took care to sleep on the other side of the campfire from Baptiste, a good thirty yards off.

That night Baptiste vowed to stop the drinking that had so clouded his judgment. Vogelweide, sensing something had changed, was strangely solicitous. "Try some of my nog," he said just two days before reaching St. Louis.

"No, I've had enough," Baptiste said and looked away.

"Are you sure you don't want some?"

When Baptiste didn't answer but instead removed the scrap of the New Orleans *Picayune* from his pocket and started reading it again, the painter said, "I don't know why you trouble yourself about it. Just a bunch of poorly dressed bumpkins trying to impress a hawk-nosed ruffian with bad drink and even worse food."

"That may not be the only show," Baptiste said.

After they took on provisions below St. Louis, Duke Paul and Vogelweide decided to continue upriver toward the Manitou Cliffs without further delay, passing up the chance to regale Clark and the President with tales of their *wanderjahren*. They could certainly visit Clark, and Baptiste, at a later date, they argued, which tickled Baptiste: Better than anything, they had learned how to navigate around trouble.

Vogelweide and Duke Paul were so preoccupied with Nalowepa-wa they took no notice as the party swept by Clark's white house.

But Baptiste's heart beat faster upon seeing the little shack disappear behind them in the reeds as they floated toward the bend nine miles upriver where they'd agreed Baptiste would leave the party and begin his own journey.

In less than forty-eight hours, I will present myself in front of the great explorer and cartographer William Clark with news of his adopted son and his long-lost daughter, Lizette.

With the Missouri River visible in the distance, Baptiste said good-bye to his hosts. He gave the seven guides under his direction final instructions and good wishes, and handed Duke Paul a map pointing to the paintings of the Manitou, not at all concerned that the nobleman would ever take the trouble to climb to any of his favorite haunts.

A soft rain began to fall, and though he hardly expected it a terrible loneliness swept over him as he stood outside the carriage with his violin and bag.

"Adieu then," Duke Paul said, his coach loaded with all the heavy baggage and his new boy, wet as a new butterfly.

"Thank you, your highness, for all you have taught me," Baptiste said, bowed, and waved his men forward. Then he called Nalowepa-wa aside.

LEAVE NOW OR I'LL SLIT YOUR THROAT MYSELF, Baptiste said.

The boy opened his eyes wide with fright, then with suspicion.

THE ONE WHO MAKES PICTURES SAYS YOU'RE ENVIOUS, Nalowepa-wa signed.

I MEAN IT. Baptiste showed him his knife.

Not taking his eyes off the glinting steel, Nalowepa-wa backed into the brush and disappeared.

Vogelweide leaned out from the carriage. "What's wrong? Where's he going?"

"He says he'll catch up with you past the bend in the river." Baptiste waited while the two Germans conferred in whispers.

"Well, you can't say we didn't give you the education we promised," Vogelweide said finally. He winked. "Good luck on your new voyage. Hey, it's been nearly a week, hasn't it, since you took a drop."

The carriage pulled forward and stopped again. Vogelweide emerged and tossed Baptiste a package. "I meant to give you these, as a last souvenir!" he called out. "Appropriate for any occasion."

Baptiste took the gift, shook Vogelweide's hand, and waved as the carriage pulled away. He walked to a rock beneath an evergreen and watched his traveling companions climb over a dusty rise and disappear.

Then he started off for St. Louis, defiantly barefoot in an attempt to return to his true self, though the pads of his feet were softer after six years in Europe and tiny stones announced a sharper presence on the trail. Two hours later it was nighttime, so he decided to make camp in favor of a fresh start in the morning. After lighting his fire and feasting on a small brook trout, he untied the string around the package Vogelweide had given to him, waxed to make it resist the rain. Inside was a pair of *clompen*, wooden shoes, rudely carved and identical to those worn by the peasants of Württemberg. Inside one of the toe boxes was a tiny flask of whiskey.

19

"HUNT"

—make sign for WOLF, then bring hand near eye and move it around.

March, 1830

Baptiste rose the next morning and followed the Mississippi back to St. Louis, tracking his own past. But he was not alone. For miles along the riverbank he passed the scent posts of coyotes, famous "tourists" themselves for the scats they loved to leave on lofty rocks and prominences, anything made of stone. He felt their spirits looking over the water.

Have you come all this way just to annihilate The Great Explorer? Baptiste thought. *Only a fool follows a set of tracks simply to come face to face with the animal who made them. A single destiny blinds you to all else in the forest and makes you prey yourself.* How dangerous it was to traverse the very glens and dales that were so dear to him in his boyhood with such a heart full of hate. As a boy, he'd been taught never to be so rash. He learned never to follow tracks simply to land his quarry, but rather to tune his sense of intimacy with his quarry's thoughts. What did he really know about Clark? Next to nothing.

"Whose track is this?" his mother asked him once, instructing.

"The hare's."

"Who else?"

She led him another three miles, standing still more often than moving, disappearing behind trees and holding her slim fingers over her mouth to keep from giggling before he understood.

"Ours!"

Killing was a dance without music, where predator and prey were blood relatives of the same tale, their fates forever entwined. How close hate was to love. Perhaps, Baptiste thought with a growing sense of fascination, it would be enough to "tree" Clark. He had to prepare for a universe of outcomes.

Now Baptiste was so close to home he recognized individual trees with boughs he'd swung from as a boy, splashing out beyond the rocks. The river eddies murmured their recognition, too, whispering like an audience before a concert. He was as amazed by what had remained the same as by what had changed.

As the moon faded, the Mississippi became smoky and deep brown as the whiskey he was trying to forget about in his possibles bag, in the toe of the wooden shoe. Keeping the riverbank to his left, he made his way along the final half mile toward St. Louis, deftly avoiding gunk holes and scrambling up pine-floored eminences as he drew nearer.

I will approach you softly, Clark, at a time of my choice and on my terms. I will stand tall in your presence and exchange greetings with the elegance and restraint I've learned at court. I will ask my questions softly and listen intently to your answers. Then, I will either embrace you or take my revenge.

Baptiste was surprised to find he'd reached the compound before he was prepared to face it: the white frame house, the little vine-covered shack where his mother and he used to live, the Museum of Human Beings, tiny stitches of the split rail fence he'd dug himself and pushed into position so many years before.

Not even Clark's dogs, whose shaggy bodies he could detect curled up near the well, were awake yet. The only noise was the whirring of flies just above the lazy rush of the river, and the flash of the occasional trout rising to snap at them.

He stopped under a shady spot beneath the great old oak tree where he had once lain with Lottie, spread his blanket between two of its long, deep roots, and watched the Clark compound come to life.

*Roots thrive in dark*ness, he remembered his mother telling him. *Let your quarry come to you.*

Clearly, the President of the United States was here. Baptiste counted eleven coaches and carriages near the stable, all of them black and several carrying glittering escutcheons of state. Yes, the man the cartoonists had lampooned as "King Andrew I" had arrived—Baptiste chuckled at the notion of America declaring herself the world's shining refuge from royalty.

Then he caught his breath. A tall black woman emerged from Lottie's house and walked toward the well. *It has to be you, Lottie.* With a grin, he left his shady spot and slipped to the dusty floor of the compound. With her back to him, she reached the well, pulled on the rope, and filled her bucket with water.

He drew closer, within fifty feet. The old Lottie would have been alert to his entrance instantly. It was almost as if he were stealing up on a deaf person.

He recklessly approached the edge of the shadows and tossed an acorn beside her. Lottie didn't look up, but the dogs did. They ran to him, ears back, curling around his legs until Lottie raised her eyes, stiffened, and immediately went back to her work. He held his fingers to his mouth and rushed to her side.

"It is you, isn't it?" Baptiste said.

"I'm sorry, sir, I don't know what you mean." Lottie kept her eyes on the ground as the river began to reflect the first seconds of sunrise. Then she shrugged, picked up her bucket with her long arm, and started for the house. He clasped her shoulder to stop her.

"Please, it's me, Baptiste!"

Lottie turned around slowly, still looking down.

"You look wonderful," he lied.

"Can I get you something, sir?" she said.

"Lottie, Lottie, don't you know me?"

He stooped to study the lines around her mouth, the scales on her puffy nose. She avoided looking at him with the battlefield of her eyes. Her Grand Tour had surely been as far-reaching as his.

Tonelessly she said, "Shall I tell Master you're here?"

"No, please, I'll tell him myself. I just want to talk to you, Lottie."

"If you don't need anything, sir, I've got to get back to Master's work."

Baptiste began to feel a slight irritation at her mannered servility and then shame when he realized he was blaming her for her fate. She looked up briefly as if she could read his mind. Then she moved her hand to her eyes and brushed something away.

"Lottie, did you marry?"

She nodded her head very slowly. "I married a good man," she said. "I've had three children but buried two."

As if looking into Svigula's crystal ball, Baptiste saw the gentle mound covered with leaves where his son now lay in the Black Forest.

"How's Hepsibah?"

"Mother died two years after father." She pressed her lips together. "I always wondered if you'd heard."

Baptiste saw tears on Lottie's cheek.

"Well, if there's nothing else, sir."

He could think of nothing to say, so he looked into the branches of the oak tree. "Lottie—"

But she was already walking away. *How inadequate I am in her presence, stiff as William Clark ever was.* Baptiste had been home only five minutes and had already upset his old friend. The rest of the compound began stirring, but there was still time for one more of memory's errands.

He couldn't resist ducking into the shack he'd shared with his mother. It was still and dark, the floor damp from mist rising from the nearby river. He almost smelled his mother's scent and could have sworn she'd been there a moment before, calling to him. The lower room where his mother slept seemed only half its size, the ladder to his old loft so rotten he barely made it up for a look around.

He pulled himself up through the transom. Here as before were the individual beams of the rafters, the stultifying heat that had baked him during the summer. The hornets' nest he had once so feared in September was still here but empty and silent. Light streamed through the knothole he'd worked out of the plank over his bedroll so he could see the river.

He heard a rustle and for an instant thought of his mother tying tobacco leaves in bunches under the eaves. But it was a mother rat feeding her children. The vermin bore a remarkable resemblance to Princess Sophie as she glared at him, the intruder, with red, defensive eyes. It was her house now. How unkind it had been of him to think his old space should never have changed. He tossed a piece of hard tack to the Madonna and dropped down through the trap door.

Crossing over to the window, he wiped a dusty pane with his sleeve and peered out at the big white house that had seemed like such a castle once. Opening his possibles bag, he removed a pair of folded trousers, some white stock, and a velvet waistcoat from the court of

Württemberg and dressed in them, complete with a pair of high, narrow-heeled boots he'd bought in New Orleans.

On his way to the door, he stopped at a shard of cracked looking glass wedged in the wallboards, stared into it, and saw no trace of his earlier self. He cleaned it off and began to comb his hair, adding pomade and finishing with a cravat trimmed in lace from Bamberg.

Hiding his bag under a bush near the oak tree, he skirted the Clark property and made his way out to the mud-luscious streets of St. Louis, which had changed, yet hadn't. The Roman Catholic church looked mean and crude after the basilicas of Europe. Out of a perverse sense of nostalgia he stopped in at the East India Store.

"Good morning, *madame*," he said to Mademoiselle Vachonne.

"Good morning, sir!"

He strode through the establishment as she, with her yellowed fingernails, pinched samples of tea for him to sniff, handing him the results in tiny newspaper cones. Mademoiselle Vachonne hurried to keep up with his steps, anxious to hear his opinions about the freshness of her wares.

"Would you like to try a cup of any of these, sir?"

"Yes, this one, please."

"Oh, the *oolong*! A very discerning choice, sir," she said.

Pleased with her mark, she took a blue and white Nanking cup and saucer from the shelf and steeped the oolong with hot water from a kettle she kept on her rustic stove.

"What brings you to St. Louis, sir?" she asked, her sharp, foxlike face alert for the possibility of new customers. "Have you come with the President's entourage?"

"No," he said. "I'm looking for someone."

"Are there many people in your party?"

"I'm traveling alone."

He took a sip of the tea, and then another. He'd left a far better supply in a silver-lined caddy placed lovingly near the bottom of his leather bag, beside his violin.

"Could you describe the person you're looking for? I must know everyone in St. Louis," she insisted.

"Then do you know who I am?" he grinned. Mademoiselle Vachonne drew closer and circled Baptiste. She stared up into his face.

"No, sir, I would have remembered such an elegant gentleman."

"Do you remember accusing me of stealing from your store?"

Perhaps she took him for an Italian or Mediterranean merchant. He rubbed his eyes with his thumb and forefinger, then put on his gloves. Her eyes clouded over but she took a step back, as if they were in a dance. "No, sir, you are quite mistaken." Then a cunning, nasty look came into her eyes. She winked. "That was an Indian boy."

Baptiste walked out the door into late afternoon St. Louis sunlight. Coaches now flashed back and forth on the muddy streets, splashing mud and tobacco spittle from uncouth citizens so universally that he was grateful for the wooden boardwalks. From a sleepy outpost of just three hundred frontiersmen, this town had sprung into a trading center on its way to embracing fifty thousand inhabitants.

St. Louis was now famous in Boston, New York, and even Paris for its beaver pelts. In this new hat district, workers "carroted" furs with mercury nitrate to raise follicles on the skins, the better to shave the dark wool that was fashioned into the tall, felt hats that looked like stove pipes. He choked on the rising fog of mercury as he passed through, trying not to inhale the deadly vapors.

And so many saloons. He began to feel his familiar raging thirst for a snifter of Monongahela but would not step into a bar for fear of being accosted by a woodsman or, far worse, touching spirits before his interview with Clark. He needed to be at his sharpest for his exchange with him.

Finally, darkness covered the city as he strolled a while longer, dodging carriages and skirting groups of new citizens as he made a gentle circle back to the compound. He stopped at a stream he knew behind the grove of trees that led to Lottie's oak tree and refreshed himself. Then he rolled back the bush that covered his bag and added further polish to his toilette, brushing down his coat and waistcoat until he knew he'd be the equal of any man there. Taking his time with the ritual, he buffed his nails with Red Squirrel's pelt. *So this is the likely end for an abductee.*

From the depths of his bag he produced, charged, and loaded his pistol, a prize from Istanbul and a souvenir from his travels in the Levant. In doing this he tried to breathe evenly and keep his level of excitement as low as possible. *Just minutes from now, I will see him.*

He felt the ghost of his younger self looking on while he slipped past the chicken coop and emerged behind the horses, with no one hearing him. After that his younger self disappeared and he strode into the courtyard as Count Lucasse, fourth duke of Madagascar. What better time to bring forth the first of the gentlemen's cards Vogelweide had given him in that silver case back in New Orleans?

Walking smoothly and smiling, Baptiste entered the back of the receiving line and looked up at the bright lights of the Clark foyer. A happy party of three women and a single old gentleman closed in behind him. There was no turning back.

He gained the stairs and was saluted by two young soldiers acting as sideboys. Nodding, he handed his card to a butler, who cleared his throat as he scrutinized the spidery words. Baptiste watched him work the German syllables over in his mouth. After an awkward moment, the servant simply waved him in.

Baptiste slid to the left and stuck his hand out to the first man in the receiving line for Clark and the President, an urgent, friendly fellow who introduced himself as former Deputy Secretary of War Walter Inness. He was small, square, and wore a tight blue uniform dating to his participation as a colonel in the Battle of New Orleans. Now he and his young wife, Louisa, were residents of St. Louis, with interest in one of the hatting firms.

"This is a great day for St. Louis," Inness boomed, then dropped to a whisper. "Too bad Lewis couldn't be here to share it with Clark tonight. Wouldn't it have made him proud to see what a fine young fellow his namesake has grown into."

Hearing that, Baptiste looked up the line and recognized young Meriwether Clark. The boy across the breakfast table was a man now. *I wonder if he will see any of the boy in me.*

But the line was moving too fast for further considerations, and just ten people away from him Baptiste detected William Clark, his red hair like a fading sunset. Clark was the second tallest man in the room. President Andrew Jackson, to his right, had nearly two inches on him. They stood like two tall pines on the blue Persian carpet. Baptiste's mouth dropped open when he realized that the very frail woman standing between them was Clark's wife. *How you have aged.*

Baptiste quickly dropped out of the line as a new waltz saved him from the next round of handshakes. He saw Inness's wife, Louisa, to his right, sigh wistfully to her husband while he shook his head no. Baptiste knew the look from his days at court and ducked into his opportunity as if it were a cave in the rain.

"*Madame*, I sense you . . . would like to dance?"

She spun back hopefully to Inness. Relegated to reception-line duty by a wink from Clark, the lesser luminary was unable to oblige her himself. With a grunt the old soldier nodded, bowed, and turned to greet the next guest in line while his lady fanned down a blush. Baptiste bowed in turn, took her by the waist, and led her across the room in a gentle whirl, three-quarter time, as they spun past the Clarks below the chandelier and into the great ballroom beyond, which still carried the new sawdust smell of its recent construction. Clark had gone to enormous trouble to prepare for this reception,

Baptiste thought darkly, but Louisa, a fine dancer, refused him much time for ruminations.

"You're from . . . Madagascar?" she asked mid-swirl as they reached the ballroom's far corner.

"My family owns property there," Baptiste said.

"But isn't it all jungles?"

"There would be jungles," he said, "if the mosquitoes ever gave them room."

"So you have a plantation?"

"We had a cottage . . . covered with vines. When my mother died, my father and I traveled to Europe. So we come here by way of Malta, and Saxony, and Vienna."

"So that is where you learned to dance!"

"Judging from your grace, *madame*, I should have come first to St. Louis!"

They were trudging through a stolid "Boston" waltz. It was so slow Baptiste felt as if Louisa and he were pushing and scraping a funeral bier to the four corners of the room. Relief arrived, however, when the diminutive orchestra shifted to a *balance valse*. He enjoyed it himself when they whirled around the room like dead leaves on a river. Louisa dabbed her forehead with a lace handkerchief as her skin glowed.

Then Clark and President Jackson entered the ballroom, which began to twirl with the music.

Bidding Louisa adieu, Baptiste boldly walked up to the faint frame of Mrs. Clark, and before she could protest, swept her onto the floor.

"You are a wonderful hostess, *madame*, and your orchestra is *exotique*," he said as he sensed her heart flutter in her tissued chest like a mad bird dreaming of escape. He finished quickly so as not to be cruel, but he achieved his purpose, which was to look directly into her eyes. *She does not know me.*

"Have you met my husband?" she asked Baptiste with confusion and alarm.

"I look forward to greeting him, later tonight," he said.

The evening blurred into switched partners, wine and cake, and then, like clockwork, the tour of the Museum of Human Beings. Baptiste sat on the very bench where he'd first talked with Duke Paul as he watched Clark conduct his fellow guests through an abbreviated tour of discovery. Then he slipped behind a mud hut as the last trickle of guests bid their host farewell from the museum's side door. Last to leave was the President, who crossed just steps from Baptiste and repaired to the second floor via the grand staircase.

Baptiste stood still beside an antelope and became a part of Clark's exhibit. Far from the mad whirl of the waltzes, time was rigid here. He could hear the ticking of the clock down the hall.

Clark, alone in the museum, did not hurry. Instead he seemed deep in thought. He walked to a large mural of the Corps of Discovery just five feet from Baptiste, put his hands in his pockets, and fished out some tobacco.

Baptiste had stared at the painting that held his interest countless times as a boy, pondering its meaning and trying hard to recapture what it felt like being strapped into that confining pack. The Expedition crew was assembled along the banks of the Snake River. Behind them, the snowy peaks of the Rockies kissed the sky. Their party of weary explorers and their dog stood to the left of the picture. Then there was a gap, and the artist had painted his mother and himself, looking across the distance at their friends. Baptiste, just inches away, watched Clark shift his stance and stare more closely at his mother while Baptiste tightened his grip around the Turkish cavalry pistol, prepared to shatter his skull. Clark scrupulously packed a thumb of tobacco into the bowl of his pipe. A plume of sulfurous blue smoke filled the air as he struck a match on the end of his boot and lit the tobacco, still contemplating the painting.

"Hello, Pomp," he said.

20

"tell/bring the word to me"

—place open right hand palm up in front of mouth; then draw toward the lips with a quick jerk.

The voice, so familiar, stunned Baptiste, and the years slipped away. *So much for the great Indian stalker.* If Baptiste held any illusions about inheriting his mother's gift of stealth, they were shattered now. Somehow, he thought, without lifting a finger, Clark held the upper hand.

"Hello, Father."

Clark took out a handkerchief and removed a speck of dirt from the painting's gold frame. He took two steps in Baptiste's direction but did not extend his hand, acknowledging that Shoshones loathed the custom. Baptiste stayed in the darkness with the other exhibits, unable to move.

"You're quite a dancer," Clark said. "But then I always told you that."

Baptiste stared at him. Clark refused to participate in any drama that was not of his own design. He was so absently privileged he seemed nearly cheery.

"Where are you staying?" Clark said finally.

Baptiste shrugged. "Sir, did you get my letters?"

"Yes, thank you, Pomp, I enjoyed them. They were very edifying."

"Did you ever think to reply?" Baptiste took a bold step toward Clark and realized the top of his head still barely reached the great explorer's chin. *How could he not condescend to me?*

"I'm not much for letters, Pomp. Let's go into my study." Clark led the way across the creaking boards into his library, where so long before he'd advised Baptiste to follow his real father, Toussaint, into the woods. Baptiste sat across from Clark at his desk, anxious that he was letting his chance for a confrontation slip by.

"Sir, I have seen Lizette."

Clark blinked.

"Your daughter, sir. I have seen her, in New Orleans. Little Lizette, my half sister."

"Pompey, I do not know what you are talking about."

"My little sister, whom you had Toussaint take away."

"I remember how you grinned from your mother's back, and how dearly she loved you, and how sternly you held to your mother's neck with your fat brown arms."

"Yes, sir."

"Wonderful little Pomp! How you and your mother could swim!"

"Sir, Lizette is alive. She is living in a brothel in New Orleans."

Clark sat in silence, studying Baptiste's physiognomy. He appeared not to have heard. Baptiste raised his hands and brandished his pistol to alert Clark to the consequences of his anger.

"Do you feel no responsibility for her?"

Clark smiled distantly and shook his head, as if told of an adventure he didn't understand. The books shelved behind him were exactly those, in exactly the same order, that had been behind his head during their last interview.

How can this man be so far away when he is sitting directly across from me? Baptiste marveled. There were so many questions he'd asked Clark in his dreams: How much he'd paid Toussaint to take Lizette away, why Lottie was still a slave when most other slaves of the enlightened had been given papers, if he'd ever received word of him from Duke Paul . . .

Still Clark let the weight of his silence press on Baptiste's shoulder.

"Sir," Baptiste said, "I am now proficient in eight languages and could be a great help to you as your secretary. I am an accomplished musician. I have absorbed every subtlety, every nicety of the European court and traveled as a gentleman for years as a member of the royal party."

I have suffered Duke Paul's visits in the night. I have found Ekaterina, and I have lost her, my son, Lizette, and myself in the process.

"Yes," said Clark's disinterested voice, dismissing thousands of candlelight hours of reading and practice. He smiled, shrugged, and stood up as if to leave.

"I guess no matter how many languages I can lisp it in, 'mongrel' means the same thing," Baptiste said.

"Pomp, how you've learned to hate me." *I suppose it's my fault,* Clark thought. *The best way to cripple a man is to make him grateful.* "Look at yourself, scowling like that."

Baptiste stood up and brought the pistol level to Clark's face.

"I should kill you," he said.

"That's not why you came here, Pomp. Why don't you ask me what you came here to ask?"

He was right. Baptiste cocked the pistol.

"Did you love her?"

Clark was very quiet. His red hair was thinner now, and a good deal whiter. Liver spots disturbed the skin on the explorer's face, and as he scratched his nose, Baptiste could see great veins in his hand standing out in blue, like a fork on Lizette's forgotten river.

"When I first saw her . . . I mean the first time I really saw her, she was bathing under the great falls. She climbed up on a rock, stood still a moment as if listening, and dove in. The falls crashed into the water and drove the mist all around her body. I was ready to lose everything for her . . ."

Waterfalls, Baptiste thought as he listened to Clark, and almost as if they were there to witness it again, real and imagined, the sound of the falls rushed back to them, boy and man.

"The night before, Toussaint, red with drink, had beaten your mother because he got it in his mind she had fallen in love with Sergeant Gass. I found her hiding beneath a blanket, confused, convulsive, bright marks on her chin, eyes, and ribs. I severely rebuked Toussaint for this."

Where was I? Baptiste thought. *I was just a few yards away, dancing. I was and will ever be the Expedition's little dancing papoose.*

"The next morning, I happened upon Janey as she stood alone, staring at a long, narrow waterfall. She began to disrobe at the side of the river, unwinding her skins of beaver and otter—so glossy against her rosy flesh—and venturing first one gamine leg into the swirl, daintily followed by the other. With an aching grace she stepped deeper into the stream and closed her eyes in relief as water from the cool pool acted as a balm to her pain. Her rib cage, so like a bird's, bore the blue stigmata of your father's most recent attentions."

Are you not my father, "Father" Clark?

Baptiste's finger now rested on the trigger. He moved the barrel to Clark's left eye, but the explorer seemed not to notice.

"Did your attraction not arise partly because of how defenseless she was?" Baptiste said very softly. *Sweet and inarticulate as a little deer, she possessed a noble intuition. She was an Indian princess of the Diggers, and so you could enter her without bothering to make a journal entry.*

Clark shrugged. "I stepped closer to her. The water ran off her, chilled by the closeness to the cliff which rose up beside both of us. From a rock I picked up your mother's belt made of blue beads. She did not attempt to cover up in the gloaming, the gloom of those early times rushing all around her in the shape of the falls."

Something was happening to her while she stood in front of you, Father Clark, Baptiste realized with a flash. She was wondering if there was a single worthy person in the world and she was deciding, standing here in front of this false white man, that it was me.

Me, the one who now makes her roll in her grave. Back then I was just two yards away, resting on a nest of her clothes, but I was without sin. I hadn't disappointed her yet. I hadn't consorted with Duke Paul.

Clark lowered his voice in reverie. As if he'd gone back in time with him, Baptiste now witnessed the seduction he had seen, but not understood, so many years before:

"And can you feel that, lovely one?" Clark said.

"Yes," Sacagawea said.

"What are you thinking about?"

"I am thinking about my son."

"And not about yourself, about the terrible things that have happened to you?"

Her voice was small, hoarse. "No!" She looked over at her papoose, his eyes wide and dark as the cloudy water beneath a frozen pond. "My son."

"He is fine. Don't worry about him."

Baptiste looked at Clark in his boiled shirt, lost in his study, staring past him as he continued to talk. *You humiliated my mother in St. Louis, impregnated her, then sent her away to die. You threw Lizette away like rubbish.* The young man felt blackness all through him, and through the mist of the waterfall he called to Clark:

"You turned her into a traitor."

"She led us through the Lemhi Pass, inhabited by her own people, of her own volition," Clark said. "We'd given up hope, but she recognized a long rock formation in the shape of a beaver that she'd seen traveling. She knew she might be killed by her own people as a traitor for revealing their summer hunting grounds, but she did it to save us, and she even followed me here, even though it made her—"

"Did you love her?"

Clark swallowed. His mouth tightened. "I loved the whole Expedition, what the hacks like to call the Voyage of Discovery. I loved being the celebrated explorer. But that's the rub." He walked across the room and looked directly into a silhouette of Meriwether Lewis in an ornate tin frame. "Once you reach the Pacific, it's nothing but bookkeeping. Meriwether couldn't take it. Did you know, years after the Expedition, he was called to Washington by President Jefferson to explain unauthorized expenses? On the way he stopped at an inn near Natchez, deeply troubled. Poor bastard. I couldn't even get to him. They found him early the next morning in a chair, his pistol in his lap and a bullet in his brain. *Felo de se*. It's just a fancy word for suicide."

"Was I a son to you?"

"Is that what you've come all this way to ask?"

This young man's tragedy began and will probably end with drink, Clark thought of Baptiste. *Look at those angry eyes, the way he can't stand still. His near inability to experience happiness. There was a time when you seemed to have limitless potential, Pomp. I have to blame myself for even considering this experiment. Some wild creatures can never be tamed.*

"Haven't I always told you so?" Clark said.

"You never have, sir."

Alcohol and delusions of grandeur. Not to mention Toussaint's bad blood. The young man you could have been . . .

"I remember," Clark said, "the first time I saw you dance."

What was innocence, anyway? Baptiste's mouth opened slightly. Either way, he was released from Clark. He left Clark still sitting in the study and walked into the night rain. His head was thumping, and the rushing sound of the waterfall, which had abated during his last moments with Clark, now increased until it was nearly deafening. With his bag slung over his back, he headed into the city of St. Louis and had made it across Broadway to Jefferson Avenue before he looked up to see an enormous coach thrashing through the night right at him. The roaring in his ears was abruptly silenced by the impact as a jolt of blinding pain knocked him to the ground. He tried to roll away from the second spinning wheel before losing consciousness.

21

"STEAL"

—hold extended left hand in front of left breast, back of the hand facing up, pass right hand under, and close to left hand until right wrist is close to left palm, right index finger extended. Then draw back the right hand, at same time crooking index finger.

Baptiste woke to daylight in a slimy cell of stucco walls covered with moss. Dimly he sat up and struggled to put his boots on, but then a fiery pain exploded in his head, whereupon he instinctively reached up and found the top of his skull wrapped in bandages.

He fell back upon his bed with a groan and hibernated for an unknown span of hours before he stirred again to the drowsy realization that his boots were being very skillfully removed. This was being done in such a loving, considerate manner that in his semi-consciousness he pointed his feet, the better to help them slip off. In his half dream he imagined only a mother could have been so gentle.

But fathers can be gentle, too. Baptiste's head pounded, his vision was fuzzy, but when he struggled to his arms to see who was in the room with him, he was face to face with his dear father, his real father, Toussaint Charbonneau.

"*Mon fils,*" Toussaint said and tucked the boots under his sleeve.

The trapper took a quick step back. Baptiste recognized the filthy buckskins, the goatlike walk. He remembered the fetor.

"Give me back my boots!" Baptiste choked out in French and just beat Toussaint to his possibles bag, at which the Frenchman tugged mightily but left behind as he disappeared into the hall. By the time Baptiste retrieved his pistol from the bag, he found himself laughing in frustration and aiming at a crucifix just above the empty doorway.

"Stop, thief!" he called. "Somebody help me!"

A graying man in a priest's collar came directly to his room. The man had kind eyes. Baptiste could barely move his head now for its pounding.

"*Qu'est-ce que c'est?*" the priest asked in a continental lilt that put trapper French to shame.

"Did he get away?"

"Yes. Has he upset you?"

"Yes," Baptiste laughed until his head hurt more. "And he has stolen my boots."

"Oh," the priest said, frowning. "Yes. He seemed in a hurry. But you're in no condition to follow him anyway."

Baptiste leaned back into the pillow with gratitude.

"You'll be here at least another week. I can get you some new boots."

"*Merci.*"

Baptiste looked around the room, still dazed that just seconds before, Toussaint had been there. What coincidence had brought his *père* to him? It was like a visitation from hell. Baptiste conjured the image of him again, and for an instant he half reappeared, his eyebrow ridges prominent, his forehead sloping, his large jaw agape at Baptiste's having awakened to see—or had he dreamed?—him. Baptiste had almost expected to catch sight of a cloven hoof as the hairy biped escaped through the door with his boots. *He knew it was me, and yet he's taken my boots, my last means of transportation.*

"Where am I?" Baptiste asked, looking around.

"*Nous sommes dans la mission de Saint-Louis,*" the priest said.

"Why on earth did you let him into my cell?" Baptiste asked. "What was he doing here?"

"I don't know how to explain this," the priest said, "but your father, for all his outrageous vulgarity, has quite an affinity for churches, as well as a rather superstitious fear of God's retribution. It's not a coincidence that all of his curses beg for intercession from the Church. It was he, and he alone, who insisted you be baptized here immediately on your arrival in St. Louis."

"My head hurts," Baptiste told the priest.

"Yes," he said patiently.

A week later, Baptiste's skull was still mending, but midway into the third week he was able to shovel coal for the mission, which he did for another three weeks to show his gratitude.

Father Mercier told him he'd been found in the street after being hit, but the coach had rushed ahead unrecognized. In fact, he was overrun by a second coach which at least stopped, with its driver dragging him to the side of the road in a heap in the rain. He remembered hands picking him up and the grateful feeling of being carried, barely conscious, into the mission beside his old school.

Then sleep and Toussaint—Morpheus stealing his consciousness and that devil stealing his boots. Somehow it made him even more irked to think that Toussaint had stolen them not to wear but just to sell.

"They won't even fit him," Baptiste told Father Mercier.

"Yes, my son," the priest said.

"Damn him to hell. How dare he call himself my father? He made my mother a slave. So did Clark. Damn him to hell, too."

Father Mercier's eyes were so gray they looked like the sky just before a rain. He regarded him silently, crossed the room, and returned with a cool cloth dipped in water from a basin. He gently swabbed his forehead and said, "Your mother was never a slave."

"You knew her!"

"Not well. I was here for nine years after seminary but was sent to Charleston barely after you started school. I saw your mother only a handful of times. No matter what others called her, she carried a nobility about her that was impossible to ignore, as if part of her were somewhere else, high in the mountains. As if she knew heaven.

"Toussaint, for all his faults, did give you life, which is a precious gift no matter how it is given. And as for Clark, it was he who registered you as a citizen of these United States and his ward. It was your mother's greatest, and last, desire, and it was a promise that he kept."

At least some promises are sacred. In St. Louis's tumult of souls, not much was lost on the priests. At the mention of his mother a second time Baptiste had to turn away.

"Forgive me," was all he could say.

Finally, he was ready to go and said goodbye.

"Where are you going?" Father Mercier asked.

"I have to leave your protection while I still have a stitch of clothing left," Baptiste said.

The priest smiled and nodded.

"Yes, but where?"

"Up the street," Baptiste said and waved vaguely at the crowds of people from the mission's narrow front steps. He walked down the muddy thoroughfares of St. Louis and with genuine disinterestedness did what any good citizen would do. He set out to vote.

22

"MAN"

—elevate the right index finger, back of hand facing out, in front of face.

May, 1830

Baptiste felt as though he'd finally shed his *lanugo*, his birth fur, when he went to cast his ballot for Roland Merthes in a special runoff for Congress following the death of Lyford B. Whittefield.

Approaching the new City Hall, he saw a crowd of beaver hats and on its vibrating edge learned the occasion for the hubbub. As the line advanced to the inner door he studied the posters tacked along the hall with each of the candidates' advantages writ large in cartoon. Thus influenced, he couldn't wait to be convinced Marion Sharp Hunt should win by a landslide, and his opponent Merthes was a murderer, a liar, and a skunk. Hunt bragged he'd single-handedly won the War of 1812. But Baptiste was swayed back to the other side when the war hero cast aspersions upon his opponent's "dubious bloodlines."

The sun rose higher in the sky, and some of the men began to take off their jackets as Baptiste reached the registration table and gave his name to the two men seated there, the older of whom hrumphed before sifting through a stack of records.

"I haven't yet declared a party," Baptiste added.

This made him a bit more interesting to the crowd of aldermen seated in a cluster of unmatched chairs around him, and some of them leaned in to hear.

"Wait a minute, I don't see you just yet," the clerk said, then peered at Baptiste over his spectacles. It took both of the clerk's hands to lift the heavy district papers and shift them to the other side of his journal's spine.

"Got to check the old records." The clerk turned and pulled a weathered green ledger from a shelf behind him. It was much smaller. He pored through the columns, flipped a final page, and stabbed a finger into the middle of an entry. "Here you be!

"Jean Baptiste Charbonneau, you're in the right district." He peered up. "Says here you were registered as a resident in 1812."

Baptiste felt his mother's presence in the room, like sun coming through a window, if sun could have carved its way through all the tobacco smoke. The clerk gave him a funny look and pointed to a scrawl on the paper, which he recognized. "Says here, 'ward of William Clark.' You were an active party member back then, listed in several rolls." He eyed him significantly. "You are a Democrat, by the way. Pretty lucky—a Métis getting to vote. But as you were registered by General Clark himself as his 'son' . . ." He regarded Baptiste sourly, then spat amid guffaws from the line behind him and handed Baptiste a white piece of paper. Baptiste went behind the curtain, stood up as if to urinate, and did his civic duty.

Something had changed in him. The decision was sudden—like a child breaking a window. He thought with odd care of the godless

Toussaint ensuring he was baptized the moment he was in St. Louis and then Clark, cribbing his name to get credit for an extra vote. Then he passed through the crowd and headed back to the offices of John Jacob Astor's American Fur.

Astor had emigrated from Baden as a boy. Tracing the footsteps of Clark, he'd found money where Clark had found the Pacific. *Maybe I will find what I am looking for in the wilderness, too,* Baptiste meditated. Bells jingled when he opened American Fur's front door. The room was rich with the smell of skins. A very old man looked up from his desk.

"Yes?"

"I'm looking for work," Baptiste said.

"Well," he said, "we've got some of that. Come in here, if you'd like. I've got some papers for you to sign. Then we let you loose with the five dollars."

"I beg your pardon?" Baptiste asked. "Do I need to pay to sign up?"

"Just come in here, young man."

Baptiste sat next to a lad named Warren Ferris on a long wooden bench. They were given a slab of stale tobacco to pass back and forth while each waited for his turn at the table with the old man. *That hunk of tobacco's been around a good deal longer than either of us,* Baptiste thought. *Who knows how long it'll be here after we're gone?*

By suppertime, thirty prospective trappers had assembled. "Go ahead and spend this," the old man told them, "all of it," handing each of them five dollars and directing them to the Astoria Bar across the street. In the shuffling nervousness they seemed to bring in with them, Baptiste hardly recognized himself in the large mirror glimmering over the polished walnut bar. He could almost see his mother's waterfall in its wavy, silver surface. It was his last stop before the unknown. *I have to go out there. My destiny is out there, somewhere. The wilderness might be my last chance somehow to find myself.*

"You, sir," said a gray-haired whore who appeared at his elbow. "Give me just one of your silver dollars and I'll teach you a lesson you'll thank me for one day."

He gave her a dollar. She got up and left without turning back.

"I guess she did teach you a lesson," Warren Ferris snickered as they enjoyed their greasy hash enriched with bear, which stuck to the roof of Baptiste's mouth.

"It didn't take," Baptiste said and fished the last two dollars out of his pocket. He didn't need them where he was going. He gave them to an old man sitting beside him.

"You're an odd one," the old man said.

"What can you tell me?" Baptiste asked softly.

"Never, never, leave one of your brothers behind." He crossed himself. "You boys heard of a man named Scott? Man suffered an intolerable death, left by his chums to die just before the snows. He'd caught The King's Evil."

So the poison of Europe is still spreading, Baptiste thought—*tubercular scrofula with lumps on the neck and a paralyzing shortness of breath.*

"How did he catch it?" Baptiste asked.

"It catches you. Stay out of cold streams, is all I know. This fellow Scott, he was given some provisions but was too sick to accompany the others. We were starving and had to rush on in pursuit of a herd of buffalo. Our conduct was loudly condemned here in town. Now you boys don't ever do that to each other, all right?"

You were there, Baptiste thought. *You left him.*

The man put both dollars on the bar and purchased a bottle of rum. He slouched toward the door. "If you leave 'em for dead, they never really die, don't you see? Stay with them till they go. Keeps 'em out of your nightmares."

The *engagés* nodded their solemn agreement, swore drunken fealty to each other, and slept on the sawdust floor before departing in the early hours the next morning, Baptiste among the most remarkable in his mish-mash of elegant lace and buckskins, having traded the rest of his European *habiliments* away.

Two months into their adventure Baptiste and Ferris were fishing along the tributaries of the Green River. Ferris still wore the tattered overcoat he'd run away in three years earlier. At campfire the young trapper told stories straight out of *Lives of the Great Romans*, only he was the hero and everything happened in Buffalo, New York.

Worst of all, Ferris, tall, liver-lipped, sharp-nosed, eyes close to-gether—actually weasely—hadn't the slightest idea of how to fish, but he reeked with good luck.

"What brings you out here?" Baptiste asked his friend with irritation as he saw his partner's fishing twine tighten again. Ferris had already caught three trout to Baptiste's nil.

"My mother," Ferris said. "I was eighteen, and she caught me smok-ing." He splashed downriver and pulled up a fourth wriggling fish. He plopped it down beside Baptiste's empty bag. "In Buffalo. You know Brightloom Street? Well, I was smoking a pipe on Brightloom Street. She screamed at me in front of thirty men standing in front of Lightheux's Bar."

"Your mother."

"Of course my mother."

"So?"

Ferris laughed. "So I left Buffalo. That minute. She'll never see me again."

You showed her. Baptiste pulled out his pipe and lit it as Ferris packed up his fish. "Here," Baptiste said. He took a puff and held the pipe out to the boy.

Ferris blushed. "Oh, no! I mean, no thanks! It isn't half as fun now I can smoke any time I like." He fidgeted. "What brings you out here?"

he said, resorting to Baptiste's own stilted question. "You being an Indian and all, seems you could do this wholesale."

Ferris leaned over, picked up his sack of fish, and shifted yet a few feet more downstream. "Don't take this the wrong way, but an Injun killed my stepfather's first wife," he said as the river grew silent for a moment. He splashed a few yards into the brown swirl.

"And where was that?" Baptiste said, waiting for him to say Buffalo.

"In Buffalo," he called over to Baptiste, as if this connected all things.

"Ah."

A paroquet flew in and landed on a tree above them.

"I'm sorry," Baptiste said half an hour later. "But for the record, I never knew your stepfather's first wife. Still, I have to ask, if we're talking about your stepfather's first wife, what happened to your mother's first husband, your father?"

"The bastard ran off with an Injun squaw."

"You mean someone other than you voluntarily left Buffalo?"

"I only left because three's a crowd."

Ferris told Baptiste he'd followed the Ohio River to Cincinnati, then Louisville, and finally St. Louis, where he'd courted investors to help him found a fledgling "school of numbers and letters." A handful of children had signed up, but not enough.

"I ran out of funds," he said, "and they were about to run me out of town. I heard American Fur was looking for people fool enough to sign up at a bar on Broadway. You know, the one run by the big Irish lass."

Ferris and Baptiste enjoyed setting their traps together, experimenting as they went, and hunted as partners. Some deeper secrets of the trade had been grudgingly imparted to them as promised by the old-timers traveling with them, but not enough to guarantee the choicest skins. Even the most experienced of the American Fur trappers ran out of luck during the last half of November, though, when game seemed to have vanished from the woods. By December their provisions were running low. Corn and hard tack had done little more than whet their appetites for the last week and a half, along with some carefully rationed dried pork.

They were walking back to camp after a frustrating day tracking a particularly elusive elk when they heard it, a rumbling sound like that which the Romans heard one rainy night when half the Coliseum crumbled after the Ostrogoths stole all the iron rods that held it together. That sound could be heard in Florence. But no one had ever written that it lasted longer than five minutes.

This faraway rumble was lasting a lot longer. Or was it the sound of an ocean? Could it be heat lightning? The smell of ice was in the air. It was none of these, but it did seem somewhat . . . meteorological.

They'd seen fragments of horn flashing in the grasses for days. Now a ceaseless thunder made its approach. Here, on the other side of Loup Fork, they saw the first wooly buffalo, all snort, steam, and lather, an anomaly so far ahead of the herd that he seemed to be outrunning a cloud of dust. His enormous brown eye flashed, as if he wanted to warn them. A second later another bull and then a third flashed past them: hooves, humped backs, shanks, horns. Soon they were in danger of being trampled to death by a raging river of bristly wool, as infinite and restless as the Mississippi.

Baptiste and Ferris stood behind a tree as the earth shook below their feet. Stretching out over the grassy plain was "savage nature in its primeval state," as Ferris muttered—a mass of buffalo so large, and so black, that they could see nothing else. They'd hunted for them for days, even nights, and joked that the only thing they could find was the mythic Great Bear of stars. Now the prey had found the predators.

"How do we tell the others?" Ferris said.

Baptiste held up his hand. "I don't think that's at all necessary."

Ten miles of plain were now black with muscle amid a storm of turned earth. Ferris was seized by their urgency. "By Jove, they are glorious!" he said. "Like a sea of dark forms, moving, plunging, rolling, rushing life."

The ground pitched and rolled like the moving decks of the *Smyrna*. Dust clouds and bits of mote cloaked and alternately revealed the scene. Baptiste had to grasp a sand burr, one of the stippled sworls of grass so sharp they sometimes cut through his moccasins, to keep from being lifted entirely into the air. The great brutes bellowed and snorted as they rushed past; Baptiste and Ferris couldn't help but bray back at them, laughing.

By late afternoon the next day Ferris put his head down and moaned, "When will it stop?" It had been a full thirty-six hours since the first "scout" had passed them by, and there was still no sign of the end of this train. When the last buffalo disappeared over the horizon near twilight, Baptiste's ears rang with the silence.

On a crude travois, he and Ferris dragged one of the many fallen animals back to camp, where they met the other trappers. There had been no need to kill any of the shaggy beasts; enough had been trampled to feed them for weeks.

With his first bite of buffalo meat, Ferris became sluggish with its heaviness. When he fell upon his second helping, he said reverently, "This is the most luxuriant banquet of beef I have ever encountered." Baptiste, Ferris, and their comrades enjoyed the mouth-watering steaks rich with fat, and the wild onions they'd gathered by the river bed.

Ferris spoke for all of them: "Hunger is a capital sauce."

The buffalo brought another side effect, seventy Sioux on horseback, the five leaders of whom rode into camp a few hours later while Baptiste was standing watch.

"*Leve!*" the Sioux leader shouted roughly from horseback, using the admonishment the trappers used to rouse each other.

"What is it?" Ferris asked.

What indeed, Baptiste thought.

Though generally known to be casual about property rights, these Sioux sniffed the air, incensed that Baptiste and company had been feasting on their meat.

Baptiste took a deep breath, approached the leader, and offered him Virginia tobacco, skinning knives, and iron fishhooks.

"*N'importe*," the Sioux sneered in French.

Ferris tried to cordel the mules, who were wide-eyed and jostling nervously as if wolves were in their midst.

"You travel at night?" Baptiste asked the leader in French. Most tribes were reluctant to do this.

"I am not afraid of the dead."

Finally Baptiste offered them his pipe, and they dismounted. The leader, looking Baptiste straight in the eye, unrolled a ladies' evening cloak that could only have come from a hapless traveler, and unfurled it with a snap before spreading it on the ground. He sat down, crossing his legs to smoke. His comrades squatted in a ring around the fire.

After tossing a piece of buffalo dung on the flames, Baptiste fell silent. In time the leader grunted with approval, returned his pipe to him, and stood up. The others followed, mounted their horses, and wheeled away for the forest. They were already leaving when Baptiste called out, "Do you know where I can find the ghost of the white trapper from American Fur?"

The leader halted and bared his teeth. "You must mean Monsieur Scott." He mimicked Baptiste in Sioux to his party, to laughs. Then he grinned and motioned for Baptiste to follow. The protests of the other trappers fell away as Baptiste jumped onto his sorrel and began to trail the Indians into the night.

"You're a fool," a senior guide called out. "They'll kill you, and on company time."

Some of Baptiste's other comrades spat in disgust, as if he were abandoning them for his own kind. Baptiste wondered, *what do I care about Scott?* He was full of fear himself, but his blood pulsed with excitement. Traveling against the moon, he could tell they were heading north toward the Wind Mountains, his mother's country.

They rode and slept, slept and rode. Breaking off from the larger hunting party after midnight, Baptiste, the leader, and another Sioux approached the shadow of Nose Mountain, a needle of rock that rose to a height of three hundred feet.

"Many Gros Ventres and Arapaho warriors are preparing to ambush your party at the foot of the Black Hills," the leader told Baptiste in French. "It will be their privilege to kill you if you venture farther west."

"*Merci,*" Baptiste answered, distributing tobacco to them from his possibles bag.

As morning approached, they plunged through lively streams and shallow shoals. "Your seat is *élégant,*" the leader called to Baptiste. "Must be the horse. *Comment est-il appele?*"

Baptiste laughed at the jibe. No matter which of the horses he was issued, he'd resolved never to drown in the loss of loved ones, and never again to become attached to his mount. "I call this one Just Transportation."

An hour after sunrise, Nose Mountain stood out like a cross in the nave of a church. Solemnly, the trio stopped and gently skirted their horses around a pack of supplies on the ground, too unlucky to touch. *Is there a problem?* Baptiste thought with a smile. *Considering your earlier puffery, I thought you and the dead were great intimates.* The warriors stiffened with disapproval as Baptiste jumped to the desert floor and opened the discarded satchel, which contained a small Bible inscribed with the name Scott stamped in gold and generations of his forebears scrawled onto the frontispiece, a knife, a tin cup, and some trading beads. Baptiste had already seen the zigzag path, in places acutely clear, that Scott had taken . . . *where?*

They walked slowly behind the footsteps as if Scott's ghost were actually leading them to Nose Mountain. There, leaned against the base of the peak's vertical shaft, was a skeleton picked clean to the eye sockets but for some violet skin and hair clinging to the back of his left ear like moss on a rock. His rictus was so unluckily comic that the Sioux warriors would approach no closer than fifty feet. Baptiste stopped, almost in surprise. Scott must have been extraordinarily tall and lanky. In life, with his toothy grin, he might very well have resembled Vogelweide.

Baptiste returned to his chums on the fur brigade, and on his recommendation they marked a course a good deal south of Nose Mountain. Though they were sure they were being trailed, first by the Sioux, later by the Blackfeet, and always by the Crows, they were permitted this route that avoided the Indians' preferred hunting grounds and proceeded without delay. They barely slept. They carried so much buffalo flesh with them that they ate nothing else.

As the weeks passed, Baptiste felt good losing himself in the stoic luxury of travel. Ferris alone among the white men could speak languages aside from French and English, and then so gingerly that Baptiste kept his European modes of expression locked up in his heart. Besides, the vicissitudes of court life seemed very small out here.

The only indulgence he dusted off on occasion was Ekaterina's violin, the Guarneri that begged to be played now and then when Baptiste was at his loneliest, when their party was at rest and he was out of earshot, protected from discovery by boulders or waterfalls where the wind or the rush of cataracts might conceal his sound.

So it was with some surprise that he felt Ferris approach him one morning while he was sitting behind a high outcropping, fiddling around with Ekaterina's ballade, enmeshed in the part that sounded as though faeries were jumping and floating on leaves in the river. Baptiste stopped playing and looked up at Ferris's dark hair, sunburned face, and crooked grin. Ferris's eyes danced.

"I know who you are," he said like a little child.

"Really, Ferris," Baptiste said. "Who am I?"

"I should have known it long ago. The way you track, the languages you shed like snake skins. Right up there with Jesus Christ himself, you are a most famous babe."

"What about Romulus?" Baptiste smiled. "And Remus."

Ferris scratched his head. "Moses," he said dreamily. "Did Buddha even have a mother?"

"Heracles strangling the serpents who had insinuated into his crib, Louis the Dauphin, I'm way down the list."

"You don't have any excuse for dawdling around, gaping at these mountains like some kind of tourist instead of pulling your weight, and leaving all the trapping for me to do," Ferris joked. "This is your dooryard."

It was true. Fifty miles to the east they'd passed Council Bluffs, named for Clark's famous tête-à-tête with the Blackfeet high atop a plateau Baptiste could still see from up here. He half remembered it from his infancy. Certainly he remembered the condors, big and blue-black as the Arabian rocs that swirled over the castles at Malta. The ground actually cooled under their enormous shadows. If anything, they were bigger than he remembered them.

"Ferris, I'd appreciate it if you kept this to yourself."

"No use," Ferris said and stepped back.

"Why?" Baptiste stood up very quickly. Ferris blinked but now held his ground.

"Your father's telling everybody. He's getting drunk with the senior guides right now!"

Baptiste packed up his violin and ran the mile or so to camp, descending through brush and fallen trees. Leaves flashed across his cheeks as he rushed downhill to his childhood, or his mistaken impression of it. He already knew he would be speechless, flushed with a confusion of hatred and embarrassment, when he saw Toussaint. *What do you want with me? Did you forget you'd stolen my boots?*

Baptiste's face was scarlet now, because he was just beginning to realize he'd traveled a thousand miles to get away from himself and failed. He had over three hundred dollars in skins in his cache, which were absolutely safe beside those of his fellow murderers and scoundrels but in desperate peril with a family member nearby. Toussaint in camp! He had to reach Toussaint before he could do any more damage.

23

"QUARREL"

—bring index fingers, pointing up, several inches apart, opposite each other, in front of body, level with shoulders. Now, by wrist action, move right tip toward left, then left toward right, alternately, and repeat. Make motions sharply.

June, 1831

"*Mon fils!*" Toussaint cried and held his arms open. The blue arrowhead retrieved from the whale dangled from a leather thong around his thick and greasy neck.

Closing his nostrils to the reeking miasma that engulfed Toussaint, Baptiste embraced him and embraced him again until his comrades began to twitch and glance at each other. Still he held on. After ten seconds or so, the sire of his cursed luck began struggling to get free, but Baptiste was far too affectionate. He had a plan to rid himself of Toussaint forever.

"*Mon père!*" Baptiste said. Crushing Toussaint in his arms, he gave him the evil eye with exactly the Jettatore squint he'd been taught in Malta. "Never has there been a father such as this!" Thus he began his curses, a litany of inordinate praise. He grasped Toussaint all the harder and glared at him, projecting all the *jettatura* he could muster.

To the others he sputtered, "My dear father came a great distance to visit me while I was sick in St. Louis, and now we are reunited! I haven't had a chance to thank him until now."

As his comrades backed slowly away, Baptiste squeezed again. Toussaint's yellow eyes flickered. His lips turned green.

"Father," Baptiste repeated feverishly and held him hard enough to burst his heart. He could feel the change in Toussaint as his eyes darkened with the knowledge of his son's hatred.

"*Mon fils,*" Toussaint said very quietly.

"Look, Papa," Baptiste said. "You are fainting from happiness."

Noting the flash of fear behind Toussaint's eyes, Baptiste fixed his loving gaze on him yet a third time and launched into another malefic compliment.

"So unmatched is your prowess, you will capture great herds of buffalo every day for the rest of your life. And in matters of love—"

With a surprising surge of strength, Toussaint jumped back and spat three times into the ashes of the fire. Baptiste could see he was impressed because this was new. Toussaint had lived in the woods so long he had moss growing on his north side. Smiling as he watched Toussaint try to brush the bad fortune off his buffalo wrap and out of his beard, Baptiste took a long look at his face. Though the Frenchman's hoary hair still stood out furiously against patches of dark on his skin, Baptiste could see islands of white hair, too. In spite of his vigor, Toussaint was now an old man with a lot to answer for.

"Where did you take my sister?" Baptiste said under his breath.

"Which sister would that be?" Toussaint said.

"You know who I mean. Lizette."

"Ah, the red-headed one who cried like a wild cat? So long ago, *mon fils*. I took her to a farm where children could play in the fresh air down on the river."

"Your abduction started her on a miserable life. Did Clark tell you to do it?"

Toussaint nodded. "Remember, *mon fils*, it was more of his concern than mine." A presentiment animated his eyes and he said, "What's more, she's alive. Do *you* have any living children to present to their grandfather?"

Baptiste said nothing.

"Eh, *mon fils*? What's that? Old Toussaint sometimes does not hear. Look at the great strong son I have!" he called back to the others over the darkness. "We'd better have a drink."

"I'm not thirsty, Father."

Toussaint, for his part, had an unquenchable thirst, and as a group they sat down to their meal. Crunching bones in the darkness, they shared the loneliness that thirty men and one satyr can spend together.

"Remember, *mon fils*, I took Lizette where I was recommended to take her. I just did what I was paid to do."

"Tell me how my mother died."

"You only think you want to hear it," Toussaint said.

They looked over the ridge and heard the Platte River crashing through the blackness. A flock of crows flew over them, and Toussaint crossed his chest.

"Bad luck to dwell on it," he said.

"Worse not to."

"You're a magician, aren't you?"

"And you're a beast."

"Animals are *monsteurs*, but evil is peculiar to the human heart."

"How did my mother die?"

"She died of the morning dew, *mon fils*. Why don't we leave it at that? Gummas all over her, chancres all over her mouth when she called your name. *Mon fils*, there are some things that as a little boy you were not supposed to see: English diseases, the Old Joe. The only skin still fresh was her *vagin*. She used to blister it raw, then scrape away the rotting flesh herself. She kept it cleaner than an eye."

He turned to walk away, but Baptiste kept following him.

"She had the yaws even when I won her, playing the bones with Le Bourgne and Black Cat. I never met a squaw who didn't."

Baptiste's stomach turned at the thought of the yaws eating their way across his mother's skin.

"It is a miracle you were born uninfected," Toussaint said, surveying Baptiste's eyeballs and the tip of his nose.

"I am infected, sir, with a different disease."

"Eh?" said Toussaint. "You look to be in good health, apart from feeling morbidly sorry for yourself. But you may still have the yaws, papoose. What if you were not the 'carried' but the carrier as well? Who knows, *mon fils*, you may yet be an 'ambassador' after all!"

Baptiste stared at him.

"Oh yes, I've heard about your desire to work with your precious Jefferson, who not only has the yaws but the clap himself. All of your founding fathers—Genr'l Washington, Benjamin Franklin, were consumed with the sickness of love."

"Of course, you have it," Baptiste said.

"Your Clark, so clean in his ways. Like your mother, like you. The question is, do you carry it well? How long is your *pipette*? Bring it out. Let's have a look."

"I will bring out my knife."

"You should show some pride, *mon fils*. But not everything is inherited. Next best thing, can you track?"

"I am perhaps the worst tracker ever to enter these woods, so it appears that I have inherited much of you," Baptiste returned to his *jettatura* stare. "I was hoping you could give me even less direction."

"Ah, *mon fils*, you are like the lover who never gives a straight answer to anyone or anything. *Mon Dieu*." He made the sign of the cross. "Can you track?"

"No."

Baptiste spat into the ground in front of him. He wanted to learn about his mother, not swap stories with a drunk and a rapist.

"To be a good tracker, *mon fils*, you first have to know what you're looking for."

Baptiste stared at the narrow blue arrowhead around Toussaint's neck. It had serrated edges carved expressly to rip the heart out of a bird.

"Your mother was just a girl, *mon fils*, and one of my favorites. She believed that you and Lizette would not carry the disease. But toward the end her disease made her like a genius. The worse she got, the more she seemed to know."

"What did she know?"

"She saw you as a man, walking on the black desert. On that night you will feel alone and unhappy, but she wants you to know you will never be alone. To her you are like a little sparrow, flinching in the cold. She wants you to know she will never leave you . . . and to listen to Old Toussaint. That is the exact truth. Look at me in the eyes. I do not lie. You will always have Old Toussaint with you.

"Your mother, she had nightmares. She said that you, at age six, were coming to find her from so far away. People wouldn't listen to her. You realize, *mon fils*, how unlucky it is to talk about the dead. Well, that was what she began to do. She began to see them during her fevers. She said she saw them stirring and rising out of the lake and taking flight like her name. She claimed she could describe them, down to the scars on their bodies, as they ruined her sleep." He crossed himself again. "Part of her greatness was her wildness," he said. "But she was crazy."

"She was too young to die."

"You are wrong, *mon fils*, she was an expert at it."

"After you stole my boots, where did you go?"

"Do you dare call your own father a thief, *mon fils?*"

"*Merde.* I saw you."

Toussaint stretched out on the ground, turned over, and went to sleep. A few hours later Baptiste kept his eyelids closed when he heard Toussaint get up and brush his practiced hand across the bag that held Ekaterina's violin. Unimpressed, the Frenchman ducked into the darkness and disappeared.

Baptiste called out after him. "No lover of music, eh?"

What am I hunting? Baptiste thought. Like the *Candide* he carried in his possibles bag, he'd begun his life in a state of innocence, been expelled into the great world by the indifferent hand of fortune, and found civilization reprehensibly uncivilized. He longed to find his father, but who was he? Clark? Toussaint? The force of Nature which seemed to stare at him wherever he fled? Only he could find his place in the world, it was true, but that would require more hunting.

For years, every June, a trappers' Rendezvous had taken place in Pierre's Hole, a twenty-mile valley almost devoid of trees. Sheltered by a wall of pine-studded rocky peaks, the grassy bowl beckoned like a *circus maximus* of the spirit world. Here, with all the refreshing coolness it suggested, a cluster of effluents joined to create a great fork in the Teton River, presided over by three striking, snow-capped summits, Les Trois Tetons. A young Iroquois trader nicknamed "Pierre" by his Hudson's Bay employers was killed after showing it to his hunting partner, who'd tried to collect a reward from three different tribes for finding it. Indians called it The Missing Land.

By the time Baptiste's group of Astorians approached the Rendez-vous, five thousand Indians had gathered in the valley, ready to trade. From the north, Captain Ghant descended with fifty men resplendent upon as many Spanish horses he'd bought from San Raphael's troops in New Mexico.

"How can you see from here that they're Spanish?" Ferris asked Baptiste of the horses.

"Fetlocks short, necks long, and do you see how they plunge down the mountain?" Baptiste said. "Can you not detect the distinctly Spanish flare to their nostrils?" Also, Andrew Dripps had told him.

They picked up speed down the hill while Ferris continued with his enthusiasms.

"Mr. Provenu is bringing his equipment all the way from Fort Union, on the mouth of the Yellowstone," said Ferris, "and the manager, Bill Sublette, is camped over there, with the other companies and one hundred men, selling every manner of new thing from St. Louis."

"Manager! I know Sublette from my last foray into the fur business," Baptiste smiled. "I'm surprised he hasn't been murdered yet."

Ferris also pointed out the elegant figure of Sir William Drummond Stewart, who was accompanied by bagpipes as he marched in with his deputation of Scottish Highlanders. The two men watched a ghostly figure with his chin in the air named Nathaniel Wyeth materialize, followed by a dozen men whose deference to their leader approached religious fanaticism.

Black Robes—Catholic missionaries—entered the plain as well, absurd in their hot cassocks. *Everyone has brought something to sell.* For a moment Baptiste felt a pang of regret because it seemed as if these coarse merchants had come to set up shop in Eden.

Mother, he thought while Ferris ran ahead of him to a vista with even better views of the camps. *You could not have foreseen this. I'm glad you don't have to see the shame of what you have done.*

Scudding clouds appearing out of nowhere foretold the arrival of rain. Leaves showed their silver undersides on the trees. Horses lifted their heads. As Baptiste and Ferris descended the winding trail, the valley grew larger. They reached the floor of the enormous plain and felt a great fetch of wind seething its fingers through the grasses as if an unknown force were composing an aria there.

24

"TO MEET"

—hold hands opposite each other, pointing upward. Bring hands toward each other until tips of index fingers touch.

All of a sudden the heavens cracked open and lightning shot across the sky with an eerie blue flame. Rain whooshed into the valley, turning everything to mud.

"God has spoken!" Ferris laughed. He caught up with Baptiste, and they ran for the nearest tent. As they rounded the corner, they saw there was a crowd near the entry flap.

"What's going on?" they asked a man in a coonskin hat.

"Shut your trap," he said. "Can't you see, Doc's getting ready to open him up? Poor bastard."

When Baptiste and Ferris pushed their way into the tent, it looked as if Dr. Marcus Whitman, dressed from the waist up for the opera, was getting ready to carve a turkey. Silver instruments flashed in his hands. The hapless patient was quite delirious with drink. He moaned whenever the scalpel brushed too close to this pearly tendon or nicked that pulsing artery or grazed the dull gray sheath of a nerve. Rain pounded on the tent as Baptiste and Ferris slid in next to a young military officer with his arms crossed and a severe bearing.

"Light that," the doctor ordered an Indian maid, motioning toward an oil lamp. She touched a phosphorous match to the wick, making all of them glow.

With horror, Baptiste realized that the doctor was poised as if to feast from the back of a live human being.

"Who is that?" Baptiste and Ferris asked.

"Shut pan and sing small," the doctor's assistant snapped and gave them a menacing stare.

"Poor bugger's name is Jim Bridger," the young officer said, leaning in. "The Doc's pulling an iron point from an arrow that hit him right between the shoulder blades."

"War party?" Ferris asked, agog.

"More like a rum party. Wouldn't you know, he'd only been here three hours before there was a bar fight in the mess tent."

Baptiste looked at the beery crowd in filthy dusters around him and was reminded of the white coats that had surrounded him in the German *versuchstadium*. Only this time he was part of the crowd getting prurient pleasure from someone else's exploitation.

"William Sheridan," the dark moustached officer said to Baptiste and Ferris, offering his hand.

"Who the hell else is here?" said Ferris. He looked to his left. "You must be a reporter," he said to a gangly man taking notes in a leather-bound ledger. "You must know who else is here."

"Not a reporter but I am a writer. Washington Irving."

"Warren Ferris."

"Well over there, that gentleman is William Fremont," Irving said, "and yon, that hesitant youth is the child of William Henry Harrison— Old Tippecanoe."

Irving's voice trailed off.

Behind the Harrison boy, in the far corner, was a large black man in the ceremonial buffalo robes of a Crow chieftain. He was so dark of aspect it seemed as if half of him were still outside, walking in the night. Seven young maidens curled and slept at his feet or hugged at his legs.

Ferris pointed. "Who's that darky who's got himself all up?"

"That's the famous Beckwourth," Irving said. "Head of the Crow nation."

So it was he! Baptiste reached into his bag and pulled out the old newspaper scrap about Clark's soiree with the president. On the obverse was the tidbit about Beckwourth's exploits.

Beckwourth was the son of Sir Jennings Beckwourth, an English plantation owner, and his ebony lover. Sir Beckwourth had confounded his Virginia neighbors when he'd taken both mother and son into his home and educated the boy well beyond his station. Further, Sir Beckwourth had three times gone to court to have young Jim no longer called a slave. The courts having refused him, the family removed to St. Louis.

The younger Beckwourth had been groomed to become a great gentleman, so of course he was destined to be a moody troublemaker, joining a group of fortune hunters bent on discovering lead mines in the Upper Missouri. Returning penniless, Beckwourth embarked with General William Ashley's troops to trap near the Continental Divide. He'd disappeared and for years had been thought dead. Instead, he'd been adopted by the Crow nation and joined their ranks as a brave. He'd fought so heroically in countless wars against the Blackfeet that he was awarded with the distinction of highest power. As chief of the Crows, Beckwourth had negotiated to trade with American Fur thousands of skins, which the Crows guarded at his command in subterranean caves the location of which only Beckwourth would disclose at times of his choosing. Baptiste looked at the man in charge of over thirty thousand braves, the man who had refused to remain in the

East and be looked down upon as "James, a mulatto boy."

"Well, if there's anything worse than an Injun with a chip on his shoulders, it's a 'Sinian who thinks he's an Injun," Ferris laughed and slapped Baptiste on the knee.

"Thuk." An arrowhead makes a distinctive sound when it is pulled from a man's back and dropped into a tin cup. Bridger howled. Baptiste might have winced when the doctor held the piece of metal up with a flourish, followed by a wave of applause, but instead he paid no attention because in the din one of Beckwourth's Indian maids came over and, taking Baptiste's hand, led him to her love.

"Hey you, I have something for you," Beckwourth said.

"What is it?"

"Come outside."

Up close, Beckwourth's buffalo robe was richly decorated and lined with the brain-tanned skins of at least eight lush young calves. Baptiste reached out and touched the hair, which was so glossy it sparked at his hands. His hand disappeared into its darkness as if he had plunged into a mirror, or a stream. It no longer surprised Baptiste that his mother's people believed that a buffalo was the one animal whose soul lived not inside his heart but shimmered outside his body, like an aura, in and through its wool. Beckwourth held out a small stone and gave it to him.

"I was up on the Wind River. I picked this up from your mother's grave," he said. The tiny white stone, no larger than an acorn, burned a hole in Baptiste's hand. He almost dropped it.

"Who told you to do this?"

"Your father."

"He gave it to you?"

Beckwourth smiled and shook his head. "I have known your father for a long time. We saw you coming," he said without boasting. "We saw you at the Green River, and at Porteneuf, and at Chimney Rock."

When he said "we" he meant the entire Crow nation. Some of the maidens he was with in the tent reappeared in the darkness a few steps off, but Beckwourth motioned them away.

"I have just completed business with Sublette," he said. "He's taking all of our furs to St. Louis and guarantees $4.25 a pound."

"What value could you give to money out here?"

"Hardly the value you give a stone," Beckwourth laughed. "Here, let me see it."

Baptiste gave him the smooth white stone, and with a mighty heave Beckwourth threw it high and far through the gathering darkness until he saw it splash into the Teton River. Baptiste took a step toward it, but Beckwourth stopped him.

"She is everywhere," he said.

"Are you leaving soon?" Baptiste asked.

"Tonight," he smiled. "I've been leaving for three days."

Night fires flickered for miles across the basin, and a mile from where they were standing Baptiste heard music, a melodic chanting that echoed from the wall of rock to the north and fell invisibly to the grass like fireworks over Rapallo. Collecting Ferris, who had welcomed the rest of their group and had seen to their horses, Baptiste wished Beckwourth well and headed toward the sound of Shoshone rhythms and a roar of chanting. Beckwourth waved, turned back to his women, and headed into the night.

"Nectar of the gods," Baptiste said to Ferris, who handed him a bottle of rye as they walked through the tall grass. "Where'd you get it?"

"From Sublette," he said. "There's enough to go around."

There's never really enough, Baptiste reflected sadly.

"Look at them," Ferris said of the dancers. "They look like goblins from hell, don't you think?"

By the time they reached the dancers, Baptiste wore only his loincloth and moccasins. He finished his bottle and, laughing, broke from the sphere of Ferris's fear. He knew these dances from childhood. He closed his eyes and tried to float over to one side of his existence, but just as Candide chased his innocence across the globe, he had not been able to track his own here. He'd just broken rhythm with the dance when he heard Ferris scream.

Like a madman, Ferris was running toward their horses. Their horses were running, too. Behind Baptiste, everyone else kept dancing. The whiskey wore off him as he sprinted past Ferris, up an escarpment, and toward the figure of a thief in the night.

The thief had mounted a horse—*his* horse—and was racing away, leading the others. Baptiste could not catch him the way he was going, so he caught him the way he was *about* to go. The thief felt Baptiste had fallen on him from out of the sky, but he'd really scrambled up a rock, seen the man passing below, and soundlessly leapt into space.

Falling through the night, Baptiste found himself alone with the silence of his musical compositions and the whole world stopped, as if it were just the piano, himself, and the loud pedal.

He hit the man on the horse and immediately they were on the ground, with the horses dancing over them and flashing away. Baptiste rolled over, looked the thief in the eye, and did not recognize him. The thief very alertly picked up a rock and hit Baptiste over the left eye, which knocked him nearly unconscious. The man raised the rock again, for the last time.

Then, for a flash, Baptiste saw Toussaint. With a lunge, Toussaint knocked the fellow over with a dark object that dropped him to his knees momentarily before he turned and ran for the woods. Baptiste's head cleared as he gave chase, but then he ran into a tree. At least he thought it was a tree. Maybe the tree was something in his inner consciousness preventing him from seeing what happened. When he woke up it was raining, and his comrades from American Fur were congratulating him and returning the long knife he had planted in the rascal's back.

"Where is the thief?" he asked.

"He absquatulated," said Dripps, somehow gently.

"Where is Toussaint?" he asked.

"We didn't see Toussaint," they said.

"Ferris," he said, "did you see my father?"

"No."

"I used this knife?"

"We saw you."

It was his knife. It made no sense, so it must have happened. Then his comrades parted, and he saw Toussaint, an Indian club suspended from his left arm. Carved on its tip was a scowling mountain lion's head. Baptiste stood up, and Toussaint looked him up and down with amusement.

"Can you tell me, *mon fils*, what possessed you to wear that Indian costume out here?"

"You saved my life," Baptiste said under his breath. More confused than ever, he spoke so all could hear: "You stopped the thief from killing me. Toussaint saved my life." *Father, would you steal even my hatred for you?*

The rapist, thief, and savior turned to address the small assemblage while slamming his hand onto Baptiste's back. "What are fathers for?" he started to say, but a fit of coughing bent him over and muffled his words. He dropped to one knee and coughed some more, wiping the phlegm on the sleeve of his deerskin jacket.

"You are sick," Baptiste said.

"No, *mon fils*, I am thirsty! I am dry as dust."

To Baptiste's mortification and amusement, Toussaint stayed with them and regaled them with stories most of the evening, drinking and boasting while Ferris asked him for lies about the great woods. Many an eye rolled as they learned about the eleven cougars Toussaint had slain during the Lewis & Clark Expedition, "and that was just on the way out, *mon fils*. One of them nearly had you in his mouth. He was completely black, except for a white ring on the tip of his tail. That cat knew how to die bravely."

He took another swig. "I weep for that cat."

"Next to man," Ferris asked Toussaint, "which do you believe is the most intelligent species?"

Toussaint took a deep draught of his whiskey and assumed a thoughtful expression.

Disgusted by the Frenchman's expansiveness, Baptiste picked up his blanket and crawled under it to go to sleep. *Damn you, villain, will you give me no peace?* He tried to wrap his head twice with his blanket so he wouldn't hear.

"Above him or below him?" Toussaint asked.

Baptiste never saw the thief again. Usually horse thieves were put to death, given "the black gown," but this one was returned to Wyeth's party, bound for Oregon, and there was much talk when their entire group disappeared. *Why, with so many witnesses, did he insist on stealing our horses?* Baptiste wondered. He darkly reflected that civilization is a performance, staged even when no one is looking. The horses were secondary to the thrill of doing the deed.

Baptiste checked his possibles bag after Toussaint left, as a matter of routine. Inside it he found a small white stone with soft gray scratches, a scuffed moon. It looked exactly like the stone Beckwourth had made the motion of throwing away.

The Rendezvous broke up. Baptiste and his fellow *engagés* did a lot of trapping as summer turned to fall, then winter and spring. Time seemed to enter a great river, then rushed to the rapids.

25

"LOST"

—make sign for HIDE.

April, 1836

Baptiste could not remember the exact day he disappeared into himself. He skinned thousands of creatures, each animal's spirit spilling out with the flash of his knife. In spite of his sympathy for his kills, Baptiste succeeded in never looking one of them in the eye.

As the months passed, watching Ferris drive his knife through hundreds of beaver pelts, Baptiste saw him change, too. Ferris used to make any excuse to talk, but now that his arms were red with blood, he kept to his work.

"What?" Ferris said one day when he caught Baptiste staring at him. "What?

"*Tas de merde,*" he said. No, Ferris hadn't been himself for quite some time.

For days the sky had been slate-colored and heavy as lead. Now a great wind picked up. The birds were crazy with it. Still they skinned animals: beaver, fox, squirrel, bog lemmings. Pronghorn antelope and mule deer, their eyes dancing all around their campfires. But none of them saw Baptiste.

The snow came once they hit the mouth of the Porteneuf. They cached their furs and split into two parties for more hunting, promising to meet on the Snake River, near the cascades where the waterfalls drop seventy feet in just a third of a mile. They were a personal landmark for Baptiste, as they were the very spot where Clark had first watched his mother bathe. He wondered if these were the waterfalls he heard in his head whenever he was angry.

The first group set off to hunt along the Cassia River, while the rest, under Baptiste's command, followed La Riviere Malade, the Sick River.

They struck off to the west, and by noon the next day the snow had stopped and dropped away as they descended to a vast desert spotted with cedars and basaltic rock. Farther ahead, the cedars stopped and all was black, as if the lava had spewed forth in waves as far as the eye could see.

"The craters of the moon," Ferris said behind Baptiste.

"If there's a moon in hell," Marcel Guertin, one of the older trappers, said.

"Charbonneau," Dripps called ahead to Baptiste, "you remember this?"

"No," Baptiste said. But he'd seen it before, in Dante, the heat steaming up from the rocks.

"You're not going in there!" Guertin said as Baptiste dismounted and led his horse into the black desert. It seemed the most sensible thing Guertin had ever said. Swallows apparently agreed about the danger, veering away from the edge of the lava as if they were approaching a wall.

"Maybe save some time," Baptiste said. "We're trapped-out here."

Ferris was the first to follow him, entering the lava without dismounting. "Afraid of something?" Baptiste called to Dripps.

"No," Dripps said and rubbed the tip of his beard. "It's just . . . slantindicular."

Baptiste hopped up on a rock for a better view of the horizon and unfolded his map, its cartographer none other than William Clark. Scribbles on the chart, already fading, showed a finger of the desert reaching out and separating them from their destination, the finger almost teasing him. According to what Baptiste saw, they could cross in just five hours, saving nearly a day's travel. But could he believe Clark?

"The sooner we enter, the sooner we'll leave," Baptiste said finally, returning the chart to his possibles bag. Then he cantered ahead over the black sand, hoping his comrades would follow. It took all of his resolve not to look back and see. Guertin waited longest, but finally Baptiste heard a clatter and Guertin's deep baritone saying, "God damn you to hell," and the young man felt a surge of pride. *I am the leader now,* Baptiste thought, *and this is my expedition.*

All across the lava, pockets of new grass leapt up from scraps of dirt carried into cracks and crannies by the wind. Still, the birdlessness of the lava put Baptiste on guard. Normally, after studying their swoops in the air, he could find water near places where they returned or flared out low. He checked his compass, slightly adjusted their course, and continued. An hour later, he heard Ferris's horse snort and stop. Baptiste and his horse pulled up, too. In spite of the sunshine, it was so uniformly black out here that had they not sensed the void ahead, both horses and riders might have walked another ten feet. In that case, they'd still be falling into a great crack in the rock.

"Let me try it first," Baptiste said and cantered to his right, taking the leap at the narrowest spot. The others followed, but after several approaches, Ferris reined his horse to a halt in front of the chasm.

"My wretched bag of bones won't jump," Ferris said. "He keeps looking down."

At least somebody's got some sense, Baptiste thought. It was a seventy-foot drop if he missed. "Mysterieux," Baptiste called to Ferris's horse, and as if a spirit animated its form, the dapple, so thin that his ribs showed, backed up, charged, and sailed across the abyss while Ferris hung on for dear life.

"What was it you told him?" Ferris asked.

"I called his attention to the lump of sugar I've fished out from my tea supply," Baptiste said, and gave Mysterieux his reward.

"That's why your teeth are so rotten," Ferris said. "I'll just take some whiskey."

They traveled a few more miles before sunset lengthened shadows on the rocks. Ferris bent down to a most symmetrical piece of lava, kicked it, and broke it off. "Look," he said and held it up, "a frying pan!"

Admiring its long handle, they used it in exactly that service an hour later. Heating a couple of hares they'd brought with them on the blistering bed of lava made them all the more aware that both water and shade were in short supply out here. Worse still, eating the salted rodents made one mad for water.

"Take it easy," Baptiste told Guertin when he drank too much.

"*Tas de merde.*" Guertin laughed and took three more swigs, his Adam's apple enunciating his insubordination.

Far from cooling as night approached, the lava began to steam. They all drank, far too quickly, from their beaver skins. By nightfall, they were in the middle of the fifty-mile desert, thirsty, and losing their way further with each step.

"We have to wait for the moon," Baptiste said. "Then we'll be able to see."

Half an hour later, to their delight, a shower swept through and cooled them, though it disappeared almost as soon as it came. Fortunately Baptiste and his troops had spread their blankets out, the better to catch what rain there was so that they could twist them and extract the precious water later.

Once the moon rose, green against the shattered black of the desert, a mountain took shape, white in the distance like the sails of a ship.

"Mount Jefferson," Baptiste motioned after consulting his charts. It was their first time this far west.

"How do you know?" Guertin said, squeezing his blanket over his face.

"Save your water," Baptiste said.

Of course Baptiste didn't "know" anything. Taking his horse by the lead, he started toward the mountain. Trying not to think of his water supply, he squeezed a bit more from his blanket over the back of his neck, squeezed some into his horse's mouth, and prayed for the night to cool.

"We'll rest once we find the river," he called back.

"What river?" Guertin said

The river at the bottom of the mountain, my dear fellow. Or at least a stream where the snowmelt might collect.

Baptiste turned to face him. "Don't you trust me?" he said.

"Define what you mean by trust."

The mountain loomed in the distance, seeming to retreat with their every step. It was surrounded by an ocean of lava, interrupted by juts, cracks, and all manner of rough-mouthed caverns so sharp they ripped their buckskins. It was impossible to walk in a straight line, and in spite of the night the heat bloomed over them. They sucked on bullets to keep their mouths moist, but to scarce comfort.

"Getting a little tired," Ferris said softly, but like a fool Baptiste didn't listen to him.

One by one, their horses sank to their knees like ships in the waves.

Then Willoughby, a sailor who had been getting "smaller" and smaller out here, who for weeks had complained to them of the same hornet following him, buzzing around his head, made up his mind not to take another step. Before the Rendezvous, Willoughby was the first to complain of the cold and the first to respond to the heat. More recently he'd been silent, and for days there had been a strangeness to him.

"Charbonneau," Baptiste heard Willoughby's voice come from behind him in a whisper.

"Keep walking," Baptiste said. *Crazy sailor. If there really were a hornet around your head, it might lead us to vegetation.* A mile later Baptiste heard him fall.

"Who's that?" Ferris asked.

Guertin spat. "The tar."

When Baptiste reached Willoughby he could barely talk, but his hands were swatting and brushing, ready for the "hornet." "Tell my daughters," he said to Baptiste. Then he drew quiet, as if he were still in his salon in New Bedford and had enjoyed too much grog.

"You tell them," Baptiste said. "Get up."

"Let the poor man die," Guertin said.

"Quiet," Baptiste rebuked him. *Unkillable yourself, Guertin, you would be the one to survive and describe how I had "gone native" under pressure.*

"Tell me your daughters' names," Baptiste said to Willoughby.

"Drucilla," he said and looked at the ground between his legs. Not even insects made tracks in the "sand." "Phoebe."

Just at the thought of women, two more men sat. That left six of them, all staggering, their horses following listlessly behind.

"What do we do, chief?" Guertin taunted. He motioned to the seated trappers and scratched his chin.

"We're staying here," Emil Provincher said and slumped his back down to a seat against an overhanging rock.

"You can't," said Ferris. "It's only going to get hotter."

Baptiste felt relieved that Ferris had supported him until he looked at the New Yorker and saw madness in the whites of his eyes, which were sunken into his skull from dehydration.

"*No one* stays," Baptiste said, but four of them did not move. Having given up their motion, they were turning to stone. Ferris began to sit, but Baptiste pulled him up.

"Let's see what's on the other side of that rock," Baptiste said.

"Which rock?" Guertin said. He looked to where Baptiste pointed and then back at Willoughby. "I just want to rest," he said.

"There's plenty of time to rest in the grave," Baptiste said.

"Lousy Indian," Guertin said. "Fuck you. I'll knock you into your grave."

"That's the spirit," Baptiste said. "The rest of you, up!"

Everyone but poor Willoughby got on his feet. Baptiste walked back to him. "Out here in the desert? Is this your redemption?" Willoughby got up too and started walking. But two miles later, four of Baptiste's men truly could go no further. Stripping off their provisions for those they were leaving behind, the strongest of the party headed for a long, low acclivity, which on its summit revealed views of nothing. Now Baptiste felt the desert pulling him down. To move was to live.

"Let's go back," Ferris said, "the way we came."

"We can't," Baptiste said.

Lost. No one had said it yet. He refused to believe it. But they'd traveled far too long to reverse course. If they were to survive, new water would have to be found. "Each of us still able to travel will head out in a different direction. If one of us discovers water, shoot into the air and we'll all to try to meet you," Baptiste said. Once fortified, they'd return for the others and their horses, who could no longer continue in this rough terrain.

Even as Baptiste made this final assignment, the thirst was so wild in him he was laughing by the time he waved goodbye to Ferris, who waved back as his head disappeared beneath a crater's rim. And to think they'd seen snow the morning before. For his part, Baptiste was determined to walk directly toward the white mountain and so struck off in that direction. He crossed a neck of lava and climbed straight up a short slope, only to embark on a new ocean of lava much higher and wider than he'd been surrounded by before. *Good Lord, Baptiste,* he said to himself. *What have you done?*

He was alone with the black desert, his mother, and the moon. He also had his chew, the spruce sap that might as well have been the same black ball his mother always chewed, even after it rotted her teeth.

"Must you do that?" he remembered hearing Clark say to her in their little shack in St. Louis. Their voices had awakened him from his mat in the straw loft. He spied down through the transom and saw a shirtless Clark had brought one of Miss Julia's old dresses to his mother and was halfway through helping her put it on. His mother had taken the sticky wad out of her mouth and looked at it curiously, as if it were a jewel. She pretended to throw it away, palmed it, and slid it back in her mouth.

"Must you do that?" Clark coaxed more softly as she let his hands follow hers across the rosy slopes of her chest as if she were showing him the Lemhi Pass.

Baptiste continued walking in the dark, chewing his black spruce ball on the right side of his mouth to avoid the throbbing lower left molar where he'd chewed it the previous spring. Time seemed to flatten for a while, and when Baptiste heard a gunshot three or four hours later, far to his left, he wasn't an inch closer to his white mountain. He turned and raced up a rise to stare toward the sound, but he could see nothing. He took a step closer, but a soft voice told him that the water announced by the gunshot was too far away. He turned back toward the mountain, took another step, and fell as if for months, all the way into his own grave.

He woke the next morning and felt as though wasps were stinging his side as he rolled to a sitting position. Light slanted above his head and flickered on a lost tuft of green grass. At least it was cool, though there wasn't a trace of water. With his ribs knifing into his side, he struggled back up to the surface and wondered how long exactly he'd been unconscious. Could a whole day have passed? The light he'd seen slanting into the crevice was nothing more than moonlight.

Feeling desolately lonely and hungry, he walked aimlessly through seven nightfalls until, even as he stumbled along, he found himself in a dream. It was almost as if the desert melted around him and he could hear his mother's voice in the whispering pines. His mother was everywhere in the desert, reminding him how to think. The stars were crowded with her. As he stood in the darkness, a powerful memory flooded back to him about the time she told him to catch squirrels near Beaver Lake. He was six, and already able to track squirrels not only across dirt but over granite and shale.

When he returned with three squirrels in his kit, mischief was flashing in his mother's eyes.

"I have a little present for you," she said.

"Where?"

"Look for it in the valley of the great sachem."

Baptiste looked far and wide. There was no valley in sight. There was nothing but fennel grass blowing softly along the lake's edge.

He pointed toward a distant rise. "There? On the other side?"

She laughed and held her hand over her mouth as he headed to the wooded hill to investigate. But there was no valley there, either. He slinked back, very quiet.

"Do you like your present?"

Baptiste said nothing.

"What did you see?" she asked.

"There's no valley anywhere!" he cried.

"I didn't ask you what you *didn't* see."

With his mother smiling, he retraced his steps. He'd crossed a stream and skirted Beaver Lake, which was really just a large pond surrounded by slash pines.

"Over there I saw a beaver dam," he said slowly.

"What did the beavers tell you?"

For an instant his mother flashed a dark smile that would stay with him forever. He dove toward the center of the pond, which indeed had the shape of a valley in its crystal clear depths and now revealed its secrets. At the bottom of the pond a flash of metal caught his eye—a warrior's knife!—which he stroked toward and seized from the mossy surface of a large flat stone. Years before, he realized, a stream had run down the spine of the valley, but a lake had been formed when beavers had dammed it in order to trap salmon.

Splashing to the surface, he found his mother waiting for him at the shore. To her, indeed to anyone with second sight, the valley was both empty and full, its sparkling essence connecting past to future.

"Someday, when the beavers leave, the lake will be empty and this will be a valley once more," she smiled.

Sweetened with the shiny prize, this moment was Baptiste's first brief journey into the Fourth World. With more knowledge, he might one day track his mother there, to the place shaded from time.

"You can't hunt elk in the sea," she once teased, teaching him to be aware not simply of where elk are expected to be, but where they used to be, and where they might be in the future.

So it is with a younger man, who tracks his subtler selves into the unknown.

"But what shall I do now, Mother, in the middle of this desert?" he cried aloud, cradling his broken ribs, which hurt with every shallow breath. Then, as if whispered to him from her lips, the lesson bloomed in the night like a desert flower.

"Was the black lava desert always here, son?" he could almost hear her say.

"No," he said, and sat down suddenly, thinking. The blackness surrounding him had issued from the lips of a volcano, the lava spilling out into stone waves. These waves no longer moved, but instead stood before him like statues commemorating the event, which never would have ceased to announce itself in his mother's vision.

"Silly gosling, why are you walking *into* the waves, toward their source?" he nearly heard her giggling.

A single step against the direction in which the waves were "breaking" would only bring him closer to the center of the desert. But if he followed the waves, they would carry him to freedom.

Walking out with the waves, Baptiste wondered when he'd stopped paying attention to nature. He looked up at the stars, which zoomed over his head like swifts flying in a dark barn with the doors closed. Toussaint was right. How could he find his way if he "didn't know what animal he was tracking"? When he reached the river, he fell face-first into it, the mossy tentacles of river weeds seething all around him. He drank and —

First he thought it was a passing fish. Then "it" passed again and tickled his toes, the way his mother had done to him as a child. He ducked under the water, opened his eyes, and saw a glow. He could barely make out the suggestion of a face, then faces. In his euphoria, in the blackness of the river, hands flew around his shape. He felt no surprise, for he was in the Snake River, his mother's ghost embracing him in the form of river grasses.

How I miss you, ghost. I am so very lonely without you. I hope Ekaterina is with you, and my son.

He could feel the weight of her knife at his side.

After a while all was still. Baptiste splashed to the surface and drank with new appreciation the desert's enormous quiet. Filling his empty beaver skin with fresh water, he crossed the river, headed into the forest, and before long heard two people talking. He did not call out, but instead he glided closer.

Maybe forty other voices added their accents to the tiny crashings of small animals around him amid the *plink, plink* of water droplets falling from leaves in the night. In spite of his hunger and the still-bright pain in his ribs, he pushed down his need for a possible handout because he felt too weak, and at too much of a disadvantage, to determine if these people were friend or foe. Skirting around the voices, which he couldn't make out, he headed downriver a few miles, and, secure in his loneliness, fell asleep.

The next morning as he opened his eyes, he saw a white buffalo on the other side of the river, half invisible in the rising mist. Such a portent was so absurd he wouldn't even admit to himself that he'd seen it, but he blinked and found the chimaera still there. The buffalo was a calf, so light on his feet he almost skipped. When he caught sight of him, Baptiste rushed after him as he led the way through the forest. He was out of breath trying to follow, and felt crazy for so recklessly crashing after the calf, tracking him for hours until he saw his figure cross the top of a hill at sundown. Arriving at the same place, Baptiste looked down the embankment but couldn't find him on the other side. Instead he found a pool jumping with fish. He dined on salmon that night, then found it so cool and peaceful he decided to travel deeper into the woods. Presently, he heard voices and the sound of a fork scraping beans across a plate.

"Stupid Indian," he heard the damp voice of Lucien Fontenelle say as if he were addressing him. "You think he's still alive?"

"Eleven days?" he heard Dripps answer him. Then a silence yawned so indifferently over the conversation Baptiste wondered himself if he'd made it out alive. Was he looking across at them from the Fourth World?

"Jesus Christ made it for forty," Fontenelle ventured after a while.

"Much easier," Dripps said. "He had the Devil for company."

"Odd fellow, though," Fontenelle said. "Talking to him—"

"Is like shitting on a rock!" Dripps finished the thought. "I thought Indians were supposed to like the woods."

"Ferris is taking it hard."

"He'll get over it or he won't make it much longer, either."

In time the light of their fire illuminated Baptiste as he stood there. Dripps rolled over in his blanket and caught him with one eye. He sat bolt upright. Fontenelle trained his rifle at him and Baptiste stepped behind a tree.

"Who's there?" Dripps said.

"Who indeed?" Baptiste said.

He called his name out and returned to the light. "You boys save me any dinner?"

"We thought you were dead!" Dripps said.

"I thought I'd sleep out."

"Some guide you turned out to be. Everyone else found his way out a week ago and survived. In fact, you walked right past them. They're staying with a village of Injuns," Fontenelle said, "half-breeds and squaws working for the Hudson's Bay Company."

"Willoughby?"

Fontenelle nodded.

"Guertin, too?"

"You could have found them days ago."

"Mmmm," Baptiste smiled and looked into the fire. "Why aren't *you* with them?" he asked the two men. But to himself he wondered, *why has the white buffalo led me to such a circuitous rescue?*

"Somebody's got to do some trapping around here," Fontenelle said.

"American Fur doesn't pay us for a Sunday stroll."

He pointed to the branch of a tree, hung with a wall of lustrous black beaver pelts. Baptiste would have trapped as few himself on the way back to the mouth of the Porteneuf had he not been completely transformed by his time in the darkness. He trapped three times as many, with barely any effort. The animals seemed to fall in his path, rush toward the iron jaws of his traps set in white water below gushing streams.

After seeing the white buffalo, Baptiste's luck continued unbroken as he experimented with new insight with his rusty Newhouse No. 4s, placing them in far more creative locations than he'd thought to imagine before: slipped below the water's surface under fallen logs set with a light chain so that the beaver in his fury would pull the trap into deeper water and sink to the bottom, the start of an invisible cache for Baptiste in the heart of a pool or stream.

Beavers, so smart they delighted in springing known traps with a slap of their leathery tails, despised the sight of one of their own in a trap's steel grip. Thus warned, they'd avoid the same pool for weeks. With Baptiste's new method, other beavers and predators such as bears or wolves, who would otherwise have snapped up his beavers right from their traps, never saw what he had done until he'd whisked dozens of the dead at once from their watery grave.

For three winters he ran his line of traps for Rocky Mountain Fur alongside his fellow mountain men and fought hostile natives defending their ancient trapping grounds. This required a deliberate lack of self-reflection, but this was his job and survival was involved. As the months drifted by, he developed a language of nuance somehow more eloquent than any of the courtly manners he'd acquired in Europe as he lost himself deeper and deeper into the wild.

The things I'm forgetting, he realized with a pang one cold morning as he stored a new pile of furs in one of his many underground caches. It fascinated him. It was as poignant an experience to lose culture as it was to gain it. He imagined fields of daisies burned in flash-fire. It was very strange to be Jean Baptiste Charbonneau: things were raining inside him, whole symphonies lost.

Seasoned old timers scratched their beards as Baptiste grew still more adept at hiding souls under streams. Then one icy February he got the news that Guertin and Ferris were leaving American Fur to head back east, via Loup Fork and Fort Belle Vue. Baptiste was fifty miles away, trapping with Strawberry Duplessis the day they left, but he was hardly surprised at Ferris's departure. Ferris had grown tired of the life, and Baptiste suspected he'd been thinking of settling down.

Baptiste was far more surprised a few moons later when Jim Beckwourth and his wives entered camp with a pouch of his favorite *kinnikinic* and a small white package from St. Louis smudged with the cartouche of the Department of Indian Affairs, William Clark, superintendent. He broke open the seal and saw that it was not Clark who had written to him, but his son, in a letter resting atop something soft wrapped in tissue.

26

"REMEMBER"

—make the signs for HEART, and KNOW.

February, 1839

> *November the 23rd, 1838*
> *To Jean Baptiste Charbonneau,*
> *My Father's Ward,*
>
> *I Sincerely hope this parcel finds you well, if in fact It reaches Your Hand.*
>
> *I regret to inform you that My Father, having been grievous ill for sevral weeks, passed away verry peaceably on the seventh of October. Of late I have been much consumed in the administration of His affaires.*
>
> *He spoke of you in his Final Hours.*
>
> *Yours faithfully,*
> *Meriwether Lewis Clark.*
>
> *P.S. He wanted you to have These.*
> *P.P.S. Of the 11,183 items in my father's museum inventory, 11,181 are in the hands of a swindler in Sweden.*

Baptiste peeled back the tissue to have a look, knowing already the contents from their familiar shape.

"What've you got there?" Fontenelle said, shuffling forward.

"I will show them to you," Baptiste said, "in due course."

Baptiste knew that this deep in the wilderness, with no word from St. Louis in over three months, every package was a communal joy, however private. Each of the hunters felt close to the schoolmarm who corresponded with shy Strawberry Duplessis, who proudly read her letters aloud to them by firelight. They all wept with William Hazard Stevenson, the West Point graduate, when he, and therefore they, learned his sweetheart had married a rival. Now it was Baptiste's turn to share, though the contents of this package formed a hot knot in his throat.

"Come on now, don't be the *barceler* dog in the manger," Fontenelle blurted and nearly reached Baptiste's shoulder, but Beckwourth's large hand blocked further passage. Fontenelle wheeled on Beckwourth, who was twice his size.

"*Mon Dieu*, you've got some nerve! You and that stink you came in with. Just who do you think you are? I just wanted to see what a piece of tail sends an Indian," Fontenelle said.

"Oh, there's plenty of space on my mantel for another frog-eater's pate, or is it porcine flesh you dream of, *manger de lard*," Beckwourth shrugged, fingering the human scalps lining his deerskin tunic and sleeves, and glared at Fontenelle.

Fontenelle's eyes widened at the sight of the crusty talismans. Most had the greasy *aubergine* mane of Blackfeet, but some were wispy fair, and others were even red hanks. Beyond counting coups, the decorations reeked of European shibboleth: The section of skull carefully excavated was the same spot Stuttgart phrenologists labeled the center of self-esteem.

"From the smell of you, you're perfectly content to let your pork die of old age before you indulge," Beckwourth said.

"*You* stink like a black arse hole," Fontenelle countered weakly. Beckwourth's wives tittered.

"In very sooth," Beckwourth said. "I will kill you where you stand"— his malignant sentiments were undercut by a soft Virginia lilt that surfaced from deep in his boyhood, like dust on silver—"while I sit."

Fontenelle returned his knife to his belt. "I'd kill you back, but according to your lies, you've already been killed seven times!"

Baptiste lost track of them as he gently pulled up one corner of the tissue, as if his mother's heart had been sent to him in the box. Instead, an image from his childhood seemed to reflect a kind of firelight as he lifted out the soft string of the two dozen weasel tails his mother had presented to Clark during the Expedition as a sign of her devotion. In spite of the fact that he had a full cache of pelts, Baptiste plunged his face into their dusty depths to bring back his earliest days. He began to remember the second time he saw the tails. He couldn't have been more than five.

Sacagawea put her finger to her lips.

"*Come with me,*" *she said, and Baptiste followed soundlessly as she led him into the museum, where it was cool and dark.*

"*Are we allowed here?*" *he said.*

"*Quiet,*" *she said. Stealing past the rotting carcass of a pronghorn antelope drinking from a mirror and past the canoe suspended from the rafters, swinging in the dark, she took him to the far corner of the ell and stopped in front of Clark's secretary—a hinged box with brass fittings, a slanted top, a groove for his quill, and a recessed cup for his inkwell. It was the same piece of furniture she'd famously rescued when Clark's pirogue had capsized on the rapids of the Snake River during the expedition.*

A storm had rolled the pirogue in the currents, the desk crashing into the white water, its glass doors flapping and its contents floating away while

Clark pointed and screamed. The great Toussaint Charbonneau only shrugged his shoulders and without a shadow of concern watched it hit the rocks and splinter.

But with Baptiste still on her back, his mother plunged into the river and rescued several of Clark's notebooks, a sheaf of his charts, his bottle of snuff, even this secretary, which they pulled to the side of the rapids against a fallen tree.

The mahogany desk continued with them through the Lemhi Pass, the secret passage Sacagawea remembered from her childhood and revealed to Clark to take them through the Great Divide. Reflecting the firelight in its single remaining pane of glass, the desk adorned their love hut in Fort Clatsop. When they made it back to St. Louis, it was painstakingly repaired by Clark's slaves, a bright green coat of felt restoring its writing surface.

"It's dark in here!" Baptiste whispered again to his mother, who signaled for him to be silent. "I'm afraid."

Now, with great reverence, she squeaked open the bottom drawer of the secretary, where Clark still kept some of his surveying tools. Slowly, she pulled out the weasel tails, wrapped in a thin white tissue.

They felt softer even than living rabbits he'd petted. Clark kept the shutters of the museum closed to keep his specimens from rotting, so in the dusty gloom Baptiste and his mother could barely see each other as she put the tails around his neck.

"They feel so alive, Mother. But they are dead."

"Yes," she said.

"Why are you crying?" he asked, and she crushed him into her side and cried even harder, gasping deep breaths of air. From the other side of the ell light flashed from a door, and they saw the chalky cotton nightdress, the pallid face. No one had seen Miss Julia for weeks.

"What are you doing here?" Miss Julia's tinny voice said.

"Cleaning," his mother said, rushing Baptiste out through the side door.

"Cleaning," Miss Julia said thoughtfully. Then she brightened and stepped forward. "You were stealing!"

Sacagawea stopped, the weasel tails still in her hands. "No," she said. She ran to Miss Julia and dropped the furs at her feet. "Please do not tell Master Clark."

"I'll say what I like to my husband."

"No, ma'am, please!"

"Just go, then," Miss Julia said.

"Oh, thank you!" Sacagawea said.

But Miss Julia must have told, for that night Father Clark came crashing through the shack and spoke fiercely harsh with Sacagawea. Something changed between them, for Baptiste had never seen his mother hold her head so low. Through a crack in the loft floor he saw his mother shield her face, then defiantly return her hand to her side. Baptiste buried his face in his pillow.

"I'll give you my belt if you ever enter the museum without me again," Clark said.

"But that's good, Mother!" Baptiste told her when it was all over. "He owes you a belt in return for the one you had to give to the Chinook."

27

"SACRED"

—make the sign for MEDICINE.

Now Death had dropped the furs at Baptiste's feet. He stood before his peers in the firelight and turned the package over in his hands. He was thirty-four now, callused and muscled, though the lustrous weasel tails made him feel both young and small.

Looking at them, he realized their spirits might keep him awake at night. Slowly he walked around the fire.

"What the hell's in there?" Fontenelle asked, watching. "Is that just some old rat tails? I've got fifty better pelts than that in my sack. He might as well have sent you a pack of scats. We've got plenty of that around here, too."

Baptiste sidestepped him, walked to Beckwourth, untied the cured sinew that held the string of pelts together, and handed eight pelts each to Beckwourth's beautiful attendants. He put the final pelts into Beckwourth's possibles bag.

"Thanks for your trouble," Baptiste said to him. With his comrades gathered around, he read them the letter and told them of Clark's death.

"So," Beckwourth said, "the Voyage of Discovery is complete."

Baptiste grinned. "I'm still here."

Beckwourth fingered the weasel tails hanging around the neck of his shorter wife while the taller girl brought his pipe and more of the *kinnikinic*, that rare narcotic that made the world seem graceful and unhurried. All present sat down and smoked.

"It gives me pleasure to see my ladies enjoy being adorned by fur," Beckwourth said. "Even if it's these blasted relics."

"I didn't know you believed in luck," Baptiste said.

"How much gold do you want for the skins?" the King of the Crows kept on. "Or you could enjoy either of my girls in trade."

The younger of the two, the sinuous one who was unafraid to stare, smiled broadly at him.

"No," Baptiste said. "Instead, take me to my mother's grave."

"Why?"

"Because I have never seen it for myself."

It took them nine days to reach Wind River. En route they were visited by hundreds of Flathead Indians, still as sweet as when Baptiste and Sacagawea first encountered them in the company of Lewis and Clark. In fact, the Flatheads once again brought their visitors dog meat and buffalo tongues.

Under the eyes of the Sioux, Baptiste, Beckwourth, and his wives passed Clark's "boiling kettles," steaming just as they had when the Voyage of Discovery first passed them in 1805.

Near the Yellowstone River they walked past falls and geysers, clear evidence to Sacagawea's people they were of the supernatural. Wherever Beckwourth went, Baptiste knew, hundreds of Crow warriors stayed close by, a handsome people, many of them over six feet tall. Beckwourth would always be sacred to them, even though he had passed on his role of chief. They still felt the desire to protect him, though he frequently waved them away.

As a result Baptiste came to depend upon being followed: Whenever he stopped short or turned he braced for the cracked twig, the knowledge that all Nature was freezing in position.

"How did you earn their confidence?" Baptiste asked Beckwourth.

"I gave them mine," he said. "I fought with them. I love them."

That is how the entire party, the seen and the unseen, reached Sacagawea's grave on a rainy March morning as the fog rose from the river in two layers, one dark and one light.

"Can I see the grave from here?" Baptiste asked Beckwourth.

"You can see the garbage dump from here," Beckwourth said.

The King of the Crows smiled his toothy smile and with a Virginian flourish indicated the brow of a distant bluff. Behind the bluff was a fringe of plane trees with leaves turned upside down, silver in the wind, and behind them a puff of smoke. For a moment the walls of a fort appeared in the shifting fog. As if pulled by an irresistible force Baptiste started walking up the hill.

A twinge of regret slowed his steps as they approached the pile of stones that contained his mother's remains. The closer Baptiste got, the more he realized Sacagawea was neither above nor below the ground. Her spirit, slipping between stones and bones, was more space than matter. Other mounds interrupted the landscape here, too, all of them disturbed and kissed by the wind, which had crossed great distances to get here.

"This is where they bury the sick and the animals," Beckwourth said.

"I see." Baptiste had heard that the Mandan village had been wiped out by small pox, too.

"They bury the others inside," Beckwourth said. "The whites, I mean."

Beckwourth pointed to the stockade walls surrounding Fort Manuel, so diffused in the fog they half disappeared just fifty yards away. He squeezed Baptiste's shoulder. "Baptiste, my Washi friend, where would they bury *us?*"

"Half inside and half out," Baptiste laughed.

"I guess that would make us the strongest part of the wall."

Beckwourth turned to his women. "He is both night and day. Perhaps tonight you will be allowed to comfort the twilight man," he said as Baptiste shook his head. "Are you coming?" Beckwourth asked Baptiste as they headed toward the fort. The sachem Buffalo Black Fat, named for the prized, and most edible, hump of the sacred animal, was visiting the stockade; Beckwourth had business to attend to. Beckwourth's wives longed to see the ice house, "the place that steams," as well as try the port wine and other medicine that the fur companies kept for special envoys.

"I'll be there in a moment."

"All right, then," Beckwourth said. "You love your sorrow so much. Bury yourself out here."

Baptiste stood and watched them dissolve into the fog before looking back at his mother's stones. A recollection of the plague victims buried outside the Old Castle in Stuttgart swept over him like a dark cloud, but that gave way to the very clear image of Hector being dragged around the walls of Troy.

Priam had gone to Achilles afterward and begged for the return of his son's body, but no one had ever thought to bring Sacagawea indoors, not that her spirit would have desired it. Wolves in the hills behind Baptiste launched a deep, lonely howl, and he sank to his knees in exhaustion.

He must have slept, because in the flow of time he felt as though he were with his mother in St. Louis, following something glittering and alive along the edge of the river, darting just below the surface. *What is it, Mother? What do you see?* he kept asking. Then, as he awakened, a murder of crows took flight all at once, in a ripple, like a fusillade of gunshots or dark applause. *Yes, Haih, you are here.*

The wind picked up and it began to rain, first over the river, then over Baptiste. He rose, walked around the grave, and, about to leave, he stopped, noticing some dark brown skin between the stones. He felt a rush of cool air around him and a voice inside him cried *Po'an!—Don't look!* He cursed his bad luck, because a glimpse of the mortal remains of a loved one can bring about disastrous consequences from the Fourth World. He walked five steps away, but now that he had seen something, the ghost of seeing it gave him the responsibility to see more. All of a sudden it began to rain in big freezing chunks of hail.

The hail bounced all around him and around the two small stones he moved to find not his mother's skin but the absurdly overtooled European fancy boots that Toussaint had pulled off his feet while he slept in St. Louis. They were soft and mealy, the leather almost a paste. He pried one free and saw that sacred spices had been shoved into its toe, along with the skeleton of a whiskey jack, its wings cradled into perpetual flight through death's darkness. Was this a tribute to his mother, Bird Woman, from Toussaint, however too little and too late? He quickly put the boot back under the rock and hurried into the fort to find Beckwourth.

By the time Baptiste reached him, Beckwourth had completed most of his trading. Fort Manuel buzzed with the news of Clark's death. The port Baptiste drank was cool and took him back to the night he'd spent at the consulate in Le Havre. They suffered through a two-hour song by Buffalo Black Fat about the time girls burned the second penis Coyote carried around in time of need.

Then, over breakfast the next morning, Baptiste said to Beckwourth, "Do you know where my father is?"

Beckwourth shook his head and smiled, his wives giggling without knowing why. *Perhaps it is funny,* Baptiste reflected. *After all, Toussaint is a dear friend of Beckwourth's. Perhaps I am the funniest human being ever to enter the woods. Certainly I am the most naive.*

"I am surprised you've waited this long to ask," Beckwourth said.

"It's dangerous to hurry," Baptiste said in Mandan, quoting a hunting platitude.

"I think he's in Montreal," Beckwourth said. "We will accompany you as far as Lake Huron."

They left the next morning, with horses and an extended blessing from Buffalo Black Fat. Three snowstorms and one lost snowshoe later Baptiste bid goodbye to his friends and found himself in Ontario alone, on the other side of the Great Falls, which steamed and misted so that they appeared to be a captured animal thundering its alarm. The deliberate harnessing of magic haunted him: settlers measured and surveyed the infinite, cutting a stone staircase to fathom the depths of Niagara with ropes and chisels. Roads and sleigh tracks twisting out of nearby Chippewa showed the town was just a name and no longer a great Indian tribe. Wonders were vanishing. What would Beethoven say about his New World now?

Guarded and spooked by civilization after an absence of nine winters, he realized he was a target for thieves. With this in mind, he kept to himself, spoke as little as possible, and slept thirty yards "into the thicket" as he found the Fleuve St. Laurent and began to follow it east. He'd been in the woods so long no one was going to seal him into the bedroom of an inn or tavern. Besides, there was an abundant supply of muskrats, delicious over his fires under the stars, although with every step, the deep protection of the woods seemed to fall away.

As Mont Real loomed into view, Baptiste found trappers, drunkards, sundry knaves, and washerwomen who were only too happy to gossip to him about the great Toussaint Charbonneau and his present whereabouts. Like any hunter, he listened and revealed nothing.

Now, Toussaint, I know whom I am stalking.

Montreal, Toussaint's birthplace, was, as always, blood deep in fur. Baptiste knew that the incorporators had arrived here looking for a Northwest Passage to the East Indies but stopped when they saw the rapids of the St. Lawrence River and dared not venture farther.

In that way, Montreal was founded by cowardly jackanapes, a great race of hopeless whites and Métis amassing here and whirling about in high dudgeon and mock industry. Future generations would carry their anger and despair forever.

As he walked past the formidable stone *maisons* he marveled that in spite of this these people had managed to create something almost etched in time, a Paris in the far-northern wilderness.

He checked for Toussaint at the Hudson's Bay Company, but they hadn't seen him. Military authorities acknowledged hiring him from time to time but had no idea whose payroll he was on now. Then Baptiste found a couple who thought they'd seen him that morning on the way to the new cathedral.

"Where is it?" Baptiste asked. The man, who had thatches of black hair sprouting from his ears, laughed at seeing him so lost.

"That is like asking where is the moon. Do you see the building that towers above all else, down by the water?"

Baptiste had lost his eye for churches, his places of worship being in the woods, vaulting cathedrals where the tips of great trees met half-way to heaven.

"Oh, yes. *Oui. Merci,*" Baptiste said softly, wondering how his French sounded and why the man's wife kept staring at him. *Is it because I asked for Toussaint? How had the old reprobate tricked her, or what has he stolen from her?*

He walked slowly down the *rue* to the structure that seemed to be

lowering itself into the river. Like a European cathedral, it was con-
structed of stone heavy enough to sink all of Montreal into the St.
Lawrence. The building loomed larger and larger as he approached.
He creaked open the black walnut door, lit a votive candle, and stole
noiselessly through Notre Dame, designed after the original in Paris,
toward the Latin-inscribed altar in the distance. Solitary figures bent
over and prayed everywhere. A priest polishing a brass incense burner
told him Toussaint had been there earlier.

"Can you show me where he was sitting?"

"Why, on earth?" asked the priest.

"Can you show me?"

Baptiste found the place on the pew still warm and prayed before the
enormous stained glass window of the *son et lumiere*. Carved angels
and gold-leaf *fleurs-de-lis* beckoned from the spirit world. Dead bishops
resisted the temptation to twitch. The confessional was empty. And
yes, he could smell Toussaint, his *asmodeus diabolos* stench an alchemy
of necrotic gums, piss-tanned leather, and regurgitated rum. It amazed
him Toussaint was able to surprise any animal with that spoor.

"How long was he here?" Baptiste called to the priest.

"I cannot remember," he said.

"Did he say he was coming back?"

"He always comes back."

Baptiste returned the next day. Two feet of snow had fallen during
the night, so it was easy to recognize Toussaint's satyr-like gait as his
tracks led into the cathedral, even among the multitude of *caleche* ruts,
hoof prints, and footprints from crowds flocking to mass. He watched
the exit door carefully as the congregation spoke to the dead. When he
finally picked Toussaint out he was deep in prayer. It was the only time
in his life he'd seen Toussaint without his buckskins on. Instead the
trapper wore the shadow of a shadbelly beneath a frock coat trimmed
in cracked sealskin. Baptiste crept to the bench behind him.

"I've come for my boots," he said, leaning forward.

"I am praying for you, *mon fils*," Toussaint said and looked back at him as if they were in the midst of a conversation they'd begun long ago.

All around them were stained glass *Taipo* with their hands resting on the shoulders of brown Indian children with romanticized features. The benevolent settlers were depicted as rescuing the pathetic creatures from the woods. One of the saved was a maiden with coral lips and small breasts just beginning to swell. *Maybe Toussaint was first aroused here to become my mother's savior,* Baptiste thought.

"Why do you pray for me?" Baptiste asked, slumping down beside Toussaint as the crowd began to trickle out to the mournful strains of the great pipe organ.

"You must show a little more respect in church, *mon fils*," Toussaint said before bowing his head for a final prayer.

Baptiste counted pews, seventy-seven of them. He could have guessed at the number in the second balcony, but that would be speculating and in a building like this there was too much speculating already. He had seen cathedrals far more grand in Europe and far more holy in the woods, but in spite of this he was moved by a profound connection to the souls who had celebrated milestones here: birth, the taking of the host, marriage, death. *How long does music stay in a room?* Ekaterina's question floated back to him, and as he looked up into the rafters he contemplated again that music never leaves the walls but instead seeps into the mortar between each stone.

Toussaint looked up and followed Baptiste's glance above the transept into the broken colors of the stained-glass windows. "The man who designed this building was so proud of what he'd done he wanted to be buried under it when he died," Toussaint said. "At first they refused him. So he converted."

Baptiste shrugged.

"Now he has his ecstasy, below us."

Baptiste wondered if the man were sealed directly below him and how many feet of stone separated them.

"How good of you to come share a prayer with me, *mon fils.*"

When Toussaint stood, Baptiste stood too. Toussaint was at least seventy winters now, but he walked vigorously up the aisle, genuflected as he left the church, and without a word entered into the quiet snow. Baptiste walked at his side: father, son, his mother the Holy Ghost.

"I always pray for you," Toussaint said. "Because you seldom laugh. Because your mother died before she could give you your medicine, or tell you how to get it."

Suddenly Toussaint straightened as if he had a pain in his back. They stood together and waited for it to abate.

"Why do you think you are so lonely, Baptiste?"

"I don't know, Father."

"Do you know the black rocks?"

So he must have heard about my exploits in the lava desert.

"Do you know the hanging waterfall?" Toussaint asked.

You mean Clark's and my mother's trysting spot.

"There is a little box canyon beyond the waterfall, near the river. Do you know it?"

"There is no such thing."

"Your mother told me to tell you about Coyote's canyon. Coyote saw people throwing their eyes up into a tree in the center of the canyon. Coyote asked them why they were throwing their eyes into the tree. 'It's fun,' they said. 'We can see farther. Try it.' Coyote believed them, so he threw his eyes into the tree, too, up into the leaves, hoping to see things he'd never seen before. But his eyes never came back to him, and the people ran away. It doesn't ever rain in Coyote's canyon. There is rain shadow alone because the rock walls are so high. You should go there."

"If only it existed," Baptiste smiled.

"I'll tell you where it is. A secret stone lets you in."

"All right," Baptiste said. "Tell me where the canyon is."

"Have pity on your old man. First something for my parched throat," Toussaint said.

Toussaint took Baptiste to an inn below Saint-Amabile on Rue St. Paul, where Baptiste paid for the desired spirit and watched the Frenchman down half a bottle so quickly he didn't bother to take off his coat.

"Won't you join me, *mon fils?*" he said. Toussaint sat down abruptly at a small table near the fireplace and coughed up some phlegm, which he dabbed back into his mouth with a dirty handkerchief.

"I didn't come here to drink," Baptiste said and sat across from him. Toussaint's coat was sweet with the scent of puke. Oddly, he looked hurt.

"It is a *tavern, mon fils*," Toussaint said, paying no notice to the inn-keeper, who'd kept his eyes on them since their arrival. *"Aux belles femmes des bois."*

"I know every inch of the land below the Snake near the boiling kettles," Baptiste said. "I tell you there is no box canyon there."

"It was where your mother went to get her gift."

"Women aren't allowed gifts," Baptiste said of Shoshone tradition.

"As a young girl, she saw where the elders took her brother Cameahwait for his ceremony. She went alone the next day. You must go alone. I will tell you the rock to move where you will find the opening. Ha! You are not so slim now, *mon fils*, but you might still just barely slip inside. Descend through the snow until you find a place like summer. There you will find a small lake. Swim out to the middle and you will find a little island. Fall asleep there. A funny flower will make a hissing sound."

"*A geyser*," Baptiste corrected him.

"A funny flower. It is dark red. Put some skins by the flower and go back to sleep. The flower will emit a great light that will reach out to the heavens. Go to the flower in the morning. Beside your flower you will find your magic. Put it in your belt and swim home."

Baptiste turned away as Toussaint began to scratch at some nits in his crotch, the only hygiene the old trapper practiced regularly.

"*Caulisse!*" Toussaint said. "How they torment me." He appeared to catch a specimen and held it up to his squinting eye. Upon seeing this, the innkeeper strode up to them with a purple face, shaking his head and checking furtively to make sure no other patrons could see.

"Goodbye, Father," Baptiste said. He stood up.

Toussaint stood up, too, brushing himself off while Baptiste warded off their host with three shillings. Just then two Micmac children waved to them through the window.

"Look!" Toussaint said and waved back. "Your new stepmothers!"

Baptiste came outside with him to meet Toussaint's wives. The taller of the two might have been thirteen. She was nearly Baptiste's height, with thin shoulders, a long waist, and tangled black hair. She had no front teeth; a bruise in blue and mulberry ran from her left eye to the back of her ear. The younger girl was eleven and barely Ekaterina's height. *No wonder that monster spends so much time in church,* Baptiste thought.

"What have you got?" Toussaint asked Baptiste as the silence expanded, as if it were part of the greeting process.

"Here," Baptiste said, giving him what little made his pocket too heavy. "Give it to your wives before the crabs devour the rest of you."

"Eh? Is this all you have?" he said.

Baptiste explained he had to get back to his killing. But he did have a final question.

"Why did you put my shoes under the stones?"

"Eh, what?" Toussaint said.

Baptiste stood still, refusing to repeat it.

"How you love the dead," Toussaint complained, then stared at him. "*Mon fils*, I hope I am never as old as you. Go back to your mother."

"Goodbye," Baptiste said again. *Goodbye, liar. I may be your issue, but I don't have to believe in you or your mythical canyon. Look at the bruises on your wives. They move in blue and green storms across their skin. How deep must I hide in the woods to make sure I don't become you?*

28

"KILL"

—bring right hand in front of right shoulder, hand nearly closed; strike forward, down, and a little to left, stopping hand suddenly.

February, 1842

No one could remember a winter this unrelenting. Throughout its coldest months, Baptiste worked at Bent's Fort, Colorado, for the firm of Bent and St. Vrain, furriers. After three straight days of sunshine teased with hope for an early spring, Ceran St. Vrain asked Baptiste to take a message to St. Louis.

"Right away," Baptiste smiled, sensing an opportunity to visit his old haunts while getting paid handsomely for it. Just over two months later, after fishing at some of his favorite spots along the way, he covered the last few miles into the city.

By day, the thirty-seven-year-old toured the growing metropolis, amazed that it had once again doubled its size. By night, he had some other touring in mind.

He stole up to Lottie's oak tree, slipped over to the water pump, crossed the overgrown yard and the white house with its paint peeling, and approached the ell. He tried the door of the Museum of Human Beings, but its hinges were rusted shut. *How strange it is to be back here.* The last time he'd been here, he hadn't known the feeling of spending months, years in the woods. He was barely more than a child with a pistol in his hands: the Duke of Madagascar. Still on tiptoes, he peered into a window. As always, it was black as a lake inside. But this time the lake had four corners and was neatly swept up. Apart from a little moonlight picking out the edges of a few floorboards, the interior of the Museum had disappeared, save for the single secretary that had once held the weasel tails in its bottom drawer.

"Well, there's item 11,182," Baptiste mused. *What had the Swede done with the others?*

Drifting back into town, he found the Astoria Bar still open and some of the old hands around ready and willing to solve the mystery.

"Turned out Clark, afore he died, loaned 'em, though some say he lost 'em in a card game, to a skunk named Albert Koch, who was after Clark to take all that stuff on a tour of Europe. Now the whole kit's been missing five years. His son, Meriwether, can't do a thing about it. Try as he might, he hasn't been able to sue Sweden to get some of his possessions back. Why do you ask? You figure you got a claim?"

"I've got a claim to this glass and the rest of this bottle," Baptiste said pensively. "Assuming you don't want some of it yourself."

Already in his cups, he kept drinking until the tavern emptied and he found himself alone. Rain outside lashed against his face, but he was too far gone to care, so he weaved along Jefferson Avenue, cutting right after deciding he wanted to see the reflection of the North Star in the water. It was well after midnight before he realized that in his selfishness he hadn't seen Lottie or thought to ask after her. The Clark compound had been emptied of all souls, regardless of pride or privilege, so where could she be? *Everyone's lights are out; I can ask about her tomorrow,* he thought. Besides, he felt sleepy after wandering to the top of a desolate hill in sight of the big white house in the rain. Actually he didn't remember exactly when he fell into a deep asleep.

When he awoke at dawn, he realized with a sense of guilt and dread that his inebriated footsteps had guided him to the slaves' graveyard. He jumped to his feet, unnerved by the bad *poha.* Before the very spot where he'd come to rest was a cross rudely carved with Lottie's name, age, and death date of a year before. Even then she seemed to be taunting him, because above her lonely appellation the words *At Last, Free* were scratched into the cheap poplar. He let out a lonely howl.

"Good for you, Lottie," Baptiste said in a rough voice and wept as the sun showed its first rays over the river.

Someone else had spoken for Lottie, so Baptiste determined that while he was alive he would do what he could to secure justice for his mother. That night, dusting off his most eloquent English with a courtly hand at campfire, he penned his first letter to the Department of Indian Affairs in Washington, demanding restitution for Sacagawea's unpaid services as a guide and early death under the "supervision and care" of Clark. *Only money has resonance with the Taipo,* he remembered.

> *To the Director of the Department of Indian Affairs,*
> *Plenipotentiary for the President of the United States*

Baptiste licked the nib of his pen and dipped into his bottle of ink, shaking it to allow a few dark drops to sink into the moss beside his piece of vellum.

> *Dear Sirs, I write to you as the surviving heir of Sacagawea,*
> *the Shoshone guide commissioned for services by the Lewis*
> *and Clark Expedition, who proved invaluable to them in . . .*

He stopped and blinked back a tear. Then he ripped up the page and started with a fresh one:

> *It is a sad truth that the conquered idolize their conquerors.*
> *How rarely do we demand the justice we deserve? My*
> *mother, Sacagawea, has been dead for thirty years, and the*
> *great injustice visited upon her as the shining guide who*
> *led Lewis and Clark to the Pacific grows larger with each*
> *passing day, hour, minute . . . The government of the United*
> *States paid $15 million for what is now being called the*
> *Louisiana Purchase, and yet not a cent was ever directed*
> *to her or her estate to recognize the efforts, the risks, and*
> *unrequited bravery she displayed in revealing the wonders of*
> *that wilderness to the Voyage of Discovery at the most terrible*
> *of personal costs . . . When establishing the price of her*
> *contributions, should one not therefore ask himself, what was*
> *the price of Lewis and Clark's survival?*

With this, Baptiste jotted down a simple invoice for $500.33, the same amount awarded to Toussaint, and "the sum of seven thousand dollars" in restitution for her mistreatment and early death. Sealing the letter with hot melted wax and impressing it with the grand escutcheon of the royal family of Württemberg—unmistakable for the roots at its base surmounted by palm leaves at its crown—he handed it to a trapper heading back into town. *How refreshing an act of futility can feel,* he mused before slipping back into the forest.

In the months that followed, when St. Vrain twice assigned Baptiste to escort adventurers and their parties from Bent's Fort to St. Louis, Baptiste told his charges he didn't want to continue into the city, that there were still a few fish he hadn't caught in the lower Missouri.

"What? You've led me near a thousand miles to get here safely, but you don't want to spend a few nights in a warm bed?" a fellow named Leeds begged of Baptiste, the steeples of St. Louis in sight.

I had enough of warm beds in Europe, Baptiste thought.

"Let me at least buy you a drink," Leeds said.

They'd made the trip in a record sixty days, carrying pelts especially chosen by the Crow nation for the wife of Henry Clay.

"No," Baptiste said. "I've already seen St. Louis." He stretched. "Now, buy my furs," he said of the personal stock he'd brought along to trade in addition to the Crows' present for Mrs. Clay.

"I have my own to worry about," Leeds said.

"Not at this price."

Baptiste sold him his pelts at a discount and handed him a letter stuffed with money to post for Lizette.

Baptiste's reputation as an eccentric spread, but he barely cared. He spent weeks alone, courting death in forbidden territory, trapping for beaver in streams belonging to the Blackfoot tribe between visits to Bent's Fort for a swig of port and the chance to swap yarns with Jim Bridger, the illustrious arrowhead "patient" at the Rendezvous. Then, when he least expected it, Baptiste earned a promotion of sorts when he was commissioned to lead the expedition of Sir William Drummond Stewart as chief guide.

He and Bridger were placed in charge of seventy men, including Captain Ben Bonneville, a West Point graduate who'd "overstayed his leave" from the army and was enchanted into the woods, and Washington Irving, who still could learn nothing and listened to no one out there. Stewart had selected Baptiste out of sentimentality, but most of all because, as Stewart liked to say, he was "the only Injun who could hold his liquor" well enough to give lessons in tracking and signing during the hunt.

Stewart, seventh baronet of Murthly and nineteenth Lord of Grandtully, was tall, thin, wore a black cape, and had long black hair and a black moustache which he grew into a dramatic black beard. His stories of Murthly Castle in Scotland, in which he starred as a terrible rake, entertained them all, particularly Father DeSmet, the besotted Catholic missionary who enjoyed addressing thousands of Indians who could not understand him, and Jim Beckwourth, who appeared in camp at odd intervals and swept through them with his presence, like rain.

The first day Baptiste guided Sir William on a hunt he thought of Ekaterina instructing him on waltz steps in the silence of the Old Castle. In both still-hunting and dancing there is a quarry, and as heady as a German *schottishe* or a date with an elk might be, they must never be rushed.

WE'RE MOVING TOO QUICKLY, Baptiste signed to Sir William, who refused to sign back to him but instead plunged ahead to make a little nest for himself in the grass. WE MUST MOVE VERY SLOWLY THROUGH THE WOODS.

They'd traveled too rapidly and too far along the Snake River, advancing through the brush, disappearing into bushes, and sliding behind trees with only an hour elapsing while they'd covered at least three hundred yards. Otherwise, they'd done well, the sun at their backs and fading. They were hunting upwind, so their prey couldn't smell them. The light was gray, that time of the day when deer half invisibly step out of the semi-darkness to feed.

Baptiste scanned the woods for horizontal lines breaking the vertical lines of the trees. And then they saw them. *Five, with more following.* Without giving them a chance to approach, Sir William swung his rifle round and fired, missing the deer as if they were ghosts.

"What did you say?" Sir William asked Baptiste from inside a cloud of smoke.

DON'T SHOOT YET, Baptiste signed.

"But a deer already saw us," Sir William said.

Actually, close to twenty had seen them. Baptiste moved so close to Stewart he could count the black hairs in his nostrils. Baptiste's buckskins were comfortable, relatively waterproof, and quiet for this excursion. But Stewart's equipment clacked as if he were a party of surveyors. The deer had bounded out of view long before Stewart pulled the trigger.

"Watch the woods, not the deer. Besides, 'that' wasn't your deer," Baptiste said.

"What on God's earth do you mean he wasn't my deer?"

Stewart had insisted upon wearing his tam-o-shanter, not to mention bringing along a supply of his beloved Scotch whiskey, which clanked with his every step. Now he stood up, towering over the crouching Baptiste, hands on hips, impatient. Behind him, two does and a fawn skipped safely to cover.

"You think the world is your deer," Baptiste laughed. Stewart had been a lieutenant in the 15th King's Hussars and fought at Waterloo as a young man. He'd been highly decorated and been made a captain at just twenty-two.

"I realize Scotsmen deserve praise for their conspicuous gallantry," Baptiste said and stood himself, dropping any pretense of still hunting, "but there is such a thing as being—"

"I am, sir, a brutish, inconspicuous Scot." Stewart swigged from his bottle and handed it to Baptiste. The twig Stewart stepped on made such a loud report that a fox bounded into the woods from across the river. His next step dislodged a pebble which rolled down the bank, plopping into the water.

"We are a British Marching Band," Baptiste said.

"Nothing British about it."

"Your clothing must be quiet, sir."

As if to silence it, Stewart smoothed his metal canteen. As he did, the sun flashed off its surface and knocked a woodpecker out of a tree. But there were still fresh deer tracks, and deer sign, around them. In spite of everything, something could still happen right now, at dusk. The beauty of the woods was that something was always about to happen.

"You can't just walk," Baptiste said. "You might as well beat the bushes. You are driving your game away through the woods."

"Have it your way, Baptiste."

"Put your weight down slowly, with each step."

"Like this?"

"Like this," Baptiste said. "All right. Now what are you looking for?"

"The deer?"

"No. You are watching the woods. You can't watch for something you haven't seen. Think of what you miss when you see a single star. You are looking for horizontal lines, because they might be deer sleeping. A deer's back is horizontal, while the trees, and all this grass, are vertical. Look around more, and try to sense a break in the pattern. Move slowly and stop more often. Avoid rub lines. When you see a perfect place to move, stand still."

"Funny way to hunt."

"It worked in Lexington and Concord."

"Not my assignment, old man."

"It's the only way to hunt. Otherwise, they'd call it killing, or catching. You have to surrender your desire for the result. You are not here to kill a deer today."

"I'm here instead to kill my Indian guide."

"Don't look up."

"All right, I won't."

"I mean, don't move your head. Instead, look up with your eyes. Do you see him?"

Stewart's eyes bulged and his hollow cheeks turned purple. His back straightened and he craned his neck so Baptiste could see the tip of the black birthmark on his neck creep over his collar.

"Don't move," Baptiste said. "He'll come farther out the branch."

"We've got to shoot him!" Stewart said.

"We have not got to shoot him," Baptiste said. "He hasn't made any mistakes yet."

The puma advanced without a sound toward the edge of the branch, which bowed under his weight. He was nearly ten feet over their heads. As his eyes met Baptiste's he knew he'd made his mistake. He yowled and sprang, and the sky became black with his shadow. The cat flew through the air, an easy target. It was very difficult for Baptiste to keep his knife at his side and wait for Stewart to raise his rifle and catch the beast just two feet overhead. In fact Baptiste had to dive to the right at the last possible moment. The cat hit the ground, dead, where he'd been standing. Stewart's bullet had found its home, and so had Baptiste's knife, quite unseen by his charge.

Baptiste hummed a short song for the puma while the elated Stewart circled the cat and prodded him with his rifle barrel. Then Stewart sat on a flat rock and finished his first flask of Scotch. The cat's soul steamed out of him, as if to join the mist collecting over the river. Baptiste had brought his own supply of spirits, and he joined Stewart for a drink, hunters through whiskey and glass.

"My seventh cat," Stewart said, "but my first in America. Funny how they're dappled when they're young," he said, looking closely at the cat's dark gold fur, the black tips on his ears. "Then the spots disappear. What is he, twelve feet long with that tail?"

Half an hour later as he hefted the cat's dead weight onto his back, Baptiste joked, "I know you're disappointed about missing your deer."

"Yes," Stewart said. "Where do you think my deer is now? Will he follow us and watch?"

"No. But you have seen him. You will always be with him. It will cause him to do different things. In a way he really *is* your deer."

"Do you think he's rejoined his herd?"

"Yes, but his life has changed. Maybe you saved him from the cat."

Blood rolled out of the puma's mouth, so Baptiste adjusted the way he carried him around his neck, holding his rear legs below his right arm, his forelegs below his left.

Baptiste must have half imagined it, but he believed he could hear the puma's heart beating, not all the time but sometimes. The cat, hunting them, had almost covered them in his jump. Baptiste looked at the trees surrounding camp, drinking in the sound around their tents.

He kept waking all night. He went out and dressed the cat, his wounds very loud around him. But they would not drown out his heart. The morning after, he could still hear it, even after the cat was skinned.

Butchering the puma was such a private act that Baptiste and Sir William kept their distance for a few days. In the meantime, there were other members of the expedition to divert their host: Ludwig Banf, "a bug hunter," according to William Sublette; Rorik Seden, an expert on birds; even two Cuban noblemen, all invited here by Sir William as guests. But late one night at campfire, warmed by Old Orchard, Sir William asked Baptiste to tell a Shoshone tale beneath the Algerian tent he'd ordered them to pitch for him. No one since Ekaterina had been curious enough to ask for a tale, so Baptiste stirred the ashes of his memory and out popped the Monster Owl.

"A young Shoshone brave was stolen from the land of his people by the Monster Owl, who carried him across the great sea to a city made of bleached human bones. The young brave yearned to go home, so he spoke to the owl: 'Oh, Mighty Owl, this is a place of death, and after I'm gone there will be nothing left for you to eat. On the other side, where I come from, in the lush nights, there are giant mice that run free in great herds through the sweet grass—bright blood rushing beneath their hides. Let me show you.' Ignoring him, the owl drew closer and bared its claws, so the brave said, 'Oh, Mighty Owl, I forgot to tell you, the mice are all blind, so they will not see your great shadow under the moon. Let me show you.' Sensing that the owl was still not convinced, he cried, 'Oh, Mighty Owl, I forgot to tell you, the mice are also all deaf, so they won't hear the rustle of your great wings as you swoop from the top of the tree. Let me show you.' So the owl relented and took him back across the water. No sooner had the brave touched down on his native shores than a great eagle descended from the heavens, and with one slash of his cruel talon snatched the owl up into the sky and carried him away. 'Oh Mighty Owl,' the boy sang after him, 'I forgot to tell you, we have Beya Qee Na here, too!'"

There was silence across the campfire before Stewart slapped his knee and guffawed. "That's a fine story! Where'd you learn it?"

Baptiste took a minute gathering his thoughts. He stared over the flames. "Sir William, have you met Duke Paul of Württemberg?"

"Well, yes, I saw that shit-eating, boxheaded Hun in New York, at the docks. He was returning to Germany." He paused. "He had a young Assiniboine with him, maybe fifteen. The boy's eyes were very wide."

The Assiniboines are from the Dakotas, Baptiste thought. *How did Duke Paul make it this far and back without my detecting it? How has this eluded me?*

"Was there an artist with him?"

"A lot of people. I can't remember." Sir William stretched and turned his head. "Your boy, stolen by the giant owl. Whatever happened to him?"

Baptiste stood up. "I'll let you know."

"It is a damn fine children's story," Stewart said, "but we're not children."

"Well, you're the one who asked for the story," Baptiste said.

Among the guides Baptiste managed for Sir William was the youngest son of William Clark. Callow Captain Jefferson Kennerly Clark, just eighteen, had red hair like his father and stood even taller, the resemblance strengthened by translucent skin which made him look like a wax figure. Jefferson had been born to Clark's second wife while Baptiste was in Stuttgart and, like his father, was all but blind in the woods. *What has sent him out here?* Baptiste thought. After a day-long buffalo hunt, Baptiste assigned him to the watch and visited him later that night, carrying him some dinner from their fresh kill.

"Jefferson," Baptiste called. The boy jumped so high he blushed brightly by the time he came down. "I brought some food."

Young Clark nodded and took the fire-charred tin. Behind them a hanging valley lay in darkness, and in the distance Baptiste thought he could hear a narrow waterfall. Clouds scudded in from the east, their hulls dark. Even though he could not see them he could hear a flock of ducks taking off low to the water, and he felt his mother close by.

Be kind to him, Baptiste. Only a coward lords his superiority over another.

"Might rain," Baptiste said, as if they were chatting in St. Louis. As if twenty years hadn't passed since he'd been part of Father Clark's world. Young Clark kept his eyes on his plate, as if he'd lost something on it. Like his father he had blue eyes, and he was also heir to his father's slender blue hands.

"You did well on the hunt today," Baptiste said.

The youth seemed comfortable in the silence that followed, though Baptiste often heard him laughing with his friends in camp. He was not a spiritual soul to judge from appearances, and he never parted from the intimates he had among the young trackers.

"Have you any word from St. Louis?" Baptiste asked him.

"I suppose Meriwether'd write, if I ever wrote him," young Clark said. "You must have many letters, from him and my father, from before. Father was such a voluminous correspondent!"

"Truly," Baptiste said.

He lit his calumet and took a few puffs. It was very dark now, and out of the distance he could feel the wind rise. He handed his pipe to Clark, who took a small puff before quickly returning it to him.

Baptiste paused. "Did your brother ask you to come out here?"

"No."

"Good Lord, Jefferson. Why did you come then?" Baptiste stared deeply into his eyes. This boy didn't look lucky. *After a while you got to tell the lucky ones, the ones who could get killed seven or eight times, like Beckwourth.*

"Money's good." Unlike Father Clark, Jefferson had a quick smile.

"Yes, the money!" Baptiste laughed. "It's wonderful. But none of us is expected to live to spend it."

"He used to talk about you," young Clark said as if gently settling a beaver trap into the rapids.

"Your father?"

"Yes."

"In what respect did he talk about me? I do not remember him as a talker."

"He said you are the last member of the Voyage of Discovery. He said I could do worse than to follow your example, even though you hate him in your heart."

"What did he say exactly?"

"That you blamed your mother's death on him. That you went crazy. That you went tracking her into the woods, even though she's dead. That I might learn from you."

"He said I was . . . what?"

"Like your mother. That's why Toussaint took her back to Fort Manuel. That it runs in your family. You went crazy in Europe. Then you came back and tried to kill him. What happened that night?"

"Nothing happened that night."

"You don't seem crazy."

"You don't know me very well," Baptiste said.

"Well, it's your business," he said. "I'm new out here."

Jefferson's relief appeared behind them, out of the night. "Who's there?" the relief's voice said.

"Just us, Pickering."

"Well, you can stay out here if you want to," Pickering said.

"No," Baptiste said. "Your turn now. It's getting late." He and Clark stood up.

"Anything out there?" Pickering asked.

Owl was out there. Coyote, too, blinded by the girls. Wolf was out there. He put many nights in a buffalo bag and when Coyote looked once he fell in. Baptiste's mother was out there, and a few miles away there was a lake with a small flower in it that opened when no one was looking and every so often sent a brilliant flame into the stars.

29

"SOLDIER"

—bring closed fists in front of breast, thumbs touching. Then separate hands horizontally.

January, 1843

It was the day after a wolf moon, with a partial eclipse staining the upper half of the lunar surface like tea. "Baptiste," Sir William Stewart asked as their horses walked through the snow. They had come to the end of their hunt together. "Have you ever been to Scotland?"

"No, sir."

"You must come! I'll take you from Edinburgh to Inverness via Stirling."

Baptiste shook his head.

"Last time I went home I brought a single buffalo," Stewart said. "But this time we will enter court with half a dozen buffalo and twice as many braves. We will take bobcats and Canadian tufted lynx. Never will there have been such a spectacle."

"It sounds wonderful, Sir William."

"So you will come?"

"Oh, no, thank you."

On his sorrel ahead of them, Kit Carson repacked his *kinnikinic* and spat.

"Why on earth not?" Bill Stewart persisted.

"I just don't need to go," Baptiste said.

"But why?" Stewart said.

Later that night, at supper, Sir William kept prodding him until, frustrated, Baptiste replied, "Must I invent a reason?"

"Yes."

They all must have been drunk. Baptiste pulled a buffalo skin over his head, stood up, and looking through the slits in its eyes pronounced in a low voice, "I will tell you, Scot, since you are of that ilk. You are a dark, addled people, still angry at being conquered. You have been weakened ever since the English stole your Stone of Destiny from Edinburgh Castle and hid it in Westminster Abbey. For nearly six hundred years, none of you has had the daring or the ambition to try to steal it back. Sir, I have to take Samuel Johnson's opinion on the matter when he says, 'Let me tell you, the noblest prospect which a Scotchman ever sees is the high road that leads him to England.'"

"Spiffing, you're thinking about it," Sir William said. "I'll ask you again tomorrow."

"Sir, if Scotland's so beautiful, what are you doing here?" old Emil Provincher asked.

"I'd like another mint julep," Bill Stewart said. They all enjoyed the beverage, fresh with the wet leaves Baptiste had sent young Captain Jefferson Kennerly Clark to fetch near the source of the Wind River.

"I am grateful to you, sir, for asking me," Baptiste said far too late, provoking a scowl from Stewart, "but I really can't go."

Kit Carson spat. They all got under their hides to go to sleep. Half an hour went by. Then Carson sat up. "Bill. What the hell is a Stone of Destiny?"

Four years and many trapping expeditions later, in Bent's Fort, Baptiste ran into his old friend Bridger.

"I'll buy you a drink," Bridger said, "that is, if they serve Injuns here at the bar."

"The Indians here built the bar," Baptiste said.

"You know, Stewart left right after you," Bridger said. "Just like a Scot to get bent out of shape over a rock."

Baptiste said nothing.

"Remember Clement, the half-breed with the dark brow from Montreal?" Bridger said. "Damned if he and six of his old clan didn't go all the way to Scotland with Stewart."

Baptiste laughed. "Now there's a show." If Stewart was looking for another moody Métis to substitute for him, he'd made a sly choice. *How long did it take Stewart to realize Clement was just the sort you'd never want to show off in Scotland, or anywhere else?*

"Provincher, too," Bridger said. "St. Vrain told me they left from New York and sailed to Glasgow, all in buckskins and Hudson's Bay blankets."

"Interesting they thought to show the flag." Neither Baptiste nor Bridger had any time for Hudson's Bay. The trading company was notorious for directing its agents to stalk braves while on their hunting parties, then jump them and steal their furs.

"Made it all the way up to Bill's castle in Inverness. It's almost in Norway."

"Ah."

"Bill let the Indians free to be with the Scottish girls, who loved their long dark hair. Planted buffalo grass in the valley behind his castle, you know. You should have gone, Baptiste. Talk about living the life."

Bridger turned and looked at Baptiste directly. "Say, what are you doing now?"

"Not much."

"I hear they're looking for scouts for the Army," Bridger said.

"How much do you get by the head?"

Bridger laughed. "It'd be pay enough to see an Injun in uniform. Besides, I don't want the job."

Bridger tossed a package to Baptiste labeled "U.S. Army." Inside was a blue woolen Army uniform fabricated in Worcester, Massachusetts, complete with buttons, boots, and hat.

The United States had entered the War with Mexico. Baptiste knew California, Utah, Colorado, and New Mexico were there for the taking. It was a race against Mexican soldiers to seize and defend the new territory. President Polk, with no troops in the West to answer the challenge, negotiated with Brigham Young to put five hundred of his most unstable Mormon settlers in uniform, arm them, and send them to claim the state of California ahead of the Mexicans.

"Your commanding officer is Lieutenant Colonel Philip St. George Cooke," Bridger said. "St. Vrain's already put you in. You're the lead guide, by the way. So you've got to get down to Santa Fe posthaste. You only have nine days to get there." Bridger shook his head. "An Indian in the army."

"I'm not an Indian. I have no medicine. I have no spirit animal."

"I didn't say you were a good Indian."

The wind whistled through the pines and a presentiment came to Baptiste. "You haven't seen Beckwourth, have you?"

"No," Bridger said. "But that doesn't mean he isn't here."

30

—make sign for WALK and for SEE, fingers pointing to ground.

October, 1846

Just as Baptiste had dressed in new clothes to cross the Atlantic with Duke Paul, so did he change into his blue United States Army uniform with bright red guide's jacket for Uncle Sam. He'd worn finer attire, but he certainly knew what to do with these. The most difficult concession was to swap his silent moccasins for heavy hobnail black boots that creaked when he walked and his invisible buckskins for the flash of a popinjay. Why did the haberdashers insist on uniforms that were easy to see? He already knew the answer. It was to keep them from shooting themselves.

"Jean Baptiste Charbonneau, guide, reporting for duty, sir." Baptiste clicked the heels of his boots the way they had in the Stuttgart barracks. His uniform was spotless. From his work with Duke Paul's troops he knew how to drill. The only thing he didn't do was cut his hair. Baptiste remained at attention while Lieutenant Colonel Philip St. George Cooke got up from the charts he was reviewing, approached, and circled him.

"Yes," the colonel said. "The Germans would do that, wouldn't they? I've heard of you, you know. Meriwether Clark speaks well of you and commends to you his best wishes."

"Thank you, sir."

"You have the further recommendation of Major Robert E. Lee, Meriwether's neighbor in St. Louis and a school chum of mine, who has followed your most unusual career."

"Yes, sir." A Clark had praised him in public! The surprise was like a blow to his chest. He didn't know a Robert E. Lee.

"You may most certainly stand at ease, corporal. Approach this window if you will."

Baptiste did as he asked and saw much of the Mormon Battalion had already been assembled: five hundred men, all cavalry; forty-five wagons; twenty uniformed women paid at half a man's salary to wash clothes; and a number of wives put on the rolls as privates and issued blue scarves to denote their participation.

"Well, sir, do you think you can do anything with these people?" the colonel asked.

"No, sir," Baptiste said. Surely he wasn't going to make an army of these. *After all, they are Mormons.* "But I can guide them."

The colonel laughed and asked, *"Has visto mucho de Santa Fe?"*

"No, sir, but I don't expect we're staying here long," Baptiste said. "I understand we're in a hurry."

"Yes, sir, we are," Cooke said enthusiastically. He slapped Baptiste on the shoulders, grinned, and warmly shook his hand. "Now take a look at these," he said and directed him to routes he was plotting on a topographic map unrolled across a table.

✦ ✦ ✦

In spite of their vast differences, Baptiste felt as though the colonel and he had provisional admiration for each other immediately. God had told the rest of the Mormon Battalion to be here, but the colonel and he were operating out of lower imperatives as directed by the colonel's commanding officer, General Kearny.

"You know of course that history is in vain to find a longer overland march than the one we are attempting?" the colonel asked him.

"No, sir," Baptiste said. There was Xerxes' drive from Samarkand to Athens in 380 BC. Hannibal's stroll from Carthage to the outskirts of Rome came to mind. But the greatest parallel was the First Crusade— from Orleans, France, to Jerusalem—led by Sir Godfrey of Bouillon with Peter the Hermit as his guide. "Godfrey became the first King of Jerusalem after reaching his destination," Baptiste said. "His first act was to kill twenty thousand infidels in the streets." He couldn't resist a smile. "Sir, what do you plan to do when you reach San Diego?"

The colonel raised his eyebrows. "Ah, that fits, and there must be others, Trajan possibly and forgotten Mongol marches across the Gobi Desert. Perhaps we've never heard of braver armies still who never reached their goal."

"Moses led Israel through the desert," Baptiste said, carefully avoiding the word "guide."

"Yes, but that was an easier row to hoe! It's twelve hundred miles to San Diego! You have to understand that to these Mormons, it is important that this march be the *very longest*. Every man must feel he is marching toward history. I trust I can have your word on that?"

Baptiste felt a distant thrill at the prospect of being asked for trust and remembered that when he was younger, it was all he'd ever hoped for from Clark. "Sir," Baptiste said. "May I choose my own mount?"

The colonel nodded. "Be my guest. It's the only thing we have in abundance. I'll walk with you down to the livery."

When they started outdoors the sun flattened any objects that dared block its light. Men, cacti, sage—they were all stunted by the process and the brightness of the desert, which dominated the landscape as no ocean could. They crossed the compound and were cooled the moment they entered the stable door. Looking at the architecture Baptiste could tell this building had once been the chapel of this former mission. Spaniards and Indians had prayed in here. Some of the horses had religious mosaics under their feet.

"Down along here, Corporal Charbonneau."

They passed a few unremarkable mounts and then he saw him, to the right, under a small arch where the penitents must have made their confessions. He towered over the others and was blacker than Vogelweide's heart. Young and flashy, he was the reincarnation of Sorcerie.

"Not that one," the colonel said. "Kit Carson said we ought to shoot that animal and save ourselves a lot of trouble."

"Yes, I do want him," Baptiste said. "I want him very much." *I believe your name to be TukaniH, Dark of Night.*

The colonel didn't seem surprised. "Watch him overnight then, in here," he said. "Then, in the morning, if you still dare, he's yours." The colonel stopped and looked into Baptiste's eyes, trying to see months ahead into the march. *Will you let me down?*

Baptiste stood still and let him peek inside. He peered as long as you'd ever want a man to peer into your eyes. Then the colonel winked at him according to military training, and it came to the new recruit. *This man has planned it all: the horse, the opportunity to let me enlarge myself with my history lesson.*

Baptiste met the other guides under his command. Who would turn up but his old chums the Two Antoines?

"Did you ever travel to Europe?" Baptiste asked the younger Antoine, unsure if this was a part of his history that he wanted to reveal.

"You'd never catch me on that godforsaken continent," he said. "I wouldn't wish that on a fly."

Leaving them, Baptiste checked in with the paymaster. This interlude particularly fascinated him. Fifteen dollars a month was the first regular money he'd ever earned.

From that first day, the Mormon contingent, perhaps seven-eighths of them, kept to themselves, worshiping in odd circles every morning and night, hiding in their wagons. God was all around them, in the clouds, on the wind, in the insects that crowded in to inspect their footprints in the desert, but these men trusted in Brigham Young.

Overhearing some of the Mormon officers, Baptiste decided it was a master stroke of President Polk to enlist these people. It made the brain dance: *Brigham Young really thinks he's a god, and these minions suppose he is, too!* During his days with the Gypsies he'd tricked people into believing Rinko was dancing instead of remembering the hot coals under his feet, but he'd never fooled crowds on a scale like this. The serene "friendliness" of Young's followers made Baptiste wonder at their zealotry even more.

Looking at the "troops" under their command, Baptiste realized the desert was not going to be their greatest obstacle. Some of these Mormon adventurers would prove themselves brave men. For others, the desert would bring out hidden frailties. Together they united in their suspicion of him, the Red Skin. Well, maybe that was his purpose.

"It's all right," some of the soldiers reassured their wives if Baptiste drew near. "He can't hurt you. He's working for us."

"But he looks just like an Indian," Baptiste heard a child pipe up behind him as he bent over a bowl to wash his face. "Will he use a tomahawk to cleave my skull?"

"Shhhh!" her mother said. "You're one of the elect. God will protect you from the devil."

Glancing down into the reflection of his own dust-streaked face and glittering, red eyes, Baptiste caught a glimpse of the devil himself.

He expected the colonel to relax uniform requirements for all of the guides, as was the practice, once they began their passage, but he did not. They stood watch resplendent and biblical. Baptiste's men and he were in uniform the entire distance.

Every night they set two echelons of lookouts on high points of land to warn them if they were being stalked, or worse, outraced to the Pacific by Mexican soldiers. They sensed the army, everywhere. There were many false sightings, but after a while the Mormon Battalion grew bold. All they had to do was reach the Pacific to claim all of California.

The Mexican *soldados* were not the only ones who tracked them during the early months. Members of all the plains cultures monitored them from behind trees and rocks. Unknown to the others, Baptiste had become aware that their passage was being watched with interest by Blackfeet, Sioux, Nez Perce, and Navajo. When they got within one hundred miles of the great salt lake, Lieutenant Colonel Philip St. George Cooke suddenly put down his spyglass and hissed to him, "Charbonneau. Look at those bushes. They're moving."

"Those aren't bushes, sir. They're men."

In fact they were Utes, sadly one of the first great tribes to accept rum from the white men in trade for pelts. The rum had proven to be poison to them. Upon realizing they'd been spotted, the bold among them crawled closer, groveling with their bellies in the dust, begging like children for their thirst to be quenched.

The colonel was dumbfounded. "Why on earth would men be out there? Where would they come from?"

Baptiste turned bright red. "They're Indians."

"Oh, yes, so they are," the colonel said. "Well, of course they're men, of a primitive sort. But you know what I mean. The thing is, what should we *do* about them?"

"The first thing we should do is hide our maids," Baptiste said and looked across a row of wagons at young Sarah Prinney, daughter of one of the Mormon officers, as she washed her hair. The top of her blouse was wet, too. The young woman was actually steaming in the sun.

The colonel was silent a moment.

"Corporal, they're not our maids," he said quietly. "If you go within five feet of that calico you'll get the strap within an inch of your life."

She seems an outsider, like me, Baptiste thought, *but she is fresh and unspoiled by the jealous gossip of her married, disappointed friends.* Lush as a newly opened horse chestnut, she held his gaze in hers longer than he'd have thought she'd have dared, free from shame. Even from a distance Baptiste could pick her out with her glossy brown hair and blue cape.

"Aren't those very precise distances, sir, in a desert so vast as this?"

"Are you threatening me, sir?" the colonel asked Baptiste.

"Of course not."

"Then what do we have to do about these scoundrels?" The colonel offered Baptiste the glass, but he waved it away. It magnified images but took away their character. He could see their movements very plainly without aid.

"We don't have to do anything about them," he said. "They've followed us for over a week."

"Well, should we stand for that?" the colonel asked.

"We may be standing *because* of it. In a sense they're buffering us from enemies who might stop our passage. I'd worry more if they started to disappear."

Baptiste knew that would signal the arrival of Apaches, who would not touch whiskey, which made them terribly dangerous. The Crows and the Apaches had become wealthy by refusing alcohol and stockpiling ammunition instead. The Cheyenne and these Utes were another situation altogether. He was embarrassed for them.

"How is it, Corporal, that you can see into the future like this? Seeing bushes turning into 'men' and such."

Baptiste considered. "No one can see into the future. It's all I can do to see into the present."

"Do all you Indians brag like that?"

"If we're misguided and encouraged. If you give us enough liquor." Baptiste drank an undisclosed substance from his beaver bag and offered some to the colonel, but he waved it off, just as Baptiste had waved off the spyglass.

"Well, what does the present tell you about these rascals?"

"That we're near water, or they wouldn't be here. That there aren't many of them, or they would have approached us. They're clearly fascinated by us, or at least the Mormons. You realize our troops are singing, don't you, sir? It's as if we've invited the Utes here. They're also curious about why we don't go in out of the rain."

He wheeled TukaniH around.

"What rain?" the colonel demanded.

The wind had picked up, but that wasn't Baptiste's cue. A blue wall was blowing into them from the east, and the temperature had dropped several degrees. The Utes had already scattered. Worse still, a three-legged javelina was about to cross directly in front of their path. For a moment it stopped and considered them with a menacing grin.

31

"BEAR"

—hold partly closed hands alongside head to indicate large ears. Add to this a clawing motion with hands in front clawing downward.

Now that the colonel had declared a certain young woman off-limits to Baptiste, he found he could not take his eyes off her. She became the perfect object of desire for him—one he was not allowed to touch.

Two nights later he saw her washing linens at a stream.

"You're a bit far from the wagons," he said, looking behind her at the Utes, who still followed them like dogs and sat just yards away in the grama grass. In spite of their timidity, they posed a danger to her.

"Oh!" she said. "I didn't see you come up."

Or hear me.

The next morning Baptiste mounted TukaniH and rode directly into the throng of Utes. Behind him he could see the concerned somato-type of the colonel monitoring his progress. From the little red bluff his perspective suited him. It was Olympian.

The Utes were a disgrace. They spoke perfect Spanish. "We will kill you," the one called Devil Rod said, "unless you bring us bowls of your black soup." The man's spitting, as well as his feminine screech, denoted his high position as sachem.

"What do they want?" the colonel asked Baptiste when he returned.

"After-dinner coffee."

When news reached them via Kit Carson that California settlers had revolted against the Mexicans ahead of them and needed immediate troop support, General Kearny took one hundred of their fastest dragoons and headed north immediately through the Sierra Nevadas. He took their best mules and supplies. He ordered Carson, who was exhausted, to show him the way. When Carson explained that his horse was all but dead from eight hundred miles of travel, General Kearny gave him TukaniH.

"So he's taking my horse?" Baptiste asked the colonel.

"Sir, he is the army's horse."

The colonel stared at him, daring him to reply.

Baptiste said nothing, and this was just the kind of thing that made people think he was a cold bastard. *What was the point?* For all a horse's sensitivity, Baptiste never knew of a horse who died of a broken heart because he had a new rider. Besides, he liked Carson more than he ever liked a horse. If anyone was deluded, it was the colonel to think that TukaniH could belong to any mortal or any institution devised by man, including the United States Army. When it really came down to it, wasn't one weight on his back the same as another? He watched TukaniH's tail flipping as he disappeared over the horizon.

That night, the colonel and Baptiste agreed that their wagons, families, and leftover soldiers could not follow the same harsh, northern route Kearny would take with his men. Baptiste was sent into the desert alone to try to discover a softer, second route.

"Your mother did so for Lewis and Clark," the colonel said. "Now let's see what you can do for me."

Baptiste nodded quickly but ransacked the empty closets of his mind for a reason why he would want to do anything for a white man who, like Father Clark, was not an expert on anything but manipulating his men and taking the credit. Why should he perform for this tall, privileged fellow with his high forehead, elderberry eyes, and long black beard?

For an instant he thought of Toussaint calmly watching Clark's writing desk shatter in the rapids. Until this moment, he'd always considered this an act of cowardice.

Baptiste traveled alone in the desert on a mule, looking for the secret passage called Guadalupe and shivering in the talking dark. During his second week out, he spoke often with his mother and prayed for a vision. On his third week alone, he began to feel someone following him but tried to fight off these moods as desert loneliness or ecstasy. He became very watchful for "him." This dangerous business became even worse when the desert seemed to take on a different character, and he began to talk to the spirit he imagined following him.

Barely ahead of "him," he saw birds and the slopes of two arid mountain ranges meet, as if they were part of an exotic painting, at least in the Orient of his imagination. Shadows softly darkened the folds in the mountains as they spilled down to level ground. It was the secret pass, though some specks at the bottom of it seemed to be moving. In fact they were two specks approaching from a great distance, which became two riders. As they approached, their features sharpened, as if they had come into focus under one of Duke Paul's microscopes. With the wind blowing their hair in time to the flowing manes of their horses, they blended into a single nightmare organism as they passed a mesquite tree and slowed effortlessly to a stop. He noticed their touch was so light on their horses it was as if they were reading their animals' minds.

First of all, your approach is genial. Now I can make out your effusively washed hair, another Apache trait. Unlike any tribe Baptiste had encountered, they performed this ritual daily while refusing to comb it. *Your hair is pretty as a girl's, you two Apaches, though it is wild.*

"Hello, White Eyes," the talker said in Spanish, suspiciously softly, in a faraway Castilian lisp. "You've picked a marvelous day to die," he added in the whisper a gentleman might use to ask for the sugar.

He was full of fun, this one. He kept grinning, trying to seduce Baptiste into fear. Funny: Whenever two men are together, one of them is the talker and one is the watcher. *If you have to shoot, kill the watcher first.*

"Señor White Eyes to you," Baptiste said.

"Traveling alone?" the talker wanted to know. This one ought to have been a salesman in St. Louis.

"Come all this way to ask me that?" Baptiste said. "And you," he said to the watcher. "Bonehead. You've followed him here just to hear him ask it?"

The watcher, by far the taller of the two and distinct because of his green headband, followed Baptiste's hand into his possibles bag while he slowly brought out a bottle of rum. No strategy there. By now Baptiste was just thirsty. A smile of derision crept into one side of the watcher's face.

"One day your people will discover peyote, Boston," the talker said in a caustic voice. "Why don't you try some of this?"

It would have been impolite to refuse "this." The peyote burned quickly in Baptiste's throat, and he nodded. "You were telling me what this place is called?"

"I told you no such thing," said the talker. "Look at you, Washi. You ride out here on this mule to insult us."

"Nevertheless," Baptiste said. "You were frankly rude. You were forcing the name on me. You were making me most uncomfortable. Now because of your lies I begin to believe it is *not* the magic place I have heard about all my life."

"Oh yes it is," the watcher said proudly. "Guadalupe."

Baptiste knew this most beautiful of words. It was a vision thousands of Mexicans and mestizos believed in and were ready to die for. Miracles followed the legend like rain showers. Guadalupe was both a statue that had disappeared for six hundred years before being found in Spain and the name the Virgin Mary had called herself when she appeared to a Mexican Indian and spoke to him in Nahuatl. Guadalupe, the apparition had said softly. He'd heard the word years earlier from Duke Paul. The Spanish pronunciation bore a remarkable resemblance to Quatlasupe, a serpent-killing Aztec goddess who smote her first demon long before the birth of Christ. *What have you done here, Guadalupe?* Baptiste thought. *You have opened these mountains for me as a divine and gentle revelation.* He looked at the almost embarrassing hole in the mountains and wondered how many spirits had worked in the Fourth World to create this. A black condor sailed slowly through the pass and disappeared behind a canyon on the other side. The wind was so strong out here it fluttered their clothes and flattened them against their bodies.

Baptiste got out his charts and with chagrin realized he wished he had Clark's astrolabe. "Tell me," he said and dismounted. "How far are we from the source of the Gila?"

"Not here," the watcher said and pointed to a different place to talk. "Over there."

Had he not diffused the Apaches' anger? Were they still going to kill him? Slowly Baptiste's guides led him three quarters of a mile into a rock formation until they vanished like the heathen devils they were. At least that's what the colonel would have said. So many things in the desert could trick the eye. But instead, in a great cleft of falling red rock, his hosts treated him to some shade, more prized than water. They sat down, he followed suit, and they questioned each other well into darkness. Only the talker slept, stirring and leaning against the red rock. The watcher threw some red sand on the talker's hair and laughed when he didn't move.

"Now," said the watcher. "We'll play the bones for your life, Boston."

Baptiste said nothing.

"Wake up," the watcher nudged the talker. "We're playing the bones."

"He's mine," the talker said, brushing the sand out of his hair. "Throw."

Baptiste held out his hands, and the choosing began. The first time he beat the odds when the watcher opened up his fingers to find the white, and not the black, bone.

"Not my day to die," Baptiste said.

"What you've won," said the talker, "is the right to try again."

"I appeal to your sense of fair play," Baptiste said to the watcher.

"We'll play that game later, Boston," the talker said. "Right now we're playing bones."

I am not nervous. The Gypsy Svigula had told Baptiste never to be nervous about luck, because nervousness creates the bad luck. He looked through a channel in the rocks and feigned boredom. From his resting place he had extended views through the secret pass and saw green grass beckoning from the other side.

He beat the two Apaches at bones all night. They shook their heads, and he yawned a lot. He was anxious for them all to fall asleep, for he didn't believe he could be killed in a dream.

"Don't go," the talker, whose real name was Rain-Too-Lazy-To-Fall-To-The-Ground, said the next morning. "We haven't killed you yet."

+ + +

Grateful for his release, Baptiste raced back—to whatever extent a mule could be raced—to the colonel and the Battalion waiting in Albuquerque, and together they began to cross the desert following the Rio Grande before cutting north to where he'd first seen the Apaches and the Guadalupe Pass. But upon their return they missed it. Or it disappeared.

"What do you mean you can't find it?" the colonel said.

"This must be it," Baptiste said. "I know I was here!" He rode for days looking for his grandiose delusion. Neither the secret pass, nor any helpful Apache, was in sight.

"I am deeply disappointed," the colonel said.

They had to take everyone up over the twelve-hundred-foot lip of a canyon, using pick axes to carve a narrow channel for the wagons and descending via an ingenious system of ropes devised by the colonel. Even so, the surrounding mountains were seven thousand feet high. Thousands of settlers would take this route to California.

In the desert, Baptiste was often dispatched to find water. In places where he was not successful, he left messages tacked to cacti: "No water. Jean Baptiste Charbonneau." He must have left fifty such messages in the remotest parts of the desert. He was delirious in writing these, because the desert knew it had no water.

The Battalion encountered many sandstorms en route, but the one by the Gila River in California blinded them the most. Baptiste climbed above their wagons onto a small promontory to see if he could see ahead.

"How far does it go?"

Baptiste heard the colonel's voice far below him and was about to answer when he had the sensation of his imagined follower nearby. He tried to regulate his breathing and find the horizon through the sand when a heavy claw raked his chest and knocked him down. For a moment he saw the flash of a shape and recognized a grizzly, maybe

ten feet high, maybe twelve. Baptiste fell unconscious, but the bear
followed him into his dream. *The smell of wet fur, blood, and bear-scat.*
Are you Akoai, the great bear of the constellation I saw in Malta? Are
you the ghost of Rinko come to find me? He half-flickered to consciousness, rolled, and heard the flash of his carbine. Another flash. When
Baptiste shot his nightmare through the heart and neck nothing happened at first, though part of him imagined the bear begging for mercy
in several languages, suavely in Italian, Parisien. But when the bear fell
away and Baptiste dodged his falling mass, two other bears appeared
behind him. *My God, maybe I deserve this hell, to have to fend off endless*
predators, massed to take revenge on me. Then come and get me. Baptiste
screamed but heard no sound. Then he plunged his knife into a bear's
belly and rammed it up to his chest with the sound of upholstery ripping. The bear's hot entrails soaked Baptiste's arm, and he rolled the
monster off the cliff.

"Baptiste," the Two Antoines joked, "we counted. You called for more
ammunition in five different languages."

"You didn't understand any of them?" he said.

"Your French still isn't very good," the elder Antoine said. "You must
learn to speak with more élan. All we heard was screeching like a girl."

Three beasts, three escapes. Mother must be very close. Baptiste felt
dizzy, giddy with euphoria. Balter, the cook, had to give him a second dressing for his wounds in just half an hour because the first one,
wrapped around his chest in gauze and cotton, turned bright red.
When the sandstorm stopped, Baptiste watched as, one by one, the
Mormon children were conducted past the dead bears and told to give
thanks to their divine leader.

Because they were starving, some of the Mormon men broke early
from their prayer circles to help the Two Antoines skin the bears.
Now this was new: Was he still hallucinating, or did the bears, hanging from a wire strung between two wagons, look eerily like human

corpses? Baptiste closed his eyes but woke at the smell of bear haunch being cooked over the fire and the sound of scraped plates. He gratefully accepted his share and leaned back against a stone. Inside the circle of wagons, he felt an odd flush not so much from his victory but from seeing young Sarah Prinney look at him from her seat just a few feet away. She hungrily smacked her lips as bear grease ran down her rosy chin.

He smiled. He'd at least earned the right to speak with her. He simply picked up his plate and moved closer to the young beauty while the others talked. She smelled so sweet and fresh—lemon verbena and lavender.

Looking down into her plate, Sarah said, "Were you afraid?"

She wore a veil embroidered with tiny flowers for protection against the dust. The veil was a little crooked, and Baptiste longed to tuck it behind her ear. They were just inches apart, but to touch her face he had to reach across memories of Ekaterina and Lizette, and all the years in between. He knew it wasn't this girl he longed for but the almost-remembered feeling of daring to hold another human being. It would be so difficult to feel that kind of love again. A slight breeze kicked up, cooling them. Almost as if she had created the breeze, or received it as a blessing from Brigham Young, she smiled at him.

You are too precious for the life planned out for you, for I have heard you will just be one of many wives, Baptiste thought. *There is something bold and wild about you. I would like to tumble into that hair.*

"Weren't you scared when the bears attacked you?" she asked again.

"No." He smiled. "Yes."

She narrowed her eyes and tilted her chin. "Is it true that your mother was a squaw?" She reached out and stroked his arm, but Baptiste recoiled at that term which meant so little and yet so much.

So that was it. His attractiveness was the exotic color of his skin. *I am nothing more than a risk you are taking.* He pondered for a second whether taking advantage of her rebellious streak might actually be worth having the colonel take a shot at him. After all, he might miss. *Are you raving mad?* He looked down and saw a single drop of blood staining the flesh below his bandages. *My mouth dry. Sure signs of a fever coming on.*

Sarah looked directly at him and shook out her hair. No one was looking. From here he could touch her face. He could do it if he did it right now.

"Here, let me straighten that," he said.

In reaching over to adjust her veil he felt a forbidden thrill from sloughing her soft cheek, and then the colonel grabbed him by the nape of the neck and threw him against the side of the wagon.

"I told you to keep your eyes to yourself, half-breed," Colonel Cooke said.

"That's good advice," Baptiste said. "You should have given it to Coyote."

"Half gentleman, half animal," the colonel said. "You are drunk." In front of all he picked up Baptiste's plate and spun it out into the desert. "Keep yourself to yourself, too."

"Better drunk than a coward," Baptiste lashed back, in Latin. The Mormons rushed back in fear, as if blown by wind, because they had been told that only Satan spoke in Latin. Sarah Prinney continued to regard him curiously but from behind two young men, as if she were peering at a lion in a cage.

"Veneer of an education," the colonel said. "It's sad. You can give them the vestiges of civilization but they have no interior world."

"Not one you'd understand," Baptiste said.

"Quite an unusual situation, really," the colonel said, no longer addressing him.

"It's not an unusual situation at all," Baptiste called over the crowd. "Even the worm will turn when trod upon."

He felt the roar of the waterfall in his head. He pulled himself up and stood looking at his fellow travelers, the night at his back. He kept backing up until no one but the stars behind him could see him. *And you, Haih.*

He returned after midnight and saw a lamp lit in the colonel's tent. The colonel was bent over his diary, recording the day's exploits and no doubt embellishing his own role in the bears' conquest. *Little wonder the Taipo so prize the written language as a benchmark of civilization,* Baptiste reflected. *Lies are so much more enduring when they're in print.*

The colonel punished Baptiste by ignoring him, but gave him no further discipline. Weeks passed, and the cacti gave way to green farmland as the Battalion rushed westward. Mexican families shivered and took cover at their approach, but they saw no Mexican soldiers on the day they "captured" California. Nor did Baptiste see Sarah Prinney again, except on the other side of groups of the faithful.

The sense of the ocean, and San Diego, intruded on every moment of his thoughts. Just as he had felt it as a child he now felt the frisson of the ocean's presence as a kind of cerebral storm coming his way. He felt the tang in the wind and had difficulty sleeping as they drew near their destination. He climbed up through Mission Valley, and there it was, Fort Stockton, a place he had built, piece by piece, in his mind. The younger men chuckled as he began to run not into the fort but past it. Bushes scratched his face; he did not care. He flew up the narrow trail to the eyelid of the world and stopped. Blue was everywhere, not just as a color but as a breeze. *How could one feel a homing instinct for the infinite as opposed to the comfortable?*

Here, from his perch on Presidio Hill, Baptiste saw the Pacific once again foaming before him. He sucked the salt air deep into his chest just as the sun set fire to the edge of the horizon. The gash of blue in his head reunited with the spectacle before his eyes. Soft grasses around his feet bent in the breeze, which might have fetched all the way from Japan. Fetching, that was it: a breeze coming from far away, like the past.

Baptiste looked down at his buckskins and moccasins, which the colonel had finally given up trying to make him discard. He was too young the first time he saw the Pacific and too old now. He mused he was older than Clark was when he set eyes on that vast boiling heaving ocean: swarthy, with well-packed muscles, and in his mid forties. Who knows what the Mormons were thinking when they hit the ocean and didn't ascend into heaven with the angels. The sun rolled like a lemon off a blue table. They stood alone in the night and now could merely hear the Pacific, deep with loneliness, shifting, infinite, green-warm in the indigo depths and shallows they could not see. Baptiste was blind, like Coyote. He had given away his eyes.

Here I am, Mother, he said to himself, but he needn't have bothered. A flock of birds took off from the water below, flapping low to the waves and then ascending to the heavens.

32

"MILKY WAY/GHOSTS/DEAD MEN'S ROAD"

—make sign for DIE, for TRAIL; then with right flat hand fully extended sweep in a great curve across the sky.

February, 1848

Everyone was awarded a position, in order to spread the Battalion's influence and protection along the California coast. As a reward for his service Baptiste was commissioned *alcalde*, or mayor, of the mission at San Luis Rey. The mission was a lovely tiled Franciscan ruin with sunken gardens, a bell tower, views of the ocean, and long, low arched stables running to the southwest with room for no fewer than sixty horses.

He worked there for six months and saw his handwriting return to form. He didn't know how many communiqués he signed with his swashy signature, *Jean Baptiste Charbonneau*.

One morning Baptiste awakened to hear the same Scarlatti passage pounding in his head that he'd heard just before losing Ekaterina.

He'd had a premonition someone was coming. Now he looked up from his desk to see Jim Beckwourth standing no more than a foot away from him.

"Well," Baptiste smiled. "Dark God," he said in Crow. "For months I've been hearing of your exploits in the Sierra Madres. That was you, wasn't it?"

Beckwourth looked straight into Baptiste's eyes, then leaned back and crossed his arms. "Your father finally fucked his last squaw," he said.

Toussaint's dead. Baptiste eyed Beckwourth for a moment, then smiled.

"You are not just a great liar," Baptiste said, taking strange comfort in a friendly Crow ritual, "you are the greatest liar who ever lived."

Beckwourth pushed a brain-tanned buffalo bag no larger than a closed fist across Baptiste's desk. When Baptiste said nothing, Beckwourth said, "I thought you'd call this good news."

"Good news is bad luck," Baptiste said. "Don't bring me presents from the dead."

He threw the bag back at Beckwourth, who caught it easily in his left hand.

"I saw him," Beckwourth said. "He'd been married the day before, to a young Assiniboine girl. He brought her into the fort, along with his other two wives. He was generous with her and let us all share in the *chivarie.* Every man in the stockade *yokoG wette* with her. Then he died himself, 'under her buckskins.'"

"You were witness to no such thing," Baptiste said.

"I swear to you, Toussaint is dead." Beckwourth left the bag on the table near where Baptiste had laid his head on his arms.

Beckwourth slipped out the door to flirt with some of the mestizo beauties who'd begun to gather outside the office once word got around that he'd arrived. Baptiste picked up the leather pouch and started unwinding the rawhide clasp. Crumpled in its dark interior was a bolt of colored linen from which wafted the unmistakable stench of Toussaint. As Baptiste unfolded the filthy rag he realized it was a very old Old Glory with thirteen alternating scarlet and white stripes and twenty-four white stars embroidered on a deep blue field wrapped around something sharp. *Oh, good, my inheritance,* Baptiste thought piquantly. A gem, perhaps, or a piece of stolen silver? Instead it was Toussaint's damned arrowhead, with intimate notches along its side for hunting birds. He sniffed it and was thankful it didn't carry Toussaint's aroma, then dangled it from its greasy cord of buffalo gut to let the sunlight plumb its depths, blue but somehow darker than obsidian. He studied it.

It was both a crude instrument of survival made by a desperate people and the work of a fine craftsman. Where once it flew through the sky, it now flew through the years. *Dear Mother, only you in all the party were not surprised to see it in the whale. Your people traveled for hundreds of miles to mine for these at sanctuaries of great medicine. How you slapped me when I asked, why bother? Why not buy a smelted one manufactured in England from Bett's in St. Louis?* This piece of steatite had swung from Toussaint's neck for forty-two years. *Why did you keep it?* Suddenly the harsh words between Clark and Charbonneau at the Pacific's-edge campsite came back to him. *All these years I'd just assumed it was yet another thing you'd stolen from my mother's people, which had always embarrassed me because they hadn't even ventured into the Bronze Age. But now I realize it was the first thing you stole from me. Funny I never asked you about it, Toussaint, but that was our way. I've never seen you without it; it would have been as ridiculous for me to have asked why you'd kept your beard or your arm. And I proba-bly wouldn't have wanted to hear your answer anyway.* Baptiste looped the arrowhead around his neck and felt it cool the skin over his heart. *Has it ever pierced the heart of any of your other foes, Toussaint? So many victims have seen it swinging from your neck, all the way to the poor adolescent fending off your latest attack.*

Beckwourth stepped back in the door. He smiled when he saw the arrowhead on Baptiste's chest. "Your father was piss proud of that," he said. "Refused to take it off that time we got skunked near Boiling Kettles and we had to burn all our clothes."

Baptiste held up the flag and shook it, as if to discover something else inside. But there was nothing. He spread the flag out on the table. Beckwourth took out his knife and started scraping under his fingernails.

"He was a New Frenchman," Baptiste said. "Why would he value this?" The flag's spangled crimson and blue were darker in creases that revealed Toussaint had carried it a long time. "He had no use of borders any more than a hawk."

"Why does that bother you?" Beckwourth asked, grinning.

"As far as I could tell, his allegiance was only to money, and his concept of motherland was defined by how far he could trap," Baptiste said, knowing Toussaint had found a way to cheat him again. His face grew hot as Beckwourth draped the flag around his shoulders.

"He always liked the stars," Beckwourth said. "It looks good on you, *'mon fils.'*"

33

"BEYOND"

—bring extended left hand, back of the hand facing up, in front of
body about ten inches, fingers pointing to right; bring extended right
hand, back of the hand facing up, between left hand and body, same
height, fingers pointing to left. Swing the right hand outward and upward in curve beyond left hand, turning right hand back down.

"Mon fils"—that was it—and Baptiste began to hear Toussaint's words
the way Ekaterina was haunted by the last beat of her father's heart.
No one had loved him like this horrible reprobate, his mother's grace-
less captor and rapist, whose very scent he'd hated all his life.

How many times had he shrunk from Toussaint's embarrassing
"mon fils"? How many nights had he sworn his revenge upon him?
Alone on his bed, deep into the night, Baptiste translated it into every language he knew: *filius meus, figlio mio, iben, καμάρι, mi hijo, mein
Sohn,* my son.

*He alone insisted I be baptized and given the name that made me feel so
absurd riding mules in the desert. He alone prayed for me, worried about*

my medicine. He alone in the New World thought of me as someone other than Sacagawea's son.

How I hate you, Toussaint.

Baptiste reverently tacked his stained American flag behind his desk and returned to his correspondence.

He worked long and seriously as *alcalde* of San Luis Rey. In the early weeks he believed he'd found a new life worthy of his education. Then he realized he'd signed on to be the Devil's secretary.

California settlers under his purview had "hired" hundreds of local Indians to farm for them, but so severely disciplined them by docking their pay for minor infractions that many of them would have to work the rest of their lives to catch up. Meanwhile, subsistence food was charged against their future earnings to put them even more deeply behind.

So enthusiastic about becoming Christians, these people were being ruthlessly tricked. He knew slaves when he saw them. *You can see it in their eyes.*

It came to a head with a rancher named Donovan, who'd demanded the imprisonment of a worker named Dominic St. Jacques for trying to run away.

"Wouldn't you?" Baptiste said, looking up from his desk. "If you were a slave?"

"I don't know what you're talking about. I've got friends here, you know. What are you doing?"

"I'm calculating how long he'd have to work for free to pay you back," Baptiste said. "I'm up to March 13, 1917."

"Are you going to lock him up or not?" Donovan said.

"I am not."

Baptiste attempted to revoke any existing disciplinary setbacks of wages imposed by other ranchers. The governor was called in. In the end the ranchers got the better of Alcalde Jean Baptiste Charbonneau. He was mayor for just eight months when he'd had enough.

Everyone was resigning from their posts, positions, jobs, and family around that time. Gold was discovered on Colonel Sutter's farm, where Baptiste had often visited. The "miracle," just seven miles away, gave rise to a fever. Even Beckwourth was not immune.

"But what interest could you possibly have in gold?"

"Didn't you learn anything in Germany?" Beckwourth said. "Searching for gold deflects gentlemen from graver bewilderments about love, honor, or justice. The accumulation of wealth without introspection is the defining achievement of the European whites. Their shield really is made of gold. Seen this way, gold truly is a precious metal. Aren't you tired of feeling bad, Baptiste?"

Baptiste had never felt so disillusioned. Everything had lost its luster. For an instant he thought of Meriwether Lewis, a dark inn, and a pistol.

"Let's go get some gold," he said.

He and Beckwourth prospected together for over ten winters, living on Murderer's Bar. People all around them made spectacular fortunes, but from the beginning Baptiste couldn't find any of the precious commodity. No one could miss gold better than the team of James Beckwourth and Jean Baptiste Charbonneau. One spring morning Baptiste stopped in at Greenie Daly's for supplies.

"There's a letter for you," Greenie said. "Came last Monday. Lucky you stopped by."

Baptiste stared at the envelope. It was precisely addressed by a woman in spidery India ink. Her tiny handwriting imprisoned each curve with an icy control.

"Need someone to read it for you?" Greenie said, but Baptiste had already torn it open. Out fell a ten-dollar silver Mex and an old handkerchief monogrammed with a single florid L.

January, 1859

I thought I would send these to you and tell you that Lizette is gone three years now from a horrible sickness that took many of my girls and a number of our best servants too. We are sorry for your grief but in good conscience can no longer accept your letters, as we have used them up until now to settle Lizette's debts to us. Please accept this recompense for what we've had to use ourselves beyond that. Things are very hard here of late. I do remain

Very truly yours,

Francesca Peña

Baptiste gave the silver Mex to Greenie against his and Beckwourth's overdue balance and tied the handkerchief around his neck. As if Baptiste had brought it in to be assayed, Greenie weighed the silver Mex and put it under a magnifying glass. Then he looked suspiciously at Baptiste.

"Who did you kill for this?" Greenie asked.

"I had a little sister," Baptiste told him. "She died."

"I didn't believe a bastard like you even had a mother, let alone a sister," Greenie said.

"I can't believe it, either," Baptiste said.

"Sorry, chief," Greenie said, crediting their account but no doubt thinking *even in the mail, silver is the best he can do.*

The mineral lost its luster for Baptiste, and for Beckwourth, too. They drank a lot, they lost their claims, even their mule. To make ends meet, Beckwourth showed some tourists around, but since Baptiste had already reached the Pacific, his guiding days were over.

As Baptiste aged, he—at last the mule—developed an exceptionally strong back, which was useful to help all the new arrivals unpack once they reached the gold fields.

Chinese coolies, refugees from the aftermath of the opium wars, arrived in waves over the area from San Diego to San Francisco. Baptiste felt *simpatía* for them immediately and admired—and thereafter mimicked—their very unusual ways of carrying immensely heavy objects balanced between their shoulder blades with the aid of a single leather harness. The mud- and excrement-filled streets of San Francisco convinced him to do what the Army couldn't—though they fit him like a second skin, he tucked the velvety pads of his moccasins into his possibles bag as he found that the wooden shoes he'd been given so long ago by Vogelweide were just the ticket for scuffling around under his burdens. In the neighborhood they began to call him "the Indian who wears wooden shoes." Baptiste was strong, still virile, and happy. He no longer had to pan for the wretched ore. There was nothing he wouldn't carry on his back.

He heard a little girl watching him say, "Why is that old Indian carrying such a heavy couch?" But there was no such thing as a heavy load. There was only an unbalanced load.

One green afternoon Baptiste was carrying a cottage piano up three flights of stairs. Perfectly balanced with his coolie strap, it put his chin just eighteen inches above the ground, but that was the *méthode*. Slowly, below the piano's small shadow, he ascended the stairs to the third-floor parlor. He put it "near the bay window," as instructed. He smiled and bowed when he set it down, with just a fleeting look at the rosewood finish and ivory keys.

Several minutes must have passed because when he looked around he found himself alone, with the footsteps of the other movers echoing two flights of stairs below. He never intended to play; all he did was slide onto the bench and stare at the keys.

But all of a sudden Middle C burned into his brain like the sun at noon. *There are two possible outcomes,* he told himself. *You can turn around and not touch the piano or you can barely touch the keys, just for a moment. No one will hear if you slip into this piano very softly. There. Sonata quasi una fantasia,* Moonlight. *Ekaterina, you have always loved the idea of not wasting sound. I will lower myself below the cattails and into the warm water of your* Moonlight Sonata, *trying to play it the way you did when I first saw you. I will drift away with the current,* adagio sostenuto, *feeling the stars around me, but only for a moment. My love, I cannot bear that you are so far away, but I feel as though you are somehow traveling to me through these chords across a great distance, a lover's touch.*

"Wait!"

Baptiste heard the sound of a young man racing upstairs two steps at a time. In an instant he was off the bench and into the hallway. The man brushed past Baptiste as he charged into the silence in his wake.

"Where did he go?" the stair-climber demanded. He had oily, curled hair and a thin moustache. His hands were nearly as slender as a girl's.

You are so urgent, young maestro; what a wonderful fool you are.

"You there," he asked Baptiste. "Where did the artist go who dared play my piano? He must be old, it was from . . . another era." He raced to the windows, then turned to Baptiste. "What's wrong with you, don't you have a tongue?"

"Where did I go," Baptiste said softly. He started down the first flight of stairs. Porters were whipped if they even granted themselves a peek at the luxuries they carried. The lash had never touched his back, and he wanted to keep it that way.

"Look here," the man called down. "He can't have vanished into thin air. What happened to the man who was up here?"

You still can't see me, can you? Baptiste made his way to his foreman and lowered his back for his next assignment, a Saratoga trunk headed for the same floor. It was heavy enough to be a coffin that was occupied.

Cities sprang up around the gold fields. In time the docks were forested with masts, even Russian ships from Sitka. Baptiste stooped below a load of crates headed to the second floor of a warehouse one day when, with his eyes on the ground, he saw a tag with a weathered Rhineland customs stamp dangling down in front of him.

He considered it as he settled the load on his back and carried it to the required place, as he waited to be told "over there," or "no, over there." The next two boxes had foreign markings, too. As he placed the last in a corner, he was able to read *gepack und proben gehoren Duke Paul of Wurttemburg, 203, item specimens.*

More specimen boxes were overseen by a dramatic young Choctaw with kohl-lined eyes, sporting a purple satin waistcoat. *Nalowepa-wa, the boy who replaced me? No. That was thirty-five years ago.* Retaining his penitent crouch, Baptiste kept his eyes on the ground.

Two of the boxes proved very light, containing, the label read, "preserved cave swallows." These were followed by boxes of bark: *cedrela odorata, Bursera gummifera.* He recognized *Brasiliastrum americanum,* the *caiba,* the genuine *guyac.* When he hefted the box labeled *Cecropia peltata* he guessed the party had been to Cuba. Then came crates of paintings, and under their weight he smelled fresh oil. He fancied he could detect the aroma of the individual colors: aquamarine, rose madder, burnt sienna, lamp black, viridian.

Baptiste had been moving luggage for nearly seven hours when, bent below a box loaded with hand-curried Austrian saddles, he saw the extreme points of two boots curling upward in medieval style. They might as well have been the shoes of Rumplestiltskin, or Der Strummelpeter, the Teuton with the dirty, long fingernails.

The shoes were tooled in blue crocodile, the decorative squares dyed alternately in lavender and peacock.

"How are you doing under there?" a voice above him said. "That is you, isn't it?" The voice paused. "I heard the wooden shoes. How nice to know one's gift has been appreciated and not passed off under some-one else's Christmas tree."

"I tried to pass them on," Baptiste answered in German. "But they kept coming back."

"We're on our way to Alaska."

"I understand it is beautiful," Baptiste said.

"Yes," the voice said thoughtfully. "You would understand."

Baptiste stood there motionless under the weight, his chin almost skidding against the ground, when the voice continued airily, "Duke Paul isn't doing well. He's over there."

Baptiste craned his neck *over there*. Duke Paul was a frail old man now. The red-lipped Indian boy was helping him into a carriage.

"Does he know I'm here?" Baptiste said foolishly and then cursed himself for never understanding about the world.

"It's been very difficult for me," Vogelweide continued. "Duke Paul needs to be medicated four times a day. He has seizures, pisses his bed. So of course now we have to go see your American gold fields. You know, the shimmer of the new. Do you think it will be very harsh in Alaska?"

"At least you've been painting. I can smell the paints," Baptiste said.

"I have to handle everything. I am condemned to be his nursemaid for the rest of my life. I see to his bodily needs, his correspondence, you have no idea. I stopped painting long ago, Baptiste."

It was just like Vogelweide to have already forgotten that Baptiste was standing still, carrying over two hundred pounds of specimens on his back.

"Then whose paintings are they?" Baptiste asked before he could stop himself. In the distance he saw the new flavor, sliding into the carriage beside the Choctaw boy and Duke Paul. The artist was narrow, el-egant, ascetic with piercing blue eyes and a long purple neck. He had very long blond hair and appeared to be in his twenties. Tucked under his arm was a traveling palette smudged on the outside with rose and cream.

"His name is Mollhausen," Vogelweide sighed. "He is Duke Paul's Bamberg discovery. He is the painter now. But someone needs to see to the boxes. You're just lucky you got out when you did."

Baptiste didn't say anything, but rather stooped and continued to lis-ten. Beyond the smell of Mollhausen's oils he could smell Vogelweide's perfume, a retch of cocoa palms.

"I mean, look at you," Vogelweide said petulantly, even jealously. "You're free."

Under his weight Baptiste looked to his right and, past his trunk's shadow through two tenement buildings, saw the wind-ruffled needles of an immense stand of evergreens beckoning to the forest beyond.

34

"DREAM"

—make signs for SLEEP, and SEE, and GOOD.

April, 1865

The guns of the Civil War barely rattled the wooden blinds in California. Meriwether Lewis Clark became a Confederate general. So did the son-in-law of Colonel Cooke, Jeb Stuart. What illustrious shame, Baptiste thought, had lain in wait for the mysterious Robert E. Lee who'd recommended him to the colonel so many years before.

After sixty winters, Baptiste had lifted one piano too many. He wrenched his back working in Auburn, California, and so took a job at the Orleans Hotel, conveniently close to the bar. He thought as a desk clerk he could keep watch over who was in and who was out, a guest register for his separate selves.

Overseeing the baggage of so many guests and working with so many immigrants, Mandarin brushed off on him, and he couldn't help but warm to the language after he fell in with a Xiongnu woman whose husband had fallen mysteriously from The Great Wall. There was a rumor around the bar that he'd been pushed.

Chou Zixian came from the land of a thousand butterflies, along the ancient Silk Road. "Eternal caravans travel across the mountains to the lost city of Hami," she said, "chains of tawny camels with golden eyes. At night, a bell jingles on the last camel's tail so you know when he's gone."

"You're lying," Baptiste smiled and reached out to stroke her long black hair.

"Why would I?" said Zixian, pulling away from his touch.

"How long can you hear the bell after it rings?" Baptiste asked, though he knew. He imagined a lonely tinkle in the giant silence of the Chinese desert, a sound drowned by infinite wind. He smiled to think back to Duke Paul's caravan in the lower Missouri, so many years before.

Zixian shrugged. "My mother told me about it. I was always asleep."

Chou Zixian had many other lovers, too, for she was adept at scheduling. "Call me Zee-see," she ordered them with a dismissive jab of her left index finger to intercept their clumsy attempts at her name. But Baptiste always thought of her as "Chou Zixian" and hoped she'd keep at least a private dressing room in her heart for Jean Baptiste Charbonneau. She'd crossed a great desert to get here. So had he. She gulped rice wine like an adventurer, but she would not smoke any herb for all the harm opium had done to her family in China, though Baptiste pointed out that gravity had caused her the greater suffering. She scorned his tale of Hsi and Ho, who discovered California by sailing across the Eastern Ocean in a leaky, creaky boat.

"But didn't *you* discover it, Baptiste?" Zixian asked, fluttering her green-painted eyelids and inhaling the after-vapor from a bottle they'd been sharing. Baptiste particularly enjoyed gazing at the silk-screened label. It was a sketch of a small flock of geese, just beginning to flap their way off the surface of the water.

Sometimes Zixian would turn her head a certain way and he'd catch a glimpse of his mother in her almond eyes and hair as blue as a crow's wing. He convinced her to sit for an asthmatic photographer, but when the wheezing incompetent presented the couple with the smoky daguerreotype, Baptiste was disappointed to see he and Zixian were only two blurs.

Late April, 1866

When the news reached the West Coast that President Lincoln had been assassinated, Baptiste started painting the hotel's fireplaces and mantels black from the top floor down at the rate of just over two mantels per month. Putting the finishing touches on the twenty-ninth mantel in the lobby, he caught sight of Major Nat Begin and his dull-eyed nephew, Billy, drinking in the hotel bar. For days Begin had been bragging about his connection to the Montana gold fields. Baptiste knew that Begin, who wore polished army boots and a tired herring-bone tweed as though he were still in uniform, had been questioning the hotel's owners about him, too. Begin waved for him to approach.

"I know who you are," Begin said. "I served with Colonel Cooke at Bull Run. Spotts and Wilderness, too."

"Thank you for your service to your country," Baptiste said quietly. "Made a lot of ghosts, have you?"

He shrugged and turned to leave, but Begin caught his arm.

"Look, I think that Cooke's a bastard, too." Begin kicked out a chair. "Have a seat."

"I'm working."

"No one will see you if you sit down," Begin said. "You're the only one here."

You'll see me, Baptiste thought as he sat down very carefully. Baptiste judged Begin to have seen forty-five winters, his nephew half that.

"'Part gentleman, part animal,' the colonel called you," Begin said and pushed a glass toward Baptiste.

"Humanity in confusion," Baptiste replied, "though as a toast, I prefer 'Cheers.'"

Young Billy, who'd never been within a foot of an Indian, watched him warily.

"You've heard about the Montana gold fields," Begin said.

Baptiste risked a look into his eyes. *Yes, you really believe you can trick me.* "If there's one thing we've got in abundance here, there's always plenty of talk."

Begin poured Baptiste a drink from the bottle on the table. "You oughta come out," Begin said. "Say—you could be our guide."

"Now there's something to beat the Dutch," Baptiste laughed. "I make a better wine steward. Call me if you want to know the best merlot to go with your venison, if you need a linguist to translate Hidatsa into Portuguese. It was really my mother who was the guide."

"I'd like you to take us there. Me and my nephew, Billy."

"It seems like you've got it all figured out, so why would you need a guide?"

"Oh, I know where to go," Begin said. "I'm just not sure how to get there."

Funny, Baptiste thought. *My problem is exactly the opposite.*

"I'm perfectly happy right here," Baptiste said. He lifted his glass and watched its amber contents glint in the afternoon sun. "This is all the sparkle I need."

"Oh, you're coming," Begin said.

The reluctant guide: A guide has to believe in his ultimate destination, Baptiste mused. *I'm as negative as a sink hole.* Through the window he saw carriages working their way through crowds of newcomers.

Moreover I'm tired. My luck, my poha, *has almost run out.*

"Sorry, not in this lifetime," Baptiste said.

"I'll do it," Baptiste told Begin over a glass of whiskey two weeks later. "I'll get you to Montana. Seventy dollars cash right now for my guiding services—one way."

Baptiste had refused his offer so many times that Begin couldn't remember if he'd really wanted him to go.

"Why now and not a week ago?" Begin said. "Didn't I ask you five times to go on this trip?"

"That's five more drinks you've stood me," Baptiste said. "I wanted to make sure you really had money. My fee is half down. A body never knows when the future'll call. Maybe I'm just another crazy 'Injun,' but it's now or never. I don't want to die holding up this bar."

"Capital. Here's a third," Begin said, handing him a leather purse, ever more suspicious of Baptiste's accepting his invitation. "You're still in the game. What are you going to do with your portion of the gold?"

When Baptiste told Zixian about his plans, she snatched the bag of coins away and gave him the sweetest of her evil smiles. "When?" she asked. "I need to know when you're going because a girl's still got to make a living."

Baptiste knew the answer, because he'd had visions of the entire trip several times the last few evenings while drinking with her.

"You fool," she spat in his face. "If you think I'll be waiting for you when you get back, you're crazy."

"Funny, my love," he said, wiping his face with his handkerchief, "but you were the only reason I'd even considered going in the first place." Slowly, he poured both of them another two fingers.

The next night, she stormed angrily into his room while he was packing. "So you're really going to go through with this trip to hell, aren't you? Don't bother leaving this behind," she said and tossed Ekaterina's violin onto the bed. "I won't be responsible for a good-for-nothing box that only wails."

She let out a strangled sob and slammed the door behind her. Stepping into the hall, Baptiste pulled her back inside with him. Warm side-by-side in bed, he made love to her and they drifted off to sleep.

He dreamed he was trudging north of the Snake River, near trees so tall he could only hear their peaks as they whispered to each other in the sky. He struggled to wake up and tell Zixian, but even in his dream he remembered with her temper it was best to leave her asleep when she wanted to sleep. Sometimes he couldn't even move Zixian to save his life. She had a way of growling and snapping if he tried to disturb her sleep. Once she told him, by way of apology, "In my small mountain village the bandits would suddenly come thundering through in the middle of the night, and it was 'Up, up, up, man, woman and child,' for us to serve them, to pay tribute, to kow tow on our knees in obeisance. I've risked life and limb to come here for a good night's sleep," she said. "I can't bear any of this disturbance."

So he dreamt alone. There were trees and then a darker section of the forest. He was afraid but went in anyway. A large stone covered the entrance to his box canyon.

He found the tiny island, swam to it, and left his wooden shoes beside the red flower that gushed white light into the stars. When he tried to return to the place where he'd left his shoes, he'd found they'd disappeared.

In their place was a bone carving of a man with two large eyes. When he picked it up and looked at it more closely, he realized it was himself. *So this is my medicine, my magic,* he marveled. *I, too, like Mother, can see into the future. Perhaps that's why she had to die so young—she discovered as a child what it took me six decades to learn.*

He woke up in a fever and stumbled over to a rickety table below the window. With his back to the slumbering figure of Zixian, he hunched over the candle so as not to wake her and began to write.

> *To Sir James Beckwourth, King of the Crows (emeritus),*
>
> *I am hopeful that this reaches you in health. I have taken the liberty of leaving your name as a contact with the management of the hotel.*
>
> *As I head out on my latest commission, I realize that this last trail I follow may be the Milky Way. If so, I leave my other possessions, including revenues from certain real and imaginary St. Louis property I inherited from Toussaint, to Swinbot, a gentleman well known in New Orleans society, in the hope that he will remember Lizette's grave with flowers. The violin I always carried is actually Italian made, and very valuable. Please take it to auction and divide the proceeds between yourself and the Mandarin woman Chou Zixian. Do what you'd like with the arrowhead I've worn around my neck. To the Clarks and their heirs I convey my very best wishes. But in exchange for the blurred daguerreotype of her sweet face that I hope will be buried next to my heart, it is to Zixian that I leave my American flag.*
>
> *In friendship, Jean Baptiste Charbonneau*

The next morning he was gone.

Baptiste's month-long passage with Begin and Billy across the California desert to the Owahee River in Oregon Territory proved harrowing. It was as if he knew what was going to happen at each turn but was helpless to stop it. Fording the wide river at the narrowest point, he stumbled on a rock and fell in.

A shiver set the stage for spring pneumonia. Even worse, Baptiste felt both a gnawing loneliness and the growing sense that the three of them were not at all alone. With every step he knew that they were now being followed. *This trek,* he knew, *is going terribly wrong.*

Several miles later Baptiste began perspiring so fiercely that Begin and young Billy almost had to drag him into a deserted shelter that was little more than a stone-and-mud-packed coop with a fireplace and a thatched lean-to called Innskip Station, on the southwest edge of the same black lava desert he'd been lost in so many years before.

"Goddamn you, do you expect everyone to carry you on their back?" Begin huffed.

It was a good joke, Begin, even the first time I heard it.

"Where are the Innskips?" Billy asked fearfully as Baptiste pulled himself into a chair.

The whole Innskip family had just up and left.

"Not a soul here," Begin said, looking out the window as night fell. "Billy, you might's well get a fire going."

You couldn't be more wrong, Baptiste thought. Wind was picking up, whistling across the emptiness. *I wonder if you ever hit a single target for the Army, Begin. How can you be so blind to what's right in front of you?*

A war party was out there on that damned black lava desert. Baptiste had sensed them for miles, unseen and unheard, massing now and gathering in groups, waiting. He and his traveling companions had barely beaten them to the door at twilight only to find no hosts armed and ready to shelter them, just these four walls made of mud and stone, a dank floor, moonlight. Everywhere you turned you could catch the whiff of death.

Baptiste was surprised to see some elegant furniture here. The interior of the station had a woman's touch. They must have left in quite a hurry.

Begin shook a small china cabinet open and put some plates on the table. He ransacked the storage bin and set out some jerky and a couple of shriveled turnips. The silence made the room seem to spin slowly clockwise.

How can you eat? Baptiste wondered. Then he felt some hunger himself.

"I think you should know, we're not actually alone at all," Baptiste said. "There could be as many as fifty strangers out there."

"Really," Begin said. "What do they want?"

Almost twenty minutes passed as they gorged on the stolen stores. Then Begin began to drink. He downed a large clay mug before fixing a drunken stare at Baptiste.

"Enough of this waiting," Begin said. "You're the Washi. Why don't you find out what those bucks want?"

"Nat, let's just wait them out," Baptiste said, unsure himself of what to do. "If they have business with us, they know where to find us."

Begin pulled out his revolver and waved it, aiming somewhere below Baptiste's left eye.

"It's not technically a duel if only one of us has a weapon," Baptiste said.

He controlled his breath as Begin eased off the safety of the barking iron he'd "forgotten" to turn back in after being discharged from the Forty-Seventh.

"Get up," Begin said. "I'm sick of your Indian horseshit."

"Before the sweet course?"

Above them a portrait of the Innskips' missing daughter, Eugenia, stiff-necked and prickly, looked down. Baptiste had seen the same virginal torso and blue velvet dress on at least fifteen other portraits. Only Eugenia's wandering eye made it distinctive.

Baptiste watched Begin drink more whiskey. The soldier slid the bottle across the table, but Baptiste shook his head no. *Remember, Begin? The last time I drank with you, I agreed to this trip.*

"What would you like me to ask them?" Baptiste said. Maybe they'll tell us what they think of *Candide*. Baptiste gulped down a bite of dried jackrabbit and pushed some morels across his plate. *A last supper? I've had worse.* He wiped his forehead with Lizette's monogrammed handkerchief.

"Where'd you get that?" Begin said.

He's seen me use it fifty times.

"A gift from the grave."

Baptiste folded the scrap of cotton and tucked it neatly into his pocket.

Begin watched Baptiste as if he were meat going bad. Rising from his chair, Begin walked around Baptiste, lifting a strand of his long, still-black hair with his gun barrel as if to demonstrate he was a savage.

"You could just go out there," Begin said, shoving his weapon into his belt. "Talk with their leader."

"You assume I speak their language."

Baptiste looked into the darkness beyond the stockade, the dividing line between civilization and a retreating sense of who he was. No doubt there was a leader, and he, resembling Baptiste, stood in the cool desert, watching. Baptiste stood up and hacked a dry cough. *Lungs on fire, but I'm still drowning. If you forded a river the way you did this morning, of course a demon was going to climb into your chest. And now you're being dispatched on another fool's errand. Sending me out there is like sending a Chinaman to turn a Turk.* A shiver ran halfway up his back, but he shook it off.

"They'll probably kill me," Baptiste said.

"If they don't, I will," Begin said.

If I go will you then trust me? What would it take? "I'll have a better chance if I go tomorrow, in daylight," Baptiste said.

"The longer you wait, the more there'll be," Begin said. "Maybe you'll join them and overpower us."

"How we'll dance," Baptiste laughed. "Won't the savages and I prize that foul, sweaty linen shirt of yours we've been gagging on for weeks."

"Now that's what I'm talking about," Begin said. "Nobody likes an Injun with a chip on his shoulder and a smart mouth."

Yokopecca, Baptiste remembered and smiled.

"Just what is your problem?" Begin asked, staring at him. "Better you go tonight." Begin, reaching down to his side, touched his gun.

"Join me in a last cup of tea?"

Begin grunted.

Baptiste got up and walked to Mrs. Innskip's diminutive cabinet, damaged when Begin broke the lock. He took out a blue and white cup. On its glassy bowl a Cantonese courtesan with delicate hands was forever tiptoeing across a footbridge. He pried open a tin-lined black walnut tea caddy and spooned the mysterious fragrance of oolong into the cup. Without discussing it, both he and Begin knew there was no way the Innskips would have left this precious cargo voluntarily. Baptiste shuffled to the fireplace, brought the kettle to the table, and trickled hot water into the cup, his hands shaking. He stirred the dark liquor and settled heavily into his chair for his last rites. He saw his reflection in the tea as he raised the cup to his lips. Begin shifted his weight from one leg to the other.

"What, no tea for you?" Baptiste said.

"Quit your stalling."

Baptiste picked up his canteen and rose from the chair. He nearly fell out the door into the darkness. Trudging past the horses, he felt their warmth and moist breath. He crossed the compound, then looked back to see Billy at the window. Baptiste waved his hand to him, but as soon as Billy saw him he looked quickly away to continue his "watch." *So this pretty business of sending me out here had already been decided between my two comrades.*

"*Au revoir.*" Baptiste gave him his best Washi shrug and slung his possibles bag, which held the only objects in the world that still meant something to him, over his back. There was something perfect in the irony that as one of the "hard ones," possessed of moderate magic and debased his whole life for being an "Injun," he was now going to fall victim to an Indian attack. *Will they attack the French or Snake side of me?* He had a sense of his own body attacking itself from the inside out, ripping his darkness wide open and exposing the paisley seams.

He opened the latch of the stockade gate and the desert stretched before him like a vast black sea. The mountains gleamed in the distance, but he couldn't see his feet. It was like stepping out on stage for a recital, with the hushed audience out there, invisible, waiting. He thought he saw a flash to his right, but when he turned quickly it was gone. He wanted to look back again, but he'd learned the hard way that looking back only makes you stumble. With his blood pounding in his ears, he took his next step into the void, the memory of the tea like warm earth in his mouth. *I must consider my audience. If nothing else, they might admire my gosses for crossing the empty desert alone to see them.* He strode the stage to his audience, and in the reflexiveness of the night desert, his audience was both they and himself.

I feel you with me, Mother. You would know what to do. Could you introduce us?

Baptiste could feel him coming up from behind, a younger man. *You've been following me from a distance, but you are here, like snow barely falling on the mountaintops, across the years, inevitable: my killer. Apropos of your presence here I'm walking deliberately, one foot ahead of the other, the taste of tea from China still on my tongue.* Baptiste reached the tree line and felt him close by.

I'll keep walking and you'll keep following, he thought, brushing past branches now amid the mooncrust of lava rocks and sage. The reassuring firelight of Innskip Station dropped out of sight as the trees closed in on him.

Baptiste took three more unhurried strides and felt his follower's presence fall more closely into step behind him. *Don't turn around. It is dark as a mineshaft out here.* The stealthy racket behind him rustled closer. *He must be a neophyte, new to tracking. No doubt he's been sent out here, just like me, him for his* jeunesse, *me for my old age. I can take my time. Enjoy the proper digestion of my tea. Consider further how the tea arrived here, on the great clipper ships. There is nothing either of us can do to change what will happen.*

Baptiste reached the edge of some ponderosas and juniper trees in a little swale, crossed into the middle of it and stopped. His other half stopped at the edge of the forest and watched him for a while, staring across the blue sage. Baptiste felt the hair bristle on the back of his neck.

He continued into the clearing. Then he hit something soft and knew instantly what it was. It wasn't a sleeping figure; it was a corpse. Its chest was concave, its shoulders sunken, its body collapsed into itself and holding its bones like a bag of tools. A woman's tool bag, in this case. He stepped over it, amazed he hadn't smelled anything; then, almost as an afterthought, the lilac perfume hit him, ghostly this time. More lilacs? Could this be the missing Mrs. Innskip? Then he hit half a bump, presumably Eugenia. He took three steps and ran into another figure, a man in a camblet coat. It was like running into furniture in the dark. Baptiste sniffled, looked down, and in the moonlight caught the corpse's eye, its lips curled in a sneer which he instinctively returned. Baptiste stepped over it and headed with deliberate speed through the wet grass toward the center of the circle, feeling his heart race. *Will I see my tracker for a moment before the flash of his knife, or will he just kill me?* Funny vanity, but he'd always hoped a woman would kill him. Shouldn't killing be an intimate act?

Now Baptiste felt another presence, to his left. Not much time. He lowered his bag. The rattle of contents inside made his first follower jump. *Come on, where is that shaving mirror. Ah.* He took the mirror out, held the lake trapped inside it over his head, and reflected the moon into the wall of trees. Then he bounced the lake's spirits all around the darkness while they watched. A fourth came, and more. Baptiste reached into the bag, took out his violin, and eased it under his chin.

Whenever an opportunity arises to play Beethoven and you let it pass, you'll kick yourself for letting the moment slide, Baptiste thought wryly. *Besides, I'm in the New World. Finally I am fulfilling Beethoven's challenge.* No time for rosin—the dark vibration stunned the air. Baptiste's different selves surrounded him, watching. Presently one of them came close to him, the young man. According to custom Baptiste let him address him first.

"When you reached the ghosts, why didn't you stop?" His mumble was close enough to Shoshone for Baptiste to get the gist of it. He relaxed a little.

"Because I am a ghost."

The youth sprang back, recomposed himself, and withdrew to his companions. These boys had not seen a lot of trappers. They were susceptible, charming. Then he returned.

"Why have you come here, ghost?"

How many people have asked me this in the last month, including myself? Baptiste thought. Through the tamaracks the moon danced on the Cascade Mountains, with Mt. Jefferson behind them, and Baptiste raised his bow toward their snowy peaks, dislimned against the blackness as if they too were ships moving through space.

"My mother was born there. She was the greatest of the ghosts." And she was. Caught between this world and the next, between her ancestors and the white invaders, the wild and the tame. Baptiste coughed. His new friend, imitating, coughed back.

"You're just a sick old man," he said.

"Yes," Baptiste said. "What a wonder it is that such a thing can happen. I am the spectral cold ghost. Consider my situation. But do not talk directly to me or all your people will suffer my sickness." As if to make his point, a wraith of clouds curled around the moon. Baptiste half turned and for the first time got a look at his interlocutor. He was beautiful, with mysterious skin, so untouched and unspoken to he could boast no shells around his neck from trade with Pacific tribes. What is innocence, really? A pity you have to lose it first to know. His long back was adorned in skins—he must have been seventeen. He grinned nervously, and from the brave's sour breath Baptiste knew he was from one of the tribes who, like his mother's, were known as "shit-eaters." After squatting, she wiped herself with a single eel-slick finger and licked the digit clean. Like a wild cat, she sought the musk of her quarry but unlike Begin depended upon the absolute cleanliness of her skin so she would leave no trail. Easy to ridicule: The "shit-eating grins" that so astonished the early trappers were not so much expressions of doomed innocence as a canny kinship with nature.

Baptiste's new friends had a parting shot. *Esprit de escalier*—spirit of the stairway in the woods as it were. Something about the nature of his spirit animal. Baptiste was doing so well, and now they wanted, what? He took a breath and began the catechism:

"My spirit animal is the beaver, who travels through water. When I lean against the tree my spirit flies through my body, runs down the sap of the tree, hurries through underground streams, and crosses the river where first you saw me. It emerges from the depths as a mossy arm that reaches out of lake or river and overturns the canoe of my enemies." A little windy, but it would have to do.

All of a sudden they were touching him, thumping his bow, daring to look directly into his eyes. He thought he saw the slash of a knife and his mind raced. The young one circled around him in pleasure.

"Why did you kill the Innskips?" Baptiste motioned to the dark patches on the grass. He couldn't decipher his answer, but it was in-souciant, something to the effect of, "What would you do with an Innskip?"

Baptiste was out of ideas, wheezing with pneumonia, the fluid in his lungs making it harder and harder for him to breathe. He had nothing else to offer. As spectral tracings of the Manitou began to float before his eyes, he realized that, like it or not, he was going to be witness to one last revelation.

He saw the Orleans Hotel in Auburn, and on its filthy street, a line of wagons was pulling away. As he peered into the last wagon, a woman was leaning over a new-born babe. The child's plump arms reached greedily toward her slender neck, and as mother and child turned to regard him in the sweetest of tableaux, Baptiste was sure he recognized the lovely oval ivory face of Chou Zixian. She whirled her dearest young prize, wet with promise, in her arms. Hanging from the baby's neck was the blue arrowhead. *Beckwourth*, Baptiste marveled. *So you did get my letter.*

As her son squealed with delight she said in a musical voice, "How I love you, little Jean Baptiste. I have always loved you. How I loved your bastard of a father, too."

She held him close to her face and said the words. *"We will always be together."*

Try as he might to follow them, Baptiste realized he could not, as they were separated by a great dark river. So he began to climb up a cliff, which he realized was one of the cliffs of the Manitou. He'd known the way since boyhood. He nimbly ascended through the secret passage as if he were a young man again and then up toward the sun through the middle rocks. The pictures were more difficult to decipher here of the elk from the outer universe, the pictures of great birds with men in their mouths flying over Stuttgart, Bamberg, and Berlin. At the summit, across a great distance now, he thought he could still see the tiny lights of the wagon. Everything began to dim and flatten out in black, and he exulted to learn he was now on Chou Zixian's desert, the wind coming from the most distant stars, watching the long line of camels passing and waiting to hear the bell.

Postscript

The Manitou Bluffs were blown to pieces in 1892 to create the St. Louis spur of the Missouri-Kansas-Texas Railway on the north bank of the Missouri. Little Manitou Rock, on the south bank, was dynamited in 1902 by the Missouri-Pacific Railway. The last recorded sighting of the pictographs was in 1823. No trace of them remains.

Duke Paul's son born to Sophie grew up to rule Württemberg, but the royal family of Württemberg will forever be remembered as the forebears of Albert, Duke of Württemberg, the German general who employed the first weapon of mass destruction when he introduced the chemical agent mustard gas to modern warfare during World War I.

On September 6, 1943, 338 American B-17s of the 8th Air Force's 384th Bomber Group bombed Stuttgart and destroyed the museum that housed Duke Paul's specimens, notebooks, paintings, and records of his travels with J. B. Charbonneau.

William Clark's home and Museum of Human Beings were razed in 1851. It is now the site of the Gateway Arch and surrounding parks in St. Louis.

Baptiste is very much in circulation today, still forever carried on his mother's back on the Sacagawea $1 coin.

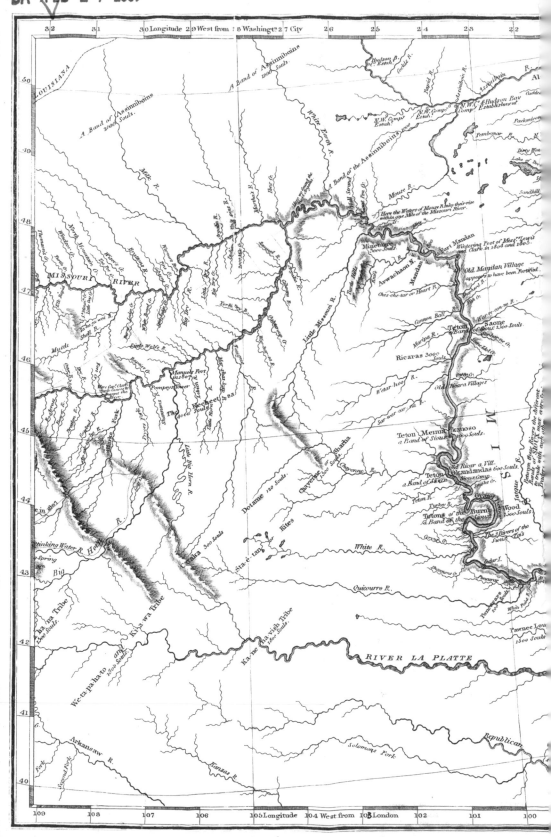